NOTHING PERSONAL

MIKE OFFIT

NOTHING PERSONAL

A NOVEL OF WALL STREET

THOMAS DUNNE BOOKS
St. Martin's Press
New York

THOMAS DUNNE BOOKS.
An imprint of St. Martin's Press.

NOTHING PERSONAL. Copyright © 2014 by Mike Offit. All rights reserved. Printed in the United States of America. For information, address St. Martin's Press, 175 Fifth Avenue, New York, N.Y. 10010.

www.thomasdunnebooks.com
www.stmartins.com

LIBRARY OF CONGRESS CATALOGING-IN-PUBLICATION DATA

Offit, Mike.
    Nothing personal : a novel of Wall Street / Mike Offit. — First edition.
        pages cm
    ISBN 978-1-250-03542-4 (hardcover)
    ISBN 978-1-250-03541-7 (e-book)
    1. Investment bankers—Fiction   2. Investment banking—Corrupt practices—Fiction.
3. Serial murder investigation—Fiction.   4. Self-realization—Fiction.   5. Wall Street
(New York, N.Y.)—Fiction.   I. Title.
    PS3615.F34N68 2014
    813'.6—dc23

                                                                    2013030271

St. Martin's Press books may be purchased for educational, business, or promotional use. For information on bulk purchases, please contact Macmillan Corporate and Premium Sales Department at 1-800-221-7945, extension 5442, or write specialmarkets@macmillan.com.

First Edition: February 2014

10 9 8 7 6 5 4 3 2 1

For my wife, my parents,
my brother, and my children.
Everything good that is in me
comes from them.

NOTHING PERSONAL

PROLOGUE

❧

Dark Harbor, Maine, 1992

From across the bay, he could see the wake before he could make out the boat. It was a Boston Whaler, coming out of Camden harbor with the throttle wide open. Plumes of spray leapt from the bow as it took the top of each wave, catching the low sun in an arc of gold. Warren knew that there would be two people on board, one his employee, the other his wife.

The porch of the main house had a sweeping view of the bay. Perched on a bluff above a cove with a double dock on pilings over the dark, cold water, the house had been the first great "cottage" to go up on Islesboro Island, made for a Scotch-Irish Boston importer who'd kept a seventy-five-foot steam cruiser tied up all summer, only venturing to cross the bay when absolutely necessary. He'd hated sailing and ships, though they'd earned him his fortune, and named the house somewhat sardonically Whales End. In the years after its construction, Dark Harbor, as this part of the island came to be known, became a favored location for large summer houses owned by the Northeastern elite. The wealthy New Yorkers, Philadelphians, and Bostonians would schedule countless sail races in the bay, and the hired crews would create diversions for their daughters and wives while the men donned captain's hats and lusted after a series of ornate silver cups that sat in a case at the Tarratine Club.

More than any other place, Warren viewed the house as a home because he loved the severe weather, the isolation, and the perfect images that constantly appeared—the sleek patina of the well-oiled teak on the classic Chris-Craft runabout he used for hops around the bay, a small American flag snapping vividly in the breeze at the boat's stern, in relief against the midnight blue of Penobscot's choppy surface. It was peaceful here, and the world could, for long moments, seem pure and serene, unchanged from the pristine wilderness known to the Abenaki tribe who had plied these waters for centuries.

The trip that had brought him to this place, along with the woman on the Whaler, had started a long time before, in a landscape dominated not by the shapes of nature or the forces of erosion. That had been a darker vista of glass and steel, bristling with wires and singing the aching and distant tune of money. Perhaps it was the ghosts of those who had died that shimmered for a moment in the mist from the Whaler's bow and then dissipated on the disturbed surface of the bay. But, whether it was fate that had steered them, or force of will, he knew as he stood here that he had come through, and that, surely, he would never go back.

One

⁂

New York, 1984

Count Lorenzo Corelli certainly didn't look anything like his name. He was balding and stout, with a jowly face that receded into a weak chin. He dressed more like an old economics professor than an Italian nobleman—understandable, as he actually spent eight months a year teaching micro-economics at Columbia Business School. His students were obligated to sit through Corelli's tedious examinations of "the dismal science"—today, that meant how bananas would theoretically be priced on an island with no other products and only monkeys as consumers. It was left to the students to figure out how this model might someday be applied to an actual job in the real world. For his part, Corelli rarely tried to enliven the material, having long before decided that, even in so inexact a discipline as his, he would grade generously those who simply recited his lectures on all exams without thinking or dissension. This practice would, he reasoned, prepare them well for life in most of corporate America.

At the front of the amphitheatrical classroom, Corelli sat at his desk, occasionally rising to scribble on the blackboard, while some of his students took notes, others dozed, and a few at the back whispered and giggled. One of the members of this group was Warren Hament, his long brown hair and black jeans distinctly out of step with the pervading aura of a working weekend at IBM headquarters. Hament was twenty-five, about five feet ten inches, with an athletic build and wide, even features, his blue eyes lending his face an intensity that did not match his sardonic, easygoing manner. The remnants of a deep suntan made him appear much healthier than most of the other students, many of them a pale, greenish white in the harsh fluorescent lighting. The only times that Warren seemed to focus on Corelli were during his occasional segues into a disapproving pontification on the economic policies of the new president, and his prediction of a powerful and lasting depression by the end of his first term.

"The so-called Reaganomics solution to the middle and underclasses' problems," Corelli was expounding, "is 'trickle down'—simply to put so much food on the tables of the wealthy that a few crumbs will fall to the floor, where the huddled masses may fight for the scraps."

"He sounds kind of bitter," Hament whispered to Eliza Roberts, who sat to his left.

Eliza smiled and brushed back her short, black hair, leaning closer to Warren. "From what I hear, Reagan's going to sign an executive order deporting all economists to Haiti to work on banana hyperinflation."

The last provoked a stuttering laugh from Chas Harper, a seat over from Eliza. "Jesus, Eliza, if he did that, there wouldn't be anybody left in Cambridge." Harper's voice held a mixture of Old New York and the Maine Coast, and his white-blond hair, prominent forehead, and ice-blue eyes confirmed the lineage of forty-room cottages and Hobe Sound winters.

"No loss," Eliza, an MIT graduate, responded, "except that I'd sell my L.L. Bean stock."

Corelli stopped in midsentence and peered over his glasses at the group in the back of the classroom. "If you three in back have a dissenting opinion, you'll get every opportunity to express it on the final exam. I might remind you that all three of you may have to delay your careers a few months if you don't amuse me as much as you evidently amuse yourselves." Corelli's scathing tone perked up the front rows, and faces turned to see what response might come from the clique. Warren was one of the few students who dared to disagree with the professor during classes, taking issue with him on economic as well as political points.

"Thank you for pointing that out, Professor Corelli," Warren responded, not wanting to disappoint the crowd. "Any more delayed careers in this room and we'd be able to start an economics think tank."

More than a few titters broke out.

Corelli stared at Hament for a moment in indecision and chose to laugh with the joke. His expression betrayed mild annoyance, but he'd usually seemed to enjoy the occasional debate. "Mr. Hament, if we had a department in playing the dozens, I would nominate you for the chair. If you don't mind, though, I would like to get on with this class."

"By all means, sir. We are anxious to hear how it all winds up on Monkey Island."

Corelli heaved an exasperated shrug and went back to his dissection of Reagan's tax cuts and policies.

After class broke, the small group made its way out to the lobby of Uris Hall. Harper poked Warren on the shoulder. "Hey, Hament, I hear you're quite the tennis player." A slight gap-toothed smile crossed Harper's face.

"Oh, boy. Am I about to get invited to play doubles against you and some ringer?" Hament knew that Harper, despite his collegial and somewhat goofy manner, was intensely competitive and generally a good athlete. He'd worn Warren down to a gasping wreck on a morning jog and had a Junior Olympics ski-racing jacket that Warren assumed was real.

"No, I thought you might want to visit me over spring break down in Florida. My grandfather's got a place, and I'm going to need a doubles partner for the tournament at the club." They were walking through the main gate to the campus, heading across Broadway.

"C'mon, Chas, you're going to import a New Yorker to knock balls around at Hobe Sound? What if we win? Wouldn't that look great on the trophy? I can see it—1924 champions: Tilden and Cravath; 1974: Laver and Wickersham; 1984: Harper and Hebrew." Hament was grinning. He'd heard about Chas's family having palatial vacation homes and was excited to be invited to see one.

"C'mon, there's no way anyone would know, except for that hair." Chas pointed at the locks trailing down Warren's neck.

"Right! But what about this?" Warren pointed to his nose as the pair stopped to look for a taxi.

"Hah! Doesn't seem to hurt you with the ladies! Besides, mine's twice as big and busted. Listen, Eliza and a friend of hers are going to be coming down for a few days. Oh, I forgot to mention that there's also a Swedish family next door with four incredible-looking daughters who like to hang out on our beach." Harper's smile was now big enough to sail in.

"You know, it's funny. Ever since my great-grandpa came over, it's been an overriding goal of the Hament family to collect the Hobe Sound Blue-Blood Title Belt. Or whatever." They flagged down a cab and gave the driver Chas's address on East Eighty-Third Street. The two had discovered during orientation week that they lived six blocks apart and shared a ride up and back every day. Chas lived in an expensive high-rise with a doorman, while Warren's apartment was a walk-up in a dark brownstone, but it was much cheaper, and he loved the high ceilings, big windows, and elegant mouldings.

"And maybe meet a few hot blondes?" Harper smiled and gave him a shove.

"That too. That too." Warren nodded. Harper was known to never tire of chasing girls.

—❧—

Warren Hament had come to Columbia Business School almost a year and a half ago, on what seemed like good advice. His childhood and schooling had hardly trained him for any productive employment. His father, a tennis coach, had given him the only education he knew—a game good enough to make him admired at country clubs around Millbrook, New York, where he'd lived until he was ten, and the scourge of junior tournaments in East Hampton, where they'd moved when his parents divorced. But once he'd come up against the California and Florida kids with their personal trainers, nutritionists, and entourages, his casual work ethic and big topspin shots were simply not enough.

After four years at Brown, idly infuriating the tennis coach and barely passing his courses, his first paid job was as an intern two days a week at a Madison Avenue art gallery. He had learned a lot about the cutthroat art world, and a lot more about the gorgeous, well-dressed socialite art-history majors who gravitated to the Madison Avenue milieu. As an attractive, and straight, young man, he got a fair share of attention. He'd struck up a brief friendship with one woman, Roxanne Nahid, whose father was an immensely successful commodities broker. They'd met in the lobby of Christie's, where she worked in Special Client Services, a group of dilettante private shoppers for serious collectors. He was there to deliver a check for the gallery, and she was intrigued by the bright, fit young man with an honest and open face.

Although she'd lost interest in Warren after several nights in her family's Fifth Avenue apartment, he had ventured to look for breakfast one morning while she slept in and encountered her father in the spectacular glass-enclosed terrace overlooking Central Park. Lucien Nahid, an intense, white-maned Iranian, had taken an instant liking to Warren, who asked endless and intelligent questions, and invited him to see the world of commerce at perhaps its most fundamental level. "You don't need an Ivy League pedigree for this world, young man. That is only necessary for my daughter" was his startlingly frank evaluation. The next day, Warren met Lucien in the lobby at seven o'clock and rode down to the World Trade Center in the backseat of a navy-blue Rolls-Royce.

With a visitor's badge pinned to his jacket, Warren quickly learned the language of the commodities exchange's trading pits. It was an elemental world of bids and offers, winners and losers. In few jobs was success or failure so clearly defined at the end of every day, where office politics were distilled to the unbridled pushing and shoving of bodies immersed in the frenzy of screaming that accompanied the sustained hysteria of the open markets. Nahid was right—it seemed to require no special training or degrees.

Warren visited the exchange several times over the next few months, and Nahid, who seemed disappointed his daughter had moved on, even allowed him to enter a few orders for gold futures contracts after opening an account for Warren with his life savings of $6,000. Warren was surprised to see that he started to make some money. One morning, a rumor of a major artillery attack on Israel had driven gold prices straight up, and Warren had made a quick $4,000. That was more than his father made in a month of eight-hour days on the court. Within two months, Warren's account held almost $40,000.

In that same span, he'd seen several faces come and go, like high rollers at a casino. Henry Greenberg, an overweight accountant from upstate New York with a Fu Manchu mustache, had come into the pit on a Monday as a

new member of the Exchange. He told Warren over breakfast that he had
sold his bookkeeping practice to buy the seat, convinced that his method of
graphing price movements could accurately predict short-term market trends.
After two days of carefully marking each trade on a sheet of graph paper, he
had suddenly exploded in a flurry of action, arms flailing and his shrill,
nasal shout booming, buying contracts wildly. He was right—the market
had "broken through long-term resistance" on the chart and was climbing.
By the end of the week, Henry's account had swelled from $200,000 to al-
most $2 million. When he got to $5 million in just a few more weeks, Warren asked him why he didn't just quit. Henry admitted he was hooked and
wanted to make $50 million. Within two months, his account was in nega-
tive territory, and his membership was sold the following week to settle his
debts. The four Cadillac Sevilles he had bought for his family were repos-
sessed. Warren never saw or heard of him again.

There were others, such as an ex-fireman from Brooklyn who was tied in
with a big broker at Montgomery Trading, and who always seemed to know
in advance when the big customer orders were coming. Jimmy would suddenly
buy fifty or a hundred gold contracts, and a moment later, Montgomery's
heavy hitter would appear with an order to buy five hundred or a thousand,
always allowing Veneziano to sell him the last lots at the highest price. Warren figured Veneziano's front-running made him at least $700,000 in the
time Warren observed, and he only wondered how much of this was passed
back to the Montgomery broker in a fat envelope.

He was quickly instructed that no good could come of discussing what
was happening so openly. "Warren, all markets incur 'friction,'" Nahid had
said. "All transactions have costs, whether it is a fee, a tax, or fraud. It will
always be this way. It would be unwise, or even dangerous, to interfere."

For the honest brokers, executing customer orders at $3 a contract could
be a nice and honest living, but only the traders with their own cash at stake
made the big money—or lost it. It didn't matter to Warren. Despite the
money he was making, he had no real taste for the pit, just as he hadn't enjoyed
the trip to Atlantic City he'd taken with a few other traders. His grandfather,
a bookie, had inoculated him against gambling in all forms, and what he was
doing was almost purely gambling. He figured out a way to make a reliable
income trading "spreads"—relatively safe trades that exploited small

changes in the relationships between different delivery months, and he found his strategy made him a tidy income without the big swings that could wipe him out.

The real change came for Warren one afternoon when he'd started a conversation with a well-dressed man who came to the floor only occasionally, one who seemed to command the respect of all the traders and brokers, and the only person on the floor who consistently wore suits made of natural fibers. Ned Johnstone worked for Merrill Lynch, and over a Diet Pepsi in the lunchroom, he'd patiently explained the difference between an investment bank and a stock brokerage house and told Warren the key to getting a good job on Wall Street was to go to a top business school. Brokerage houses made most of their money selling investments to middle-class individuals, mostly at big markups. The investment banks were the "class" of the Street, the middlemen between the biggest corporations and financial institutions and the vast pools of capital that were held for investment by insurance companies, pension funds, and big professional money managers.

"The question is," Johnstone said, "how important is money to you, really? All of this is based on the same drive—greed. You're not saving lives or making art."

Warren leaned back in his chair. "I never really thought about it before. But now that I've made some, I like it. But this place is just plain nuts. It's all risk, no certainty. I don't know how these guys can stand it."

"Warren, you can make over a million dollars a year at an investment bank if you're any good at it and never risk a cent of your own money. You might get fired, but even then, you'll probably get hired somewhere else." Johnstone smiled a little. "The best thing that ever happened to me was getting fired by Smith Barney."

Warren let out a low whistle. A million dollars a year? That was as much as Ivan Lendl made playing tennis! "Jesus. You think I'd have a shot at a decent school?"

"You went to Brown. With your experience down here, you'll walk in. You're a good-looking kid and Lucien Nahid likes you." Johnstone waved at Warren. "I'd get out of here as fast as I could if I were you."

Like so many things he did on impulse, Warren had called Columbia University that afternoon and asked about the admissions process for the

Business School. He was told to take the GMAT, a standardized test used like the SATs to evaluate applicants. Another call to the Educational Testing Service in Princeton got him the registration forms, and four days later he went as a walk-in to an auditorium at Pace University. The majority of the other people in the testing room looked dead serious and slightly nervous. A nice-looking, tall brunette came and took the seat next to Warren, smiling at him. The proctor checked everyone's ID and went through the rules. Warren realized he hadn't brought any pencils! He raised his hand, and when he asked the proctor if any were available, the girl reached over and poked him, then tossed him a crisply sharpened pencil with the International Paper logo printed on the shaft.

"You wake up late or something?" she asked him. He shrugged, smiled, and thanked her. Warren knew he had a knack for standardized exams and finished each section quickly, comfortable that he had done well. After he finished the last section with fifteen minutes to spare, he'd run across the street and bought a $60 roller-ball pen and managed to catch the brunette before she got to the subway.

"I wanted to return the favor," he said, extending the Montblanc box.

"Are you kidding? That's like a confirmation gift or something!"

He liked her big smile. "I'm Warren." He leaned toward her and put the box in her hand. "And I wrote my phone number on the bottom . . . there."

"Well, Warren, I'm Deborah." She was still grinning and opened the box. "Give me your hand."

"My hand? Jeez, we've just met!"

He let her take his right hand in her left. She turned it over, opened the top of the pen with her teeth, and wrote her phone number on the meaty part of his palm. "Maybe you can give me a call and explain to me how you finished every section of that test half an hour before me. Did you actually *answer* any of the questions?"

"I guess so. Who knows? Are you free for dinner tonight? Does International Paper let you out for meals?" She really was pretty, and he liked the way her hair fell across her eyes.

Deborah stepped back and gave him a long once-over. She nodded. "You're pretty cute. Pretty sure of yourself too. You think you can figure everything out so fast?"

Warren smiled and looked down, a little embarrassed. "I'm not that quick, and I don't get phone numbers from girls like you very often. I didn't want to let you get away."

"You're good! Modesty and flattery are a lethal combination. I live on Forty-Ninth and Second. Call me at six thirty and we'll meet at seven thirty. You got that, Warren?"

"I'll be early."

Deborah looked at him for a second and smiled. "I just hope you're not always in such a rush!"

His almost perfect score on the exam, together with a nice letter from Johnstone, and a pleasant interview through which Warren remained charming and enthusiastic, had secured Warren a place in the January class at Columbia despite his slightly lackluster grades from Brown. His date with Deb had also gone well, and he had seen her once or twice a week in the three months since the test. She was hoping to go to Kellogg at Northwestern University in Chicago or UC Berkeley Business School, so they both knew it wasn't likely to last. She got in to NYU and Berkeley, and Warren was disappointed when she told him she would be moving to California. IP had an office where she could work part-time across the Bay and would pick up her tuition. He always liked having a girlfriend and couldn't stand going to parties or out to clubs to try to meet girls. Deb was smart and funny, and with her long legs and high energy she was a lot of fun in bed. But, he was in New York for good, and he couldn't convince her to stay.

When he got the acceptance letter from Columbia, he called his dad, who had moved back to Millbrook, New York, after he'd left for college. He taught at an indoor tennis club four days a week and also worked with the team at the Millbrook School. "Jesus, Warren, I never thought you'd have any interest in business. You only read the sports pages and the funnies."

"I think you're the only person left alive who calls the comics *funnies,*" Warren had said into the phone, smiling.

"Well, your mother thought you'd do something in the art world. She figured you had a nose for it—the 'commercial instinct' is what she called it."

"Dad, I think the only people less honest than art dealers are probably commodities traders," Warren said with a tinge of disdain for the thievery he'd witnessed.

"Warren, I'm not sure you're going to run into a whole lot of honest people in the finance world. My pops always told me the only straight people he'd ever met were bookies. They told you the odds, paid when you won, and you knew up front what the vigorish was."

"Yeah. Don't I recall Grandma saying something about being able to buy a mansion with all the dough Gramps blew on the horses?" Warren loved the way his dad used the language of the twenties and thirties.

"Nobody ever said you could beat a straight game. That's probably why everyone's trying to get the fix in all the time. And Pops never bet on anything."

Warren laughed a little and thanked his father for the advice. His own grubstake had grown to almost $75,000, which, even after taxes, meant he had more than enough money to pay his living expenses and tuition. Money wouldn't be a problem, at least until he figured out what he would actually do with an MBA.

"I always figured you'd be okay. Maybe I didn't hand you a lot of money or a family business, but at least I didn't beat you up over your lousy grades, kiddo. I remember someone telling me Albert Einstein flunked math."

"Yeah, well, that wasn't exactly right, Pop. He was a brilliant student. But your heart was in the right place. And besides, money would've just made me miserable. Look at all the rich kids we knew. And how will I ever get rich if I didn't start out poor? Where's the motivation?" In college, he'd had several friends who went on to run their family businesses. All of them complained about it, yet most of them also immediately sprouted huge egos and paychecks while everyone else was struggling just to pay the rent. His resident adviser at Brown had moaned and whined about the soul-deadening work at his family's multibillion-dollar Midwestern real estate company, but three years later he had abandoned linguistics for a senior job with his dad, a giant penthouse on Lake Michigan, and a seat on the board at the Art Institute of Chicago.

Warren also got to see firsthand the problems of kids with lots of money but bad family lives. He spent his junior year at a private high school in Manhattan, and of the twenty-one boys, almost all from immense wealth and old families, four had committed suicide before graduation. His dad saw it too. A garment executive had built three tennis courts at his Long Island home so his son could practice on the same surfaces that the Grand Slam tournaments were played on. The boy's total winnings as a professional wouldn't have paid for the fences. Warren's father, Ken, had tried unsuccessfully to get the boy interested in his family's clothing business, but having been told all his life how great an athlete he was, and then realizing that he was not even average among the elite, the boy became a coke and heroin user and almost killed himself in a car accident on the European tour stop at Bordeaux. The boy's father had shrewdly taken advantage of the trip to the French hospital as an opportunity to buy and ship home a few dozen cases of wines from the great château, and a new Porsche the boy crashed soon after his recovery, killing a Yale undergraduate.

"Yep, well, maybe you're right there, kiddo," Ken said, sharing the unspoken thought. "I guess I always had a master plan and just didn't know it! Anyway, let me know how you're doing. I've always heard economics is a regular joy."

"You bet, Pop. Listen, all I know is you've got to suffer if you want to sing the blues."

two

When Warren got to the Hertz counter at West Palm Beach airport, the only vehicle available was a white Lincoln Town Car.

"Excuse me, but are you certain you don't have anything available in any size that is a bit less immediately ethnically identifiable?" Warren asked the girl who was struggling with the endless ID number on his New York license.

"What?" She seemed confused by his request.

Sometimes Warren wondered whom he thought he was amusing.

After a few minutes filling out the new computerized forms, and a brief shuttle-bus ride, he was winding his way up the coast toward Jupiter Island and Hobe Sound at the end of a warm, sunny day. Although he spoke about Hobe Sound as if he'd been there, Warren's only knowledge of the place had come from oblique references in the gossip columns, and the occasional mention of it by the wealthy women whose horses he'd groomed as a kid in Millbrook and at the equestrian barns out in Bridgehampton. It was evidently the winter home to the old-money WASP establishment, much farther up the social food chain than Palm Beach.

With his map in one hand, he mentally followed Chas's instructions until he found himself crossing a small bridge. Shortly thereafter, a police car appeared in his rearview mirror, and only a few moments later he was signaled to pull over with a brief blare of the siren.

The uniformed and armed man who emerged from the vehicle came up beside Warren's window and tipped his hat. "Excuse me, sir, but I don't recognize your car. Who are you visiting?" It wasn't clear to Warren if this man was actually a police officer or simply a private security guard.

"Hi. My name is Warren Hament, from New York, and I'm visiting the Harpers."

"Oh, yes. They're up the road about a half mile on the right. The gray columns. Thank you, Mr. Hament."

The man turned and walked back to his car, and Warren noticed as he drove on that he was followed and watched until he had pulled into the driveway. The short coral-gravel driveway opened to a circular car park that held an old Volkswagen Bug, an aging Mercedes sedan, and a Ford station wagon. The façade of the house was neoclassic, of cut limestone, surrounded by dense vegetation that made judging its dimensions impossible. As he rang the bell at the broad teak door, the security man was still watching from the road, waiting to see him greeted.

Galbreath Harper had founded the American branch of his family's London and Edinburgh bank in 1935. What had been a small investment advisory grew into a major private bank and investment manager by the early 1950s. They were respected for their honest advisory work, and banking acumen. When he failed to have any sons and his daughter evinced no interest in the business, he sold the firm to a German bank for a reported $270 million. Since then, he had been an economic adviser to two presidents and had amassed one of the best collections of Pre-Raphaelite art in the world. He had donated a great deal of it to the Boston Athenaeum and made the seed contribution toward building a new wing, named for him, to house the works. Chas was proud of his background and did nothing to hide it. The Harper's money came from an era when bankers actually helped build companies and create new and viable businesses. There was no doubt that he would work with his family's fortune, although he might spend a few years learning about investments at a bank after graduation.

Like many of his generation who had succeeded after the Depression, "Gal" Harper built himself winter homes in Islesboro, Maine, and tiny Hobe Sound, Florida. His house, like all the other great structures along the beach, was referred to as a "cottage," although it had nine bedrooms and was built of Indiana limestone in the style of a Roman villa. From the moderately scaled entry, a grand square foyer opened, its cream-marble floors worn smooth, but highly polished. Through a broad opening directly ahead was the parlor, or living room, decorated in bright yellow chintzes and a finely woven coir carpet, with fifteen-foot-high arched French doors that opened out to a panoramic view of the Atlantic Ocean. The furniture was oversize and comfortable looking, and every table held a small collection of objects. Warren was invited in to wait in the living room, where he was drawn to a group of tiny, albino sea creatures nestled at the base of an imposing Chinese vase that had been wired as a lamp. He gingerly lifted a minuscule crab, its shell as smooth as stone, and every feature crisp, reproduced in perfect detail.

"My grandfather found those in Dakar. They're all made of ivory—before it became illegal. Neat, huh?" Chas had come in from one of the wings.

"Incredible."

"Yeah, they were made for some prince about three or four hundred years ago, and now here they are in our living room. You want to take a swim?" Chas was in a pair of the most garish swim trunks Warren had ever seen. They were surfer length and baggy, with bright blue, orange, and fuchsia flowers everywhere. In them, Chas's lean, taut body looked almost sticklike.

"If you're going to wear those, let's hit the ocean. No shark will come within a mile of us. Bad taste." Warren had noticed that Chas loved to be teased about his preppy clothes and purposefully played up the outrageous colors so popular with that crowd.

Chas laughed and directed Warren out to the foyer, then through a door that opened to a long, columned stone pergola. The house extended from two long Ls around a court, which contained a broad limestone patio with steps leading down to a massive swimming pool. To the left of the pool facing away from the main section of the house, the pergola fronted a row of guest suites. A matching pergola across the pool fronted steps to the beach, and the Atlantic Ocean. At the far end of the pool, a sculpture of a nude female figure at the center of a fountain created a gentle splash of water, which echoed within the court and blended with the sound of the breakers.

"That's a Frishmuth, isn't it?" Warren asked, pointing at the fountain.

"Jesus, Hament, Corelli is right. You do know everything." Chas opened a door to one of the guest rooms. "That's a Frishmuth, all right. Gramps evidently knew her."

"Nah, I don't know *everything*, I just paid attention in art history because the professor was so hot."

Actually, Warren's mother, Susan, an art historian, had taught him about painting and sculpture before she and his father had split up, and he'd kept the passion through school and an unpaid internship at the Guggenheim during the summer of his freshman year. When she had moved to Cambridge, she gave up custody of Warren to Ken, and since Warren's brother, Danny, was at boarding school and spent his summers working in the top hospitals and labs in Boston, Danny wound up much closer to their mother. Warren stepped past Chas into the bedroom, a large, bright space with muted, pastel-upholstered furniture and the anomaly of two twin beds.

"Pretty shabby accommodations, wouldn't you say?" Part of Chas's charm was the way he professed amazement at the luxury that surrounded him. The windows on the far wall looked over a small, formal garden filled with roses and vines climbing over bright white arbors. The property was grand and yet the scale somehow livable, and every detail had been meticulously planned.

"Not bad at all. But I see you've provided at least one obstacle to my love life. Maybe you can prep me. What's the best line to use when I'm on this bed, the girl's on that bed, and I've got to get one of us to move? Really, I'm lost here. Help me."

"Hament, I have faith. If you manage to get some girl back here, she'll probably volunteer to push the beds together for you."

"She may have to after this stupid tennis tournament. Let's swim." Warren shucked his travel clothes and pulled on a brand-new pair of Polo boxer swim trunks. Two nights before, he'd carefully removed the horse-and-rider logo, which he hated. There was something grasping about that trademark, given that Ralph Lauren was the son of a Jewish housepainter named Lifshitz and had probably never been within fifty feet of a polo pony. But there was no denying he had a genius for classic style.

After a race up and back in the pool, which left Warren the surprisingly winded winner, they toweled off, and Chas told him to change into his tennis clothes and they'd go practice a bit. Warren went back to his room and pulled out one set of Fred Perry whites that he'd laundered the night before, and his two Head racquets. He'd arranged to play against a pro at Crosstown tennis courts over the days before break, hoping he could shake the rust out of his game. The savings from his commodities earnings were getting a little lean, but he still had enough for tuition and rent through the end of school, and to keep up the checks he'd been sending to his dad every month. His mother's new boyfriend, a lawyer, had relieved any need to help her, although, after meeting him, Warren doubted that would last too long. His dad never asked for any money, but Warren knew the alimony and his age were wearing on him. Warren hoped his mom would get remarried.

Chas was waiting for him in the white Volkswagen, with the top down and the radio on. He was wearing the kind of sunglasses that reflect the world in purple.

"It's only a half a mile, but we've got to save your strength." Chas gunned the reedy motor and shifted into gear, barely pausing at the gate before pulling out onto the single road that served the islet. They sped down the narrow lane for about a minute before Chas guided the car into the Hobe Sound Club. The grounds were perfectly manicured, and the clubhouse immaculate. Every piece of wood had the same patina found in the locker rooms of the Meadow Club or Shinnecock in Southampton, where Warren had played in tennis tournaments and caddied for his dad playing golf with clients, and the awnings over the terraces were as crisp as the ones at the Millbrook Golf and Tennis Club.

Chas and Warren were met by a sandy-haired, middle-aged man in whites, whose attitude of deference and familiarity quickly identified him as a member of the staff. "Hey, Chas, good to see you! Long time. I've got you two gentlemen set up with Ray and Austin Karr. Should be a good match if your friend here can play the game."

"That's great, Bill. This is Warren Hament." Chas patted the man on the shoulder as he extended his hand to Warren.

"Bill Asher. I'm the excuse for a tennis pro around here. Good to meet you."

Warren returned the firm grip. "I might be looking for some tips later. It's been a while."

"Well, once the Karrs get done with most people, they need a stiff drink more than any tennis tips. You're all on court four." Bill winked at Warren and waved over his shoulder as he headed into the pro shop. At the door, he paused and threw Chas a can of balls. "Go get 'em, Harper."

"For some reason, Chas, I get the feeling that people around here take their tennis pretty seriously." Warren was beginning to be glad he'd practiced.

"Well, if these two beat us, you'll get to hear all about it at dinner tonight—all night. My mom's invited them." Chas led the way to the court. From the lawn, Warren could see the Karrs warming up. They were obviously father and son, one in his late fifties, the other in his late twenties. The two looked like an advertisement for something, only better. Ray Karr was about six feet one inch tall, and fit, his legs solid slabs of muscle, his gold-and-gray hair setting off a deep tan on a handsome, weather-beaten face. His son was about the same size, with short blond hair and a long, fine nose, atop which perched a pair of sunglasses virtually identical to the ones his father and Chas wore.

"God, playing with you three's going to be like getting stopped by a team of Nevada state troopers. You guys all get your glasses at the same place?" Warren poked Chas in the ribs with the butt of his racquet. They stood still for a moment, and Warren sized up the opposition. The older man had graceful movement and powerful strokes, but was an overhitter with limited control. The son had obviously taken plenty of lessons with Bill, his strokes long and fluid, but his rhythm had a tentativeness that suggested he would tense up in a match. Warren noted Ray's backhand looked suspect, and that even in practice his son took relish in driving the ball to that corner and pouncing on the weak response.

"Okay, Harper, I'll take the backhand and serve last, I come to net on everything, we hit pace to the old man's backhand, short to his forehand, and spin to the kid. By the second set Ray'll be telling him he was illegitimate, and by the end, the kid's going to think he's right."

Chas turned his mirrored gaze to Warren and said, "I just knew I was going to enjoy this."

three

❧

The walk from the guest room he'd been assigned was pleasant, his shoes making a sandy, scratching sound on the stone path. The evening was warm, with a slight breeze off the ocean. His skin was flushed from the sun, and the exercise made him feel fit. Just one day of the good life, he thought, and I already feel like a million bucks. Then he corrected himself—better make that a couple of *hundred* million bucks. The Harpers weren't just a successful family. They were a dynasty. This was a nice place to visit, but whatever it took to make this kind of money, Warren was pretty sure he didn't, or maybe didn't even *want* to, have it.

The minute he walked into the living room, Warren was relieved at his choice of clothes. He'd considered white pants with a white shirt and blazer, but that made shoes difficult, and he didn't want to look ready for sailing. After a few moments of deliberation, he went with old Brooks Brothers khakis, a blue oxford with rolled-up sleeves, and a pair of slightly worn Tretorn tennis shoes. He carried the blazer in case.

His outfit closely matched everyone else's, except for that of several older men, who were wearing pants and jackets in indescribably iridescent colors. He remembered a line a caddy had once told him: "Golf is just white folks' excuse to dress like fools." For a certain set of people, no excuse was necessary.

As he walked into the room, he snagged a small hors d'oeuvre from a tray that was laid out and one of the maids took his drink order. As he made his way toward a group of six people on the patio, Cornelia Harper lassoed him with a practiced arm.

"We meet at last. I'm Cornelia, and you have made Chas a celebrity. Straight sets from Ray Karr is absolutely biblical." It took about one millisecond for Warren to like everything about this woman. He knew it was an art, but every gesture, every word, was somehow meant to put him at his ease and make him feel welcome.

"Well, I think the Karrs were a bit off their game today. I guess the new blood confused them." Warren had been led into a group sitting comfortably in plumply cushioned rattan chairs. Cornelia leaned against the arm of one, and Warren mimicked her as he spoke. His drink arrived, and he gladly gulped it before he was introduced.

"Warren Hament, this is Gran Beal, Jim Metcalf, the Karrs, whom you know all too well, and Frances Benson. Warren is Chas's new doubles partner and is evidently *also* carrying him through business school." Warren shook hands all around, and after a polite moment of small talk gravitated to Austin Karr, the closest to him in age.

"Sorry about that lob. I had no other play." Warren had caught Austin out of position during a key point and made him look bad with a topspin lob over his head late in the match.

"Hey, it was a good shot. Besides, Harper's been trying to win this tournament for years. He just needed a good partner. You're way out of our league." Warren was surprised at the compliment. "And, hey, it's good for my old man to get a whipping around here once in a while. Most everyone's too boozed up to teach him a lesson."

"Tell me something, is there usually an audience like that for friendly doubles tournaments down here? I felt like we were at Wimbledon." About twenty people had wandered over and watched the match, and they'd even wound up with a few younger kids as ball boys. Warren had played a lot of matches, but was unaccustomed to applause from a gallery.

"Everybody down here watches everything. *Everything.*" Austin finished his drink and waved for another. "And there's no such thing as a *friendly* tournament. You're going to love it."

"I guess that depends. Where do you live if it's not 'down here'?"

"I'm up in New York too. I sell fixed income for Morgan."

"No kidding? I was thinking about looking into sales and trading jobs when school's over." Warren had started studying the investment banking firms, trying to pick the one that would allow for the fastest advancement. He had decided that being in corporate finance, where they advised big companies and worked endless hours, wasn't for him. He wanted to be on the trading side, where the daily action was, preferably in the mortgage or futures area. "I was thinking about Weldon Brothers." Warren also finished his drink.

"Weldon!" Austin snorted. "That's a tough shop. Real competitive, bottom-line traders' house, like Salomon. You better be ready to hit the ground running there, boy, and watch your back. For a salesman like me, that place is no picnic." Austin shifted on his feet.

"What about Goldman?" Warren asked. They had a reputation as the smartest, most ethical firm on the Street.

"Ugh. Great place if you can get a job. A close friend of mine has been there for four years. If you're on the partner track, it's a gold mine. But, Jesus, the things he says they do for a buck. It's unbelievable!" Austin shook his head.

"Like what?" Warren was curious.

"Well, he told me this amazing story. Basically, they were hired to advise a big finance company on a sale of some assets, and evidently then told the client one portfolio was so bad no one would buy it, except Goldman, as a favor. So, they bought it themselves and a few weeks later sold it for like a fifty-million-dollar profit. So, maybe that was the plan all along. They knew the portfolio was worth a ton more. It sounded to me like they never even showed it to anybody until they had bought it! He makes it sound like they do stuff like that all the time."

"Jesus. That's scary. Why would they do something like that? It's got to be illegal." Warren was stunned. Goldman touted itself as the cleanest and the best.

"Yeah. I know! Hey, anyway, that's what he told me. He was probably just making it up or boasting. Who knows what they really do? All I know is that partners there can make eight figures a year! The minions make less than the competition pays, but there's that gold ring out there if you work twenty-four/seven for like ten years." Karr's voice had gone from sardonic to almost awestruck.

There was a moment of silence while Warren contemplated the conversation and the contact he had just made. During the lull, Eliza Roberts and a beautiful, reddish blond-haired girl came in from the patio.

"Whoa! Who are they?" Austin's eyebrows shot up and he gestured to the pair.

"The dark-haired one's Eliza Roberts, and she goes to school with Chas and me. The other one, I hope, is going to fall helplessly in love with me." Warren was staring at the newcomer, wondering where she had materialized from.

"Wow. Get in line." Karr snuffled a laugh nervously as the two, both in summer print dresses, approached.

"Hey, Warren! Heard you were the big stud on the tennis court today. Trying to hustle these poor WASPs?" Eliza gave him a push on the shoulder as he stood up, momentarily knocking him off-balance.

"Hey, take it easy on me, Eliza…Jeez! This is Austin Karr, one of Chas's victims. Eliza Roberts." Warren gestured between the two before he turned toward the newcomer. "And so I may never forget, who on earth are you?"

"I'm Larisa Mueller." Her faced flushed slightly, and she shook Austin's hand.

"Hey, Hament, wake up. Larisa's in our macro class." Eliza punched him on the shoulder.

"You go to Columbia?" Warren said incredulously. "I can't believe it."

"Well, if you spent a little more time around school and a little less screwing around, you might know a few more people." A lesser shove punctuated Eliza's barb. "And what do you do, Austin?" She turned on him, batting her eyelashes, speaking in an exaggerated Southern drawl.

"I, um, sell bonds in New York." He looked down into his drink as he spoke.

"And tell me, is that something to be ashamed of?" Larisa had detected the hesitancy in Karr's voice and seen his eyes drop.

"Well, around here, guys like me are just the indentured servants." Austin gestured with his drink.

"Yeah, scraping by on a half a million a year," Eliza rejoined in a mocking tone.

Cornelia Harper interrupted the conversation by announcing dinner was served. To his vast pleasure, Warren discovered he was seated directly between Larisa and Mrs. Harper. The dinner conversation centered around politics, with virtually all present noticeably conservative Republican in viewpoint. Warren seemed to find a willing ally in Mrs. Harper while he engaged in a debate with the senior Karr about the merits of President Reagan's policies. Warren felt they didn't go far enough, and that government spending cuts across the board would be the only sure way to avert a disaster at the end of a brief rainbow of prosperity. Mrs. Harper seemed to feel this was a capital notion, so long as the bulk of the cuts came in social and entitlement programs, accompanied by bigger tax cuts for the higher-income brackets. Ray Karr evidently felt that all the poor, blacks, and Hispanics in the nation should be relocated to a vast military encampment in North Dakota and assigned to manufacturing any product that a bountiful supply of cheap, unskilled labor could benefit, while also busting all the labor unions in the country. "We'd give 'em food, clothing, shelter, and birth control—more than they'd ever get themselves." After a few minutes of this unappealing conversation, Warren let it drift away, so he could focus on Larisa, who had remained mostly silent.

"So, how is it we've never met at school?" Warren took advantage of a shift in the flow of talk to the far end of the table to speak quietly to her.

"I don't know. I guess I'm always in the library." Her even features were not perfect, but the strong chin, grey eyes, and name conveyed a sense of an Aryan aristocratic elegance.

"Well, that's one place you'd be completely safe from me. In fact, that's about the only place on earth you would be." He looked straight into her eyes to judge the response.

"Such a sweet talker," Larisa said a little derisively. "I thought all you were interested in was busting Corelli's chops, or chatting with these neo-fascists."

"I've had this affliction my whole life. I have a hard time keeping my mouth shut. Especially when I'm trying to impress someone with my intelligence and wit."

"Is there anyone else around as smart and witty as you?" Larisa's lips were soft and full, almost pouty.

"Nobody is." Warren gave it his best Bogie impression.

"*The Big Sleep*. Doghouse Reilly." She caught his reference to the classic movie.

"Well, there's something we have in common! I guess you do get out of the library once in a while." He lifted his glass of red wine and saluted her before he drank. "And what brought you down here?"

"It seems Chas wanted a chance to make a pass at me and had to travel a thousand miles to do it."

"Oh? And how did Eliza feel about that?" Warren had assumed Chas and Eliza were seeing each other, but neither of them ever discussed it.

"She's probably slightly pissed that you're making a pass at me and not her. I was supposed to be for Chas."

"Wait a minute. Eliza? Since when?" Warren was surprised, and flattered, not to mention a little piqued by the crack about his own pass.

"Since a long time ago. She's such a girl, that one. Come on, I always see her grabbing your arm and whispering to you. You mean you didn't notice that?" Larisa had a remarkably condescending tone, but Warren noticed she made her comment while grabbing his arm and whispering in his ear.

"Well, I might have to see about that. Jeez. Eliza. Who'da thunk it? But let's talk about you. Where are you from? What do your parents do? What are your goals in life?" Warren drank off the rest of his wine, confident the waiter would refill the glass before long.

"Born in Lake Forest, grew up in Charlottesville. Daddy was a doctor and research chemist at the hospital and my mom was in HR at UVA, but they got divorced, and my mom's remarried in Palo Alto. As for me? Major success, power, and a pair of those small, round sunglasses." She toasted him back. "What about you?"

"The New York area. Mostly retired tennis-pro father, mother's a teacher, sort of. I don't have a clue about goals and never really did. I guess I wanted to be a tennis pro too. All that changed a few minutes ago." He bent at the waist in genuflection.

"You're a flatterer. But I give you credit, you're paying more attention to me than to my host."

"So, you were for Chas, eh? Isn't that a little demeaning? I mean, to be the ascribed consort of the great scion? I wouldn't take you for it, though I bet you look great in a bathing suit."

"Nah. Chas's cute and incredibly nice, but cut me a break. I mean, he has no *edge* at all—none. And, he sure as hell doesn't have your vocabulary—*ascribed consort of the great scion?*—and I hear he just windsurfs for days."

"Yeah, I'd heard that too. I'm looking forward to seeing it live. He told me his favorite thing is to windsurf all the way across Penobscot Bay in Maine when the water's so cold that if you fall in, you live about twenty seconds, and the wind is up, and there's a mighty chop, and the will-o'-the-wisp is a howlin'. Or something like that."

"Are you feeling okay?" She was laughing, and Warren liked the way her full upper lip curled under to show her even, white teeth.

"Never better! I think it's dessert time. Isn't that so, Mrs. Harper?" Warren had sensed that their laughter had attracted the hostess's attention, and he turned to address her.

"Oh, I just let everyone worry about that on their own time, Mr. Hament." She laid her hand on top of Warren's. "And I would say from the sound of things over here that you do okay on your own time."

Larisa blushed, and Warren smiled. "In this atmosphere it would be pretty hard not to."

"I'll make a note of that." Cornelia smiled back and glanced down the table toward Chas, laughing with Eliza and Austin Karr, who looked to be getting on pretty well.

After the dessert, Warren and Larisa wandered down to the esplanades of columns that fronted the Atlantic. The tide was coming in, and the breakers were washing up only a few dozen yards away. A salt breeze was coming onshore just strongly enough to put the slightest chill in the mild air, and Larisa folded her arms across her chest as they stood and talked.

"This is pretty incredible, isn't it?" Warren said, waving a hand toward the house.

Larisa nodded. "Unbelievable. It's hard to understand that people can have this much money."

"I know. I mean, I knew that Chas's grandfather was rich, but I've never seen anything like this."

"Well, he was an investment banker, right? So maybe someday you'll have a spot just down the road. You and Cornelia can have an affair."

"Right. In your dreams."

"How about yours?"

"Right now, my dreams aren't focused on money or Cornelia Harper," Warren said, his gaze level with her pale grey eyes.

Larisa returned the stare with a crooked grin. "Charmer."

They stood in the night air for a few moments. Tiny droplets of salt spray clung to the silky blond hairs that covered Larisa's forearms. He reached across and ran a finger gently across her arm, making the moisture coalesce and wet her skin. She shivered slightly and turned toward him. He didn't say anything as he took her in his arms and kissed her softly, and then more forcefully. She wrapped her arms around him, and he felt her tongue dart behind his teeth. His body couldn't help reacting to her.

"Hmm. I see what you mean about focus." Larisa backed off the kiss just enough to speak.

"Ummm, yeah." He was a little embarrassed, but riveted to the spot.

"Well, at least I know where you stand." She released him and stepped away. "I think this might be very interesting."

"Interesting? It might be interesting? Just exactly when do you think it might actually become . . . interesting?" Warren could see the outline of her body in the breeze as she stood leaning against the next column. She was taut and muscular, defined yet inviting.

"That's part of what makes it fun, isn't it? Patience? Surprise? Spontaneity?" She was looking at him dead on with her wide-set eyes.

"I have a feeling this is going to be a long weekend." He half groaned.

"I certainly hope so. We don't want to disappoint Cornelia, now, do we?" Larisa laughed and took his hand, leading him back inside.

The group had divided into small conversational circles, the nearest of which swallowed Warren and Larisa when they came back into the room. The man who was introduced as Jim Metcalf was holding forth on politics and economics, but his eyes seemed to linger appreciatively on the front of Larisa's dress.

"Anyway, what these fatheads in the Congress don't get is that Reagan's finally got it right. You've got to stop feeding the welfare system and start giving the private sector incentives to perform and grow. These assholes better get onside, or they're going to get their butts kicked." The others in the group nodded and murmured assent, though Warren guessed most of them were hoping Metcalf had talked himself out. His blue blazer was flecked with bits of ash from his cigarette, and his face was flushed under his wavy gray hair from the sun and drinking.

"Hey, our economics professor says that the deficit will be a couple hundred billion a year by 1990, and there'll be riots in the cities. Of course, he also seems to think that Jimmy Carter was a misunderstood genius." Warren tried to break the obvious tedium.

"Listen, it's those moron economists who got us into all this trouble in the first place. And forget about the deficit. We'll grow our way out of it." Metcalf dismissed the national debt with a wave of his hand. "If I'd have listened to economists, I would've sold all my orange groves years ago. Best thing I ever bought."

Warren perked up at the mention of oranges. He'd made a nice profit trading orange-juice futures once. "Oranges? You own orange groves?"

"I own more orange trees than Tropicana, sonny. More than anyone outside of Brazil." Metcalf said this while staring directly at Larisa's chest.

"Wow!" Warren replied with a slight edge. "That's impressive. I guess you must do a lot of business in the futures markets?" Warren stepped in closer to Metcalf.

"A lot of business? Sonny, I pretty much *am* the futures markets!" Metcalf waved his hand, and cigarette ash described a snowy arc toward Larisa. "In fact, when I trade, everyone else better get out of the way!"

"So you hedge?" Warren couldn't quite understand whom Metcalf wanted to impress. Everyone knew he was wealthy, but Chas's grandfather could buy and sell Metcalf several times over.

"Oh, sure, I hedge—or play around a little . . ." Metcalf winked, but Warren wasn't sure at whom.

"Play around?" He couldn't see the harm in encouraging Metcalf..

"Lemme tell you, the greatest thing is when there's a cold snap in Florida. Drives everyone crazy! I love it. The markets go wild!" The man was clearly enjoying a private joke.

"Wild?" Larisa joined in, which seemed to turn up the lights even brighter.

"Oh, yeah, lemme tell you! You see, the USDA calls us if there're freezing temperatures to ask what kind of crop damage we might have." Metcalf dropped his voice into a conspiratorial tone. "So first we buy up a ton of contracts, then tell the USDA the freeze is gonna kill all the oranges! It's like candy from a baby!"

"So you make money on your futures contracts and on your crops when the crop loss estimates drive prices up?" Warren replied, purposefully talking like a simpleton.

"You're not as dumb as you look, sonny! Yup! We tell 'em fifty, sixty percent crop loss, and it's like a moon shot! Of course, it's not our fault if the freeze wasn't as bad as we thought, now is it?" Metcalf was actually rubbing his palms together in glee. "Easy money, lemme tell ya!"

"Doesn't the USDA check on your estimates?" Larisa seemed awestruck.

Metcalf let out a roar. "*Check?* With *who?* They've got like three people in the whole state! Hahaha! Nah, those pencil pushers just call us and ask!"

Warren had suspected that growers manipulated the markets every couple of years and made fortunes off speculators who didn't have an inside connection. Tariffs kept foreign oranges out of the United States, and Washington lobbyists made sure that the tariffs stayed in place. It was all one big inside game. Warren didn't even know if it was illegal, or how anyone could prove anything.

"That's *fantastic*," Warren said with heavy sarcasm. "What an ingenious fraud!"

It seemed Metcalf finally realized that he'd pretty much admitted to being a con man. "Hey, what's your name again?" Metcalf looked at him with a scowl.

"Warren Hament," he replied neutrally.

"Hament . . . Hament. Your family from Denver originally?" Warren knew there was a socially prominent family in Denver named Hamment "No, sir. Only one *m*. My grandparents were from Baltimore."

"More like from hunger." Metcalf looked at the curtains when he made the insulting insinuation.

Warren knew exactly what it was, an anti-Semitic slur, and he felt his blood rise. "You're right. I don't guess I have the impeccable pedigree that you so obviously possess. You probably have AKC papers and everything. Do you have all your shots?"

Metcalf stood still, speechless.

Larisa stifled a giggle. Warren took her arm and led her toward the couch.

"Jesus, Hament. Make friends and influence people." Larisa had a big smile on her face.

"Wow. He gives capitalism a bad name." Warren finished his last drink. "I gotta get out of here before I get so drunk I invite Cornelia skinny-dipping. I'm in training for the Hobe Sound Wimbledon Open, or something, you know."

"Oooh, you athlete types get me all worked up." Larisa took Warren's arm and whispered in his ear, "I can hardly stand it." The hairs on his neck stood on end.

After making the rounds and saying good-nights, Warren wandered off toward his room, with Larisa and Eliza also heading to their bedrooms. He felt awkward and blew them both a kiss at his door, disappointed that he'd missed the chance to get Larisa alone. He fell into bed dizzy, after a brief wrestling match with his toothbrush and his pants. It had been a fascinating day. The Harpers were at the top of the food chain and fit seamlessly into the old-money world that Warren had viewed from the periphery most of his life. Metcalf was from some old WASP family, but he was as crooked as a guy selling fake watches in the Grand Bazaar in Istanbul. Even so, Warren liked most of these people. They seemed extremely comfortable in their own skin, and most were completely open to new social or business contacts, as long as you didn't try to join their clubs. Best of all was Larisa. She was almost too good to be true.

The sun, exercise, and wine overtook him, the open windows admitted the sea breeze, and the sound of the fountain gently crested the surf, lulling him inexorably to sleep.

four

※

Warren woke to a perfect Florida morning, and breakfast was served on the patio by the pool. A uniformed man brought Warren coffee and juice, and a table was laid with a big bowl of fresh raspberries and strawberries, and a selection of cereals poured into soup tureens. Warren ladled out some Rice Krispies and Rice Chex, dumped the berries on top, then filled his bowl with milk. Several copies of *The New York Times* and *The Wall Street Journal* were on the table, and Warren idly perused the basketball standings. The Knicks were in fourth place and going nowhere. He flipped to the front of the paper and read about a bus crash in India. It did seem there were an awful lot of them. A kid at Brown had collected each news item in a notebook, and he had well over a hundred.

Chas came bounding onto the terrace from the beach, dripping wet and drying himself with a huge, yellow towel. He plopped down at the table and drained a glass of juice.

"Okay, how far did you swim?" Warren knew Harper had almost unbelievable stamina, and an absolute devotion to the endless repetition of any endurance sport.

"Don't know. Maybe three miles. Not much surf today. Did a couple hundred sit-ups though. Push-ups too." Chas loved to tease Warren about his lack of commitment to working out.

"You're amazing. What, did you get up at five o'clock?" Warren shook his head.

"Nope. Quarter to six. How'd you get so lazy?"

"Mine are a cerebral people. We exercise our minds and rest our bodies." Next to Chas, he felt indolent.

"Yeah, that's how Israel got built in the middle of the desert. Well, eat up, our first match is at nine thirty, second round's at one. Semis and finals tomorrow. No time to dawdle." Chas hopped to his feet. "I'm taking a shower. I'll meet you out front in forty-five minutes."

Warren put his sunglasses on and grinned up at Chas. "Yassir, boss."

Harper tossed his damp towel lightly into Warren's face and waved. "Aloha."

Warren stretched out in the chair, soaking in the warm sun. He could never figure out why his father had settled in the Northeast. Florida, California, Arizona—*those* he could understand for a tennis pro and coach, but New York? He idly contemplated what life would have been like growing up where it was always summer.

His reverie was interrupted by the dripping of cold water onto his forehead. He opened his eyes and saw Larisa's face, upside down, holding a melting ice cube over him. He groaned.

"Wake up, lazy bones! It's a beautiful day!" She had a big smile on her face, and Warren sat upright. She was wearing a one-piece, black Speedo bathing suit cut high on the hip, which showed her body off to good advantage. Her legs were long and slim, her stomach flat, her breasts full. There was a sleekness to her that seemed almost seal-like. She pivoted away from him, took three long strides, and executed a graceful dive into the pool. There was barely a splash, and she didn't surface until she'd reached the far side.

"Do you have gills or something?" Warren doubted he could make it halfway to the other side underwater. He had to shout.

She swam back briskly, with the smooth form that seemed more than casual. She looked up at him, her hair now slicked back from her face.

"You look like you swim a lot."

"Actually, I was a rhythmic gymnast in school."

"Wow. That's amazing. I have absolutely no idea what that means, but it sounds like it could be very painful."

"Not really. C'mon, come in. I'll race you."

Warren got out of the chair. "What is it around here? Everyone wants to compete. 'Let's race,' 'Straight sets from the Karrs.' Whatever happened to sport for sport's sake?"

"It's more fun when you're trying to beat someone."

"As long as you win, right?"

"It's better."

"I suppose. The Olympian ideal. I'm supposed to race a rhythmic mermaid. Hah!" He eased himself into the pool and swam a lap, which still left him a little winded. He begged off the race. They climbed out and stretched on the warm stone coping, the air still except for the sound of the surf drifting in. Warren peeked at her, lying still, the water beaded on her legs, which were slightly flushed from the exercise and the sun. He rolled onto his stomach and crawled the three feet to her. He leaned over and, as she started from the sudden shadow blocking the sun from her face, kissed her. She kissed back and put a hand behind his neck.

"I'm glad I met you, Larisa Mueller," he said, withdrawing slightly.

"Mmm. Me too." She smiled smugly and closed her eyes again.

"You coming to see the tennis?"

"Nope, I'm going to work on my tan. I have faith in you two. Bring us home a medal, a prize, a trophy."

"I will make the fair lady proud." He stretched.

She sat up and wrapped her arms around her knees, her eyes meeting his in a even gaze. "Can you believe anyone would ever leave here?" She broke an arm free and swept it broadly around the pool and house.

"It is kind of hard to assimilate. I keep thinking we're at some big hotel in the off-season, so no one else is around."

"The service is better than at any hotel I've ever been in."

"I guess that while some people were thinking about Vietnam or Korea or marching on Washington, there was a whole class of people who just kept the money machine rolling. Now, all the others have decided to buy in, but all the good seats are taken. It's like Corelli says, the masses will be left hunting for grubs."

"Are you really going to try to get a job in one of the investment banks?" She cocked her head to one side.

"Sure. It's not like I have any kind of a head for real business. I barely made it through all those case studies and systems analysis courses in school. There's really nothing productive I can do for a big company that actually *makes* something. So, I'd rather just sit down at the card table every day and see what I can do with whatever I'm dealt."

"You think it's like gambling?"

"I don't really know. Trading commodities was nothing *but* gambling. It seems that the guys who trade bonds at least have to use their minds sometimes."

"Yeah, and it happens to pay well."

"That's a big plus. I never really thought about money until I made some, and now it doesn't seem like a bad thing. I tried the art world, and it seemed like the only honest places are the museums, and I just don't know enough for that. What about you? What are you going to do? Are your motives so pure?"

"I'm not sure. I may wind up interviewing for an investment banking job. I *definitely* like the idea of getting paid well. I mean, I went to law school at UVA for two years, but I hated it, and it was so expensive, so I took a job at Sandoz in international marketing and reporting. Anyway, I probably could adapt to Wall Street pretty well. I had to deal with them all the time. What a pack of animals."

"Ha!" Warren laughed. "I don't know if the Street could adapt to you."

"How's that?" Her forehead crinkled.

"Smart. Articulate. Beautiful. Gentle. I don't know how they'd handle it."

"Oh, you don't know me. I'm not so gentle all the time." A slightly evil smile played across her lips.

"Are you saying that you'll do anything to get what you want?" He grinned at her and feigned horror.

"Absolutely. Ruthlessly."

"And when do I find out if I'm something you want?"

"I think I'll leave it up to you to figure that out for yourself. The element of surprise."

Warren smiled, then looked at his watch. "Well, if I don't get changed and meet Chas, I'll be on the menu tonight." He got up and looked down at her appreciatively. "Or..."

She smiled and tossed her towel at him. "You keep your mind on the tennis, I'll manage the melanin. Git along now."

Warren and Chas had an easy first match, playing two brothers who argued quietly between themselves about court coverage. There was plenty of time to kill, so they drove back to the house and joined the girls and Cornelia on the beach. Chas's mother was in fine condition, her slightly heavy-boned body taut from a regular exercise regimen. She had commandeered a half dozen lounge chairs and a room-size white tent from the pool house, and the staff had erected it all. In the tent was a buffet lunch, complete with a bar. Warren took a quick swim in the surf to wash away the sweat, then dried off and heaped a plate with lobster rolls and salad.

After a brief exchange about the walkover match, Mrs. Harper gave Warren some tips about the afternoon's opponents, who included Jim Metcalf, who evidently had a weak net game.

"Oh, great, you mean I get to play against Mr. Metcalf?" Warren had felt a bit of regret about their conversation. Metcalf may have been an anti-Semite and a market manipulator, but Warren was a newcomer and a guest.

"Don't worry. He doesn't expect to win. Just be nice."

Warren sat in the sand and ate, and the conversation drifted on the midday sun and the ocean breeze, with no one making an effort to be clever, but simply enjoying the good food and the warmth. It was hard to feel any pressure or tension in this setting, and Warren snuck a glass of wine when Chas wasn't looking. Cornelia talked to Warren about Millbrook and horses for a while, but he wound up dozing contentedly.

The afternoon match was sluggish, and Warren's mind was not focused on anything except how to get Larisa alone that night. They barely beat Metcalf and his guest, a strong player from California, thanks mostly to Chas's boundless energy and his diligently hitting drop shots to Metcalf every chance he got and the older man missing almost every volley he attempted.

"Thanks for carrying me, partner," Warren said as they toweled down. Metcalf had evidently forgotten the conversation from the previous night—in fact, he didn't even seem to recognize Warren at all.

"No problem. Just be ready tomorrow," Chas replied, smacking Warren on the back. They showered and changed, then drove back to the house. Drinks were on the patio, then Eliza and Larisa got into the Volkswagen with them for a drive into Palm Beach for dinner. They met up with a group of six others, all friends of Chas's with family homes up in Hobe Sound or in

Palm Beach, including two of the Swedish neighbors Chas had mentioned in New York. Everybody drank with gusto, and they made a big game out of cracking the stone-crab claws and sucking out the meat. It was a fun, sticky, and briny meal. Larisa sat next to Warren at dinner, and he kept leaning over, being sure to make as much contact with her leg as possible. By the time they climbed back into the car, slightly inebriated, he was holding her around the waist. Eliza had paired off with Austin Karr again, and Chas seemed to have hit it off with the older blond Swede, a model in Paris, and all of them decided to go back to the Harpers' for a swim. To make room in the small car, Eliza sat on Austin's lap, and Larisa sat on Warren's. With her long hair spilling over his face, and the bouncy suspension of the car, she kept adjusting her bottom, and he was pretty sure she was doing it on purpose.

Everyone piled out at the cottage and headed toward the living room and screened porch. Warren grabbed Larisa and slowed her down, letting the rest get inside. He then led her around the side of the house on the path to the rose garden, which was softly lit in the moonlight.

"Are you kidnapping me?" She laughed at him.

"Maybe. At least leading you down the garden path. Literally. C'mon, I'm a little tired of all the company." They came to a small grassy area surrounded by tall arbors overgrown by mature climbing roses. A wood bench was thoughtfully placed beneath the central arbor, and they sat there.

"What's wrong with the—" she started to ask, but he cut her off with a kiss. The kiss intensified, and soon she had half climbed on him and had her hands inside his shirt, stroking his chest. His own hands ran down her short dress, then up over her haunches. After a few minutes, they eased back.

Warren couldn't help saying exactly what he felt. "I know we just met each other, but I want you to spend the night with me."

"You sure say what's on your mind."

"It's an affliction sometimes. But, we're not kids. I think you're great. I think you're beautiful and I want to spend a lot of time around you."

She snuggled back down into his arms and kissed him lightly. "I think you're pretty great yourself. To be honest, I was happy when I saw you here last night."

"God, I can't believe I never noticed you around. Have you been dating anyone?"

"Nope. Saving myself for you."

"I do appreciate that." A kiss.

"Think nothing of it. How about you?" Another kiss.

"Not lately. Not for a long time as a matter of fact. My last girlfriend dumped me and moved three thousand miles away. Before that, in high school..."

"Okay. I don't need to hear about your first date. I like you just fine." She ran her hands through his hair. "But you need a haircut."

"Was it my looks or my charm that got you?" Another kiss.

"I think you're sweet." Another, interrupted.

"Sweet? Guys aren't supposed to be sweet."

"Well, I think you are. Cute too. Don't complain. Work with me here. If I like sweet, go with it, okay?"

He laughed and hugged her close. "Let's get out of here." He helped her up, and they picked their way through the garden back to his room. At the door, she hesitated.

"Work with me here, okay?" He opened the door. She paused, then a wicked smile creased her lips before she grabbed him and wrestled him inside, kicking the door closed behind them. She didn't seem to even notice the other bed.

They fell back, and she kissed him hungrily. She was on top of him and straddled him, bringing her knees up under her. She ran her hands down his arms, and he tensed slightly.

"Umm, strong, huh?" she said, twisting her lips away from his, and pressing her weight down on his wrists.

"Strong enough." He let his hands stay pinned as he strained his neck upward to meet her lips.

She stayed just out of his reach, and her tongue darted out and ran across his lips. "I'll be the judge of that." She suddenly moved across his body, sliding her left arm under his armpit, and snaking her hand behind his head. Her right knee pushed underneath him, and he found himself gripped in a tight wrestling hold, unable to move, as she pulled his right arm back and underneath him, her weight on him. He could not get any leverage, but he didn't struggle too hard.

"Don't tell me you're giving up already," she said, her lips at his ear. She nipped the lobe with her teeth.

"I never give up."

She eased off the pressure a little and slid her left foot up his leg, until she reached his crotch and used her heel to press against his bulging erection. "Hmmm, what are we going to do with that?" she whispered.

He tried to turn, but she tensed again, freezing him. He relaxed, and her foot moved again. The sensation made him groan, and she tightened the grip of her arms, stretching his joints to the point of discomfort.

"Easy, girl, easy. I'm gonna need that shoulder tomorrow." He didn't mind the game. Instead, he was intensely aroused.

"Earn it."

He did, surprised that he had to use almost all his strength to break her hold. When he did, she was at him like an animal, tearing his clothes off, biting him, her breath short. He rolled on top of her, and she writhed under him, making him pin her to the bed with one arm while he jammed his right arm between her legs to hold her still long enough to slide inside her. He found a stamina he had not expected, and their instincts led to an almost desperate, violent coupling. When he finally lost control, she pushed him away, and his body arched, then collapsed, and he lay panting and sweating on the bed, the sheets a tangled mess, their clothes everywhere. He tried to think of something to say, but he could barely make a sound.

Larisa stretched alongside him, their breathing slowing at the same pace. Eventually, he reached for his shirt, to use as a towel, and she pulled him back and kissed him hard, then softened.

"You have a lot to learn, Warren Hament. But I'm a patient teacher."

He kissed her back and said nothing, letting the endorphins and fatigue carry him away. Whatever she wanted to teach him, he was willing to learn.

five

❦

The trip back from Florida at the end of the week had been full of anticipation. He had an amazing new girlfriend, and school was drawing to a close. The eighteen months had been a small part academic jawboning with the likes of Corelli, a fair amount of drudgery in accounting and math, and a bit of useful discussion, mostly in Sol Fisher's finance class.

Fisher had been a senior investment banker and a partner at Goldman Sachs and retired to a full professorship at the Business School, his millions tucked away. His lectures lingered only briefly on the actual mechanics of finance and usually wound up in discussions that revealed the engine that drove Wall Street.

"It's actually pretty simple," Fisher had said in his first presentation. "A real investment bank simply acts as a conduit between big companies looking to raise capital and big institutions looking to invest it. Let's say Ford Motor needs a couple hundred million bucks to build a plant in Wisconsin to make pickup trucks. In the old days, they'd go to Morgan Bank or Chase Manhattan for a loan. And the banks would make a big spread, since they were the only game in town, and their source of money was cheap deposits by their customers. Then, investment banks stepped in. We'd tell Ford we could get them the money a couple of percent cheaper, by selling bonds. Or virtually free, by selling stock. So, we'd go to the big pension funds and insurance companies and peddle Ford bonds, or Ford stock, and they'd save a mint versus borrowing from the banks. The investors were happy because they got the bonds of a topflight company and got to earn more interest than they could get from US treasuries or by depositing it. We'd earn a big fee. Then, we'd excite the investors even more by being willing to trade those bonds. That made it possible for them to sell the bonds if they didn't want to keep them, or to buy more, or swap them for something else they liked better. Suddenly, investment bank traders were buying and selling Ford, Chrysler, AT and T, you name it. Our bankers, who advised the borrowers, got paid big fees. Our traders made money. The investors got choices and liquidity."

"But isn't that too simple?" One of the front-row students had raised his hand. "Wouldn't all the investment banks compete for the same business, and wouldn't that competition take the profits out of it?"

"Good question. That's the force that makes it more difficult to be an investment banker today than ten years ago. Competition. Brutal, backstabbing competition. The only way to win is to be smarter, come up with trickier ways to raise the money and shave a few hundredths of a percent off the cost of borrowing that money. Structured finance, it's called. Bonds with warrants to buy stock, stock that pays interest like bonds, stock that isn't equity, bonds that aren't really debt, bonds that pay interest with more bonds—whatever!

"Some of the companies stress trading—willingness to commit a lot of their own money. Others focus on making customers happy—a relationship backed up with lots of greenbacks. Whatever gets you over. Lots of drinks and dinners, ball games, and golf outings. But it pays. There are twenty-eight-year-olds at Morgan Stanley or Weldon Brothers making a million dollars a year, for God's sake. And the irony is, every single one of them thinks he's *underpaid*!"

That kind of talk was incendiary in a room full of students of the higher forms of capitalism. Many who hadn't thought about a career at an investment bank realized they could have a shot at making much more money there than in the industries they were working in before business school, and much more quickly. Of the graduates in that year's class, 60 percent would apply to Goldman Sachs, and only two or three would be offered a spot.

"Of course, nowadays, there's a lot more to it than just raising money for big industrial companies," Fisher continued. "There's junk bonds, which are used to raise money for dicier companies. There's foreign-currency bonds, derivatives. And then there's the whole mortgage-backed securities markets."

"Isn't that the Ginnie Mae market?" a front row voice piped in.

"Yes. That's one part of it. Ginnie Mae is one government agency that guarantees mortgages against default, so investors can buy them with no credit risk. Mortgages are a lot more difficult to figure out than most bonds, though. When a company sells a bond, they agree to pay interest on it for ten or twenty years and not pay it off, or 'call' it, for most of that time. A call is when the bond can be repaid by the company that sold it after a certain amount of time, but before its maturity. That way, if the company can borrow less expensively, they pay off the higher-interest-rate bonds and sell new, lower-interest-rate bonds.

"But, unlike most corporate or treasury bonds, which can't be called for a long time, most mortgages can be prepaid at any time, if the borrowers refinance, or the houses are sold or burn down, or even if the borrower defaults and the government or insurance companies step in and pay back the lender. So the securities can be called away. This has a big effect on their value because the investors who bought the mortgages can get their money back when interest rates are much lower, and that's bad, or even when rates are much higher, which is really good. So, people trade them around a lot, always trying to stay a step ahead of prepayment risk. The firms that have good research and analytics on prepayments get a lot of business from the biggest investors—pension funds and big-money managers. Someday soon, you're going to see Wall Street invent ways to make big bucks off that risk. But that's another course altogether."

After class, Warren met Larisa for lunch. It was a warm day, and they sat on the steps of Uris Hall. She had brought a sandwich with her, and Warren grabbed a cup of clam chowder from the student snack bar across the green.

"Fisher's class this morning was really good," he said, slurping a little.

"Wait. What? Who are you? You *actually enjoyed* a class? Where is my boyfriend, and what have you done with him?" Her upper lip curled under when she smiled, and Warren couldn't resist bending over and giving her a kiss.

"Umm. Onions in the tuna. Yummy!... Yeah, he was talking about mortgage-backed securities trading at the Wall Street firms, and it sounds like something I might really like. I didn't know that kind of thing even existed." He was serious, his eyebrows even a little furrowed.

"Yeah, we learned about that in my capital-markets class last month. Sounds really complicated." She had finished half her sandwich and took a big chug on a can of Coke.

"That's what I like…complicated! So much of the stuff we've learned about seems so dull. None of this finance math or statistics seems particularly hard. Hell, most of it is just division and multiplication." He had finished the soup. "Plus, commodities trading was pretty much just guessing where the market was going to go, or wasting time with charts and stuff. It seems like trading mortgages would actually require using your brains and getting paid for it."

"And you have such a cute brain. So big, and so fast, and so modest." Larisa poked him in the ribs.

"Hey, Fisher said you can make a million a year in a job like that. And that you can get to that kind of level fast. I wouldn't mind that kind of pay." He remembered Ned Johnstone had said the same thing.

"I wouldn't mind that kind of money myself," Alicia said, "but I had no idea you were such a greedy little devil."

"I didn't know you were such a greedy little devil."

"Neither did I, really. I mean, when we would go visit my dad's clients, the way some of them lived was mind-boggling. I gotta admit, maybe I even resented it. My dad worked so hard, and we couldn't dream of ever living like that. But maybe I could actually succeed at this. Whatever the hell 'this' really is!"

"Well, from what I've seen, you usually figure out a way to get what you want. After all…" She spread her arms wide and glanced down at herself.

"Ummm, I seem to recall *you* jumping me." Warren moved in for a hug.

"Cutie, I *always* get what I want!" Larisa squeezed him hard in her arms. "You never had a chance."

❧

In early spring, dozens of firms scheduled on-campus recruiting meetings for jobs that started in August 1984. In addition to the general meetings, most included a formal interview schedule. Warren spent a lot of time talking with Claire Tompkins in the Career Counseling Office, and the two of them had decided that investment banking, on the sales and trading side, was for him. He was outgoing, smart, and personable and had some experience with the markets. She was confident that he would get a place at one of the top firms.

"Listen, if you get shut out of the bulge-bracket firms, it's not like the second tier don't pay as well—some pay more. Just go for the best first." She'd recommended Weldon and Goldman as the two best places to work from the reports of graduates. First Boston was in the middle, powerful but somewhat disorganized. A classmate told a story about interviewing with Goldman that gave Warren some doubts. The guy had been set up by his uncle, a powerful banker at Lazard Frères, to meet with Robert Rubin, the head of equities. Rubin had kept the kid waiting over four hours in his office, only to then blow him off. "I got sick of looking at that picture of him and Jimmy Carter, and he never even so much as apologized after having told his secretary at least five times he'd be down in five minutes!" Goldman sounded like a place that didn't treat junior people well.

Warren got hold of annual reports and went into the library to check periodicals. He learned about Salomon's economist Henry Kaufman, called Dr. Doom, whose interest-rate forecasts moved the markets, and John Gutfreund, the round, cigar-chomping head of the firm, who made billion-dollar bets in the bond markets without blinking an eye. Weldon was famous for its mortgage department, the only one able to compete with First Boston's, run by Larry Fink, and Salomon's, headed up by Lew Ranieri and Mike Mortara. Warren tried to memorize the names, and to get a sense of the culture of each firm. Goldman pushed itself as an ethical company, which seemed oxymoronic to the nature of the business, but intriguing despite the stories he'd heard from Austin Karr in Florida. He agreed with Claire's hierarchy and decided to make Weldon his first priority and First Boston number two. Though he doubted he had a shot with Goldman Sachs and Morgan Stanley because of his college grades, he signed up to meet with them during their on-campus interviews.

Austin Karr, who had kept in touch since Florida, sent Warren's résumé to a friend at Weldon, and they had given him an appointment for a full day of interviews at their offices, which allowed him to avoid the on-campus interviews altogether. He'd also talked to Ned Johnstone about Merrill, but Warren had decided afterward that the firm was too huge a bureaucracy for him.

Generally, he felt the prospects were fairly promising. After all, the Street was starting to do well again after a long lull. The stock markets had picked up a little steam, and interest rates had been volatile, making trading houses profitable. Salomon had made record profits two years in a row. There'd be plenty of jobs—he hoped. Warren's grades were excellent—he made dean's list, and only Serena Marchand had a higher GPA among the top students interested in a trading career.

Larisa had been very much in favor of the career choice. She had met some of the people at the investment banks on campus, even though she wouldn't graduate until a full semester after Warren, and was extremely impressed at the amount of money they made. It wasn't unusual, she learned, for a new hire to be making a mid-six-figure income after only two or three years. That sounded great to Warren—his savings would pay his rent for the year cover his final tuition, and carry him maybe another couple months, but things were beginning to feel a little tight. He just hoped he'd make it through the first round of interviews and get at least a couple callbacks. He felt that Ned had given him some great advice. It was almost impossible to get a job at one of these prestigious firms without an MBA. Though he had never imagined himself capable of working in a regular nine-to-five, or in this case maybe seven-to-seven, job, the prospect of making as much money as people who had spent a decade at a law firm or building a medical career made it seem like a great investment.

Warren checked his closet. He had an Italian suit that was inappropriate, but the conservative, charcoal, nailhead-wool, single-breasted Brooks Brothers suit his mom had bought him as a college-graduation present was perfect. He made a special trip to Saks for a new white Oxford shirt, and Larisa surprised him with an Hermès tie. The blue and red silk set off the gray flannel, and it had cost more than his shoes, which hadn't been cheap.

On the morning of his first interview, he suited up and checked himself in the mirror. A clear-eyed, young Wall Street moneyman stared back. He had even shaved off his usual stubble. Larisa gave him some final advice. "Warren, you don't always have to say exactly what you think all the time. If someone gets you mad, or you think someone is an idiot, just keep it to yourself. Turn on the filter! Maybe even count to five or something." She was right. Trading barbs with Corelli or pointing out a mistake by his stats TA might be fun, but sometimes it was better to just shut up.

The tense bubble in his gut wouldn't go away, but he figured there really was nothing to be too nervous about. Almost nobody got a job at Weldon, so he might as well try to relax and learn from it. He stuck a few résumés in his pocket, just in case someone hadn't read it, and headed out, prepared, as best he could, to do battle.

six

❦

When he got out of the subway at the Bowling Green station, Warren was relieved. To people who had grown up outside New York, the subway system was a daunting, frightening underground inferno. Warren had never gotten used to it even though he had spent months living in the city with his mom almost every year. Once back on the street, he found his way up to Old Slip, and the offices of Weldon Brothers. He felt reasonably assured he knew what to expect—the placement office at school had taken everyone through practice interviews, and he had handled himself well. He had done his research and knew the names of most of the department heads and important people, such as Pete Giambi, the highly regarded, young fixed-income research head who specialized in mortgage-backed securities.

Weldon Brothers was acknowledged as one of the premier investment banks in the world. It had been founded by two brothers early in the twentieth century to compete with the firms started by Marcus Goldman and Samuel Sachs, Orthodox Jews who had begun a company that financed trade receivables, and the Lehmans and Schiffs, aristocratic German Jews who were raising money for shipping companies. The Weldons, two distinguished-looking young men whose father owned a regional railroad in the South and virtually controlled the import of coffee beans into the Northeast, had seen a need for a Protestant trading house. Founded on such inegalitarian motives, the firm, by the time Warren came to interview, employed forty-two hundred people in seven countries, had assets of almost $47 billion, and generated a pretax profit of approximately $400 million a year, after paying the average midlevel professional compensation of some $400,000 annually, most of that in year-end bonuses. It occupied a solid niche in what was called the "bulge bracket," the top six firms used by blue-chip clients to raise money in the stock and bond markets. First Boston, Salomon Brothers, Goldman, Morgan Stanley, and Merrill Lynch were its main competitors. Warren had investigated each company and felt Weldon best suited him, with its strong mortgage-backed-securities department, and its aggressive trading image.

❧

One Old Slip, just above the Salomon Brothers building on the East River waterfront, was a massive tower that commanded a sweeping view of the harbor and the monuments to money that had been erected in lower Manhattan since the nation was young. Warren crossed the windswept plaza and pushed through a set of revolving doors into a cavernous, granite-clad lobby with an immense and powerful Frank Stella painting suspended on the far wall.

The security guard in the lobby called upstairs, and Warren was given a pass to the nineteenth floor. When he got off the elevator, a sleek reception hall with burnished wood trim and the firm's logo in large brass letters greeted him. The woman at the console took his name and asked him to take a seat.

After a few minutes, a short, heavyset young man in a billowing white shirt and red tie emerged from the glass doors and headed toward him. "Warren?" The man's hand was extended.

"Yes. Are you Rich?" Warren stood up and gave a firm shake.

"Yup. Rich Symanski. You're right on time." Rich's attitude seemed congenial enough.

"Thanks. It was an easy trip." Warren noticed Rich had a sheaf of papers in his hand. Symanski caught him looking.

"This is a couple copies of your résumé and your interview schedule. Hope you're ready for a long day." They were making their way along the perimeter of the trading floor, a cavernous, double-height room that contained about three hundred modular trading desks with no partitions or walls, just stacks of video monitors and computer screens. The open floor was a nest of activity, with dozens of young men in white shirts and ties holding phones to their ears, some yelling out numbers, others pointing to the small trading screens. A few women were scattered around. The tall windows were tinted dark against the bright daylight, and the fluorescent lighting gave the scene a greenish cast. To their left, a line of offices, each with a glass wall, fronted on the floor. Absolutely no place in the entire room had any real privacy.

"Here's your schedule. We're starting you off with the toughest part first. You survive that, you move on. You'll finish with Jillene Manus, head of HR. Hey, I'm the oldest Weldon trainee ever. I'm famous." Symanski handed Warren a typed sheet as they walked.

"What do you do now?" Warren took the sheet and scanned it, noticing Symanski's name was not on it, and wondering why he would be proud of coming so late to the game.

"Oh, I'm just starting on the convertible desk. Not cars. Bonds. Convertible bonds." Rich giggled to himself a bit.

"Well, I suppose they're not so great for those rainy days." Warren figured a little humor might ease his tension. He knew what convertible bonds were; Fisher had covered them a few weeks before. And bonds were supposedly safe investments, literally good for the proverbial rainy day.

"Hey, hotshot, think you were the first to come up with that one?" In fact, Symanski had never heard that play on words before, and Warren could tell by his tone.

"Nah. Just learning as I go," Warren said in a conciliatory tone, minding his girlfriend's advice and holding back from adding a sarcastic *Aw, shucks*.

"You're learning pretty fast, rookie. Now, here's Bill Pike's office. I'm going to do you a favor. Someone must have had it in for you to start you with him first. He's the biggest prick in the place. Only one out of ten get past him. He'll piss all over you. Just do your best not to let him get to you. After him, you're on your own to find the guys on the rest of the schedule. I might be tied up." Rich knocked on the door and cracked it. He leaned his head in and spoke briefly, then ushered Warren in past him. "Warren, this is Bill Pike. He's in charge of fixed income—that's bonds. Bill, you've got Warren's résumé on your stack there. He's from—"

"Jesus Christ, Symanski, that's enough. Get your fat, fucking lard ass out of my office already and go make some money, will ya? What are ya, a goddamn secretary or something?" Symanski started to object, but Pike cut him off. "Yeah, yeah, I know. Just leave me and Wonderboy here alone. Go take dictation or something." Pike picked up a golf putter that was leaning against his desk. Symanski grinned, tittered, and ducked out. "Fucking fruitcake, wouldn't know a bond if it tried to blow him in the bathroom," Pike muttered under his breath, then looked up at Warren with an appraising glare. "So, you wanna work for Weldon, eh?"

Pike was easily fifty pounds heavier than Symanski, though no taller, and his gut rolled over his pants. He wielded the putter like an ax and paced around the room, which was at least fifteen by thirty, with a huge partner's desk, a seating area with a sofa and three chairs around a coffee table, and golf balls scattered across the floor. He didn't offer Warren a chair.

"Yes, sir." Warren was a bit off-balance. Pike's hostility was like a big, angry wave perennially about to break.

"Now there's a deeply considered answer. 'Yes, sir.' I didn't see any military service on your résumé there, Wonderboy. I saw Columbia and Cornell. Let me ask you something: Why might you want to work for Weldon?" Pike's walruslike face loomed closer as he swooped past on his orbit toward the bank of blinking screens behind the great desk. Warren didn't correct him about having gone to Brown and not Cornell. Pike didn't seem to be the kind of guy you'd want to correct, to put it mildly.

"Everyone recognizes it is the top trading house on the Street, Mr. Pike. If you want to trade, anyplace else is second best. I want to trade." Warren tried to sound confident—he knew from reading the newspapers that Weldon and Salomon were always competing to be considered the biggest, ballsiest trading house. He figured a little flattery might ease Pike up a bit.

"*You want to trade. You want to trade.*" Pike's whiny imitation was halfway between a school-yard taunt and a lament. "What the fuck makes you think you even *know* what it means to trade? What makes you think you know *any*thing? You're just some goddamn kid who's going to come in here and be the hottest fucking piece of shit we've ever seen, eh?"

Pike reminded Warren of a lot of professional hockey players later on in their careers. He'd seen them at Rangers' games. Surly, scarred, short-tempered. He could imagine Pike in a Red Wings uniform, trying to smash in the teeth of some first-round draft pick.

"Um, no, sir. I've just found trading fascinating, I'm extremely interested in mortgage-backed securities, and—" Warren was about to say he just wanted a chance to get into the system, but Pike cut him off.

"You've found trading fascinating. Just exactly what the *fuck* have you traded in your illustrious career, Mr. Hament?" Pike had stopped, bent over, at the screens, perused them, and looked up at Warren.

"Well, I traded metals and some other futures on the COMEX and NY-MEX, and a few financial futures through a friend who is a member of the Chicago Board of Trade—"

"Financial futures? Let me tell you, Wonderfuck, you don't know fuck-all about financial futures. Did you know that I *created* half of the fucking futures contracts? Did you know that? I hate guys like you. Fucking locals. Scalpers." Pike was pacing again, his voice heavily laced with disgust and anger. "We eat guys like you for fucking lunch. Man, Weldon could just fucking *crush* you like dust if it wanted to, did you know that, you fucking Wonderputz? A bunch of fucking parasites." Pike seemed ready to pop a blood clot. Warren was nervous for real, beginning to wonder if this was just a "stress" interview, which the placement office had prepared him for, or if Pike actually didn't like him for some reason.

"Um, Mr. Pike, I didn't mean to suggest that I could compete with Weldon. . . . I haven't traded anything for almost two years." Warren could see no other option but to be almost submissive.

"Yeah, and if you were ever to work at Weldon, you might never trade anything again. We tell you if you sell or trade or wash windows, we tell you when you have to go to the bathroom. You fuckwads think you know it all. You know jack shit. Jack *fucking* shit." Pike finished his soliloquy by plopping down in his chair, behind the desk, in front of the screens.

"Yessir." Warren blended the words on purpose. Pike had just said *"if you were ever to work at Weldon."* That wasn't the kind of thing you said to someone you didn't think had a chance. Warren decided to play along and be superhumble. "And that's exactly why someone like me would consider it a great opportunity to work at Weldon. For the chance to work with experienced pros like you, guys who've been through it all and are at the top. Where hard work and some guts might pay off."

"Ho-ho-ho, Mr. Warren Hament. *Brown* fucking University. I like it. 'Experienced pros?' You making a little fun with me, asshole? Very nice, scum-bag. I like it. Now get the fuck out of my office." Pike turned his back on Warren.

Warren took a second to figure out how to respond. He just went with it. "Might you tell me where I could find Mr. Dressler?" Carl Dressler, head of mortgages, was the next name on the list. Warren would be ten minutes early. Pike had been playing with him—the Cornell "mistake" was some kind of test.

"Out there. Call that fat little faggot Polack. He's your nursemaid, isn't he?" Pike pointed toward the trading floor.

"Thanks. Nice to meet you." Warren was soaked with sweat, but had the sense that Pike liked to see how potential hires stood up under the abuse.

Pike flashed him a grin. "The pleasure was all mine, son. Close the door, wouldya?"

Warren stood outside the office for a moment to regroup. The onslaught of crudeness, vulgarity, hostility, and bigotry was not what he had expected, even in a stress interview, but he felt he'd done okay. Being around the crude-ness of the commodities exchange had built up some immunity, but the rela-tive peace and decency at Columbia had made it a bit of a shock.

He headed back toward the reception desk, where he asked for Syman-ski. The receptionist handed him the phone.

"Did you love him, big guy? Was he great?" Symanski was obviously eat-ing, his words muffled.

"Terrific. It was a lovefest. Thanks for the tip. What should I do now? Go see Dressler or just hang myself in the bathroom?" Warren was trying to adopt the collegial tone. "You free to bring me over?"

"Save that for later. Carl's on the floor. I see him from here. Wait. I'll get him. Meet us in the office two down from Pike's. Just wait there."

Warren hung up and backtracked. As he passed Pike's office again, he saw him putting at the distant sofa leg and noticed a collection of balls, all five feet or more short, and all left. He went into the open office down two doors.

After Warren had spent a few minutes alone thinking things over, Carl Dressler walked in and shook his hand. Dressler ran the mortgage-backed-securities department, which was clearly the hottest area in the firm. Word had it they were making money hand over fist. He was surprisingly muscular, with long, thick hair, but an incongruously, nasal voice with a San Fernando Valley twang. He peered at Warren through round, wire-rimmed glasses.

"Hi. I'm Carl Dressler, I run the mortgage desk. I see you're at Columbia." He pulled up a chair and gestured for Warren to sit.

"Yes, sir. I graduate in May," Warren answered neutrally.

"What do you think you might like to do?" Dressler s manner was so different from Pike's, Warren had to take a second just to slow down from the frantic assault to a civilized interview.

"I think I might like to trade mortgages for you, Mr. Dressler." Warren couldn't help but smile when he said that because he believed he meant it. He instantly felt comfortable with Dressler and already liked him.

"What makes you think that? And call me Carl." Dressler steepled his fingers and pressed the spire against his pursed lips as he focused on Warren.

"It's obvious the two growth areas on the Street are mortgages and structured products. It's between Weldon, Salomon, and First Boston for best in both businesses, and I personally think Weldon's going to come out on top." Warren's conversation with Austin Karr and his reading were paying off.

"Why's that?" Dressler had a small grin on his face.

"Because of you. And Pete Giambi. Between your desk and his research, I don't see who can beat you. I'd love to be a part of that." Warren tried to make his enthusiasm sound as real as it felt.

"You've done a little homework." Dressler suddenly shifted the topic. "Where are you from?"

"I grew up mostly on the East End of Long Island and then upstate."

"Upstate?"

"In a town called Millbrook—it's near Poughkeepsie."

"I know Millbrook," Dressler said, waving his hand. "It's where a few of the investment bankers keep their wives' horses." He added derisively, "Are you some kind of polo player?"

"Not really, sir. I ride a little because I used to take care of people's horses during the summer. My dad was a tennis coach and liked to buy and sell houses. My mother's a teacher."

"She moved around with your father?"

"No. Actually, they were divorced a long time ago. I spent the school year with my dad in Millbrook and then on the East End, and summers with my mom in Manhattan. She had the summers off, and my dad had to travel a lot."

"What kind of teacher?"

Warren was surprised at how curious Dressler was about his family. "She was an art history professor at NYU."

"Impressive. Do you have any brothers or sisters?"

"Yes. I have an older brother, Danny. He's a doctor—actually a cancer researcher in Houston. He's older than me. He went to boarding school, so I didn't see much of him after sixth grade."

"Are you married?"

"No. I have a great girlfriend at Columbia, though."

"A father who taught tennis, and a mother who teaches art history. She must be something of a scholar. How did you wind up here? Why are you looking to become a trader?" Dressler's tone was mild and inquisitive, almost psychiatric.

"I kind of wandered into it through a friend who got me trading on the COMEX and NYMEX." Warren's answer was rehearsed, but he managed to make it sound fresh. "Also orange juice and metals. I made some money, and I liked it, but it's very limited, and you really need big capital to be anything more than a little scalper. So, I decided to go back for my MBA. I did well enough to pay for school and a couple of vacations, and now, here I am."

"What did you learn in business school? Why did you go?"

Warren laughed a little. "I wasn't exactly sure why I went until this semester, to be honest. I knew I wanted to do something different, but I didn't know exactly what or for whom. A trader from Merrill advised me B-school would be useful. When I learned about MBS in Professor Fisher's class, I realized that was what I had been looking for. Something that demanded thought and analysis and wasn't just making wild bets on the markets, or slowly working your way up some corporate hierarchy. And besides, without an MBA, I doubt your recruiting office would have scheduled me at all. I guess I could have found a cheaper way to learn about fixed-income markets, but school was fun—there seemed to be more girls than tests." Warren liked Dressler's manner and found it easy to talk to him.

"So, you majored in English literature in college, traded some futures and made a few bucks, then went back to business school and now you want to trade bonds. Seems logical. Why not? Do you really know anything about mortgages? Do you have any idea what real trading is all about?"

"Well, I knew my dad was always having trouble getting a mortgage," Warren joked, and Dressler chuckled. "I've done a lot of studying. Read about optionality and the different prepayment models. How every MBS pool has unique characteristics, and there are real opportunities to make money through hard work, not just dumb luck or guts. I was a competitive tennis player, and I learned the hard way that really succeeding usually means really applying yourself. I am willing to work harder than anyone when the rewards are there. And, honestly, I want to find a way to make a lot of money that doesn't require ten years of working up some kind of political ladder. I understand a bit about MBS coupon spreads and relative value. But at the end of the day, trading mortgages seems to me to be all about understanding prepayments. After that, I figure that sales and trading is all about communicating, and that's something I've always been able to do reasonably well."

"That's a pretty good answer, and a pretty long one." Dressler smiled. "Yeah, you definitely have the communication thing down. How'd the communicating go with Bill Pike?"

"I think I got his message," Warren said with a regretful look.

"Nahhh! Pike doesn't really hate you, he just resents all the young kids coming in here every day. He's a dinosaur. He loves to rattle rookies." Dressler shifted in his seat, and Warren sensed that the interview was just about over.

"Well, he succeeded. But he still pulls all of his putts short left. Maybe I could help him with that." Warren smiled as he said it.

Dressler met his gaze, smiled back at him, and nodded. "Maybe you could, at that."

Warren started thinking about his name under the Weldon letterhead.

seven

After his interview with Dressler, Warren worked through four more sessions. The men got younger and obviously less senior as he progressed. He'd enjoyed talking with Jed Leeds, a young mortgage trader, and Hart Campbell, a new salesman who had graduated from Wharton a year before. The last name on Warren's list was Pete Giambi, and after fifteen minutes discussing everything from the Philadelphia Flyers to prepayment models, futures, and forward pricing, Giambi, the head of mortgage research, cut off the interview.

"Who else are you talking to on the Street?" His high forehead and round glasses imparted a slight sense of age to the youthful face, and a small smile curled Pete's lip.

"Well, I was planning on seeing Goldman and Salomon, but Weldon is my first interview and my first choice." Warren decided to commit because he felt his day was going well, and he genuinely liked Giambi. He was enthusiastic, obviously brilliant, and they had a lot of common interests. And Weldon was everyone's choice as the "hot" firm for new MBA's—a bulge bracket leader that allowed Associates to advance quickly in growth areas.

"Let me ask you something. If we offered you a job right now, would you take it?"

"I'm not sure. That wouldn't exactly be smart of me, I don't think. I mean, what good trader wouldn't check out the interest away at other firms?" Warren had picked up some of the trading lingo from Leeds, whose speech was peppered with it.

"You're probably right. Look, with your trading experience and skills, I think you'd do well at any firm. Honestly, the top firms don't pay new hires any differently no matter how good they think you are. The only thing they can offer you is the promise of a job in the department you want after the training program. That's your ticket to moving up to the next level in pay quickly. I spoke to Carl Dressler about you before you came in. I think you could get Jillene to promise you a place in the mortgage department if you took a job here right away. That's pretty unusual."

Warren knew that few people came into the top firms with a secure job placement. Once they got into the training program, they'd have to prove and sell themselves to department heads in the hot areas. It wasn't unusual for 10 or 20 percent of a training class not to get placed in the firm at all and to be fired within a year. Giambi was telling Warren he had a good shot at coming into Weldon with a place trading mortgages. There was no better or more desired job on Wall Street. To be in the fastest-growing sector of the fixed-income markets at the firm considered the best in the business was a virtual lock on the fast track to big bonuses and promotions.

"That's a pretty attractive idea." Warren understated it, and stayed calm.

"Look, there's no need for you to spend any more time interviewing here, unless you want to. I'm going to pick up that phone as soon as you leave my office and tell Jillene to hire you and offer you a job anywhere you want it. Carl liked you, and I think you're the best candidate I've seen so far this year. You'd be amazed how few MBAs have any trading experience. Even Bill Pike thought you took abuse pretty well, and that's an important quality in this line of work." Pete stood up. "I'm not supposed to do this, and I'm certainly not supposed to tell you all this. But I hope you'll take the job. Jillene will make you commit before she actually offers it to you, though, so you better make up your mind before you see her." Pete put out his hand.

Warren shook it and smiled. "I believe the appropriate response is 'You're done.'" Leeds had explained that was how traders universally said that a trade was confirmed.

Warren took the elevator up to the forty-first floor and sat down in Jillene Manus's office. She was the head of Human Resources and Professional Services, and in charge of the recruiting and hiring of business school students. She came in and shook his hand. A tall, heavy-boned woman with gray-flecked and frosted hair, she had a gravel voice harshened by a Rhode Island accent and chain-smoked Kents.

Warren watched her write some notes in his file, her script precise and rounded. "You've got the Brearley swirl."

Jillene looked up. "I'm impressed."

"My mother was a Brearley girl." He couldn't help but smile when he said it. His mom had always been proud of her link to the prestigious Upper East Side girls' private school. Warren had learned to copy the rounded letters perfectly to forge excuse notes when he cut classes or had to sign a bad report card.

"No kidding."

"Yup. Class of... maybe 1949?"

Jillene smiled. "A little before my time. What's she do now?"

Warren filled her in, and Jillene pushed back from her desk.

"Well, sounds just like a Brearley girl. I must say, it wasn't the most practical-minded place. I majored in philosophy at Smith, for God's sake." Jillene paused a moment. "Anyway, Mr. Hament, it seems you have had quite a day at Weldon Brothers."

Warren grunted.

"And, much to my amazement, both Carl Dressler and Pete Giambi want me to break the rules. I have a question."

"Yes?"

"If I offered you a job, and I'm not saying I will, would you take it?" She looked at him quizzically, leaning in, with a pencil touched to her lower lip.

"Umm... that depends." Warren was grateful to Giambi for preparing him for this little game.

"Yes?"

"It depends on whether I'd have a guaranteed spot in mortgages if I wanted it."

"Let's say that, assuming you pass all the tests and registrations, not to mention our background check and a drug test, you did. Would you accept?"

"Can I ask the pay?"

"You can ask." She grinned coyly.

"Can you give me an idea?"

"We're competitive with the top payers on the Street for a new associate."

"Well…yeah, I guess I'd have to say I'd take it." Warren was a little overwhelmed. He'd walked in the building scared about interviewing at a bulge-bracket investment bank and was walking out with a job. An actual job, probably before almost anyone else in his class had so much as interviewed!

"Well, then. Congratulations. I am offering you a job in our 1984 training class. We will actually start you in the summer, and you're expected to be placed by mid- to late fall. The base pay is forty-seven thousand, and you can expect a bonus of five thousand more if you are successfully placed, and significantly more if you contribute immediately to the firm's bottom line. Obviously, there's a full benefits package—health care and such. We will pay all your expenses for preparing and testing and registering with the various exchanges and regulatory bodies and, if you need, give you a clothing allowance of two thousand dollars. You live in New York, correct?"

"Yes."

"Then you don't get moving expenses. We provide all the training materials, and you can have lunch on us every day, and dinner when you're here after seven, which will be most of the time. That's for as long as you work here. You'll get a carrel in the training room until you're placed, and temporary business cards. We begin in mid-June, so you'll get a two-week break after graduation. We recommend that you get a lot of R and R, because you're going to work your tail off once you start. You get ten days' vacation your first year, and another week after every two years to a maximum of six weeks. Any questions so far?"

Warren shook his head no.

"Good. I'll have an offer letter out to you tonight and will expect your signed acceptance by early next week. If you turn me down, you will never work at Weldon. Your paperwork will be processed when you start in June." She picked up the stack of papers in front of her and tapped them to straighten the pile. "It doesn't usually work this way. You're lucky. Honestly, I think serendipity may have played a role here."

"Serendipity? How?" Warren wasn't sure what was coming.

"We interviewed a young lady last week who I thought was very impressive. As luck would have it, she has had to withdraw. A terrible story."

"Terrible? Why? What happened?" He was a little off-balance.

"She fell down the stairs at Uris Hall yesterday. Broke her collarbone and a few ribs and got a terrible head injury."

"Uris Hall? She went to Columbia? Who was it?" Warren looked up, surprised.

"Serena Marchand. Did you know her? She was very interested in mortgage trading too." Jillene thumbed through another stack and pulled out her résumé.

"Serena? She got hurt? I didn't hear. Jeez, that's terrible. Is she gonna be okay?" He hadn't been to school since the previous morning.

"Well, her adviser called and said she was in critical condition, was not going to be able to take finals, so we may not be able to consider her for the entering training class."

"Wow. God." Warren wasn't sure of what else to say.

Jillene stood up and put her hand out. "I have just one question left for you."

Warren stood up, took her hand, and raised his eyebrows. "And that is...?"

"When you get on the floor, are you going to be good, or are you going to be great?"

"Both, I hope."

"Good answer. Welcome to Weldon." They shook hands. Jillene's grip felt like a steel vise.

eight

❧

When he got to her apartment in Chelsea, Warren was disappointed that Larisa wasn't home from classes yet. She had been more nervous about the interview at Weldon than he was, and neither of them had dreamed he would come home with an offer. Goldman Sachs was known to pass a potential hire through as many as forty separate interviews over four or five weeks. Warren knew Larisa would be ecstatic. She'd left the key for him with the super, a lethargic man in a mechanic's uniform with JIMMY embroidered on the pocket. His name actually was Carlos, and he made Warren wait for five minutes while he searched for the envelope.

As soon as Warren got through the door, he tore off his suit jacket and tie and rummaged through the refrigerator for a beer. As usual, nothing was in there except some old yogurt and a bottle of white wine. He took out the wine, threw away the yogurt, and found a clean glass. The cork came out easily, and once his glass was filled, he sat down by the phone and called his father.

Ken Hament had followed Warren's advancement with amazement. The world of finance left him totally cold—he understood it about as well as programming a VCR. The amounts of money seemed unreal to him. Warren had told him if he got a job at one of the big firms, he hoped, after his first six months, to make close to $100,000 a year. There was no answer at his dad's house, so he left a message and flipped on the TV. To his surprise, the phone rang less than five minutes later.

"Hey, kiddo, it's yer pappy!"

"Hey! Figured you'd be out and about all day." Warren was used to his dad's unpredictable travel schedule, and knew it might take him four or five days before he checked his messages.

"Actually, I was down your way yesterday. Didn't want to disturb you, what with the big day and all."

"You were in the city? Jeez, I woulda loved to have dinner or a drink with you! What made you take the long drive? Important client?"

"Something like that. I had to see the Dunlop factory rep for the club. They've gotta give us more of a break on our orders."

"You were always a hustler, Pop. Still, it would have been nice to shoot the breeze. But I have some good news!" Warren recounted in detail what had happened at Weldon. When he told his father his starting pay, his dad let out a low whistle.

"Well, Warren me boy, don't let it all go to your head. You're a smart kid—Christ, you and Danny are the two smartest people I know other than your mother. You're more like your grandpa than me. He was a tough SOB. You got his head for numbers too." Ben Hament had been a successful bookie in Baltimore when it wasn't strictly illegal and fought off the Mafia for almost ten years before they shot him in his living room. He retired immediately. "Just stay humble, and keep your head down. Those big companies can be murder."

Warren stifled his usual impatience with his father's advice. He'd coached Warren to play tennis with control and tone down his power. Despite himself, Warren knew that his inability, or unwillingness, to take his father's counsel was probably what had limited him to being merely a good college player, but nothing more.

"You gotta figure the same qualities that'll make you a success in the slaughterhouse could also hurt you. Take opportunities, but try not to step on too many toes, or somebody will want to get you. Try to keep that razor wit of yours in your pocket." Ken couldn't help but give advice. Like Warren's grandfather, Ken referred to Wall Street as "the slaughterhouse." Even to a bookie, the action on Wall Street seemed geared to grinding up people and taking all the money.

"Thanks, Pop, I'll try to make you proud." Warren hammed it up, and his father rewarded him with a hearty laugh.

"Warren, I'd be proud of you if you were driving a cab and selling pencils on the subway. You're a great son, and I love you." The older man never let a conversation pass without expressing his affection for his children. He knew that, no matter their inattention, they thrived on it, that it gave them a secure base to build on. Ken Hament had never asked for any money from Warren, and the two never talked about it. Warren was happy to send his dad a check anyway. "I wish you were here so I could give you a big hug and a kiss."

"Well, maybe I'll try and get up there during my time off. You coming to town again anytime soon?" Warren heard the front door open, and Larisa saw he was on the phone and waved to him before she headed for the bedroom. He smiled and gave her a thumbs-up.

"Nope. Unless you want me at your graduation."

"I don't see business school graduation as a big event. I was planning on being someplace like on a sailboat, to be honest. I'll only get a few weeks before I start work." Warren heard Larisa close the bathroom door.

"Ah, you kids today. All you think about is self-gratification. Come visit your poor old father, and I'll whip your butt two out of three. And if anyone gives you any guff, I'll take 'em down!"

Warren laughed. His father hadn't taken a set from him since his thirteenth birthday. "Dad, I'm afraid you've created a monster. But I gotta go. Larisa just came home."

"Some monster. Give that girl a hug for me. How you ever landed a looker like that I'll never understand!" They said good-bye, and Warren popped up as he put down the receiver.

Larisa was in the bathroom, washing her face. "Jesus, it was hot on the bus. How'd it go?" Her voice made bubbling sounds through the water.

"The bus? You took the bus? Not bad. Jeez, did you hear about Serena falling down the stairs?"

"Yeah, everyone was bummed. Evidently she's in some kind of coma. It was during classes, and no one saw it. I didn't really know her, but it's so awful." Larisa paused for a moment, then shrugged. "Anyways," she said, grabbing a towel and changing the subject. "Come on! What happened? Think they'll call you back?"

"God, that's terrible. Jesus, a coma? Poor girl. Umm... I'm pretty sure I'll go back, but not for a while." Warren made his voice sound noncommittal.

"What, they have to see everyone else first?" She sounded a little deflated.

"Not exactly."

"What then?" She was carefully blotting her face with the towel. "What did they say?"

"They said that I start in June, I'll make about fifty-two thousand through December, plus a performance bonus if I earn it. I get money to buy clothes, and I have a placement in mortgages if I want it." Warren leaned back, a huge grin splitting his face.

"'What? You're kidding! In 1984 dollars?" She dropped the towel and her jaw at the same time.

"Nope! No joke! That was exactly the way I imagined you'd look when I told you!" He felt a warm surge run through him...this had actually happened, and his girlfriend was ecstatic. Suddenly it seemed real.

"I don't fucking believe it! No way!" She screamed, jumping up and down on the bathroom floor. "Yeeee-hah!" she let out a rodeo whoop, and jumped into his arms, wrapping her legs around his waist, almost knocking him over. She started smothering him with little kisses. "Holy shit! Holy fucking shit! A job offer on your first round? A *placement*? Jesus!"

"Yeah, they made a big deal out of it. And they said I can get a decent bonus this year too, if I contribute."

"*More* than fifty-two in your first year *for six months*? That's *insane*! I made twenty-six at ITT last year, *including* my bonus. With an MBA, I might make forty all in if I go back. For twelve fucking months!" He had backed out of the bathroom and still supported her around his waist. "My little man is an investment banker! Hah!"

"Nope," he said. She kissed him. "Just a low-life trader."

She kissed him again. "That's okay, sweetheart," she said as they toppled back onto the bed, "I don't mind slumming so long as the pay's so good."

nine

❧

Frank Malloran wasn't in bad shape for squash. Not exactly good shape, but he moved pretty well for a forty-two-year-old Weldon Corporate Finance managing director. Directors worked long hours and ate far too many fancy meals with clients. Warren had been hitting high lobs to Frank's backhand, then short drop shots, to wear him out, and Frank was beginning to wheeze a bit. He was also starting to get pissed. The two weren't saying a whole lot, and all you could hear was the resounding thwack of the racquets, and the squeak of their sneakers on the maple floor of the brightly lit squash court.

"Eight to three." Warren announced the score as he prepared to serve.

"I know the fucking score," Frank growled. His side ached a bit, but he didn't want to let on.

"Hey, Frank, if you need a break—some CPR, a little oxygen—let me know. Really, there's no rush."

"Hey, Warren. Screw you. Lobbing little punk. Serve 'em up." Warren hit a soft, deep serve, which Malloran scraped off the wall. Warren drove a backhand crosscourt, which the older man scrambled after and scooped up off his shoe tops. Warren volleyed the ball hard back to the same deep corner, then took Malloran's defensive lob and killed it into the front corner.

"You were right. Lobbing's not my game. Had enough?" They were both sweating, although Frank looked as if he'd just taken a fully clothed shower.

"Enough? I'm just getting started. But Jillene'll rip me a new one if you

don't get back in time for the afternoon session." Frank opened the door to
the court, and they headed out to the locker room. "God, you've only had
three months at the firm, and fucking off already. Squash every Tuesday
afternoon with a finance guy. Shameful."

"Yeah, well, I wish this training program would end already. Who wants
to be useless overhead? I want to be a producer. Besides, I asked permission
the first time." Actually, Jillene Manus was thrilled that Warren was socializ-
ing with an MD in Corporate Finance. Warren had been rotating through the
various trading desks and finance departments. Malloran's work was mostly on
international plant and equipment investments by major corporations, and
there was usually little contact between the disparate parts of the firm. Warren had seen Malloran heading out with his racquet one day and told him he
should try one of the new lightweight aluminum models. That led to an invitation, which had become a regular game.

"Well, I wish Jillene'd retire already. That woman is forty miles of very
bad road." They'd emerged from the hallway and entered the locker room.
The racquet club locker room was cavernous, and Frank's stall was at the far
end. He was stripping as he walked. "Anyway, she can wait. You're having
luncheon with me here at my club, and we will discuss many matters of
grave import and tremendous value to you and to Weldon in building your
career." Frank was walking in his jock and sneakers now and tossed everything else into a bin at the end of the last bank of wooden lockers. "Throw
your crap in there. Jimmy'll have it laundered and ready when we leave."

"What? You're kidding me, right?"

"Of course I'm kidding you. He'll have it in a plastic bag, so it can mil-
dew under your desk. But it sounds good. Laundry takes about three months
around here. Let's hose down and then eat something. God, why do I always
pick guys who are so good at racquet sports?" Frank stepped out of his sneakers and into the shower room.

The dining room, on the second floor of the enormous Italian Renaissance building, was more like a library, and Warren ordered the crabmeat
salad. He was pleased to be eating with Malloran. A jock was always in demand
on Wall Street, it seemed. Frank was known as a straightforward and decent
guy, who kept a good sense of humor about his work and had, according to his

reputation, absorbed the occasional screwing rather than resort to back-stabbing or office politics.

"When I first interviewed at the firm, I was at Texas, on scholarship." Frank was chewing on a roll as he talked. "Somebody had messed up, and the head of Corporate Finance back then thought I was on a tennis scholar-ship, not swimming, and invited me to his tennis club—here—for a match. I was a complete spastic with a racquet, and the game they play here isn't normal tennis, it's 'court tennis.' About ten people in the world have ever played this fucking game, but he figures, 'UCLA, tennis scholarship, no prob-lem.' Makes a big bet. I think we lost every point. I tell him the screwup, and the next thing I know, he's got four guys in the pool, doing sprints. Com-petitive guy. He winds up even on his bets, I move into his department, and now I drag you here so I can get a workout and keep my girlish figure." The waiter had deposited Warren's crabmeat salad on the table along with Frank's sandwich.

"Anyway, how's it going so far?" Malloran took a huge bite of his tuna-salad sandwich.

"Pretty good. The training program's kind of a joke, but I'm meeting a lot of people—or I should say some people and some other species I'm not so sure of." Warren's crabmeat was sweet and fresh. He squeezed some lemon on it.

"Those'd be the assholes. They've been multiplying lately. They breed like flies on horseshit, and it's hard to keep up with them." Warren liked the way Frank talked while he chewed—he was obviously a guy who knew how to enjoy himself.

"I guess. I like a few of the salesmen I've met, and one or two traders, but I've gotta say that the mortgage traders are tough to take by and large." War-ren was comfortable talking to Frank, who had shared a number of scathing observations about people at the firm with Warren before. If Frank was will-ing to share his low opinions of senior management, Warren figured he could talk straight to him too.

"That's for sure. The biggest mystery is that Frank Tonelli. He should be tossing pizzas in Brooklyn." Frank shook his head. "I don't get how he runs the desk. Listen, once you get placed in a job, we'll go on from there."

Warren was silent for a minute, imagining Frank Tonelli, the head of Mortgage Trading, in a T-shirt stretching pizza dough. It wasn't hard. "You know, that visual works. Anyway, to be honest, I'm not so sure I want to take the job on the trading desk. I'm thinking about sales."

"There's nothing wrong with that. You'd be a good salesman. The traders are a crazy bunch anyway. Just don't piss off Dressler. Ask his permission." Malloran was almost finished with his sandwich. "Conover's okay for a head of sales. As long as no one is after his job, he can be a decent guy. But Dressler is the real power. And you're still a kid, for Christ sakes."

"You know, this is pretty good of you. There aren't too many MDs who would do this for a rookie." Warren meant it.

"I accept your gratitude, worthless one. You can pay me back by telling me if that girlfriend of yours has a sister." Warren had heard Frank's wife had left him for the former head of Project Finance, a guy who later made a disastrous call on the financing of a Brazilian paper factory, cost the company $30 million and some clients much more, and had been sent to Tokyo "to enhance the Far Eastern franchise."

"As a matter of fact, Larisa does have a sister. Supposedly, she's better looking, and two years older. About twenty-eight, I think."

"No kidding?" Frank stopped eating.

"Absolutely no kidding at all. She's been living in Cape Town working with some anti-apartheid group, but she's coming back to town for good in a couple of weeks. Actually, I think she was a runway model in Milan before she got a conscience. I'm not kidding. Want a date?" Warren didn't know why the thought hadn't occurred to him before. Frank was single, successful, smart, good-looking, and a likable guy. No wonder he'd always had a hard time finding a suitable mate in New York, where obnoxious traders, real estate developers, and club kids seemed to get all the girls. Karen would be perfect. She was tall, smart, and, according to her sister, not a total emotional mess. From the pictures Larisa had around her apartment, Karen was absolutely gorgeous. "She's a little into the whole third-world thing, but the right man could probably convince her someone as evil as Henry Kissinger should be secretary of state. Oh, wait, he was!"

"Well, then I'll owe you the big one."

"What's that?"

"The ultimate advice. The only thing you have to remember absolutely." Frank jabbed his fork in the air.

"You've got my attention."

"Anson Combes. Head of Mortgage Finance. He may seem harmless to you now, sitting over in his office. You probably don't have a clue what he's doing over there. I'm telling you, that guy is the fucking doomsday machine. Neutron bomb. Manson. Speck. Bundy. Right now, he's plotting to kill the pope, Golda Meir, Reagan, Mother Teresa, and probably ate his parents alive as a toddler. I'm not kidding around. Psycho killer. Bodies in his crawl spaces. Satan. Beelzebub. You want to live, you keep a million miles away from that guy. Got it?" Frank pointed with his fork again. "Am I clear?"

"Jeez. Yeah. Absolutely."

"Case closed. One other thing."

"What's that?"

"You're going to hear a lot about 'your word is your bond' and ethics for a while. They play that up big-time. But it's just for show. And they mean exactly that—*your* word is *your* bond. *They* can say and do whatever the fuck they want. Trust no one, and believe only what makes sense from the worst possible angle."

"You trying to disillusion me before I even get started, or what?"

"Come see me in five years. You'll kiss the ring, I promise you." Frank leaned back and stretched.

"Somehow, I believe you are right."

"Bet your rookie ass."

ten

◆◆◆

After spending fourteen weeks in a rotation period—two weeks in each of seven departments, learning about their businesses—Warren had been offered the promised job on the mortgage-trading desk by Carl Dressler. Warren was torn. Salesmen generally seemed to be under less pressure than traders, and with a few exceptions they also seemed less frantic, and there seemed to be fewer truly intelligent salesmen compared to the preponderance of whiz kids on the trading desks. Larisa agreed with him. One of her sister's college friends was married to a trader who had an ulcer and an irregular heartbeat at thirty-five.

Weldon had a tradition of white-shoe salesmen—well-dressed, nice-looking men who were holdovers from a more congenial time, when the markets moved slower and salesmen relied on long friendships developed with portfolio managers at major investing institutions such as pension funds and insurance companies. Some of the heavy hitters, such as Bill Dougherty and Dan McAloon, were assigned young protégés to do their computer work and back them up when they were out golfing at Piping Rock or having lunch. Warren recognized that these men were sowing the seeds of their own destruction—allowing young, aggressive sharks to infest their territories, learn their trade, and eventually replace them. The massive paychecks these men earned were out of scale to what they actually did. But, unlike most of the traders, they mostly enjoyed their work.

Warren always smiled and sympathized with the traders' complaints, while marveling that anyone working there could be so unhappy with a job that any of two or three hundred thousand intelligent, well-educated applicants would literally give up their lives for.

Malcolm Conover, the managing director in charge of sales, had offered Warren a spot on the New York institutional bond sales desk, considered a plum assignment. Several of the senior salesmen had taken a shine to Warren and liked his pleasant, unthreatening manner. Unsure of which offer to accept, Warren had asked Carl Dressler to allow him to have some extra time on the trading desk, to see how he felt about it. He'd always had success when it depended on his getting people to like him, and after a few weeks of watching the stress traders operated under, he wasn't sure it was for him. He had also noticed that Weldon had virtually no traders over thirty-one or thirty-two, while many salesmen were in their forties.

"Burnout. It's like a dog's age. Seven years for every one." Alex Stevenson, one of the senior traders on the mortgage desk, at twenty-nine, explained. He had a hawklike face, with hollowed-out cheeks and curly hair around a severely receding hairline. It was the head of a much thinner man grafted onto a round body, his stomach rolling over his belt. His thick arms and neck showed he spent time in the gym, but years of sitting all day had taken their toll. He didn't hesitate to tell Warren that he was earning $1.3 million a year but felt grossly underpaid, and he complained constantly. "This job sucks. You come in every day, and Carl's standing there asking how much money you made. You've got clients on one side trying to pick you off if you make a mistake, and the rest of the Street trying very hard to fit their foot up your ass. Somehow, you're supposed to always be right, because when you're wrong, you lose money. Now, salesmen, though, they've got a great deal! Whatever they buy or sell, it doesn't matter how the firm does, as long as they get their commission. Hey, most of the time we pay a salesman more to get us out of a bad position than for selling a winner. I'm a piece of shit for losing dough on the bonds, and they're a hero for selling them to someone. Then, when you actually have a great year, management fucks you on payday anyway."

Warren had asked Alex why he kept trading, and why he'd stayed at Weldon if the pay was so low in comparison to that of some other firms.

"I honestly don't know. I go in there every year on payday"—he pointed at Dressler's office—"ready to quit and call a headhunter, and somehow that slimy fuck talks me into another year of this agony. I should get myself some big guarantee from some horseshit retail firm like Prudential, roll the dice a couple of years, then retire to San Diego. This place is bullshit." Alex gestured at the expanse of the trading floor, the desks receding in tiered ranks to the walls of windows, easily 150 yards away, every seat filled by a young man or woman in a white shirt, staring at screens or talking rapidly into handsets or the occasional headset. In this hive of activity, shouting and laughing burst out sporadically. On one side, a couple of the treasury-bond traders were tossing a football, annoying the assistants and occasionally sending something smashing to the floor.

"What do you mean by roll the dice?" Warren had asked.

"I mean go work someplace where they give you a percentage of your profits."

"Why is that rolling the dice?" Warren didn't understand what Alex meant.

"Because you go there, they guarantee you a big bonus no matter what, and then you just take huge positions. If you win, you get a piece above your guarantee and you get seriously rich quick. If you lose, it's their money, and you leave with just your guarantee, but a rep as a big hitter—so at least you have big cojones. Other firms will still want you."

"So, why work in a place like Weldon?"

"Well, they tell you that you'll be taken care of and have a long career. Also, they have the big customers—the institutions. The percentage places are usually the retail shops. Their customers are moms and pops with twenty thousand bucks. We only deal with the big boys—you know—pension funds with twenty or fifty billion or even a hundred or more. The crap firms like Pru or Smith Barney just gouge the little guys for big commissions. Their traders usually are more like clerks. Understand?"

"Sure. Since we can't rip off the unsophisticated little guy on a regular basis, we just try to do it to the big guys. But, that generally means you've got to have some brains, 'cause they're smarter."

"Some are, some aren't. But they've all got their charms."

"Yeah, but if you're a good trader, does it matter where you work? And don't a lot of other shops have decent institutional sales?" Warren was perplexed by Alex's misery and refusal to change anything. Alex clearly liked talking about himself, and Warren felt that he was getting to see a side of the business that it might take years to fully appreciate.

"Hey, the devil you know is better than the one you don't. And, sure, Solly, First Boston, and Morgan have good sales forces, but they pay traders the same way as here. My advice is go into sales or get a percentage deal to trade while you're young, single, and have no overhead. Me, I've got a wife, two kids, and a couple of mortgages. I can't afford to take any risks with my career."

Alex broke off the conversation at that point to argue on the phone with Bill Dougherty, a senior salesman, over the value of a $75 million block of FNMA-guaranteed mortgage bonds with a coupon of 10 percent. His customer, Metropolitan Life Insurance, wanted to buy them an eighth of a percent cheaper than Alex was offering them, a difference of about a hundred thousand dollars.

"Hey, Dougherty, tell the Met to get fucked, okay? I'm sick of those guys bidding me back an eighth on everything. Just for once, let them lift me. These bonds are at least a half point cheap to where they should be, and these assholes can't get this size anywhere else." Alex disconnected the phone and turned to Warren. "You see? These fucking guys, they know I've got cheap bonds, that I made a good call when I bought them last week. If they want my bonds, they gotta come to me. I'll drop the price one thirty-second of a point, but that's it. Fucking Dougherty is just the errand boy. Bet they buy 'em." Alex had gotten a little flushed.

"Sounds smart," Warren said, then resumed their conversation. "But is it really Weldon's franchise that makes the position profitable, or is it you?" Warren had been inundated over and over with the notion of Weldon's franchise in the training classes, until the concept had taken on a life if its own. Everything they saw or heard clearly implied that it was Weldon Brothers that made the business happen, that salesmen and traders were just a part of a continuum of bodies filling the precious seats and taking phone calls like clerks.

"Ah, who knows? Look, I made this place thirty-seven million bucks last year. Let's say I'd gone to Drexel or Pru-Bache and gotten fifteen or twenty percent. I'd only have had to make ten million there to get paid maybe twice as much." Alex stopped and studied the broker screens in front of him. Every line was a bond being offered to sell or buy. "Ah, I see the Met went to someone to try to buy the bonds cheaper." He pointed at some numbers that Warren deciphered as a bid. Alex picked up the phone to the broker.

"Bid seven for twenty tens," he said, and hung up. "When the Met hears they're seven bid in the Street, I bet they'll buy my bonds ... ah, I don't have to bet. That's gotta be Dougherty calling me now." He punched another line, for the New York sales desk. The traders and salesmen in New York did business on the phone, even though they sat only fifty or sixty feet apart. "Yeah? ... Billy? How'd I know? ... They wanna pay six? Yeah, me too. I wanna pay six for more bonds, too. Six bid for a hundred million, okay? I'm at seven.... Yup. Seventy-five million to go at seven.... I'll wait." He smiled at Warren. "Okay? ... Yeah, seventy-five done at seven. Take two dollars, priority one, and call me in the morning. Thanks."

"They bought 'em?"

"Yup. At seven. Now, get this. I paid Dougherty two dollars per thousand commission. He sold seventy-five million bonds. That's three hundred grand in gross commission. Priority one means he gets the top percentage payout on commission—fifteen percent. That's about forty-five grand net pay for four minutes' work. And, he's got no positions to worry about, no losses to eat. If I'm lucky and don't blow the four hundred grand profit I just made by doing something stupid, I might see five or ten grand off this trade at the end of the year. Once he prints a ticket, nothing can make him give that money back. Sweet, huh?" Alex shook his head, evidently finding it a little hard to believe himself.

"Well, that's why we're here, right? For the glory of Weldon, and a private plane." Warren smiled.

Alex shrugged. "Yeah. Whatever. All I know is, if I wasn't doing this, I'd probably be one of those homeless guys washing windshields. I really don't have a clue what else I could do for a living." Something defeated in Alex's voice depressed Warren. That Alex had an undergraduate degree in engineering from Princeton, an MBA from Harvard Business School, and had had nothing but success as a trader didn't seem to have helped his confidence in his abilities at all.

"You know what? I think I'm going to go sit with Dougherty for a while. At least he's probably enjoying his big trade. Jesus, you just printed four hundred grand. Shouldn't you feel good about that?" Warren said, amazed.

"Sure. I feel great. Look at me. I could just bust into song or something. So Met Life bought my fucking tens. Now what? Now I gotta think of something else. Maybe we could do a strip deal. I don't know. The month's almost over, and if I don't hit one point two mil, I'll be behind last year. You know, last year was a record year. And we're budgeted to be up twenty percent this year. Isn't trading fun? I hate this fucking job. They're going to carry me out of here in a goddamn box, but I'll be all dried out, like a fucking prune, so it'll be a small, light box. Am I cheering you up yet?" Alex wasn't kidding. His shoulders were slumped, and he was staring tensely at the screens. He had been inactive for no more than two or three minutes, and you could see he was already nervous, bored, anxious. He punched an autodial button on the turret, then hung up before it rang. He scribbled a few notes, then picked up the handset to make a call, paused to look at the screens, then slammed the phone down on the desk. Warren got up and grunted a good-bye. At twenty-nine, Alex looked about forty, and Warren noticed as he got up that Alex was going gray at the temples, too.

Warren no longer had any doubts. Despite what Bill Pike had said in that terrible interview, he hoped that Weldon would let him make his own choice. He wanted no part of the trader's life. Selling seemed a far better lifestyle, and deep down, Warren had to admit he wasn't sure he could do trading or stand that kind of pressure. As Dirty Harry said, "A man's got to know his limitations."

eleven

❧

Fortunately, Carl Dressler had been supportive of Warren's decision to go into sales. He told Warren that he thought Warren would make a terrific trader, but agreed that with his "interpersonal skills" he would probably be more valuable to Weldon in sales. Plus, everyone was impressed with how well Warren understood all the mortgage-backed securities structures, which would be useful in sales. The only issue was one trader on the government desk who, for some reason, hated him. Sean O'Hara was known to be unstable, though, and a little anti-Semitic, and he suspected Warren might be Jewish. Jillene told him to forget about it. Frank Malloran agreed and had said, "If O'Hara would quit stuffing half a pound of coke up half his nose in the bathroom half the day, maybe that half-wit would be half-sane half the time." Warren vowed to try to win O'Hara over.

The first attempt had started unpleasantly. Dan Goodman, a junior salesman, had asked O'Hara the same idiotic question three times about a trade O'Hara had suggested. Even Warren understood the trade—it was nothing more than a purchase and sale to take advantage of a spike in repo rates on a bond that was temporarily in short supply. Goodman's client could earn an effective 10 percent annualized return just to lend another client some bonds for a week. The normal rate was about 4 percent.

"Jesus Christ, Goodman, what the fuck is wrong with you?" O'Hara had said. "You got shit for brains or something?"

Goodman told O'Hara to screw off, that the trader had the whole concept wrong. Everyone was a little stunned to realize that Goodman didn't understand it.

Warren was listening to the conversation with the intermediate trader, and he jumped in good-naturedly, saying, "Hey, Dan, come on! You have to get it! This is embarrassing! Jews are supposed to be smart!" The traders all snickered—only another Jewish guy could get away with a joke like that.

Goodman looked confused for a second, then blurted out, "What? Oh, no, no. You don't understand, I'm *not Jewish!*"

The sheer stupidity of his reply convulsed the entire desk, and O'Hara slapped Warren on the back, laughing so hard tears ran out of his eyes. From then on, every time Warren passed the desk, O'Hara would whine, "Oh, no, no. I'm not Jewish!"—and they'd share a laugh. O'Hara was no longer an obstacle to Warren—in fact he became a big supporter.

Jillene called Warren upstairs in early November and told him he'd been placed in institutional fixed-income sales. He'd be reporting to Malcolm Conover, his salary was raised immediately to $100,000, and he could expect a 50 percent bonus, or better, at year's end if he acquitted himself well over his first eight weeks. He would likely become a commission salesman next year. They talked briefly about Serena Marchand, who had never come out of her coma and was not expected to live. Warren was surprised by the emotion in the older woman's voice—she had only met Serena once for a short interview. Maybe Jillene wasn't so tough after all.

He couldn't wait to tell Larisa all the good news. The downside was that selling would probably involve more travel, but he hoped he might get some accounts in fun places to visit, not just New York. A lot of younger salesmen were given accounts in the Midwest or the South because the branch offices of Weldon were not tremendously strong in fixed-income sales.

"It's really not that difficult to figure out," he told Larisa as they ate their appetizers—green salads in a perfect mustard vinaigrette—at La Goulue, an intimate French bistro on Seventieth Street off Madison Avenue. The room was paneled in a rich brown mahogany with large mirrors and framed pictures lining the walls, the lighting warm and flattering. Crisp white tablecloths and an all-French staff lent the place a true Parisian feel made tactile by the mellow glint of the well-worn silverware that filled the air with the welcoming chatter of fork and knife against china plates. "Basically, the accounts are guys who get paid to buy bonds, and you get paid to sell them. We've got some pretty decent traders, especially in mortgages, and all the accounts have a lot of respect for Weldon. With some of the guys I've been watching, most of their business is just picking up the phone and taking orders, or repeating what a trader says is a good trade to a customer. And they make a ton of money just being parrots. But few of the guys really sell. I mean, they could sell anything—cars, real estate, shoes. There's a guy in LA who's amazing, and a few in New York and Chicago. It just doesn't seem like it takes a lot of brains to do this. Being smart can help, but it sure isn't a requirement."

"You really think it's so easy? Seems to me you can't even keep your notes straight." Larisa had made fun of the notebooks Warren was trying to keep. No matter how diligent he was, his organizational skills stank. He kept forgetting to take notes, or losing the whole book. "But what an amazing opportunity!"

"I don't know about easy," Warren said, taking a sip of his glass of Domaines Ott rosé. "But these senior guys literally make *millions* a year, and it seems like their most stressful decision is whether to order the Lafite or the Petrus at a client dinner. Plus, management doesn't ride them like traders or finance geeks."

"Now that's the kind of sex talk a woman like me wants to hear," Larisa said, leaning over the table and stroking his thigh. "Maybe tonight I can teach you a little lesson about dealing with management the right way."

Warren felt himself respond immediately. Her hair tumbled around her face in the soft lighting, which set her hair ablaze, caught her high cheekbones and emphasized her full lips. She had gotten even wilder in the bedroom after that first night in Florida. She liked to be physical, in control, and when he was with her, the rest of the world just disappeared. Every encounter was an amazing, exhausting workout, and she wasn't embarrassed or ashamed to do anything.

"In your case, I don't mind being...well, you know...managed," he said, leaning over to her and kissing her.

"Mmmmm. Do you think there's something wrong with me? Some guys can't handle that kind of thing." Her hand was under the table now, working its way higher.

"Some guys? You do this a lot?" Warren was only half joking. He didn't know a lot about Larisa's past.

The hand suddenly disappeared from his thigh and reappeared on the table.

"What's that supposed to mean?" She tossed her hair and sat up straighter.

"Umm...come on! Nothing! I mean the way you said that. It's like..." Warren was fumbling for words, realizing there was no way to avoid digging an even deeper hole for himself. So he stopped talking.

"It's like what? Like I'm a slut or something? Like I fuck every guy who looks at me? You know a lot of guys *do* look at me." She was flushed red, and her eyes were tearing.

"No, no. God, no! I was just kidding! I mean, you said, 'Some guys can't handle that kind of thing.' I wasn't thinking. I didn't mean anything like that!"

It didn't matter, she was crying now.

"Please, please, Larisa, forget it! It was just banter. It must be because I spend my day with a bunch of crude assholes. God, I didn't mean to upset you. Please, come on! I know how lucky I am. I'm in love with you. You know that." He was getting upset now too. He could not stand to see her crying, angry, hurt.

Her hand went from her face and took his, interlacing fingers. She tried to start speaking, but had to stop and take a sip of water.

"I'm in love with you too," she said. "But this is not easy for me. You need to understand that."

He didn't. But he was willing to try. "I want to make it easy. What do I need to do? You are an amazing girl, and I want to make everything easy for you."

"Warren, I am not as amazing as you think I am. I'm just me. I'm not that smart, and I'm not that special. You're doing so great with everything. I have a long way to go." She was wiping her eyes.

"What the hell are you talking about? You get straight A's at Columbia, you're gorgeous, you're funny, you're generous—did I mention gorgeous? Oh, and you're gorgeous too." He pulled her hand toward him and reached out with his other to smooth her hair. "And I love you. If I love you, you have to be pretty goddamn amazing."

She laughed a little, then wiped her eyes and nose with her napkin. "You are so good to me. I don't deserve it."

"Stop saying that. Why would you say that?" Warren was mystified. So many of the world's most spectacular women seemed to think so little of themselves.

"If you really knew my family, maybe you would understand more."

Warren didn't say anything. He only knew her family from pictures in her apartment—her stunning older sister who lived in South Africa, but would be coming back to New York soon; her father, who looked like a German movie star; and her mother, who could have been Garbo's sister. There was also a boy in one picture of the whole family, but he had no idea who he might be, and she had never mentioned him..

"Why do you say that? I know your parents are incredibly proud of you. I hear you on the phone with them."

"Yeah. Great. They're proud of me. I'll be rich someday, maybe. Or marry a rich guy who can take care of me," she said derisively. "My fucking family."

Warren was more than a little stunned. This was totally new ground. As if on cue, the waiter deposited their entrées and, with an innate Gallic sense of privacy, somehow picked up on the moment and retreated immediately, without even asking if they wanted fresh pepper.

Warren pushed his plate of duck aside and leaned in closer. "What's going on? I don't understand. I know they're divorced, but you seem to get along great."

She looked as if she had turned to crystal, all the color gone from her face. It was as if at any moment she could break—shatter—into fine, glistening shards. "Have I ever told you about my brother?" she asked almost defiantly.

"Your brother? No. You never told me you had a brother. I know about your sister...."

"Yeah, my sister. She got to take off to Le Rosey in Switzerland in ninth grade. I got to stay home and deal with the jocks and Jamie. Jamie Mueller," Larisa said, spitting out her brother's name as if it were sour milk.

"What do you mean? Was he younger or older?" Warren asked.

"He was two years *older* than me. But he was out of control. Lazy, arrogant...impossible. And my parents just left it to me to deal with him. I was little Miss Perfect. Straight A's, sports, yearbook editor...he smoked dope and liked to shoot squirrels and birds with his stupid, fucking pellet gun. He was kept back twice and kicked out of all three private schools in Charlottesville." She had put down her silverware and was trembling a little.

"Wow. How could they leave it up to you? You were his younger sister, not his mother." Warren tried to imagine a teenaged girl attempting to control a difficult boy her own age.

"They were too busy with their own careers. And my dad was always screwing around with a TA or someone. JJ looked just like my dad, too. I think that just pissed Mom off even more." Warren was about to ask why she used the past tense, but Larisa kept on. "So, I tried to keep him from getting drunk, or driving and getting arrested, or breaking into people's houses for fun. I swear, boys are the most pathetic little animals on the planet. So we had this big argument in senior year. He was in the same year as me, for God's sake. He wasn't going to get into any decent college anywhere, and even UVA told my dad Charlottesville was out because of his arrest record, not to mention his academic issues. Even though my mom was in their HR department! I told Jamie he was lazy and stupid and had no ambition, and that Mom and Dad were ashamed of him."

"Sounds like you told him the truth," Warren added, trying to be supportive.

"Yeah, I told him the truth." Larisa shook her head. "He went in and had a huge fight with my dad, who called him a loser. So he proved I was wrong. Guess what that moron did?"

"I don't know. Rob a bank?" Warren shrugged.

"Hah! If only. No, he went and enlisted in the army the next day. My dad tried to get them to release him, but Jamie told him to butt out. It was 1974. The fucking war was over! But old JJ wouldn't have made it to Vietnam, anyway. My dad's panic was for nothing. He got drunk the night before parachute training and somehow screwed up his equipment and died in a field somewhere in Kentucky."

"Oh, God. That's horrible." Warren winced at what this must have done to her and her parents.

"Yeah, well, my dad, who never accepts any blame for anything, dumped the whole thing on me. Said I should have never said he had no ambition and was stupid. Forget that *he* called Jamie a *loser.* Anyway, that was it for my parents. They both blamed each other and also blamed me. I couldn't wait to get out of there. We're civil to each other now, but if I could've gone anywhere else for school, I would have. Free tuition is a big deal."

"Wow. I don't know what to say." Warren was a little flustered. "I guess I should have asked before. I mean, how could I not know something so important about the woman I love?" He took her hand. "I'm ... I'm ..."

"Sorry?" Larisa finished for him. "Don't be. From then on I knew I was on my own. My brother is dead. My parents are both alone. I'm in New York, and nothing, *nothing,* will ever make me go back there. We talk like we're close, but we're not. Don't be sorry. Don't.... Hey, I'm lucky."

"Lucky?" He was confused.

Larisa reached across the table and took his hand again. "Yes, I'm lucky. I found you."

Warren wasn't sure, but at that moment he thought he could feel his heart breaking.

twelve

✦

The next six weeks passed quickly. Warren was officially assigned to the sales desk and sat in with each salesman in the group for a few days, listening, and occasionally even helping take an order or run some analytics. Warren was surprised when Malcolm Conover called him into his office for his year-end review, which he hadn't expected for at least another week, and said his bonus was going to be $70,000. Warren flushed a little. It was huge, but someone like Dougherty could make that in a week.

"Get used to making a lot of money, Warren. I think you're going to do well. You're promoted to AVP immediately, and you will start on your own accounts next week."

Warren couldn't help but wonder if all his fellow associates who weren't bombing out had been told the same thing.

Malcolm immediately changed the subject from money to Warren's new account list, and a change from salary and bonus to full commission. His initial account package included Glendale Federal and Warner Savings, two decent-size and active West Coast savings banks. Both had expressed a desire to be covered out of New York. Dutch Goering, a senior New York salesman, also covered a West Coast thrift, Golden State. In addition, Warren was assigned Monument Management, a medium-size mutual fund company, and Emerson Insurance, a smaller life insurance company in New York. But the best had been saved for last: he would also back up Bill Dougherty, the senior salesman, who covered a half dozen of the biggest accounts in New York, and two big state pension funds, Wisconsin and Ohio. Dougherty's backup, a kid named Walther, had been caught passing stock tips from Corporate Finance to his friends. He claimed not to realize it was inside information, but once the New York attorney general had been informed by a client, that was it for Walther's time at Weldon. Amazingly, he'd been hired at Drexel Burnham almost immediately.

Warren knew being assigned to back up Dougherty was a huge opportunity. It almost cemented his future as a big hitter at Weldon. When Doughtery retired or left the firm, Warren would get the list. If he could build good relationships with the accounts, he might push Dougherty aside and get primary coverage on them even sooner. Warren knew some important business was to be done with the State of Wisconsin pension—they were looking at completely overhauling their investment strategy. If he could get to know their senior people, particularly Barbara Hayes, it would serve him well.

Warren also liked Bill. Dougherty was pleasant, about six feet tall, with sandy hair that he slicked back, and ice-blue eyes, a patrician-looking fellow whose family had been figures in New York City politics and finance for several decades.

Bill was not a detail-oriented salesman, but enjoyed solid relationships with his accounts. Warren had already tried to emulate some of his style, but with more substance. Every day after six, Warren went to the gym to work out, then spent several hours reading after dinner. He spent most nights with Larisa at his apartment, since her classes started much later than he had to leave—she would generally still be sleeping when he slipped out the door in the morning. When she didn't come over after school, he occasionally went back to the office in the evenings, to study and to chat with Pete Giambi or other research people, trying to learn as much as he could about the markets.

When his bonus check cleared, he sent his father $5,000, and his brother's hospital $3,000 earmarked for the genetic research Danny was leading. Warren also sent along a note promising to stop in next time he was in Houston. He took the remaining thirty-odd thousand after taxes and bought treasury bills. Dull, but safe and liquid. Exactly what you would try to talk accounts out of buying—low margin for the firm.

Warren developed a routine. First thing every morning, he would call each account, giving them a three-minute summary of what was going on in the markets, and mentioning the major "axes," or positions, that the trading desks were pushing. He might also fax written-up trade ideas. If he got a positive response, he'd follow up with more information and calls.

His first giant trade had been with Monument. He had convinced Nathan Leonard, the senior portfolio manager, that he should sell his GNMA 10.5 percent mortgage securities to buy GNMAs at 9.5 percent. Interest rates were dropping, and prepayments would likely accelerate, making the higher-coupon bonds less attractive. Nathan had agreed and sold $600 million of GNMA 10.5s and bought the same amount of 9.50s, at a price difference of two points. This had also fit the trading desk's needs perfectly, as they were doing a structured security deal with the 10.5s. Leonard had done all the business with Warren. It was one of the biggest swaps anyone had ever done at Weldon. It made Warren a hero. He was assigned a $600,000 commission. Based on a 15 percent payout, he quickly calculated that this one trade would be worth some $90,000 in real money to him.

After Warren had completed the trade, he sent a memo to Leonard, thanking him for the business. He told Leonard that the trade idea had actually been Giambi's and suggested that Warren and Pete set up a lunch with him soon. Warren knew that, once a smart portfolio manager met Giambi, he'd do more of his business with Weldon, just to get Pete's ideas. Portfolio managers on the "buy side"—Warren's clients—were all judged on how their portfolios performed relative to an index of their peers. Good ideas that worked meant better pay and advancement for them.

Warren sent copies of the memo to Giambi and the manager of Fixed Income. Later that day, Warren was surprised when Anson Combes stopped by his desk to chat. Warren noticed that the salesmen around him all stopped talking, eager to hear what was said. Combes was short, just under five-six, but looked like a prototypical banker, reasonably fit, with carefully cut, thick, whitish blond hair, piercing grey eyes, and thin lips behind which lurked even, pointy, white teeth. He wore rectangular, black-rimmed glasses that gave him an air of diligence rather than a nerdy look, and his face had softened around his sharp features to make him seem a bit jowly. His head always seemed to be pushing forward off his neck, a posture that imparted a sense of aggression and restless energy that women evidently found attractive.

"Hey, Hament, nice trade with Monument." Combes seemed to be passing by at random and paused to congratulate Warren almost as an after-thought.

"Oh, thanks." Warren couldn't figure out how Combes even knew about the trade. He barely even knew Combes—they'd been in a couple of meetings together, and Warren made every effort not to call any attention to himself.

"Yeah, Kris Jameson mentioned it to me. Showed me your memo." Combes laughed nervously, and Warren noticed that Combes had a tic—he'd scratch his left ear whenever he laughed. This odd laugh was a sort of a hissing accompanied by a heaving of the chest. It made Warren uneasy.

Kris Jameson was the head of Fixed Income, which included the entire Sales and Trading division, a heavy man who was rarely seen on the floor, and no one was certain what he actually did. He had an office on the executive officers' level, a vast and impressively decorated room that he had completely redesigned. Rather than the floor-to-ceiling windows present throughout the rest of the building, Jameson's office had been Sheetrocked and reconstructed with large, colonial, eight-over-eight windows. The walls had been lacquered a deep hunter green, a fireplace installed, and a portion of Jameson's collection of eighteenth-century American furniture filled the space. A freezer was stocked with Häagen-Dazs rum-raisin ice cream, which Jameson consumed constantly, at least partially explaining his enormous girth. Jameson's hobby was buying and renovating historic buildings, and his purchases kept several Madison Avenue antique dealers afloat. Warren couldn't imagine that Jameson would have known or cared about Warren's trade, or that he would have mentioned it to Combes.

"Yeah, Pete did a nice job." Warren started to try to look busy. Obviously Anson's visit wasn't happenstance.

"Well, I can see you're a first-class ass-kisser. Anyway, Jameson told me we should talk about your accounts—whether we can do more business there. I've kind of been covering Golden State and Warner myself the past year on the finance side. He said we should coordinate." Combes's smile had disappeared with an almost audible snap, and now he was leaning in over Warren's desk.

"Uh, sure, Anson, that's a great idea. I didn't know you'd been talking to them. Warner never mentioned it to me. Neither did Malcolm. Or Goering."

Warren could feel his bile rising. Combes was pushing his way into Warren's account base already. It was bad etiquette for a finance officer to talk to an account without at least letting the salesman know. In fact, it was pretty much a rule not to.

"Malcolm? Malcolm's a fucking idiot. Malcolm probably doesn't even remember your name, or mine for that matter. Haven't you caught on that he's not all there?" Anson had a look of incredulity, a kind of conspiratorial smirk at how dumb Malcolm Conover was.

"Gee, Anson, I'll have to look for that in the future. Thanks for the tip. Anyway, how can I help you with Warner?" Warren avoided the trap of agreeing that his boss was a moron.

"Well, for starters, you could get Malcolm to assign you Golden State instead of Goering. He's like his namesake—a crazy German who likes to blow things up. Anyway, right now, just keep on doing what you're doing. But keep me informed about anything you hear from them. I'm working with Golden State on some more big stuff down the line, assuming they can stay healthy long enough, and I bet we can do business with Warner. See ya." Anson turned and walked off. Warren put down his pen and shook his head. Anson fucking Combes was telling him what to do.

"Man, what a piece of work, huh?" Kerry Bowen sat to Warren's right, and had overheard the whole conversation. She was a smart and pleasant woman who had been at Weldon two years, moving up the ladder quickly in sales. She covered three of the biggest insurers in Hartford and New York and had done well. "He's scary."

"You're telling me? Jesus, I hope I don't have to work with him. He terrifies me." Warren liked Kerry and, despite his best instincts, trusted her.

"Good luck. Just do me a favor and don't mention my name to him. I like my job." Kerry reached over and patted Warren on the arm.

"What is it about him that sends the chills up my spine?" Warren remembered Frank Malloran's advice about Combes.

"The guy's a real bastard. When I started, he'd just gotten divorced from his first wife. No kids. He started sleeping with the wife of an AVP who worked for him. He'd send the guy to New Mexico for a week, and literally bang his wife in his bed the whole time. So, she leaves her husband for Anson, but meanwhile he was also screwing Marisa in research. Anson had promised her they'd get married, but he dumps her and starts dating some twenty-two-year old Associate. About six months after that, he decided the department was overstaffed, so he fired seven people in late October, including the ex-husband. I'm amazed neither of them sued. Too embarrassed I guess. Nobody got any bonuses either. Just in one day with no warning, out that afternoon. Some good people too. Shall I go on?" She loved to gossip, and Warren had obviously tapped a rich vein.

"He ever hit on you?"

"Nah. I'm not his type. He likes 'em young and dumb and hot."

"That's why I thought he'd go for you." Warren smiled, and Kerry cuffed him on the head. "Wiseass. That's the last time I cover for you when you're in the can."

"Well, I guess the best thing to do is shuck and jive and try to steer clear." Warren shrugged his shoulders. "I mean, I'm just the new kid. What do I need Darth Vader on my case for?"

As with many conversations on the floor, this one ended abruptly when one of the direct wires to a client's desk started flashing on Kerry's turret. Warren sat idle for a moment. Something about the way Combes had so clearly announced his intention to be involved with Warner and Golden State was odd. It made Warren nervous. Why would Combes want Goering off of Golden State? It looked as if, despite the warning from Malloran, Warren was going to have to deal with Combes, after all. He dismissed his worries for now, since, he reasoned, there was nothing to be done, he was too new to the business to be thinking geopolitically, and most important, it was lunchtime, and he was still excited at the concept of the firm's buying him lunch every day. He realized that it was simply to ensure that no one felt the need to wander too far from his or her phone, but a turkey and Swiss on soft rye with lettuce, tomato, and mayo seemed to be calling his name. Anson Combes would wait. Oh, and a good, sour pickle.

thirteen

❦

The hours at work had reduced the amount of time Warren spent with Larisa, but she had been pretty busy with her last semester at school and had begun the interview rounds at the investment banks as well. Warren had not been shy about pushing her on Jillene—he believed Larisa would be an excellent Corporate Finance recruit. Jillene couldn't disagree. Larisa's grades were outstanding, and her desire and drive were obvious.

Weldon had set a total of thirty-four new associate positions to be offered that year. There were well over six thousand applications. Warren knew that there was a bit of a quota system for each of the top schools, with women and minorities given a slight edge if they qualified. Jillene confided in him that four men and one other woman were in the final cut for the three positions Columbia would be allotted in the Finance associate derby. They were all good candidates, with diverse work experience and strong recommendations. It would be a close contest.

The subject became an obsession in the evenings for Larisa. Weldon was the "hot" firm again because its Mergers and Acquisitions department had hired some key talent away from First Boston and gotten a lot of big advisory assignments. Their Reorganization Department, which specialized in assisting firms in financial duress restructure, had also been heating up, as sections of the economy faltered. Most business school graduates who were interested in Wall Street, which was most business school graduates, wanted a job at Weldon Brothers.

After the final round of interviews, and midterm exams, Warren had agreed to spend a long weekend skiing with Larisa and two other couples—Nino Cortez and Anna Meladandri, a pair of friends from Columbia, and Kevin Salton, whom Warren and Larisa had met at a tennis tournament in San Francisco when he was in high school, and his girlfriend, Kate. Kevin, who'd graduated two years before from Stanford business school, had recently started working for one of the new "hedge funds," which didn't actually hedge at all, but made huge speculative bets with investors' money and reaped huge returns if they paid off. Warren had been surprised—Kevin had known nothing about markets, and less about trading. He had been a mountain guide after college and focused on international corporate finance at business school. Salton hadn't been sure about what he would do when he graduated from Stanford, but he said, "Warren, there is absolutely nothing I won't do, short of killing someone, to get wealthy. I mean *dynastically* wealthy." He seemed well on his way. Evidently he was pretty much *running* the new fund.

The group's destination was Killington in Vermont, where Kevin had rented a house on the slopes and treated everyone. The drive up had been fun, with Anna and Nino splitting most of the driving. Anna was exceptionally bright and well-read, and intensely conservative in her politics. Warren had enjoyed playing devil's advocate on a variety of issues and was impressed by her range of knowledge. He was a little concerned when she told him she had applied to all the investment banks as well. She would be tough competition for Larisa at Weldon. Larisa hadn't noticed—she was busy talking to Kate about shoes and face creams—two things Warren had no idea she was particularly interested in.

The weather had been threatening all day, and just as they pulled into Kevin's driveway, the snow began to fall. By the time they finished cleaning up from dinner and everyone retired to the porch, three or four inches were on the ground.

"Nice day for the powder hounds tomorrow," Kevin said, and exhaled a cloud of steam and smoke from a fat cigar. "I know some unreal tree runs if it's still coming down."

"Thanks, but I'll stay to the open spaces. Last time I went tree skiing, I had to remove a couple of stumps from my chest." Warren was beginning to get the idea he was a little out of his league in this group. He was a decent skier, but deep powder and narrow runs intimidated him. He hadn't skied more than five or six times in his life.

"Don't worry, Warren, old Kevin knows all the best spots. I'll take good care of you."

"Hey—that's exactly what I'm worried about."

On the first run of the morning, Kevin made his taste for adventure obvious. He continually skied down the hardest line, and although he was a strong and skilled skier, he was by no means graceful and took his share of flops. Tall and thin, with his shock of red hair, he was quite a sight. Warren took his time and made it down without embarrassing himself. Larisa was phenomenal on skis. She seemed to float above the snow effortlessly. Anna skied well and conservatively, never pressing to keep up on the hardest runs, carving a steady line of symmetric turns. By the third run, Kevin was encouraging everyone to slip under the boundary ropes to ski some chutes he had learned about with some friends on the ski patrol on earlier expeditions. Warren passed, but first Larisa joined, and then Anna and Nino, who, despite his reserved demeanor, was an excellent skier, graceful and aggressive.

Warren was content to spend the day with Kate, a stunning young woman, not particularly long on conversational skills, but a joy to look at, and a prudent athlete. She admitted on a chairlift ride that dating Kevin was probably a complete dead end for any girl—he was only interested in money and thrills—but he was successful, very attractive, and a free spender. Just in the past few months he'd taken her to Colorado to ski twice, to the Caribbean once, and to Australia on a fishing expedition. Kevin's rapid ascent to high living in just a year was breathtaking.

They had all agreed to meet for a late lunch at the base lodge, and everyone looked flushed and happy. Kevin regaled them with a story about how the feral head of Fixed Income at Lehman hadn't even understood basic bond math when Kevin had gone in for his interview before graduating. The two senior lieutenants had seemed no more intelligent than their boss. "How guys like this get their jobs is just beyond me," Kevin said. "They must just be great at killing off the competition. I swear one day those morons will blow that place up."

After Lehman and other good firms didn't offer him a job, he explained how he decided to spend a few months as a climbing guide again, to pay the bills and think about what to do. On his first job, halfway up an easy ascent of Kilimanjaro, Kevin had expressed his drive to become wealthy to his middle-aged client. The man, one of the top global hedge fund managers, had told Kevin that he would set him up with his own fund and funnel money to him, and all he needed to do was follow orders and he would get what he craved. He said they often teamed up with some of the investment banks and other big funds to attack currencies or food commodities, and being able to divide up the positions among several seemingly unaffiliated firms would keep the regulators off the scent.

"Hell," Kevin said, "any one of the big boys could corner the markets in pretty much anything with the leverage the banks will give us. It's easy money! I'm talking billions with a *b*."

Warren asked if that wasn't illegal collusion, and Kevin just shrugged. "It ain't collusion unless you get caught, and trust me, the regulators aren't looking, and all of them want jobs with us anyway!" Warren laughed a little, but he was beginning to wonder if his dad wasn't right about the financial world. Was anyone running a straight game?

Soon, Kevin and Larisa were eagerly plotting the next out-of-bounds area they could explore, while Anna and Nino relaxed and sipped some mulled wine. It was an act of will to get up and continue skiing, but Nino and Anna said they would team back up with the "cruising crew" for the rest of the afternoon and let the daredevils go it alone. Before they got to the top of the gondola ride, though, Kevin and Larisa had goaded and enticed them into changing their minds.

The snow kept falling, and the temperature dropped along with the visibility, and after an hour, Warren had had enough. The snow was up to his knees, and he had a hard time controlling his skis. He and Kate skied back to the house and warmed up by the fire. The crackling flame and exertion of unused muscles lulled Warren into a doze, and he slowly passed out on the sofa, while Kate read German fashion magazines.

The noise that woke Warren up sounded like a waterfall, but it was actually a helicopter passing low over the house, its engine working overtime in the thin air and bad conditions. Though he was groggy, it seemed odd to him that anyone would be up flying in such weather, but backcountry skiers who chartered helicopters tended to be foolhardy souls, and they were probably seeking out untracked powder. He found a comforter on one of the chairs and snuggled back in for an extended nap.

In a few minutes, though, these plans were scuttled. Kevin and Nino came trudging into the house with terrible news. Anna had missed a turn, lost control, and fallen off a small cliff. Kevin and Nino had been ahead and didn't know it had happened. Larisa had been between them, with Anna in the rear, and noticed that Anna had disappeared. She had reported it when Anna didn't show up at the bottom of the hill. The helicopter had taken twenty minutes to get up the mountain, and another fifteen to find her. She had a severe skull fracture, and several broken bones, and was in critical condition. Larisa, the lightest of the three, had been allowed to ride in the chopper down to the hospital. Nino and Kevin had agreed to meet them there. Nino was a wreck. Kate helped him get out of his wet ski clothes and got him to sit by the fire and take a sip of some bourbon while she went to get him a change from his room.

"And that's not the whole deal, either," Kevin said. "The cops told us we could all be arrested for skiing out-of-bounds, and I've been kicked off the mountain for the season. Man, I'm stuck with this house, and I can't ski here anymore."

"Hey, Kev, that's very sensitive of you," Warren chimed in. "Maybe Anna will rent it from you to recuperate." He was angry at Kevin. Skiing out-of-bounds had all been his idea, and all this guy could think about was his fucking *ski pass?*

Everyone piled into Kevin's Land Rover, and they skidded down the mountain and then into town. By the time they got to the hospital, Anna's condition had deteriorated. She was unconscious and was undergoing surgery to relieve pressure on her brain from swelling. The police had notified her family in Eau Claire, Wisconsin, who were arranging to fly in as soon as possible.

Warren found Larisa in the waiting room. Her eyes were red rimmed, and she looked badly shaken. He hugged her, and she spilled tears, blaming herself for helping talk Anna into the risky skiing when she was obviously tired. Warren soothed her, saying that Anna was an adult and made the decision herself, just as he and Kate had decided not to, and Kevin had been the instigator.

"God, Warren, it was like half of her head was missing. I don't see how she's going to survive that."

He noticed blood on Larisa's ski pants and shuddered. "Ugh...I'm so sorry you had to see that. It must have been horrible."

"I must be jinxed," she said, shaking her head.

"Jinxed? Larisa, this happened to Anna, not you." Warren regretted it as soon as he said it.

"*You think I don't know that?* Jesus! Back in Charlottesville, a girl in my class was hit by a car when we went shopping for our prom dresses. I had to see that, too. I know it happened to her, but I don't understand why I had to see it." Larisa was crying, shivering, and trembling all at once, and Warren just kept quiet, holding her in his arms, until she stopped. They just sat there, holding each other, waiting.

After two hours, the surgeon came into the waiting room and introduced himself. Unfortunately, Anna's chances did not look good, he said. She had severely injured her brain in the fall and was currently unable to breathe without a respirator. Her vital signs were weak, and he did not know if she would live out the night. He told them that medicine could do nothing more for her, and that it was a miracle she had survived the fall at all.

The sad group gathered in the hospital cafeteria. They decided that Nino and Warren would wait at the hospital. Nino wanted to be sure that if Anna didn't make it, her family didn't get the call from a doctor or a policeman, but from one of her friends. If she did, they'd trade shifts until the family arrived.

As they stood up to leave, their decision was made moot. Anna hadn't made it out of the recovery room. Larisa and Kate broke into sobs, and the three young men all sat down. Warren thanked the nurse and got the family's phone number from Larisa. Nino was too upset, so Warren made the call. He was relieved when he got a family friend, who told him Anna's parents were on the way to the airport. He gave her the horrible news, and she assured him they would get it before they got on the plane. He and Kevin then went to the hospital's main office and signed the necessary forms to keep Anna's body waiting for her family, and to take financial responsibility for her bills, if necessary.

"It's just a business precaution. Nothing personal," the cashier had said. "I'm sure she had good medical coverage."

"I'm sure you're right," Warren had replied.

They had all stayed until Sunday morning, when Anna's parents arrived. They were beyond consolation. Kevin simply told them that they had been having a great time skiing, and that she'd died doing something she loved and was good at. It was the truth, and her father acknowledged it and actually thanked Kevin, despite knowing that he had led his daughter under the safety ropes and taken her where she should not have been.

The trip home was endless and depressing, with Larisa sleeping most of the way. Nino had stayed behind. Warren tried to occupy his mind with driving, and positive thoughts, such as the beautiful new apartment he had just rented, but by the time he reached the Bronx, he couldn't wait to get back to the office, to get his mind off the vital young woman who had fallen, literally, on the rocks. Maybe Kevin could just forget about it, and Warren had no doubt that most of the people he worked with would just shrug something like that off as bad luck, but what was the point of this relentless pursuit of money when there was so much more to life? Even Kevin had spent a couple years climbing mountains. What had Warren ever done, except play tennis and get from paper to paper or test to test? So far, Malloran was the only person he'd met at Weldon who seemed like a decent, well-rounded human being. Malloran could talk about art and literature and confessed that he'd been a French-movie freak in college. A Finance Associate working with him on a valuation had told him Malloran was an advanced scout Army Ranger in Vietnam, something he never mentioned to anyone. It figured—a guy who was a hero in a doomed war, and he didn't even bring it up. All the guys on the trading floor ever talked about was sex, sports, or money. Warren wondered if that's what he was going to become.

Through the windshield, the rays of late-afternoon sunlight slanted across the thin winter sky and washed up against the stone and glass towers of Manhattan. The fiery light was without heat, but bathed in it the city looked like a vast furnace, an engine that powered greed, envy, and lust and that would carry Warren to a destination he had yet to decide—if his fate would even be in his own hands.

fourteen

❧

"Can you believe this?" Warren opened the door to his new apartment; Larisa stepped into the foyer after him.

From Central Park West, Eighty-First Street runs one block from the green oasis of Central Park to Columbus Avenue as a broad, Parisian boulevard. On the south side, two long, even rows of old honey-locust trees form an elegant colonnade that flanks the Museum of Natural History and the Planetarium park. The apartment houses that line the north side of the street benefit from the open-air space and the southern exposures, with sweeping views over the West Side and Central Park to the towers of Central Park South. Warren's new home was a four-and-a-half-room aerie on the tenth floor of the building just off the corner of Central Park West. He had sublet it, with an option to buy after a year, from a soap opera actress whose business manager had stolen most of her money. Built in 1908, the building was an ornate beaux arts pile with twelve-foot ceilings and huge French windows.

"Jesus, it's like one of those great Parisian apartments!" Larisa exclaimed, spinning around in the living room. It was her first visit. Warren had moved just three days before from the tiny, dark brownstone apartment on Seventh-Seventh Street off Third Avenue he'd been living in since coming to the city. He'd told her his new place was as small as a closet, so she would be surprised.

It had been a good week. Larisa had also just heard back from the investment banks, and Weldon had offered her a spot in the Corporate Finance training class, one of the lucky twenty out of maybe a thousand applicants. She'd also been offered jobs at JP Morgan and Merrill. She'd accepted Weldon.

"Well, at least it has a nice view." From the windows, the buildings along Central Park South and Fifth Avenue stood sentinel over the park, dwarfing its trees and looming over its lawns and paths. He'd snapped the place up when the broker showed it to him.

"So, is this one of the rewards for being a big bond salesman?" She wrapped an arm around his neck and gave him a soft kiss.

"I'm afraid so. God, forget the apartment! I can't believe you're going to work at Weldon!"

"That's right. You're dating a Finance geek."

"Well, I always wanted a banker with great legs, but Paul Volcker was taken." Warren ran his hand up her calf, then up under her skirt. He leaned over and they kissed, while his hands explored.

"It's not too late. I hear he's getting a divorce," she whispered in his ear, making his neck tingle.

"That slut. She didn't deserve him. Only I can make Paul truly happy." Warren affected a heavy lisp. He had her shirt open, and her skirt mostly down her hips. They fell backward onto the sofa.

"I don't know. Don Regan has better teeth. I would have thought you'd go for the treasury secretary over the chairman of the Fed." Larisa undid Warren's belt, and he started kissing his way down her belly.

"Nah. It's Volcker I really want. But, in the meantime, I know just the thing for the girl who has everything...."

She closed her eyes as his lips reached their target.

⤜⤛

"So, who told you you got the job? Was it Jillene?" Warren had his head propped up on one elbow, and an open carton of delivery rotisserie chicken was between them on the bed.

"Yup. She says, 'Weldon is interested in you,' like it's a person or something. Then she asks, 'If we offer you the job, will you take it?' I asked her if this meant she was offering me the job, and she said no, but she wanted to know if I would take it if she offered it."

"Yeah. She did exactly the same thing with me. After she told me that I was lucky Serena had gotten hurt...." He paused for a moment. He had heard from Eliza that Serena had been taken off life support and was likely to die within days. Larisa looked up for a second, but said nothing. He hesitated, but kept going. "Maybe I should have tried that approach with you. But I'm too afraid of rejection." Warren had his mouth full of thigh meat and stuffed in a few french fries.

"As I recall, you never asked," she said petulantly.

"That's right. You basically raped me. So then what'd she say?"

"Well, I told her I'd take it if she offered it, and then she said that I was hired. Forty-two five to start, with a bonus in January. I'll be in the Investment Banking Group as an associate, on the thirty-second floor. What do you mean I *raped* you?"

"God, who woulda believed that not only would I become Joe Bonds, but I'd be dating one, too. Not that long ago, I didn't even know what an investment banker was. Only I would've bet they didn't have bodies like yours."

"Really, what did you think you'd be?" Larisa looked at him with her head cocked to one side.

"Remember? Don't you ever listen to me when I talk to you?" he whined in a falsetto, and ducked as a french fry flew by his head. "Hey! I don't know. Honestly. A tennis pro. Or bum. Or work in advertising or something. In college, they told me I was an underachiever." Warren shrugged.

"C'mon. a full scholarship to Brown, and you just hung out? You never told me how you got into Columbia Business School if you were so lazy." Larisa had worked incredibly hard at UVA and earned a 3.75 GPA. Warren's had been 2.8.

"I got really good GMAT scores, and I also had a friend who was a graduate. He wrote me a great recommendation, once he saw my GMATs."

"What do you mean by great scores?" Larisa was curious. And competitive. Somehow, this topic had never come up before.

"They were good, or at least people said so." Warren hated these discussions and was glad he hadn't had one since freshman year in college.

"How good? C'mon. I want to know how big a supergenius I'm sleeping with. Get a handle on the gene pool." Larisa was acting playful now, but he could see an intensity in her eyes.

"I don't really remember. Somewhere around seven hundred or so, I think." He tried to let it slide. He had scored a 760.

"Okay, you're not going to tell me. Fine. I got a 1340 and a 690. It was the second-best GMAT from Northwestern, according to the counselor's office." Larisa was proud of her score. She'd studied for three months preparing.

"Wow. Jesus. That's an impressive score. For someone with big or little tits." Warren tried to get off the subject with an inane chauvinist joke. It worked.

"I don't think Jillene was looking at my chest when she hired me at Weldon," she sniffed.

"Do you think she knows we're not just pals'?"

"Yeah. I mean, either that or she thinks you recommended me so strongly just to try to get into my pants. Actually, she let it slip that you are considered a star already, otherwise they'd never have let me skip the on-campus interviews. So, I do owe you something. Anyway, Weldon's evidently got a lot of that kind of stuff going on. One of the women that interviewed me started telling me all about the affairs—she said that with the hours you work, you can't help it."

"Oh, I see. It's like, after twenty hours in the office, you get so horny that you just grab the first managing director you see and hump till dawn. And then, you get a free cab ride home on the company."

"Exactly. Hey, I'd fuck you for cab fare." Larisa shoved him playfully.

"My dear," he said, rolling on top of her and crushing the carton of chicken, "why do I have the sneaking suspicion that you already have?"

fifteen

≈

In the next few months, as spring thawed the monotony out of city regimens, Warren still felt that he was on probation at work, but the action, and the size of the transactions, quickly forced him to concentrate and not worry about mistakes. To experienced people, it was easy to keep straight who wanted bids, and who wanted offers, but the language was startlingly imprecise and it was easy to get confused. Still, his worst error was only using a wrong settlement date for a small trade, a minor infraction that was caught by an assistant, and rated but a mild admonishment from Dougherty.

"Screw up like that again, son, and you'll be driving a school bus back in Binghamton," Dougherty had scolded him, half jokingly. Later that same day, the older man had stopped by Warren's desk and, to his surprise, invited him to dinner. "Not out at some lousy steak house. At my house. With my wife. Bring your girlfriend from upstairs." Warren winced. He'd been trying to keep his relationship with Larisa quiet. Warren accepted, but said he'd have to check on Larisa's availability. Corporate Finance associates hardly had time to go home and change at night. Six or even seven eighteen-hour days in a week was not an uncommon schedule.

When he'd called, she asked exactly whom the dinner was with. Dougherty was evidently a big enough name to get the nod, and she was given the evening off by her supervisor. It was unusual for Corporate Finance people to mingle with salesmen or traders, like Warren and Dougherty, who were seen as almost exotic.

Warren recognized the address as impressive, but not until he and Larisa stepped out of the taxi did the full impact hit him, and he remembered reading about it in architecture class. Seven forty Park Avenue is at the northwest corner of Seventy-First Street, a massive yet articulated art deco tower that houses some of the wealthiest people on the planet. The lobby felt like a beautifully decorated bank vault, so solidly constructed that there was no sound of the street once the front door had closed behind them. One of the four doormen took their names and nodded that the Doughertys had said to go right up. Another showed them to an elevator, as the first announced them over an intercom. Warren noticed that an armed security man, who looked reasonably alert, sat at a desk.

This was one of the truly great buildings of New York. Constructed in 1929, it was designed by Rosario Candela, an architect who specialized in luxury high-rises in the era of prosperity that saw some of the city's finest residential construction, planned and paid for before the Crash by its builder, Jacqueline Bouvier Kennedy's grandfather. With masonry and steel exterior walls almost three feet thick, many fourteen-foot ceilings, and rooms of truly baronial proportions, it was, along with 2 East Sixty-Seventh Street, also built by Candela on Central Park, considered the absolute pinnacle of apartment living. It had been John D. Rockefeller Jr.'s home, and he'd bought the whole building before converting it to a cooperative in the fifties. Warren knew that the legendary but repugnant financier Saul Steinberg had moved in, investing almost $20 million and accumulating some fifteen thousand square feet. Steve Ross, the head of Warner Bros. lived here, too. Warren had read that by 1980 a buyer would need to show a cash net worth of over $50 million to even merit consideration by the building's board of directors, who had the right to accept or reject potential buyers as neighbors. It seemed money was their only criterion, but there sure was plenty of it.

The carpeting muffled Warren's and Larisa's footsteps as they crossed the marble lobby to the faux-bois elevator doors. The elevator man delivered them to the eleventh floor, where they exited into a foyer of large-block limestone floors and cream silk damask walls. Two huge, light mahogany doors opened into the apartment, where Bill Dougherty stood, in gray flannel slacks and a white polo shirt under a yellow cardigan sweater, with the emblem of the Lyford Cay Club embroidered at the chest, to welcome them.

Warren introduced Larisa, and Bill explained that his wife, Megan, was on the telephone and would be right out. He ushered them in, through the apartment's own grand foyer, past a sweeping staircase, to a comfortable library, filled with bird's-eye-maple bookcases, where he offered them a seat and a drink. He filled their orders at a bar installed in a recess behind one bookcase.

"This is a beautiful apartment," Larisa said, still standing, as she accepted the bourbon and water, "absolutely beautiful."

"Thank you. It was my parents' house. They left it to me, along with this bad back." He made an exaggerated groan as he sat in one of the streamlined, bottle-green velvet club chairs. "Megan's done a great job redoing it, but it almost never seems to end."

As Bill was talking, Warren took in some of the details of the large, square room. On the east wall, to the left of a carved-wood fireplace, was a small frame holding four military medals, above a line drawing of what looked like Bill in an army uniform. To the right of the hearth was a painting, which Warren believed was a Marsden Hartley. Hung between the bookcases on the north wall was another, larger oil, of an immense flower, which Warren recognized as a Georgia O'Keeffe. Two Paul Manship bronzes were on the side tables by the sofa, and a cubist painting Warren could not identify was between the windows on the west wall. All those years listening to his mother describe paintings in museums and visiting the homes of his father's wealthy clients had left Warren with a reflex to catalog the details of an extraordinary place such as the Doughertys'.

"You have some wonderful art," Warren noted. "I love the Hartley."

"I didn't know you were interested. He's always been one of my favorite artists. My mother actually knew him. He was quite an *artiste*." Dougherty took a sip of his drink.

"It sounds like you had a pretty interesting family. Who was the war hero?" Warren pointed at the medal display as Bill gestured to them to sit on the upholstered sofa. The fabric looked as if it had been carved out of plush velvet into a subtle art deco graphic pattern that picked up the details and colors of the room.

"Please, sit. Actually, those were mine. I wasn't much of a hero. I just survived, so they gave me a bunch of those things." Bill waved his glass dismissively.

"You were in Vietnam?" Larisa seemed surprised.

"For two years and some." He nodded slightly.

"Jeez, Captain Dougherty. What did you do?" Warren noted the rank from the drawing. For a moment he wondered if Malloran kept his medals on display. Somehow he doubted it.

"I was with an advance artillery unit. I had about fifty-five men and eight guns. Seventh Battalion. It was relatively safe, but very loud." Everyone shared a brief laugh, and the older man changed the subject. 'Tell me, Larisa, what do you think of Weldon so far?"

"Honestly, I don't really know. I spend all my time on the computer or in the library, so it's more like being at school than actually working. If I ever worked this hard at school, though, I guess I'd have been sent to a psychiatrist or something. I haven't really gotten around yet." She smiled warmly and leaned forward when she spoke. Warren stopped for a moment and just looked at her. Her reddish blond hair was brushed smooth and swept back from her forehead, cascading to her shoulders. Her blouse, a white cotton tuxedo shirt, had a high collar that accentuated her neck and, together with the simple gold necklace she wore, framed her face in a way that made her high elegant cheekbones even more dramatic. Her gray flannel pants matched Bill's, but they were cut slightly high at the cuff to expose Larisa's perfect ankles over a pair of sensible but elegant gray pumps. A striking young woman, she exuded confidence and seemed comfortable in what could be an intimidating setting.

"Oh, don't worry, that'll change soon enough. You'll get your first direct client assignment, and you won't be a bookworm anymore. You'll get around."

"Hey, wait a minute. Am I supposed to like the concept of my girlfriend 'getting around'? What kind of a job is this, anyway?" Bill smiled and laughed slightly, but Larisa looked mildly annoyed. Warren added meekly, "Well, we all have to make sacrifices."

Then, Megan Dougherty came into the room, a tall, rail-thin woman with a big head of raven hair. Her face had an austere beauty to it, and her complexion was pale yet luminous. She was a super-annuated version of Larisa, and seemed to have stepped directly out of a Pre-Raphaelite canvas. She smiled as the men rose and shook hands enthusiastically with Warren and Larisa as Bill introduced them.

"I've heard so much about you. Bill says you've taken quite a load off of him, so I owe you a debt of gratitude for that piece. He tells me you're doing very well." She accepted almost subconsciously the drink Bill handed her. She was wearing camel-colored flannel pants and a white silk shirt, with brown crocodile loafers, all effortlessly elegant, yet slightly casual. Rather than sit, she simply leaned against the arm of Bill's chair.

"I'm still learning. Bill's helping me," Warren said, looking down modestly.

"And he tells me that you are one of the future stars, as well." Megan looked at Larisa. "You two make quite a pair."

"Some people might say that about you two. We were telling Bill how lovely we thought your home is," Larisa replied. Warren noticed how Larisa's cadence immediately adopted the older woman's speech pattern, and even a little of her patrician lilt. It was a sales technique he used sometimes, and it was pretty effective, especially combined with flattery.

"Thank you. Would you like to see the rest of it? Bill will give you the grand tour while I make sure everything is moving along in the kitchen." The invitation was not intended to be declined, and they were led through most of the fourteen rooms. The style was a rich combination of modernism and art deco, with an understated and comfortable opulence enhanced by the huge scale of the rooms. The bedroom, however, had a more classic touch, with Biedermeier furniture and an upholstered bed. The dining room featured a good-size Braque oil, which had obviously been the source for the colors of all the paints and fabrics used in the room. Warren followed from room to room, his image of Bill Dougherty changing by the moment. A million a year might cover the maintenance payments, staff, and insurance for this apartment after taxes. Clearly, the man sold bonds because he felt like it, not because he needed to. The income probably kept the help well paid and made nice tips for the doormen.

They sat down to dinner, which was served by a young Jamaican woman. Bill kept the wineglasses full, and by dessert they'd finished off three bottles of a 1970 Château Lynch-Bages. Together with the cocktails, the wine made Warren lose track of much of the conversation, except the coincidence that both Megan's and Larisa's mother had graduated from Smith. That had led to a comparison of mutual acquaintances, which led Warren to conclude

that Larisa's mother had been an aspiring socialite whose orbit had somehow transferred from Boston to the Charlottesville circuit. The strong coffee after the raspberries perked him up a bit, but the long day and the food
still had him nodding off. He had enjoyed Bill's stories about Weldon, and
everyone had laughed at Warren's various anecdotess about his school days,
and Bill howled at Warren's misadventures at military summer camp. When
Warren sounded slightly apologetic he had never served in the military, Bill
cut him off. "Trust me, Warren, you didn't miss one single thing." They retired to the library briefly, then Warren suggested it was time for him and
Larisa to go.

Megan brought them their coats and waited until the elevator came to
close the door. The elevator man made them too self-conscious to talk until
they got into the taxi that was waiting.

Larisa started. "God, could you believe those two?' Disdain was in her
voice.

"Umm, how do you mean?" Warren felt drowsy, but the bile in her voice
woke him up.

"What a couple of dilettantes. All that phony war stuff of his, and her
charity stuff. I mean, living like that, with all their money, it's kind of hollow, don't you think? And what was it with her? She used the word *piece* so
much? Like, 'Yas, that was a mahvelous piece' when you were talking about
that movie. Or, 'We try not to think too much about that piece' when you
asked about Vietnam. I swear she must have said *piece* fifty times." Larisa
was staring straight ahead with narrowed eyes.

"Yeah, that was kind of strange." Warren had noticed a lot of odd usages
in Megan's speech. He thought her less atrophied than he might have expected a woman in her position to be, with a mild wit. Her well-developed
lockjaw, that almost motionless, inflected speech of the WASP, had confused him somewhat, as he had noticed during his years playing at their
clubs that it was common among the socialites in New York and Boston, but
not generally among the Irish.

There was a moment of silence, but Larisa's animosity was palpable. "My
mother used to tell me about people like that, where she grew up in Boston.
Socialites. They spend their lives at events and inviting people over for intimate little dinners, but never have any real friends. I mean, those two never

even talked about their children. It's like they hardly exist. My grandpa called it the hornets' nest. Said they didn't do anything productive, but loved to sting each other." Warren remembered that Larisa's grandfather had been a senior explosives chemist for the Department of War and very much a part of the Virginia social elite.

Warren had seen several framed photographs of the Doughertys' boys when he and Larisa had briefly toured their rooms, but Megan explained they were both at boarding school in Connecticut. Warren knew the school, having competed against their tennis team. He had played a tall, elegant boy with perfectly tutored strokes and used heavy spin shots to dissect him until he left the court crying. Warren's dad had taught him to use this tactic when Warren was overpowered, and only the most disciplined opponent could overcome it.

"It's hard to believe that he's gone so far at Weldon, too. I mean, there isn't anything going on in his head, really, is there? How can you stand him? Doesn't he get on your nerves?" The Doughertys clearly pissed Larisa off for some reason. Warren didn't exactly love Bill, but, given his background and status, he was a pretty pleasant guy.

"Well, he's charming when he has to be. Most of his accounts like him. He comes from the days when you didn't have to be a rocket scientist to sell bonds. The most important thing was that you weren't a crook. You know, good family, right schools. Clients knew they weren't going to get bagged. Now, he just plays a lot of politics. Makes sure he gets the credit and always knows how to avoid the blame." It didn't bother Warren. He admired the man's talent for deflecting criticism. Bill never talked back to guys like Malcolm Conover and let insults from traders pass like water off his back.

"I just hate people like that. We've got them all over the place in my department. I wind up covering for them, their mistakes, or their laziness, and then they wind up taking all the credit when things work out. I swear, there's one guy, Doug Phillips, I can't stand. I mean he's just an AVP. I found all these errors in his presentation to one account, spent a whole night reworking the numbers, retyped it, reprinted the whole thing, and even rebound forty binders at three in the morning. He blows in at ten o'clock, picks 'em up, and never even thanks me. We got the fucking deal because I saved his ass, and he never says a word." She was getting wound up, and Warren wanted to change the subject. He'd been thinking about work since six in the morning, and it was almost eleven thirty. He felt bloated and sapped and was dimly aware that he hadn't worked out for almost three weeks. His pants even felt a little tight.

"Do you want to come up?" They had reached his building, and he hoped she'd say no. He wanted to take a shower and get comatose.

She sensed the weariness in his voice. "Let's skip it tonight. It sounds like you've been screwing your customers all day, and there's nothing left for me." Her job was certainly toughening her up, but that didn't mean he couldn't laugh. He gave her a light kiss as he opened the door.

"I'll make it up to you this weekend. We're going out East, remember?'

"How could I forget?" She smiled and waved as he closed the door behind him, and the driver pulled away, into the stream of traffic that barely slowed to admit him.

sixteen

❧

The Hamptons is a reference that obscures gradations of class and style in a generality. F. Scott Fitzgerald's Eggs were for only the sublimely decadent wealthy, while the four real towns that shared the common *Hampton* name encompassed every variety of inhabitant from the native Bonacker descendants of baymen and potato farmers, to poor blacks living in tumble-down shacks, on up to tenth-generation land-grant beneficiaries of King George's munificence and Wall Street lords whose jet-powered helicopters churned the air with a heavy chopping that sounded like riffling money.

For Warren and Larisa, a rented Mercury Marquis offered more earth-bound transport, its air-conditioning a gentle respite from the four-hour crawl on the Long Island Expressway to the cherished retreat. They had been invited for a weekend with Austin Karr at his father's East Hampton house, a shingled cruise ship on four acres off Lee Avenue, two short blocks from the beach. It was an unusually warm early-June weekend, and they were looking forward to some sun.

It was ten thirty when they finally arrived, and Warren had dozed off in the passenger's seat while Larisa took her turn behind the wheel, fighting the solid line of taillights from the Midtown Tunnel until it began to disperse near Commack. The crunch of the crushed-shell drive under the tires woke him, and they stumbled, bleary-eyed, into the parlor. Austin greeted them cheerily, and so, to both of their surprise, did Warren's ex-classmate Eliza Roberts, whom neither of them had seen for months. Larisa had told

Warren Eliza had distanced herself as a friend after their trip to Florida and had thought it was because of Larisa's interest in Warren.

"Hey, if it isn't the two Wall Street superstars in person!" Eliza looked great, tan and relaxed, in a pair of tight jean shorts, flip-flops, and a baggy white T-shirt. Both Warren and Larisa suddenly felt pale and exhausted.

Warren accepted Eliza's hug. "It's good to see you guys." Larisa took the hug more stiffly.

"How's about a drink? Let me get those bags." Austin snatched both bags in one paw and trotted up the big oak staircase, his Top-Siders clomping heavily. "Siddown. I'll throw these in your room and be right back."

Warren and Larisa followed orders happily, trailing Eliza, who had let her hair grow out to shoulder length, into a large, rectangular room with walls of wood planks, laid shiplap and washed white. The white marble fireplace had two logs burning, and scattered about were overstuffed sofas and chairs, upholstered in white linen with navy-blue piping. A half dozen watercolors were scattered on the walls, mostly of beach scenes, some of which Warren recognized as important, and a double set of French doors led to the covered porch that ran around the house. Beyond the porch, Warren could see a pool, lit from within, and a pool house, both separated from the main house by a broad, flat expanse of lawn. Beyond the pool and across the road were sand dunes covered with wispy grasses, and a weathered plank path led down to the beach between several driveways to houses invisible behind tall hedges. Larisa asked where the bathroom was, and Eliza pointed her to a door just across the foyer.

"This looks like tough drill." Warren plopped down in a sofa's crisp, comfortable embrace, the linen canvas softened by age and the humid sea air.

"Yeah, I've been roughing it out here while Austin's dad's in Europe." Eliza curled her feet under her in an armchair, kicking off her sandals.

"I didn't realize you two were such an . . ."

"Item? I guess we are. Actually, we're kind of engaged!"

After an oddly awkward moment of silence, Warren said quickly, "Engaged! That's awesome! Wow." He was genuinely enthusiastic.

"Yeah, well, no date yet, but we'll get to it soon. We're both so busy," Eliza said with a slight shrug, but a smile.

"Tell me about it. So, how's the job?" He remembered that Eliza had taken a position at the Markham Foundation, a heavily-endowed private charity that supported the arts in schools.

"It's great. I'm hitting up the A-list out here for donations, and pumping them all with invitations to our big reading. Austin's been very helpful."

"What are you promoting?"

"It's for inner-city kids. We have famous writers doing a benefit for a creative-writing program. We're matching donations to start up classes in six major cities. You know, self- expression to vent frustration instead of guns and knives. That kind of horseshit." She waved her hand in the air.

"Gee, Eliza, so pleased to see that you're such a believer in the cause."

"Cut me a break, will you? I actually had to go to one of the schools a couple weeks ago. In Detroit, for God's sake. I was so scared I needed a diaper. We're going to buy these kids computers and teach them to write? We should keep them all on dope and on the basketball courts, or locked up somewhere. Thank God we had along some security guys."

The juxtaposition of her attitude and the work didn't surprise him at all, and Warren smiled and tried to provoke her a little. "Aw, c'mon. You'd actually like that, wouldn't you? Don't all white girls fantasize about being held hostage by angry savages?"

"Yeah, exactly. That's my idea of a dream weekend. Forties and drive-bys. That's the last time I go to a site. I'll raise 'em all the money they want. Just teach 'em to use deodorant, and keep 'em away from me."

"Well, Eliza, I'd have to say that your caring and commitment are exemplary. The foundation is fortunate to have you. With you at the development helm . . ." Warren had adopted the stentorian tones of an awards speech.

"Can it, Senator! Hey, you don't have to hang out with lepers to build 'em a hospital, right? I put the bucks together with the cause. Good gets done. Guys like you're gonna be in ten years make a donation and get to feel better about taking all the money and leaving none for anyone else. That's my job."

"Please, don't get me wrong. It's a hell of a lot more than I do. Hey, the sixties are dead. This is the eighties. Man, I feel guilty already." He reached into his back pocket for his wallet. "Where do I give?"

Eliza smiled. "You see? You've got to direct the pitch for the audience.

You Wall Street guys are easy. Put a white woman in peril, and they're ready to pay."

Just then, Austin clomped into the room, with Larisa in tow. The two made a handsome pair—him in his regulation tan khakis and blue oxford shirt, and she in a pale blue, floral sundress with Warren's lavender, heavy cotton cable-knit sweater over her shoulders.

"Wow, what a great house. Austin gave me the tour." Larisa was truly enthusiastic.

"Are you guys hungry? There's plenty of chow in the kitchen. Marina's still around. She's the cook. Just ask her for anything you want." Warren found Austin's mannerisms incredibly reminiscent of their friend from Columbia Chas Harper's. They both had an apparent diffidence to their surroundings, a sense of disbelief at their good luck to have woken up the eldest child in a family worth hundreds of millions of dollars. They spoke about everything as if it belonged to someone else, and wasn't it all just amazing? Warren had seen the same thing in some of his schoolmates in Millbrook. It never failed to amuse him how, once the old man died, that wide-eyed attitude almost always shifted to one of total entitlement, and an air of having earned every penny of their inheritance. Actually, given the way their fathers generally treated them, maybe they did.

Austin poured Warren and Larisa beers, and they wandered into the kitchen. Warren rummaged through the huge, double-doored fridge and resurfaced with a platter stacked with pieces of fried chicken, and a bowl of coleslaw. Larisa's eyes lit up. Warren put the food on the pine farmer's table that was in the kitchen, and Austin pointed him to the right cupboard for plates. Warren sat down, and the two weary travelers dug in with gusto. Austin pulled up a chair, and Eliza started poking at the low fire that was burning in a small hearth.

"So, how's biz at Weldon?" Austin's curiosity was obviously bubbling over.

Warren swallowed a chunk of white meat. "Pretty good, no complaints."

"You're covering Monument, right?"

"Yup. I have that honor."

"Yeah, it's a joy, isn't it? Leonard is certainly saving souls with his work." Austin was their sales coverage, too, and Warren knew that he had been taking a good piece of business away from his friend. Morgan just didn't have the same kind of mortgage effort that Weldon did, and Warren was capitalizing on his firm's strength. Alex Stevenson had explained to him one day that Nathan Leonard had founded the money-management company, after leaving a big trading firm, paying a retired World Bank president $5 million to become vice chairman, thereby gaining instant credibility. Stevenson explained that Leonard's first fortune had been built as a corporate bond trader for a second-tier firm, although most of the profits he had earned his employer were the result of inventory being overvalued on the books to record phantom gains. By the time the dinosaurs who ran the company figured out what was going on, their own fortunes were inextricably tied to Leonard's. Rather than expose the fraud, they continued to reward and praise him, their own compensation ballooning as surely as his bogus bottom line. At the apex, with almost $200 million of losses hidden on his books, Leonard, still thought of on the Street as a profit machine, had left his firm to join Monumental Insurance and start their investment-management business. After three years of great earnings around Wall Street ended, his old firm had simply taken the hidden losses and blamed "deteriorating markets." By then, the executives were all wealthy men, and no one on their Board either knew about the hidden losses or cared. As Leonard himself had put it, "Hey—when did you ever hear of an executive committee member giving any of his pay back?"

"But I hear that you're Weldon's new superstar," Austin said. "How's Frank Malloran doing?"

Warren put his beer glass down. "You know Frank?"

"Sure do. He's a great guy. I used to play squash with him at the racquet club twice a week. Hell of a swimmer. He was the lead finance officer on my dad's first bond deal."

Warren smiled and nodded. It was kind of scary how closed a society this little world was. They all played the same games in the same places, spent their vacations in the same resorts. Of course some were principals, such as Ray Karr; others were simply the hired help. Over time, their institutions had begun to weaken before the tide of motivated, bright outsiders—Jewish and Asian kids with their brainpower and work ethic, the Irish with their balls and bluster. Even Ralph Lauren understood the attraction of this paneled-mahogany world of khakis and gin and was making a fortune selling it to tiny Japanese girls and, ironically, even to the high WASPs, who knew quality when they saw it. One thing Warren had come to share with Kevin was, if not the desire for "dynastic wealth," then at least the desire to live well, within the understated definition of comfortable luxury this world so effortlessly achieved. "Well, Malloran's doing great. In fact, he's been dating Larisa's sister."

"That's your sister? That knockout we saw him with the other night?" Austin said. Eliza shot him a dirty look from across the room. "Of course, she's a washerwoman next to Eliza." A piece of kindling whizzed by his ear and bounced across the stovetop.

"I'm afraid so. Been taking her rejects ever since third grade." Larisa smiled and laughed, but only half convincingly.

"Well, now that you're all practically family, we'll have to go out one night," Eliza piped up halfheartedly.

They finished their snack and the beer and spent a little while longer chatting before heading up to bed. The house had been put up in the local "shingle style," during the first big building boom in the Hamptons during the 1920s. Several owners had added to it, generally in good taste, so that it now had twenty rooms. The second floor offered a clear view to the ocean, though the houses on Lily Pond Lane, one street south, had direct access to the beach.

Ray Karr hadn't wanted a house right on the ocean. His upbringing in coastal South Carolina had taught him that wasn't such a great place to be during an Atlantic storm, no matter how much money you had. He didn't spend a lot of time in the Hamptons, so Austin had the place pretty much to himself whenever he wanted it. His younger sister was still in high school, even though she was almost twenty. She'd been diagnosed as learning disabled, and her volatile emotional outbursts led her parents to keep her at schools such as Rumsey Hall that specialized in troubled and disabled kids. Austin had told Warren about her less charitably one day when they'd grabbed drinks at the Four Seasons after work. "She was a spoiled bitch, and my parents were never even around. She had this thing they call ADD—she couldn't actually sit down and do her homework. Attention deficit disorder. Crap. My mom used to make me do my homework every night by eight or there'd be no TV or dessert. Bailey never even saw my mom—by then she was so busy with charity parties and trying to keep my dad interested in her. Bailey had ADD, allright. Adult discipline disorder. Out all night, drugs, parties. Now she's treated like she has some kind of fucking mental illness. She's just another rich kid who doesn't want to do shit. And she won't. I have to work like a dog, and she'll just get her half of everything on a platter. But it's not her fault. My mom just abandoned her, and I was no fucking use. I had my own problems." Warren was surprised at the bitterness. The Karrs seemed like the perfect success story.

Austin's father, Ray Karr, was an exemplary American entrepreneur. He had taken the inheritance of a small newspaper in Charleston and parlayed it into a significant media and telecommunications empire. He kept houses in Hobe Sound, East Hampton, New York, Islesboro, and San Diego, plus a gorgeous historic mansion in Charleston and apartments in Paris, Rome, and Cape Town. His holdings included the largest privately held block of stock in Mobil Oil, and also in Weldon Brothers. When Austin took an interest in investment banking, Ray Karr had simply made two phone calls and, with the chairmen of Morgan Stanley and Weldon Brothers on the line, had agreed that Austin would go to Morgan, and he would not be told of his family's ownership of 12 percent of a major competitor.

Austin had been doing reasonably well at Morgan, though his father had not been pleased with his choice to sell bonds for a career. Ray Karr thought a background in international corporate finance, with a focus on Latin America, would be more useful to Austin later on, but understood that his son might feel the need to carve out his own niche. In the meantime, Ray Karr kept building and acquiring.

The bedroom that Warren and Larisa shared was cheerfully decorated with blue-and-white-striped material and wallpaper. The towels even matched. Warren ran a shower and let the hot water ease his aching muscles. Between spending ten hours a day sitting in a chair with a phone pressed to his ear and another four hours sitting in the car, his back felt like mush. He wrapped a towel around his waist and stretched out on the bed, while Larisa took her turn in the bath. It only seemed like a few seconds, but he woke up in the dark. His watch said 4:00 A.M., and Larisa was sleeping soundly beside him. He crawled under the sheets and tried to nod off again, but couldn't. After he tossed and turned a few times, and Larisa began to stir, he decided to get up so she could sleep. There'd always be time to take a nap, and maybe more, later. Her smooth, naked skin stirred him, but her opportunities for a real night's sleep were increasingly rare.

As quietly as he could, he dug a pair of shorts and a T-shirt out of his duffel bag, then slipped out the door. Downstairs, in the living room, the fire was cold. He stepped out onto the porch, where the air was surprisingly warm and still. The lights from the pool beckoned across the lawn, and he decided a little dip might be a good idea. The heated pool water gave off a hazy cloud of steam in the cooler night air, a mesmerizingly beautiful halo slowly rising into the dark. The grass was clipped as short as that of a putting green, and as he crossed the lawn, he realized that part of it was actually a grass tennis court. There was a net, and two green-wire fences at the backcourts, with one side boundary framed by a ten-foot-tall privet hedge.

At the pool house, he poked inside and found a stack of big towels. He took one and put it down at the edge of the pool. Not surprisingly the pool was invitingly warm—clearly heating bills were not an issue in this house. After testing the water, he dove in cleanly, then started into a rhythm of swimming laps. It was a little difficult without goggles, but after three lengths, he had measured the pool at eleven strokes. He tried to keep track of the laps at first, then just decided to keep going until he felt tired. His mind began to wander, as it usually did, to work, and he tried to shut it out and think about more pleasant things. Somehow, Anson Combes and his pointy teeth kept popping into Warren's mind. At least he knew there weren't any sharks in the swimming pool. He knew Anson wanted something out of him, and maybe even Dougherty, but he had no idea what it could be. Frank Malloran had warned him Combes did nothing without bad intentions, and Warren was sure Frank was right. Jesus! All Warren wanted to do was sell bonds and make a living and move up. Maybe he wouldn't inherit a fifteen-room palace at 740 Park, but he could maybe buy the place on Eighty-First Street or start looking for a two-bedroom if he and Larisa decided to—

Out of nowhere, he felt hands grab his leg, and he was startled. He came to the surface coughing for air. He wiped his eyes clear. Eliza was in the pool beside him. Her hair was wet and sleeked away from her face, and she was laughing at him.

"Jesus! You scared the shit out of me! I must have swallowed half the pool." He waded over to the side and slumped against the stone coping.

"Well, you woke me up with all the splashing, so it's your own fault." She playfully splashed a little water at him. "It's kind of a strange time for a workout."

"I know. I woke up and couldn't get back to sleep. I didn't want to wake Larisa up, so I wound up down here."

Eliza was wearing a white, one-piece bathing suit, and it clung to her above the water. Warren couldn't help but notice how good she looked, and her skin seemed preternaturally dark in the glow from the pool.

"Look at us. Both trying not to wake anyone up. Aren't we a couple of sweeties?" Eliza floated onto her back, her hair fanned out around her head, and her legs, long and slim, broke the water. Warren took the three steps to the end of the pool and climbed out, picking up his towel, and drying himself off.

"Are there more towels in there?" Eliza swam to his end and climbed up the steps. In her wet suit and the bright light softened by the water, her body looked fit, angular and tight. Where Larisa was smooth and muscled, Eliza was lithe and defined. Warren remembered Larisa's telling him that Eliza had been interested in him down at Chas's house in Florida. Eliza was sharp, funny, smart. She may have developed some seriously jaded views from her work, but she was actually doing something worthwhile. Looking at her, Warren wondered how she would really fit with someone like Austin, who was actually a bit of a stiff. Warren knew she had been joking about the kids she was helping with her work—she cared deeply about what happened to them. She had always enjoyed provoking people with outrageous statements, just to test them.

"Yeah. There was a stack by the door." He walked past her to the door to the pool house to show her where the towels were. She followed him inside and took the one he handed her. Absently, she started to dry her face, then stopped. She was standing less than a foot from him, they were both damp, caught in the wavering sparkle of light from the moving surface of the pool. Warren felt a sudden surge, and they both leaned into a crushing kiss and an embrace.

Their hands were all over each other, pushing off their suits, easing down to the floor. He was on top of her, and she reached down and guided his hardness into her, slick, ready for him. Her hands held his bottom as he pumped into her, her legs coming up to wrap over his. She moved with him, moaning softly, then gasping, and brought him over the top, her muscles contracting on him, pulling him in. His back arched, and his lips pulled away from hers, every fiber contracted. He felt the eruption deep inside, her breath ragged as he filled her, every movement a convulsion until the power drained from him and he slumped onto her chest, her arms enfolding him.

They lay like that for a few moments, regaining their bearings, their breath returning. "Good Lord" was all Warren could say.

"I don't believe it." Eliza smoothed his hair. "After all this time."

"Why did we never do this before?"

"I don't know. I just can't believe it." He was still inside her, and she moved her hips to ease him out.

"Umm. I can't believe it either. I haven't slept with anyone except Larisa for over two years." Warren was starting to think about the repercussions already.

"That's nothing. Relax. I'm on the pill, and I'm going to marry Austin in six weeks. You guys are invited." She half laughed, her voice full of sarcasm. Her hands balled into fists and tapped him playfully on the shoulders.

"Six weeks? I thought there wasn't a date? Jesus. May I kiss the bride?" He leaned his head up and she gave him a long, deep kiss. To his surprise, he felt a stirring again.

"Do you know I always wanted you to ask me out in school?" She rolled him off her and propped her head up, lying on her side.

"I kinda hoped you might, but I was afraid to ask. I thought it'd piss you off. You know, we were 'friends.'" He made little quotation marks in the air.

"Well, it wouldn't have." She traced a finger down his chest and stomach. "Not at all. But Larisa's great. A bit of a man-eater, maybe, but you seem . . . *Hmmmm.* I see you may really be up to the task."

Warren just groaned. After a minute, she mounted him and took her full measure, grinding on top of him until she was satisfied and exhausted, when he let himself go.

They dozed together briefly as the sun began to come over the horizon, turning the sky a midnight blue, casting a golden glow that filled the air.

"Listen—" she began.

"I know. It's okay. It never happened." He scrambled into his shorts, and she slipped into her suit.

"I mean, the wedding, and everything. If this had happened—"

As she said it, Warren knew she was right. If this had happened in school, there would never have been a Larisa or an Austin. He stopped the thought and cut her off again. "Consider it like a bachelorette party or something. Wild oats." Then he leaned over and kissed her lightly. "But it was great."

She smiled at him, with the light shining through the window now, and he could see her here, in a few years, with her children, and he knew she had found the right place. He looked back toward the main house, a white colossus gleaming over a deep green lawn under an azure sky, the morning sun glinting off the glass, and wondered when and where he might find his own.

seventeen

❧

Not for at least a month after the trip to Austin's did Warren notice it. At first, he figured that the cleaning staff must be rearranging things at night. Finally, it began to bother him a little. He kept a file of each trade ticket in a big accordion folder, organized by account and trade date. One folder was for his trades, and one for Dougherty's. All salesmen kept copies of trade tickets in case there was a problem later. Trades were punched into the computer system by the salesman, and they would automatically be forwarded to the trading-desk position clerks. They had to be done immediately. The client would get a trade confirm based on the ticket, but not including internal information, such as commission paid. Amber, Dougherty's sales assistant, would review them at the end of each month and make sure Warren was getting all the commission he was entitled to. The problem was, the tickets never seemed to be where he'd left them the night before when he came in each morning.

Amber told him he was getting senile, and that she never touched them except the last two days of the month. So, as a test, he made a point of leaving them in a particular spot, or with little pieces of paper balanced on the folder as telltales. Once a week or so, they'd have been moved, probably opened and the papers inside them obviously looked through, the telltales scattered.

Many documents on a trading floor are "classified." Competing firms would love to know exactly what big clients had bought or sold with Weldon. They'd love even more to know what sort of inventory Weldon traders were holding, or where they were trying to sell particular items. Security was assumed to be tight, but, Warren knew, in reality it consisted of a few bored and underpaid guards in cheap uniforms who hardly ever even checked for identification at the elevator entrances and rarely patrolled the floor after hours.

"You ever see anybody nosing around my desk?" Kerry shrugged her shoulders at the innocently phrased question. "Anyone you don't know?"

"I thought I saw some KGB agents the other day, but I couldn't be sure. Big guys. With fur hats." Her sarcasm made Warren smile. "Why? Is something missing?"

"No. Not that I can notice. It just feels like things keep getting moved around."

"So? What've you got in your desk anyway? Plans for a hydrogen bomb or something?"

"Nah. Never mind." It bothered him, but it didn't matter. If anybody wanted to look at the trade tickets, they must not have much else to do with their nights, he thought to himself. The tickets told an interesting story, though. Warren's folder had started thin, with only a couple of tickets making it in each week. As the months passed, each week's section grew thicker. His volume of trades had begun to accelerate, and the last few sections were as thick as Dougherty's. Warren had turned his account list into a big producer, especially considering the relatively small size of most of his customers. Admittedly, Dougherty's trades tended to be much bigger, but that was not surprising, considering that his accounts controlled almost $400 billion in assets. Warren's totaled about $80 billion.

The older man had done little to actually help Warren or teach him about the business. Warren had simply listened in on his client calls with a "trainee phone," a handset with no microphone. He was surprised that Dougherty generally read sales memos—the marketing materials prepared by the trading desks—verbatim over the phone. Warren soon realized that his mentor actually understood little about the intricacies of the products he sold. Dougherty relied almost completely on the traders and research to tell him what to say. Bill almost never stayed past five fifteen in the evening. Warren seldom left before seven, and research and finance analysts seemed never to go home.

Warren put the folders under his desk and walked out toward the small trading-floor cafeteria for a cup of coffee. The kiosk accommodated two large coffee urns and a refrigerated display case for sandwiches and soft drinks., plus a table with a hot entrée and soup each day. Everything was fresh and excellent. Warren plucked a foam cup out of the dispenser and opted for decaf.

"What's the point of unleaded? Don't tell me you like the taste." Anson Combes had come up behind Warren and was waiting his turn.

"Huh? Oh, hey, Anson. Nah, I'm on natural stimulants. Rent. Car. Utilities. Caffeine's overkill. I'm just cold from the damn vent over my desk."

"Well, you could do what Bill does and get yourself a nice cardigan sweater. Looks like he's playing golf out there. Maybe he *is* playing golf." It seemed to be impossible even to trade small talk with Combes without him insulting someone. Dougherty's cardigans were part of his image.

"I wondered why he wore them until I started sitting down there. It's always freezing." Warren stirred some milk into his coffee and pressed a lid onto it. He was always anxious to get away from Combes.

"You know, I wanted to ask you something. It's sort of about Bill too. Got a sec?" They were paying for their coffee, and Warren shrugged his shoulders and told the cashier to cover Anson's. Anson leaned against the wall in the wide corridor and sipped from the cup.

"You know, Bill covered Warner before you did. Never did too much business with them, though. Had one really big year a couple years back, but that's it. Anyway, I was curious. It seems like his production's been falling off the last year or two. Why do you think that might be?" Anson had a slight smile, almost a smirk, leaning against the wall in the red-carpeted hall by the kiosk, his legs crossed in front of him. He looked totally at ease.

"I don't know. I mean, wasn't he in the top two or three in the whole firm last year? I think he works pretty hard, considering." Warren was tingling, all his radar screens lit up. Anson was looking for dirt on Dougherty. That could only mean Anson was trying to get him in his crosshairs.

"Considering what?" Anson's tone was sharp all of a sudden.

"Seems to me he's got more than enough money not to bother with this crap anymore. I'm surprised he even comes in half the time." Warren figured Anson must know about Dougherty's family.

"Aw, that's all horseshit. Dougherty doesn't have any money. He spends everything."

"Anson, his apartment's worth about ten times what I'll make in my lifetime."

"Maybe. But it belongs to his wife. I know he probably gave you that shit about his father. Don't believe it. Bill Dougherty's a typical Irish bond salesman. He's in over his head." Anson dismissed Dougherty with a wave of his hand.

"Well, assuming that's so, what difference does it make? I mean, Bill's carrying his weight. He may not be the smartest guy in the world, but he sells bonds." Warren regretted it the moment he said it. He could almost see Anson filing away the comment: insulted senior salesman's intelligence.

"Well, it just seemed to me that Bill had slowed down a bit, and I was curious if you'd noticed anything different, any change in his habits, or something. Maybe he just isn't working as hard."

"Hey, Anson, I can't believe he works as hard as he does." Warren didn't want Combes to think Warren was an ally in any fight Combes might have with Dougherty. Bill had been at Weldon when Anson was in college, and in the jungles of Southeast Asia when Combes was hazing frat brothers. He didn't seem like someone to bet against.

"Well, listen, just let me know if you notice anything different, if there's anything I can do to help." Combes gave a quick nod of his head as he spun on his heels toward the elevators.

"Uh, sure, Anson. I'll do that." Anson toasted Warren with his coffee cup, and turned away. Warren was flabbergasted. *If there's anything I can do to help?* That was like a great white shark offering to help a wounded codfish to shore.

Warren went back to his desk and contemplated the conversation for a while. What on earth could Anson be up to? Was he trying to tell Warren that he would help him if he wanted to go after Bill's account list? Was he intimating that Warren had something to do with it, and the whole thing was part of an attempt to blindside Warren? Besides, Dougherty's production hadn't slacked off at all. It had to be Anson looking through the trade tickets. But why? The whole thing didn't make a lot of sense.

"Hey, Senator, what's on your mind? You look kind of lost in the sauce." Dougherty had rolled his chair back and was talking over his shoulder. Their chairs were back-to-back in the large, U-shaped enclosure made up of a sectional desk with two stacked rows of phone turrets, CRT monitors, and a Bloomberg machine that rose from their desktops and gave them what little privacy was ever available on the trading floor.

"Nothing much. Just thinking." Warren had an urge to confide in the older man, to warn him that Combes might be circling, looking for a sign of weakness. Or, maybe Dougherty's reaction to the news would tell him something.

"Well, try not to hurt yourself. It's that mindless charm that your accounts love and I rely on." Bill's tone was jocular. Bill didn't really do jocular.

"I suppose. I wonder what Anson wanted," Warren said, taking a stab in the dark. Maybe Bill would give him some idea of what Anson was up to.

"Anson? What do you mean?" Dougherty swiveled his chair now, facing Warren, blocking the aisle.

"I don't know. I think he was looking through your trade tickets the other night. In the folder."

"Why would Anson be looking through my trade tickets? They've got nothing to do with him." Dougherty's voice had slipped up a half octave.

Warren shrugged his shoulders. "I dunno. Anyway, I'm not even sure it was him. Just a hunch. And he was asking about you. He seemed concerned." Warren knew he was stepping over a line here, but he wasn't sure what the line meant or exactly where it was.

Bill sat still for a moment, then let out a derisive grunt and waved his hand. "The day Anson Combes is concerned about anything except his own hide is the day I go to bond heaven. That guy . . ." Dougherty trailed off.

"Yeah. I know. Anyway, it was probably nothing." Warren got up, having another idea he wanted to act on. Maybe he could get some information elsewhere. He gave Bill a slap on the shoulder and wandered over to the corner office that Combes used. It was empty, as he hoped, and Warren spent ten minutes chatting amiably with Ann Lois, his assistant, whose desk was in front of the glass door to Anson's office. She handled everything for Combes, who was one of the few managers on the floor who had his own assistant. As the senior finance manager, Anson bridged the world between the mortgage finance group and trading. Warren had only spoken to her a few times before, but she always seemed embarrassingly grateful for human contact and asked personal questions to keep the conversation going. Anson seemed never to speak to her except to bark an order or ask for something.

Warren listened to a story about her son, who was getting ready to graduate from college. He knew she had lost her husband and didn't get along too well with her son, but her cubicle was plastered with dozens of pictures showing him at every stage from infant to postadolescent. He had grown into an insolent-looking, beady-eyed kid. Warren offered to help him get interviews with some friends at other firms, and she thanked him profusely. He told her he had to get back to his desk and waved as he walked away. He had a feeling that she might have some idea what Anson was up to, or at least he might be able to get some idea by chatting with her from time to time. Malloran's advice rang in his ears—he said to avoid Combes and Warren had tried to. But if something was going on, Warren decided he'd be better off knowing about it before it was too late.

eighteen

❧

The Franklin Delano Roosevelt Drive runs down the East Side of Manhattan from the 125th Street Bridge to the South Ferry. It is the city equivalent of a superhighway, three slim lanes in each direction, no traffic lights or intersections, and virtually no recognition of any laws—natural, physical, societal, or, occasionally, even gravitational. In many ways, it was a road that was not unlike its namesake's political party—wild, disorganized, never in good repair, but paved with the best of intentions, if not an even passable grade of asphalt. It was down that impacted artery Warren Hament, somewhat dazedly, rode every day—into the whirling tornado of paper and money that roared day and night at the tip of the island, seeming to pull all the light, air, and life from the narrow streets of the Financial District, and making anyone caught inside yearn for the open water and glinting sun of the harbor and the flats of Brooklyn beyond.

As you leave the broken highway and turn westward from the waterfront, the walls of office towers quickly close in, creating windblown canyons that tunnel across lower Manhattan at the odd angles of its seventeenth-century streets. From overhead, the buildings seem packed so tightly that all that delineates them is their differing heights and colors. Within the thousands of floors in the hundreds of buildings are the offices of virtually every major trading house in America. Hundreds of thousands of phone lines run to countless desks and computers, generating millions of phone calls, blinking lights, and moving cursors.

On one particular day, the single most important lightbulb in this electronic cosmopolis was the third from the top in the far left row of Warren Hament's telephone turret. The phone had 128 lines, each represented by a small plastic push button that flashed when ringing and stayed lit when in use. The key button was a direct line to the Investments Office at the State of Wisconsin Employees Retirement Fund. At the other end of the line was the desk of Barbara Hayes, chief investment officer for the fund. She managed an investment portfolio of approximately $18 billion, which backed the pension obligations of the state to some seventy-five thousand present and former state employees. Bill Dougherty was her salesman at Weldon, and as his backup, Warren had responsibility for the state when Bill was out. The state was Bill Dougherty's number-one account—in fact, it was one of the top three for the entire firm.

Warren had spent the bulk of his first full year working hard on his own accounts. Anson had kept nosing around Dougherty for a while, but then stopped. At the end of 1985, his first full calendar year at Weldon, Warren's bonus had been almost exactly 15 percent of his commissions, not a penny more. He had grossed $3.2 million, and been paid $500,000 in total in mid-January 1986. Malcolm told him it was a record for a new salesman, and he was in line for more opportunity this year, and that he would have been paid extra for his work with Dougherty, but there was a cap. Warren had started to ask why no one had mentioned any cap, but caught himself. His wildest hope had been to make $100,000 in 1985 when he started at Weldon. His father had congratulated him for keeping his mouth shut. "People get killed for a lot less money than a half a mil, kiddo," Ken had said. "You're pretty lucky they gave you the shot." Larisa had been ecstatic for him, pointing out that most of his classmates were lucky if they were making $50,000 or $75,000 wherever they worked. He couldn't help feeling that he'd been screwed.

Barbara Hayes, by comparison, had started to work as an actuarial for the retirement system in 1978. Her job was to calculate and update the benefit schedule for all the pension liabilities of the employees' retirement system, and to generate a cash-flow model. It was extremely tedious work and paid poorly, but like so many other state government jobs, it offered security, and a healthy pension from the same plan later on in life. With her accounting degree from the State University at Madison, she thought that being around the capitol might make for an interesting life, and the chance to meet some handsome young state senator or lawyer and to settle down. The five years of sitting at a computer console and working on spreadsheets, though, had led her to put on a good deal of weight, and her eyes had gotten worse, so that her modest looks had degenerated to a plainness that mirrored the tone of her job. The dashing young man had not materialized, and frustration and bitterness had begun to develop.

The previous fall, newly promoted to associate director in the Investments Office, she had been asked to attend a meeting with some investment bankers from Weldon Brothers in New York. The assistant to the chief investment officer, John Conklin, had invited her along because the "rocket scientists" from Wall Street wanted to discuss some fancy new technology that they said would solve a lot of the Investments Office's problems in matching up their investments to meet their projected cash-flow needs over the next forty years. Nobody in the small group in the office understood that cash flow better than Barbara Hayes.

So Warren and Dougherty had stepped out of a taxi at the steps to the state building, in their crisp white shirts and expensive suits, standing out in the drab crowd on a cold, late-fall afternoon like a beacon. They'd brought Pete Giambi, from the Mortgage Research Department, since his Midwestern twang and polished, comprehensible presentation would make their suggestions totally credible. They had come to explain something called Portfolio Immunization and Optimization—essentially a computer program into which was fed the cash-flow payment characteristics of virtually every government, corporate, and mortgage bond in existence, and the cash-flow requirements of the client's pension liabilities. After several hours of computer time, out would come the optimal portfolio—the magic combination of bonds that would meet the retirement system's projected cash-flow obligations for the lowest possible cost. Warren and Pete did almost all the talking, while Conklin struggled even to pay attention.

As they spoke and moved through the charts and graphs, Barbara felt herself floating into a state of almost euphoric bliss. She suddenly became aware that this was her opportunity to become the fulcrum around which the entire Investments Office turned. Her boss had never paid much attention to the liability schedule. He'd just bought whatever bonds seemed cheap and what the salesmen pushed the hardest. All the technical jargon had passed him by. Her CIO, Bob Mosely, was constantly jabbering about cash being king and liked to spend long lunches with his pals in the statehouse. Only Barbara saw what these Wall Streeters were after. If they were allowed to run this program for the state, their firm would get to buy and sell every single security in the entire portfolio, a huge and probably unbelievably profitable piece of business. This would happen not only once, but potentially several times a year, as the system "re-optimized" the portfolio. Barbara Hayes, if she played her cards right, could suddenly become one of Wall Street's most important customers.

"Tell me, Pete, if I were to send you a disk that contained our entire liability profile, do you think you would be able to tell us how much we are over- or underfunded at today's rates?" Barbara had interrupted Giambi as he was answering an irrelevant question from Conklin about how the system had been set up.

"Absolutely. It would simply be a matter of evaluating all the fund's assets, determining what the optimal available return on the liability structure is in today's environment, and allowing the program to tell us if there is enough value to meet the obligations. It will tell us the amount of any shortfall or any excess," Warren answered for Pete, sensing they had suddenly gained an ally who spoke this odd language.

"Well, I think I should give Warren that disk immediately, don't you, John? Don't you think the governor would want to know if the pension funds are in good shape, and to know it for sure instead of our usual estimates?" Warren saw Conklin recoil—her voice had taken on a sudden authority, and he quite evidently didn't grasp what was going on.

"If, if…if you think so, Barbara." Conklin's reply was timid, as he was out of his depth.

"Well, I do. I'm going to make getting out that disk our number one priority. And, Warren, I think you all should call me as soon as you have a run of the recommended strategy. This may be a great opportunity for us." Barbara knew that at the high interest rates prevailing at that time, the CIO's conservative, almost scared approach had left the fund with cash at the most opportune moment. Not only was she certain they were adequately funded, she felt sure the pension fund was actually overfunded.

Here was a chance to champion investing all that cash at high interest rates. She would explain that the governor could tell the press how he'd masterminded the high-tech restructuring of all the state workers' pension funds and grab some great public relations. If they were overfunded, he could propose spending some of that money on education, law enforcement— whatever suited his reelection campaign the most. She would get all the credit for this fantastic idea. She also figured it couldn't hurt to make a few pals on the Street. Her imagination jumped forward—this kind of thing could give her a shot at becoming State Treasurer. If it was big enough, she could even run for Governor!

At the same time, Warren knew that Dougherty saw this trade as his shot at redemption, what with Anson Combes breathing down his neck. Combes had, for reasons seemingly only he understood, slowly mounted a campaign against Dougherty over the past few weeks. At first, Warren was relieved that he wasn't the target, but then started to feel bad for his blue-blooded mentor. Dougherty may have defeated the North Vietnamese single-handedly, but Anson Combes's form of warfare was unfamiliar to him. Combes had senior management's ear, and he was whispering into it variations on a funeral dirge for the salesman's career.

After the five people exchanged handshakes at the portico to the state office building, Warren, Giambi, and Dougherty climbed into the waiting yellow cab.

"Jesus, what did you think of that?" Dougherty had a big grin on his face.

"I think you're about to become Malcolm's favorite salesman of the year." Giambi's tone was dry, but his eyes were dancing in his head.

"Yeah, well, Conover may think I'm hot potatoes, but if that crazy bitch does this, you're going to be an MD by the time your voice changes." Conover was a managing director of the firm, one of its most senior officers. Giambi ran the Mortgage Research Department, the group that constantly analyzed the bond markets for moneymaking opportunities that were then presented to clients as trade ideas. Occasionally, someone in research would come up with a massive, structural concept that, if it caught on, could generate tens or even hundreds of millions of dollars in revenue for the firm. Other than playing politics for a long time, making the company lots of money was generally considered the best possible way to win the coveted MD title.

"Yeah, right" was Giambi's response, as he'd grown tired of the jokes about his youthful looks.

"But, I wanna ask ya something, Petey boy. And it's important. It could hold the key to this whole show here in lovely mini-noplace, son, and you better give the right answer." Dougherty was getting the same cocky tone and Irish accent he usually got after a big-ticket sale, even though he had contributed little but his presence to the meeting.

"What's that?"

Warren figured Dougherty was going to tell them one of his war stories about how the master salesman would have to play up to Conklin to make the trade happen, so that Warren and Giambi would stay in the background, allowing all the glory to go to Dougherty. Warren started to feel less sympathy for the man.

"You might have to decide how many." Dougherty looked deadly serious.

"How many what?" Giambi was confused.

"How many paper bags you're going to need to put over her head when that tubby broad tells you you're going to have to fuck her to get the portfolio. I'm telling you, she wants you bad, Petey boy, very bad. About eight-fucking-teen billion dollars bad."

nineteen

❧

When they got back to New York, Dougherty let Warren work non-stop for almost a month putting together the final proposal to the state. Pete Giambi assigned three people to the job full-time, and with the head start they had on the rest of the Street, their presentation was clearly the winner. It didn't hurt that Warren, Bill, and Barbara Hayes had hit it off. She was continually feeding them tips on how to refine the program to meet concerns voiced in the internal meetings at the Investments Office. It seemed to Conklin and Mosely that Bill and Warren anticipated every worry or question Conklin had.

The final version of the proposal suggested the optimization of $5.7 billion in long-term asset allocation. Over four hundred separate bond positions were analyzed, and the computer, conveniently, showed a complete overhaul would generate remarkable results.. It estimated the savings to the state would be close to $475 million. A great deal of this was simply reinvesting cash in longer-maturity bonds, which, at the high interest rates prevailing, retired the pension liabilities inexpensively. Basically, Warren told Barbara, by doing exactly what Conklin had always eschewed—investing most of their money all at once, the state could show that it had retired all its pension liabilities for almost half a billion less than the state's accountants were carrying the liabilities on the books. Besides, he argued, if they didn't do it, and interest rates dropped, it could theoretically cost the state more to retire the liabilities than they had set aside. An underfunded pension plan was hardly a great re-election issue.

The meeting took place in the governor's office in Wisconsin. Pete ran the meeting, and even Warren's manager, Malcolm Conover, and the head of Fixed Income, Kris Jameson, attended on behalf of Weldon. Giambi repeatedly asked Warren to join in, to describe how the transaction would benefit the state. Warren took the opportunity to hammer home the potential political downside if they decided not to do it. Bill Dougherty sat still and looked serious, nodding his head at key moments, letting the bright young men carry the day. Afterward, he took Conklin and Mosely out for a drink and told them how, with the state being so important to him, he would never recommend that they go along with this trade unless he believed in it. Fortunately for him, they didn't ask any technical questions.

It took only two days to get the governor's approval. When the program started, it took almost two weeks to execute all the trades. Dougherty had Warren run around the floor to get levels from all the different traders and confirm them with Barbara. The traders doubled or tripled their usual spread, or profit, on each trade. At the end of each day, Dougherty would take Warren's tickets, stack them up, and count the commissions Dougherty was earning. Warren also kept a running tally. By the end of the program, it added up to almost $7 million for Dougherty's side of the trades, which meant he would earn in the vicinity of a million dollars for this single piece of business. A bump up in market rates before the trades made the savings to the state over $500 million, and Weldon's profits were well disguised in the windfall.

After the entire deal had been completed, Warren drafted a memorandum for Dougherty to sign. It thanked Pete Giambi and his team for their assistance and effort in convincing the state to proceed, Warren for his help, and gave a total of the estimated profits earned by Weldon—almost $15 million at minimum. Nobody ever wrote memos like this that shared credit for big deals. When Dougherty saw it, he pushed it under a stack of papers.

"Warren, we don't need to be wasting time on memos. There's enough paperwork around here already. Look, I already thanked Pete, and I appreciate the work you've done. Everyone is aware of it. Who needs more paper?" Warren nodded his understanding and didn't say anything. He had neglected his own accounts to make sure that this deal had gone smoothly, and Dougherty didn't even have the decency to recognize him for it formally, even with Warren writing the memo for him!

Warren had been obliged to help out, as the junior backup, but he had really busted his ass. He bit down, smiled at the older man, and grunted, "Sure. Whatever."

After a few minutes on the phone catching up with Karlheinz at Warner, who had been dealing with Kerry while Warren was busy with Wisconsin, Warren dialed Larisa's extension. He was pretty wound up, and he needed to vent some steam.

Larisa picked up the phone on speaker, a habit that annoyed Warren and really got to him now. Those fucking bankers, he thought, it makes them feel like big shots to sit back in their chairs and blabber, while I have to listen to their hollow, echoing voices. Plus, you never know if they're alone.

"Hey, sweetheart, could you turn off the fucking box?" Warren was pissed.

He heard her fumble with the button and pick up the receiver. "Jesus, what's bothering you?"

"Nothing. It's just that I hate feeling like I'm calling the goddamn boardroom at General Motors when I just want some solace from my girlfriend. You can't tell me your clients like talking to you on that thing."

"Hey, most of them do it to me. It's just my way of getting even. What do you need solace for? Is everything okay?" She perked up, obviously wanting to hear the dirt. Warren explained to her what had happened, embellishing his own role a bit, and making Dougherty out to be even more of a self-serving son of a bitch than he actually was.

"Hey, Jocko, that's the business we're in. Come on, you're the one who taught me this stuff. I didn't like him at dinner that time. So, he's a self-aggrandizing prick. So are half—make that three-quarters—of all the assholes in this firm. What's the big deal? Just be sure that everyone who counts knows you did all the work. Dougherty's days are numbered. He's a fucking dinosaur. Lunches and football tickets aren't enough anymore. You've got to know what you're talking about. It's like me with Temenosa. Those fucking assholes came in here like they knew everything about bankruptcy..." Larisa promptly took off on a full five-minute soliloquy on her dealings with Temenosa, pointing out to Warren her brilliant tactics with the court-appointed receiver, how she had negotiated a bigger fee, and even a piece of the upside for Weldon on certain asset sales. She threw in how the CEO, an extremely wealthy Texan, had tried to seduce her, and how she was now interviewing the auction houses, who were kissing her butt for a chance to sell off Temenosa's corporate art collection. Warren could hardly squeeze in a grunt or a "Yup," she was so engrossed in talking, and was disappointed that she'd turned his phone call into a chance to talk about herself.

When she had played out the scenario, Warren told her she was right, that he should be patient, and Dougherty would go the way of the Brontosaurus. She suggested a few subtle ways to undermine him with management, and Warren agreed, then hung up. He barely ever saw her anymore, with the hours she was keeping. New Finance associates commonly worked ninety-hour weeks. She had been in Texas sixteen days the previous month. It wasn't as if he had loads of free time, after all, but he did like some feminine company in the evenings.

The last time he'd gone out to dinner with Larisa, she'd gotten unbelievably angry when he called Susan, a high school friend of Larisa's, now a lawyer, a "smart girl." She corrected him to "woman." Warren said he still thought of females his age as "girls," but Larisa responded that was demeaning, as if she called him a "nice boy." He finally said that he thought of himself as a "guy," and that "men" were generally at least in their late forties. "Women" were at least fifty.

Larisa had called him a jerk and said he believed that women were incapable of being successful or powerful. He reminded her that his mother had been the smarter, better looking, more successful, and more accomplished of his two parents. She said it didn't matter, and that he had better not refer to her as a "girl" again. He agreed, then asked if she knew whether Susan had gotten the job she wanted—to be an Assistant United States Attorney and prosecutor. He said he'd always thought she was "one sharp broad." Larisa had actually gotten so mad she started crying, and nothing he could do seemed to convince her it was just a harmless joke. "Look, I have this compulsion to say the wrong thing at the wrong time," he said. He was about to add, *And I love my little girl anyway,* but managed, for once, to catch the words before they popped out.

❧

Warren flipped a pencil up in the air, and its point stung when it landed on his outstretched palm. He and Larisa had made up, although the sex had seemed almost functional, like mutual relief, a sort of stress-release valve.

Most of the time now, they actually just had oral sex and then went to sleep. He had to admit she had a real talent for it and obviously responded just as well. It wasn't particularly loving or intimate, but it left them both satisfied and sleepy. It was a sort of masculine thing—Warren couldn't remember any other girl—woman!—he'd dated who liked sex that way. She did a lot of things that most women didn't or wouldn't and generally liked to be dominant in bed. He couldn't imagine why someone so smart and attractive would want to be a man.

He wouldn't be seeing Larisa after work because he and Bill had dinner with Barbara Hayes scheduled at the New York Athletic Club. She was in town for meetings with the stock market guys over in equities, and tonight was a kind of victory dinner to celebrate the huge trade. He decided he needed a dose of something that would cheer him up, and he knew just where to get it. He dialed Dutch Goering's extension, even though he sat about twenty feet away. The square-jawed salesman was always good for a laugh once you got him wound up.

When Goering picked up, Warren got him started.

"Hey, Dutchie, whadya think of that new sales assistant?" A young woman named Dawn had just been hired in the money markets sales area. She was reasonably attractive, and well-endowed.

"Oohhhh fuuuuuckk! How'd you like to rub your fuckin' dick between those big fuckin' hootskies, eh?" Goering hardly missed a beat. No matter what time of day or where he might be, it was a safe bet Dutch's mind was focused on one subject. The way he expressed himself was something of a legend among those who had heard him on a roll. "Man, I'd like to fuckin' ride her like a fuckin' carousel pony. Oohhhh fuuuuuckk! She's hot. I'm going to fuck her too. Oh, yes indeedy, I am. And she's going to fuckin' love it. Uh-huh. Tomorrow night. It's a date, Warren me boy. But, don't worry, I'll take pictures so you can fuckin' beat your donkey next week. Oohhhh fuuuuuckk, I can hardly fuckin' wait! Maybe you'd like to come and watch?" The obscene tirade paused for a response.

"Jeez, Dutchie, I've got dinner with the state tonight. Do me a favor, okay? Just leave yourself out of the pictures, would you?" It didn't surprise Warren that Goering already had plans for Dawn. Warren just wondered whom Goering had told his wife he was entertaining that night.

"No chance. Maybe you and that fuckin' girlfriend of yours can beat off together. Man, you gotta tell me when I can jam that girl. I know she wants me. She's got nice, tasty fuckin' titties too." Every time he saw Larisa, Goering flirted with her. Warren tolerated it, mostly because Larisa always seemed totally disgusted by him, even though he looked like a Ralph Lauren model, with his blond hair and sharp, Germanic features.

"Dutchie, I told you, you can't nail her until I'm done with your sister. But your mama says I'm the best man she's had since you." Nobody could get Warren going like Goering. Warren honestly believed if anyone else ever heard one of these conversations, they'd be put in prison somewhere.

"Fuck you, Hament. I got work to do." Goering was reliable. When he clicked off the phone, Warren was smiling. He saw that Goering, despite himself, was smiling too.

Warren's good mood didn't last long. He picked up Kerry Bowen's line, and Mahmoud, the portfolio manager from a Middle Eastern Monetary Authority—managers for the royal family's vast wealth—asked him to get a bid on a $15 million mortgage bond Warren had never heard of. He went over to Danny Mordecai, who traded most of the unusual bonds in the mortgage area, and gave him the information. Mordecai had recently come to Weldon from Goldman. He walked over to Warren's desk about twenty minutes later. Kerry was out on a client visit, so Warren had to handle the whole transaction for her.

"Hey, kid, let me ask you something," Mordecai said in a low voice, "who else are they asking to bid on that bond?"

"I'm not sure, but he did say 'in competition.'" This meant the seller would ask for bids from at least two dealers, to make it honest.

"Well, I know they talk to Goldman, and to Merrill, and neither of them will know shit about this bond," Shuler said. "This could be a home run."

"Why's that?"

"Well, it so happens, I structured this deal three years ago, when I was at Goldman, and the information they have on this sheet is wrong. That deal has ten years of prepayment protection, not four." Warren realized that this made the bond far more valuable. The interest rate on the mortgage that backed the bond was high—10.75 percent—and if the issuer could not refinance it for ten years, whoever held it would get to earn that interest a long time, making it trade at a much higher price.

"Hey, Mordecai, do whatever you want. Shouldn't you tell them they have the facts wrong? I'm just the backup on the account and relaying the bid." Warren wasn't sure what he was supposed to do.

"Fuck them! They provided the info and didn't ask for verification. That's their problem. Caveat emptor, baby! Tell 'em 102.271. I bet Merrill bids par and Goldman 102.1. Hah! This could be sweeeeeet!" Mordecai rubbed his hands together. Warren did some quick math in his head, and figured the bond, with all that extra call protection, would be worth at least 111 or 112.

Sure enough, five minutes later, Mahmoud called back and told Warren Weldon had won the bonds. When Warren asked for the cover bid—which meant the second-highest bid submitted—Mahmoud told him Goldman at 102.251. Mordecai's call had been almost perfect. When Warren relayed the info to him, Mordecai let out a loud whoop.

Within a few minutes, Mordecai was back at Warren's desk. "Hey, kid, this bond will fit Emerson Insurance to a tee. You cover Schiff over there, right? Wanna make a fuckin' bolus?"

"Ummm...maybe. What's a bolus?" Warren was feeling uneasy.

"Look it up! Anyways, offer them the bonds to settle next month at a price of 114 and a half. That's plus 350 to the first call against treasuries. Insanely cheap!! And it's a great credit—that mortgage is guaranteed by the full faith and credit of the USA—Ginnie Mae. And the borrower is making a ton of money—rents are way up, so it will never default. Schiff will love this baby!"

Warren was dumbfounded. In a business where even unusual bonds would trade on a spread of a fraction of 1 percent or at most one point, Mordecai was marking this bond up over 12 percent! "Umm, Danny, isn't that against the five percent markup rule?" Warren remembered the SEC rule that did not allow brokerages to make more than 5 percent on a bond trade.

"Dickhead, that only applies to risk-free crosses. I bought this as principal. Not my fault those shit for brains didn't keep the right info."

"I don't—" Warren was shaking his head doubtfully.

Mordecai cut him off. "It's every man for himself in an unsolicited bid in compo!" Mordecai was smiling. "We're gonna make one point six million bucks on fifteen million bonds! Whooooeeee! Bet ya Schiff doesn't even back-bid us!" Mordecai walked off, then yelled back over his shoulder, "You got a fifteen-minute exclusive. I could blow these out in a heartbeat!"

Warren paused for a minute, unsure of what to do. The whole thing made him nervous. He decided to take precautions and saw Carl Dressler walking off the floor, toward the men's room. Warren got up and followed him in.

Standing at the urinal, Warren spoke looking straight ahead. "Hey, Carl, let me ask you something." Warren explained the situation. It wasn't unusual for conversation to take place in the bathroom at Weldon. Business always came first.

Dressler zipped up his fly and washed his hands. "So, who was the seller?"

"EMA. Mahmoud."

"EMA? Fucking *EMA*?" Dressler seemed incredulous.

"Yeah. EMA. The Arabs." Warren handed him a paper towel.

"Oh, that clinches it. Do the trade. Fuck those rag-head sand niggers." Dressler waved Warren off and pushed the door open.

Warren stood there for a second and looked at his reflection in the mirror. Ignoring the racial slur, if Carl Dressler didn't care how much Mordecai marked up the bonds, why should Warren? He went back to his desk.

"Hey, Warren, what's up?" Schiff was always congenial on the phone and knew Warren would never waste his time.

Warren described the bonds and told Schiff the whole story, including what Dressler had said, substituting the word *epithet* for the slur.

Schiff let out a low whistle. "Jeeeezus! That's kinda bald, isn't it?? Hmmm..." He seemed lost in thought. "God, those bonds are stupid cheap, even at 114 and a half. But, I gotta tell ya, I just don't want to have anything to do with it. Listen, I'm writing this down in my notes, in case anyone tries to get you in trouble ever. I doubt they will. But I'd stay away from this if I was you. Billy Gross at PIMCO would buy these in a heartbeat, and you can bet his salesman won't tell him the whole story. He's smart enough to see the value. It kills me to pass. Hey, I can't stand those people either. But twelve fucking *points*? You know it doesn't surprise me. Not with Mordecai."

"No? Why's that?" Warren felt disappointed, but relieved. He was probably missing out on a payday of close to a $100,000.

"Mordecai's a Goldman guy. They're the biggest pack of thieves on the

Street. Maybe in the world. I have stories on them that'd make your hair fall out."

"Goldman? I keep hearing that! But they're supposed to be the most ethical shop anywhere!"

"Oh, yeah? Ask Dressler or anyone else. They'll tell you. Those guys will do anything for a buck. Forget it. The worst. Stay away from this stinker. Thanks for telling me what was up. And make sure you let me know if anything I'm doing involves that weasel Mordecai, so I can check my pockets!" Schiff clicked off.

Warren walked back over to Mordecai and told him he didn't have a buyer.

"Are you fuckin' kidding me, rookie? No buyers? You must be the stupidest salesman on the Street! WAMCO would suck my dick for these bonds at 116! Fuck off back to your nursery, shitface. I gave you a shot. These'll be gone in two minutes. Useless fuckin' douche. Change your diaper and get outta my face!"

Warren tried to hold back, but he couldn't. "Hey, Steve, I just don't want to get wrapped up in it, okay? Rippin' an account's face off for twelve points may be your idea of good business, but I just don't want to get fired over one trade. Pay Kerry her commission and leave me out of it. The money was in the buy, too, so don't screw her." Warren was angry and knew his face was probably red.

"Screw her? I wouldn't screw that sow with your tiny dick, loser." Mordecai was leaning back in his chair, enjoying himself. "Maybe with the dough she's gonna make on this, she could pay you to throw her a bone. Get outta here before I say something you're gonna regret!" Mordecai was smiling now.

Warren took a deep breath and walked away, trying not to think about smashing Mordecai's face in with a hard left hook. He was a scrawny, balding guy who didn't appear to have a muscle in his body. In a fight, Warren knew he would beat the guy senseless. Battles here weren't decided by size, strength, or character. It was always, and only, about money. Just business. Nothing personal.

twenty

❧

The wind that swept across Central Park from the north piled up against the palisade of towers on Central Park South, intensifying the Canadian chill into a frigid arctic blast that whisked Bill Dougherty's breath away as quickly as it turned it to vapor in the night air. More than a hint of liquor was in that steam, and clearer evidence still in his gait, which was unsteady as he negotiated the broad steps of the New York Athletic Club and, heedless of the doorman's offer of a taxicab, turned east into the teeth of the gale.

It would only be a few blocks to the corner of Fifth Avenue and Fifty-Ninth Street, where hansom drivers violated the city's new ordinances about keeping their horses out in the cold, and the Plaza Hotel's bright awning lights and red carpets beckoned. The air would do him a world of good, he thought, and taxis would be plentiful at that tourist mecca, waiting to whisk him in curry-scented warmth home to Park Avenue and Seventy-First Street. Within a few strides, the glow of the AC's own lights receded to a forlorn pool on the wide sidewalk, and Dougherty, just a slightly hunched pedestrian, was cast adrift into the night, like a small craft in a gathering storm, all quiet as he headed into a nor'easter.

In most cities at night, light is safety, and numbers are preferred, but on that particular evening, Bill Dougherty had crested the wave of the greatest moment in his career, and the wine, heavy food, cognac, and cigars dulled the senses and the reflexes he had developed, but perhaps left, in an Asian jungle a decade and a half before. He was alone on a vast, blasted tarmac, in a dark wasteland of closed storefronts and shuttered buildings between the safe harbors of busy public gathering places of the night.

The money would be sweet, the rush of recognition sweeter still. He was far smarter than they all knew or could possibly believe. Old Bill, the customers' man, the salesman who got by on his relationships and Irish good looks, his family connections, and his wife's money. The biggest single-customer trade in Weldon history, with Wisconsin, and he'd masterminded the whole thing, brought the resources to bear, focused the laserlike beam of the firm's insatiable greed that sent the minions with their engineering degrees and MBAs scurrying antlike over Barbara Hayes's balance sheet until it had been transformed and rebalanced in a way any investment banker could understand, appreciate, and, most important, envy.

"'You are like the five-hundred-pound payload at the tip of a billion-dollar, ten-thousand-ton rocket,'" he said into the night audience of blowing papers and coagulated grime. "'The delivery system for all those guys at Mission Control—research, trading, sales...,'" he quoted from Malcolm Conover's "payload speech," used to motivate rookie salesmen, which also reminded them of their insignificance without the magisterial resources of the mighty Weldon machine. Fucking asshole, Dougherty thought. Empty suit.

The hunched figure whose weaving path intersected his in the middle of the block was like a cipher, a filthy, grime-covered body, with a face so coated in dirt that no light reflected from its smooth planes. This familiar vision was the embodiment of the city's excess to so many who were offended or made guilty by the gulf between success and failure that New York emphasized with such gusto. The millionaire bond salesman and the homeless beggar were as much a part of Manhattan mythology as Boss Tweed and Fiorello LaGuardia.

The outstretched hand wore a glove of unknown pedigree, and the mumbled invocation for alms paid unknowing homage to a tradition of the millennia. Dougherty's reply, downcast stare, less audible apology, and swallowed invective were in the same timeless mold, as was the quickened step, and the subtle course correction to deflect the interloper to the inside, leaving the street, and a potential path of escape, open, the unyielding granite façades safely behind the beggar.

Dougherty didn't see what made him fall, only felt his foot catch and managed to blunt the impact with his hands, which had been up at his collar. Still, it stunned him for a moment, until he felt strange hands reaching to him, seeming to try to get him stabilized, maybe help him to his feet. It took a moment to realize that it was the beggar, the hapless vagrant who was coming to his aid, and a flicker of that guilt or regret passed through his jaded mind, only to fade quickly when his body told him he was not being helped, but robbed.

"Hey!" he managed to blurt out, as he started to reach up toward the offending arms. He hadn't plotted a reaction, as the images were slow to crystallize in his brain, though adrenaline would soon clear the webs. He started to push himself upright, though the smooth leather soles of his Alden wing tips got scant purchase on the quartz-encrusted concrete and kept him off-balance before he could get past a sitting position.

The sudden punch to his chest, and the second to his throat, startled him, but there was no time for anger, or even fear, as his eyes caught the glint of the long steel blade, now wet with his own blood, and his lungs filled and his breath escaped, and the hot, dark puddle that suddenly grew steamed briefly in the frostbitten evening before the wind bore it away.

twenty-one

❧

Warren pulled a *Post* off the stack at the corner grocery before he hailed a cab every morning. He generally read the *Journal* once he got into the office, but the tabloid made for more entertaining fare during the ride in. There wasn't much of interest nationally, but as he paged through to local news, he noticed an item on the fifth page, lower right: "Broker Slain near Central Park":

William E. Dougherty, a broker for Wall Street powerhouse Weldon Brothers, was robbed and stabbed to death late last night only steps from the New York Athletic Club, on Central Park South in Manhattan, where he had just completed a business engagement. Police refused to speculate on the identity of the killer, but a witness said he'd seen an apparently homeless man panhandling in the area shortly before the incident. Dougherty evidently lay unattended for several minutes, before a maintenance worker from the Essex House Hotel nearby noticed him. He was rushed to St. Luke's Hospital, where he was pronounced dead on arrival.

A spokesman for the mayor's office expressed abhorrence for the crime and promised "the full effort of all law enforcement agencies to capture the guilty party in this heinous crime."

Mr. Dougherty, according to sources, was a highly successful salesman with Weldon Brothers and was a holder of the Silver Star for his service in Vietnam. He was married to Megan Rance, granddaughter of

Reynolds Rance, the founder of Rance Aviation, a major defense con-
tractor, and leaves two teenaged children.

"Holy shit!" Warren blurted out, startling the driver. "I can't fucking believe it!" He snapped the paper shut and closed his eyes.

"Excuse me, sorh?" the man behind the wheel said in a Pakistani accent.

"I can't fucking believe it! I can't fucking believe it!" Warren was shaking
his head now. "A guy I work with was killed last night. Jesus Christ! What
the fuck is going on here? What do I do? Holy Jesus H. Christ." Warren was
rubbing his hands over his face as the cab reached the FDR Drive entrance
and turned downtown.

As soon as he stepped onto the floor, he slowed down. What had he expected? Clumps of men in funeral garb, some kind of general outcry? The
impact on the floor was negligible. A group of salesmen were gathered near
Dougherty's desk, but most everyone else who had arrived was on the phone.
The morning passed with several brief conversations, mostly about the rise of
violent crime in the city, expressions of shock and disbelief, and an address
over the internal television system to announce the death, and to offer solace and advice on safety. At about eleven o'clock, Malcolm Conover called
Warren into his office. Conover, as Fixed Income sales manager, was responsible for handling the reassignment of Dougherty's responsibilities.

"Goddamn unbelievable what happened to Billy. Right after the biggest
trade of his career with Wisconsin. I just can't get over it." Malcolm was
speaking to the far wall as he led Warren into his glass-walled office. "How
are you holding up?"

"Well, Malcolm, it's not easy. All of Billy's accounts are horrified, and
I gotta tell you, I'm pretty shaken up. It just makes the business seem unim-
portant." Warren hung his head as he plopped into a chair.

"God. He had two kids. I saw them at the Christmas party. And Anne.
Christ, I hope he had a lot of insurance, at least. This fucking city. I told them
we shoulda moved the company to Greenwich last year." Conover seemed
genuinely upset, and Warren could see he was thinking about his own family, and what would happen if it had been him. That he'd gotten Megan
Dougherty's name wrong didn't really surprise Warren, but he was slightly
appalled that Malcolm's showing human emotion surprised him.

"Well, Malcolm, we've gotta figure no matter where the office was or where he lived, he'd still have had to come into town for dinner with Wisconsin. Barbara Hayes loves the AC, so that was where he'd've been no matter what." Warren knew that she enjoyed the maleness of the NYAC, and the sense of intruding on privilege that made her feel special.

"Yeah, I suppose you're right." Conover paused for a moment, then dismissed the tragedy with a short wave of his hand. "Well, anyway, Warren, we've decided to split Malcolm's book for now. You know everybody pretty well already, and you've been doing a good job, especially with the state. We'll have JT split the coverage with you, but you're the senior coverage, he's more backup. A familiar voice on the telephone will do the clients well, and maybe you'll even get a few sympathy trades out of it. If it works out, you'll be alone on the list." Malcolm was leaning back in his chair, looking away from Warren and out at the floor. "It's kind of seamless this way. And a big opportunity for you."

Warren let the air hang silent for a long moment as Malcolm rotated in his chair and looked Warren square-on for the first time since they'd started talking.

"I hate to have things happen this way," Warren started, "but I think you'll be happy with the job I do. Last night, after dinner, I dropped Barbara off at her hotel, and we had some great ideas on what to do next. I know that I can keep the state a top account. And I've been spending a lot of time working with the rest of the list. In fact I'm going to the Knicks game tomorrow night with Teachers Insurance, and we had dinner planned on Thursday with Morgan management. I know I can make this work out for the firm." Warren was laboring to appear earnest and humble, his heart pounding at this huge opportunity. JT was a third-year associate who was clearly going nowhere. Warren had blown by him in a few weeks. Bill Dougherty had averaged about a million and a half take-home pay a year, after taxes. His account package was now effectively becoming Warren's, and the burgeoning assets of the investment funds meant that the size of trades and the commissions were sure to grow rapidly.

"Well, then, good luck. I'll check in with you a couple of times a week to see how you're doing. In the meantime, the police department had a man here this morning, and he left his card for you to call him. I told him I thought you were at the AC last night, and he said he'd want to interview you." Malcolm handed Warren a thinly embossed card belonging to Detective Dick McDermott of the Homicide Division.

"I'll call him right away." Warren stood up.

"Good. They'll announce the services for Bill probably tomorrow. Tell everyone we should put in a good showing."

"I will. Thanks, Malcolm, I'll pick up the slack." Warren left the office and returned to his seat. He immediately dialed the number on McDermott's card.

The voice on the other end was mild and answered with two words: "Homicide. McDermott."

"Detective McDermott, this is Warren Hament from Weldon Brothers. My boss told me to call you, that you might have some questions about last night."

"Hament? Oh, yeah, Hament. Hey, sorry about your friend. That was a tough way to go. I hope he had insurance. Listen, if you want this to wait a while, we can talk later on. But it'd be better while it's fresh in your mind."

"No. If I can help in any way, I'd like you to catch whoever did it. Bill was a friend and did a lot for me. What can I tell you?" Warren sounded anxious to somehow be of use.

"Listen, Mr. Hament, we normally like to do these interviews in person. If it's not too much trouble, I can come up there in a few minutes." McDermott didn't sound particularly flexible.

"How long do you think you'll need? I've got a lot of calls to make for Bill."

"I'd say twenty minutes or so."

Hament glanced up at the clock on the ceiling beam. "Can you be here in the next half hour?"

"Well, why don't you just give me a rundown on what you did last night, starting with leaving the office." Lieutenants Dick McDermott and Roger Wittlin had settled into comfortable chairs in the syndicate conference room, which was dominated by a mahogany table easily capable of seating forty people. Foam cups of coffee steamed on the table in front of them.

McDermott, about six feet, heavy, and rumpled, led off the questioning. Wittlin, a few inches shorter, sat back a little farther, dressed neatly, thin, hair slicked back, and with a far more intense manner. He had laid a notebook on the table.

"Okay. Let's see…we had the dinner set up with Barbara Hayes from the Wisconsin Employees Retirement Fund at six thirty at the NYAC. I was writing up tickets—trade tickets—from the day and putting them into our logbooks until it was time to go. Bill stayed because he didn't feel like going home first, and he and I caught a cab up to the AC, where we met Barbara. We were maybe five minutes late and met Barbara in the lobby."

"So you'd say you got there around six thirty-five," Wittlin said, taking notes.

"Roger wants you to know he can add," McDermott cracked, and grinned at Warren. Wittlin gave McDermott a bored glance.

"Close. Yeah, about six thirty-five." Warren reciprocated with a thin smile. "So, we had a couple of drinks at the bar and then went to dinner. We spent a long time going over the big trade we just completed for the fund, and we showed her a bunch of exhibits Research had worked up, so dinner took a while. They drank a lot—Barbara likes to be wined and dined, and it was a celebration—so after the first course, the conversation kind of got off business. Anyhow, after dessert, Barbara said she was pretty tired and she'd talk to us some more when she got home to Madison."

"That's Wisconsin, Roger. About what time was that?" McDermott glanced up at Warren. "It must have been eleven or so, and we headed back down to the bar for a last drink."

"You said they drank a lot. Did you drink much?" Wittlin cut in.

"I had one vodka gimlet before dinner, which I didn't finish, maybe two glasses of wine, and one or two sips of cognac after. For me, that's more than enough. I'm a lightweight." Warren could never handle too much liquor. It tended to make him sick. He'd perfected nursing drinks while clients got tanked, and he'd used the practice well the previous night.

"So, they went down to the bar after dinner for another drink." Wittlin waved his hand like a bandleader.

"That wound up being two drinks, and we were all pretty tired by then. So we decided to call it a night."

"Yeah. What then? Who left how?" McDermott picked up the line.

"Well, Bill offered to have me drop Barbara off on my way home, since she was staying over at the Carlyle. He said he'd get a cab later, that he wanted to shoot a rack or two of pool. So, we said good-bye at the bar, and Barbara and I went down and got our coats. Then we got a cab. We got one heading the other way, but he made a U-turn. I dropped her in front, on Madison Avenue. Then I took the cab over to Columbus and Eighty-First. I got some milk at the Koreans' for my morning coffee on my way, and that's about it." Warren was surprised the detective hadn't interrupted him or slowed him down.

"You didn't see Bill talk to anyone else at the club while you were with him?" McDermott now sounded bored.

"He did wave to one or two guys. I think he said one was a former partner of his at Merrill or something like that. But he didn't have any conversations with anyone."

"Do you know what time you got home?"

"Yeah, about eleven fifty or twelve. I looked at my watch when we left the AC, and it was around eleven forty. It couldn't have taken me more then fifteen minutes to get home. I also know I was in bed by twelve fifteen. Oh, yeah, I had a message on my machine from work. Pete in Research had called with some questions about the final computer runs he was doing, so I tried to get him in the office, but he was gone. I got his machine, but 1 didn't leave any message."

"Your Research guys usually work that late?" Wittlin chimed in.

"Sometimes. If it's important."

"This was important?"

"Oh, yeah. We just traded several billion dollars for their portfolio. But I guess Pete got them done—the runs—or quit. I don't know, because I haven't had a chance to talk to him yet."

"Okay. Thanks. I just want you to think about coming out of the AC." Wittlin leaned in a little. "Did you see anyone or anything that made you notice them? Also, can you tell me anything about the cab or cabdriver? Maybe he saw something."

"Well—the cab was just a regular one—not a new car or a Checker or anything. The driver was foreign, maybe Indian or something. It had a partition in it. And it smelled pretty bad. Barbara might remember more, she doesn't... Oh, Jesus! Has anyone told her about this yet? Wow! She'll be pretty shocked."

"Don't worry about that, I've already spoken to her. She saw it on the morning news. She took it okay. Didn't remember much about the cabbie either, but we'll be able to find him by his log." McDermott glanced up at Warren to watch it sink in that they were comparing his story to Barbara's. No wonder they'd been in a hurry to interview him. "Listen, I may ask you to come in for a more complete interview later on. Just to see if one of our guys can't help you remember any tiny details. We want to find this guy before he gets anyone else." McDermott's voice had shifted from bored to hurried—he wanted to get going. He hadn't touched the coffee.

"Okay, Detective, sure. If you need anything at all... do you have my home number?"

"Yeah. I got it from your boss. Listen, think hard. I'll be talking to you." McDermott got up and shook Warren's hand.

"Thanks for your time," the smaller man added as he pushed back his chair.

"No problem. Good-bye, Detective Wittlin."

Wittlin nodded and tapped his forehead, then shook Warren's hand, almost as an afterthought. He put his card on the table. He seemed preoccupied. "If you can't get either of us, we check in every half hour. Leave a message."

❧

Warren went back to his desk a little dazed. Growing up in the Hamptons and Millbrook, where the local cops seemed to live to harass the summer people and to persecute their own ex-schoolmates, Warren had never been involved in anything more than a speeding ticket. He was glad his dad was in town for dinner that night. He always made Warren relax. Ken Hament used the same phrase his own father did whenever one of his boys would start whining about something: "That's too bad aboutcha." It made you realize that there were generally far worse things people had to endure than whatever was bothering Warren or Danny. Talking to the cops might not be fun, but it beat lying in a cold drawer at the city morgue.

twenty-two

≈

As he climbed the stairs to exit the subway, Warren was thinking how jealous he was of people who worked in midtown Manhattan rather than the downtown Financial District. He made a left at the top, rather than the habitual right—he was having breakfast with Neal Faber, a friend from his first semester at Columbia, an attorney he'd met at a party he'd gone to with Chas Harper. They'd played tennis on occasion, and met every few months for breakfast, to compare notes—Neal was working at a major securities law firm, and moving up fast. He and Larisa had gone out with Neal and a long line of gorgeous, intelligent women he never seemed satisfied with.

Seven-Thirty Broad Street, Viner and Goulet's offices, was not a particularly distinguished building, but the firm handled some of the most complicated securities deals, asset transactions, and even mergers and acquisitions work for the Street. At the security desk, the guard called Neal's extension. He was given a name tag and sent up to the 6th floor. Neal was waiting at the elevator bank when he got off.

"Hey, buddy! Welcome behind the Wizard's curtain!" Neal was incredibly thin, his head seemingly oversized for his body. The close-cropped, almost shaved hair gave him a skeletal look, but his generally happy personality softened the overall impression of intensity.

"Yeah, I might steal all your ideas!" Neal's specialty in exotic structured bonds and in how to create financing vehicles for distressed assets—like mortgages in default, or even bankrupt companies, was considered the province of the most mathematically gifted rocket scientists on the Street, and they needed extremely sharp lawyers. "But, seriously, is it okay for me to be here?"

"Dude, don't worry! Just don't tell anyone, okay?" Neal slapped him on the back. "You gotta hang out for a bit—I have to finish something, and it's taking a little longer than I thought it would, so I told them to send you up. Is that okay?"

"No problem." They were walking past an open lounge, and Warren smelled coffee. "Can I grab a cup?" He pointed at the large silver urns lined up along a counter in the room.

"Hey, sure. You know what, why don't you just grab a chair in there? I shouldn't be more than ten minutes. You have a *Journal*?"

"I don't leave home without it!" Warren pulled the folded paper out of his bag. "I don't have to be in until nine thirty, so take your time." Stacks of paper cups were next to the urns, and Warren filled a large one, splashed in some milk, and plopped down in a chair along the wall of the big room. He couldn't help but notice how shabby and crummy the space was. Weldon's lounge on the trading floor was softly lit, carpeted, and comfortable. The coffee was tended by staff from the executive dining room, always fresh and rich. The law firm's version was thin and acrid. Conover had always said that coffee was the fuel that ran the floor, and it should be the best possible—to help keep everyone overworked and caffeinated.

The front page offered nothing of much interest, so Warren dug the *Post* out of his bag and flipped to the sports pages. After a few minutes, a small group of men came in, and he recognized Les Bergeron, one of the Street's best-known traders, as well as Tim Saturnino, the founder of Bastille Investments, one of the most aggressive hedge funds around. Their specialty was buying up portfolios of distressed assets and mining gold out of them that no one else recognized. Saturnino was medium-height, with long, prematurely gray hair that fell across his forehead, and moved at almost laconic pace. The two other men were very different—one an extremely tall, rotund fellow with bristly black hair, a pug nose, and thick, black-rimmed glasses. The rapid, jumpy way he moved and talked somehow reminded Warren of a wild boar—or at least what he imagined a wild boar would look like, since he'd never seen one. He was whispering to an even taller man, easily six-six, who wore no glasses, but had what appeared to be a perpetual squint, his eyes thin slits above a large nose and thick lips set in his puffy face.

"Listen, Tim, this is in the bag—it's no issue." The feral-looking fellow gesticulated animatedly with both hands as he spoke. "They hired us to tell them what to do, and they're gonna do *exactly* what we tell 'em!"

Tim shook his head and shrugged. "Well, if we can keep this out of competitive bidding, it's gonna be a grand slam, I promise you!" He looked at Bergeron, who nodded and slapped Tim on the shoulder.

"That's what we're here for, right? We told 'em that you guys are the best in the business, you're the *only* shop prepared to step up, and they better not blow this meeting or it'll cost 'em at least twenty points! Oh, this is gonna be sweeeeeeet!" All four men chuckled.

"God, could you imagine if Rainwater or Cooperman or even Kravis had any idea this stuff was for sale, what would happen?" Bergeron had a nasal voice and an unctuous manner.

One of the men Warren didn't recognize spoke up. "Listen, guys, Les is gonna have to get a massive disclaimer and indemnity in his engagement letter. Let Grolier draft it, then we'll mark it up and 'discuss' it for a while. We'll be sure everything gets brought down to the buyer. It'll be clean as a whistle."

Warren easily deciphered what they were saying. Some company had hired Bergeron's firm to sell assets for them, and they were directing them to Bastille as the best buyer. Bastille was going to get a steal on the pricing—there would be no competition. The other three mentioned—Richard Rainwater, Leon Cooperman, and Henry Kravis—three of the biggest names in private equity—would all have loved to bid on the assets, but they weren't going to get the chance. Warren was dumbfounded. This was completely immoral—and probably illegal. The firm was obliged to get their client the best price in the markets. Meanwhile, the lawyer would be sure the legal documents absolved both of them from any claims in the unlikely event the seller of the assets ever figured it all out. Oviously, Grolier, another major law firm, was in on it as well.

"You all set for the meeting?" The tall man had spilled a little coffee on his tie and was blotting it with a napkin. "You need anything else?"

Tim waved his hands, and a smug smile creased his eyes. "Noooo, I think we're all set. We've got everything. Don't worry. *We'll even bring the sheep's clothing!*" This prompted hearty laughs all around.

"We'll tally it up when we do the secondary offering for you guys and adjust the net," Faber said, and they didn't even notice Warren as they strolled past him on their way out, coffee cups in hand. Warren waited until they were gone, then laid his paper down.

"Jeezus!" he couldn't help blurting out loud. What he had just overheard was "epic" in Jed Leeds's parlance. These men were conspiring to bilk a banking client out of what must be a huge amount of money, and then to split the profits by adjusting Bergeron's firm's fees on another deal—possibly through a sale of stock for the hedge fund later in the year. It would be impossible to connect, even if someone were looking for it. Saturnino's joke was spot-on—these were wolves in sheep's clothing. It also explained how his firm always seemed to buy assets so cheap—they were paying off sellers' financial advisers to give them the inside track. No one would ever suspect it. As Warren sat there absorbing all this, Neal came around the corner with his jacket on.

"All set, dude! What do you say to Harry's for an omlet? I'm starving! How's Larisa?"

Warren got up and put his paper away. "Give me a sec.... Damn! You wouldn't believe..." Warren hesitated. What good could telling Neal possibly do?

"What? How hot Larisa is for me?" They were already at the elevators. "I always knew it!" Neal's gap-toothed smile reminded Warren a little of Chas Harper's. The two could not be more different.

Warren waited and recounted the basics of the story to Neal over breakfast at Harry's.

Neal just shrugged. "Dude, in the time I've been here, believe me, I've seen things that make that look like the minor leagues. Those other two must have been Paul Stevens and Jimmy Salinger. Stevens is unbelievable. He advises the group that invests money for Bergeron and the partners of his firm. There is *nothing* Bergeron wouldn't do. I met his mother at my parents' cocktail-party benefit for Central Park. You know what she said? It was like 'My relationship with my son wasn't good until I came to terms with the fact that he would, absolutely, sell *me* for a dollar!' Can you believe that? His own *mom*! Then she told me about how he flies her and all their family around on his G-IV jet. She's a piece of work. Two-fisted drinker, too." Neal was devouring his omelet, two orders of bacon, a plate of hash browns, toast, juice, and anything else within reach.

"Man, I feel like taking a shower or something." Warren was still uncomfortable. "I mean, what I heard—"

"Forget it. Don't even think about it!"

"What do you mean?"

"Dude, don't even *think* about telling anyone. Nobody gives a shit. And it's probably dangerous."

"Dangerous? What do you mean *dangerous*?"

Neal speared what was left of Warren's breakfast steak. "I mean fucking *dangerous*. Listen, people get killed over twenty bucks in this town. Bergeron's firm has a whole *department* devoted to this shit, and it's in the *billions*!"

"*Department?* What are you talking about?"

"Dude, they're called the Reputational Risk Department or something like that. No shit. It's in another building, even. I had to go there last year to talk to them about a new bank client in South America. Everyone knew they were laundering money for the drug cartels, but they were connected through their government, and their trading desk wanted to do business with them. So little old me, the lawyer, goes down to Rep Risk, and there's these *huge* guys down there. I talk to one of them, and he's a former Mossad agent. Basically tells me they deal with anything or anybody who could put the firm's reputation at risk in any way. And he smiled when he said 'deals with' too. Also says every firm has something like it. The stakes are too high."

"Jesus. That's some crazy shit!" Warren had stopped eating.

"Listen, there's a reason these places make so much dough. I got a million stories."

"A *million*? I know you like to tell a story, but a *million*? Come on!"

"Trust me. Listen to this one: Over at Bergeron's firm a few months ago, they are selling a package of loans to a giant finance company from their trading position. I'm over there working on a prospectus, and I hear the trader talking to Bergeron, saying that there's a loan in the package that's going to blow up in a couple of weeks. He tells her to forget about it, and to have one of our lawyers call up the borrower and figure out a way to keep the loan afloat for a while. Otherwise, if they pull the loan, the whole sale could collapse. She says, "Les, are you kidding me? They're gonna find out for sure. What the hell are you thinking about?"

"Jeez." Warren interjected.

"So wait." Neal's eyes were ablaze. "Get this! Bergeron looks at her, then starts digging in his pocket." Neal mimed rummaging in his pants. "He pulls out a fistful of twenties and shakes them in the trader's face. And yells, 'What am I thinking about? *THIS! This is what I'm thinking about! This and how to put as much of this in my pocket as I can! And that's what you had better be thinking about, too!*' ...I'm not kidding. A fistful of fucking twenties! In her face!" Neal was slightly flushed, his amazement tinged with clear anger.

"Damn! That's... what? Naked?"

Neal went on, still fired up, "So she says, 'What about the ethics notice? What about 'the firm must always place the client's interests ahead of its own'?" Warren and everyone on the Street knew about the various compliance documents sent around every year, led by Goldman's Ten Guiding Principles. Neal kept going. "So Salinger just snorts and says, "Fucking A right. And whenever we actually do put a client first, stupid, make no mistake, it's a fucking *business decision!*"

"Nice. I guess those guys aren't..." Warren was shaking his head.

"What, any different than any of the other scumbags all over this festering swamp? Well... *wrong!* They're a whole lot better than anyone else. They get the client to *thank them and pay them* while they're *raping* them! Come on, you gotta admit, it's goddamn *impressive!* Goldman *wishes* they had the swagger those guys do." Neal was smiling again, but Warren could see the disgust in his eyes and heard the disappointment in his voice.

"Yeah, I guess you could say that." Warren wasn't really surprised by the stories, only how Neal was so willing to talk about them.

"Anyway, so tell me about what's been going on with you." Neal had already put his credit card in the folder for the check. "It's on me. They pay us less and promise us we'll all be partners someday. And they make sure it's always some Associate whose name is on any opinion or closing document so they can duck responsibility. That way they can take home six or seven mil each year and make us suckers wait until they're so rich they can buy a whole state and retire. Fuck, when the managing partner finally retires, he'll be worth at least three hundred or four hundred mil! Then he can run the US government for the benefit of his friends and colleagues!"

Warren updated Neal on his own work situation, the developments after what had happened to Dougherty, and his relationship with Larisa, and how busy he was at work.

"Damn, dude, all respect there. She is one hot babe. What have you got that I don't?" Neal bowed his head in supplication. "I guess she had you marked as a comer. Saw big things in you, and I don't just mean that cruise missile you must have in your pants."

"Well, I'm not sure a bond salesman is exactly every girl's fantasy. Don't they usually go for quarterbacks or movie stars?" Warren shook his head.

"Don't ask me! I'm just a geek rocket-scientist lawyer happy if any girl will even look at me!" Neal flashed his gap-toothed grin.

"Ha! You date nothing but the most amazing girls. I think you have commitment issues." Warren threw a small piece of toast at his friend.

"Well, this job takes up my whole life. I miss going out with you guys." Warren knew Neal often worked until 2:00 or 3:00 A.M. and hadn't had a vacation since he started. "But it sounds like what happened to Dougherty opened up a real opportunity for you."

"I guess so. But, you know," Warren sighed, "those stories you told me are sad, in a way, and a guy dying is evidently a big opportunity in this business. I'm not sure what would surprise me anymore."

The two men got up and parted at the front door.

"Back to the meat grinder," Neal said, slapping his friend on the back. "Just make sure no one is standing close enough to shove you in!"

twenty-three

✦

Jamie Holik stepped out of the elevator with the *Daily News* under his arm. He'd completed the Word Jumble on the train from Long Island and planned on doing the crossword puzzle during the day. A smudge had developed on the side of his suit jacket from the ink of the newspaper he carried every day, and the cleaner had not been able to remove it—polyester seemed to hold stains, especially the lighter shades such as the off-taupe that Holik favored.

He'd always taken some abuse for his appearance, being tall and gawky with absolutely no muscle tone, and every time he'd bought a conservatively cut banker's suit, he'd wound up with something horrible. Finally, he'd listened to Frank Tonelli, his cohead of the Mortgage Trading, and allowed Mr. Chu, the Hong Kong tailor who came onto the trading floor every six or seven months, to measure him for a few suits. Tonelli, who was about 6'6", sixty or seventy pounds overweight and hard to fit, swore by him, and at $300 each, for a custom-made suit they were cheap and looked it. On Holik's scrawny frame, the glued seams and blocky cut looked ridiculous. The sheen of the cheap fabrics added to the effect, and even in a dark blue pinstripe he looked like a kid wearing a costume. He'd gone back to his off-the-rack suits from Loehmann's.

"Hey, Scooby Doo, get dressed in the dark again?" The inevitable greeting from Tonelli had ceased to make an impression. Holik's lavender shirt and pinkish tie clashed horribly with each other and the suit, but at least the shirt was not short sleeved and didn't have a pocket flap.

Warren was sitting over a Styrofoam cup of steaming coffee, discussing the fixed-income markets with a trainee. He had built a reputation as a pleasant person for trainees to seek out, as he was patient and less abusive than most other people on the floor and had been one of the most successful new sales-men at the firm in many years. He'd been doing great with Dougherty's ac-count list the past several months, and everyone seemed to be aware of it.

Bob Thomas had introduced himself to Warren as a Columbia gradu-ate, and they reminisced briefly about business school, and Lorenzo Corel-li's banana-based economics. The young man, in his white shirt, rep tie, and three-week-old Brooks Brothers chalk stripe had stopped midsentence and stared incredulously at Holik as he passed, obviously dumbfounded by his outfit.

"I know what you're thinking. He takes down about two million a year, and you'd think he was a back office geek. It's a true American dream." War-ren sipped his coffee and took a bite out of his bagel. "One of my favorite stories, and one that is instructive too." He swallowed, then punched one of the phone buttons, which had begun to blink. "Weldon... Yeah, sure, hang on a sec." He punched the hold key and yelled out, "*Mike!* Wayne on two!"

"You were saying?" The young man wore an expectant smile because Warren had also earned a reputation as the best storyteller on the floor.

"Well, about six years ago, Weldon had a Ginnie Mae trader named Marco Levene. Marco was a great trader and made Weldon a ton of dough. This was a ways before my time. One day, Marco goes home to Roslyn, and his wife tells him the lawn guy just quit. So, he picks up the local paper, sees an ad for a lawn service, and, after dinner, this tall, skinny kid shows up, not with a Weed Eater, but with a notebook. Spends a half hour discussing their land-scaping needs, and lets the Levenes know he's learned the business from the ground up—used to work summers at the public golf links. Levene likes the kid, hires his crew. Anyway, two weeks later, the trading assistant here quits because Levene throws one of his patented shit fits and calls the kid a stupid queer in front of the whole floor. Levene is in a little trouble because the kid actually was gay, so the firm pays him like a fifty-grand settlement, and Marco's got no assistant. He goes home and tells the lawn guy he should get out of the sun and gives him forty grand starting pay. This was before we had Jillene in personnel to be sure every new hire had a Harvard MBA.

"Anyway, the lawn-mower man comes in, and three months later, the junior GNMA trader goes to Lehman for six hundred grand a year, and Levene moves Holik up to trading. Nine months after that, Levene gets a two-point-six-million-dollar bonus and retires. Carl Dressler takes about four months interviewing replacements, and it turns out the edge trimmer can trade well enough. So, about a year and a couple months after mulching the begonias for five-fifty an hour, the boy is good for three-quarters of a million a year, and now he's a two-million-a-year MD at prestigious Weldon Brothers with the worst taste in clothes of anyone in the world but Cecil, the shoe-shine guy, who's probably interviewing on the Corporate desk. A true story. All-American, guaranteed."

As Warren finished the story, and the trainee was shaking his head slowly in disbelief, Holik called two of the senior traders into his office. The three were soon engaged in a heated discussion in front of a computer screen.

"What's going on? Are they getting ready to price a new deal? They didn't announce anything, did they?" Bob was anxious to appear up to speed.

"Relax, that's just a traders' meeting." Warren grinned at the kid's nervousness.

"What kind of trade are they working on? Do you have any idea?" Thomas was almost sweet, he was so ingenuous.

"Well, Jamie is the commissioner of the Strat-O-Matic baseball league, and he's got to clear any trades that managers want to do. I know that Juterman and Bluhm were working out something involving Viola and Nixon to Symanski for Chili Davis and a relief pitcher, but I haven't been keeping up. Anyway, Jamie's probably propping something like Henderson and Martinez for Viola and a catcher. I know what you're thinking—other than this is a shitty trade—that the commissioner shouldn't be a manager too—clear conflict of interest. He sees all the trade proposals and gets to propose better trades before he approves any and might veto one in his division. And you're right. But this is Weldon, where rules are meant to be observed, preferably from a good, safe distance."

"You mean those guys are . . ."

"Wasting an incredible amount of time on an inane child's baseball-simulation game? Cheating the firm out of their full attention? Utilizing massive amounts of work and computer time and resources compiling statistics and tracking performance of baseball players in an imaginary league? Yes, that's what I mean. But in about fifteen minutes, you'll see Holik reading the racing pages, and after lunchtime, maybe, after his post-prandial dump, he'll have at least a half dozen bets down at three tracks. And he'll probably be planning a romantic weekend with his girlfriend down in AC—"

"AC?"

"AC—Atlantic City . . . feeding the slots, and playing the wheel. Tell me, isn't that what you'd do if you had a few mil in the vault and a weekend free? Head down to Circus Circus with your 'lady' or a pro and put a few hundred on the point? C'mon, admit it, that's class. Like Telly Savalas or Joe Piscopo, or something. That's what Weldon's all about. Work hard, play hard. Sleaze out over in Jersey. Know what I mean?"

"Come on. You mean to tell me the cohead of the Mortgage Trading department of Weldon Brothers, a former professional lawn mower, spends his free time playing rotisserie league baseball and betting down in Atlantic City? He doesn't get enough action here every day?"

Warren liked the way Bob summed up the morning lesson. "You forgot about the track and the pacers he owns. Listen, I'm not trying to slant your opinion one way or another, but we've got a few colorful figures here at old Weldon. It's not all white shoes and old money." Warren waved his arm expansively.

"How long have you actually been selling?"

"Was about two years this week. Seems like about fifty years."

"Well, from what I hear, you're one of the best already."

"Yeah, well, I'm doing okay. But when you're on commission, remember, you're only as good as your last trade." Warren had grossed $11 million over the months since Dougherty's death. Warren's share should be about a million and a half. This was preposterous pay for a second-year associate, and it still wasn't clear whether he was on straight commission with Dougherty's accounts. When he'd asked Malcolm about it, the answer hadn't been definitive. Every time he tried to pin him down, Malcolm would avoid the issue.

"How'd you do it so fast?"

The young man's flattery was beginning to annoy Warren a bit. "Hard work. Good looks. Naked pictures of Malcolm with an adorable young pony.

Getting a great account base because Bill Dougherty got stabbed to death on Fifty-Ninth Street. And just not fucking up. But, anyway, son, it's been a pleasure. Now I've got to go do my duty for God and country. There's chickens to pluck and fat to fry, and I've got to go wallow in the pismire."

"Isn't that all a little rough?"

"A little rough? Welcome to monkey island, Wilbur." Warren snorted like a horse and turned to his phones.

twenty-four

❧

The better things went for Warren at work, the more difficult things got with Larisa. She was now working on the bankruptcy of a real estate syndicator in Houston, and the troubles of a big gas and oil company in Dallas, and he never saw much of her. She came and went a lot, but whenever their paths crossed, she'd update him on her work and ask about his dutifully, obviously losing interest before the first punctuation mark. He was on a path to make about ten times her pay, but worked far fewer hours and traveled less. She was getting ahead as quickly as one could in Finance, but it would still take her four or five years to catch up. He figured he resented it, even though she was supportive in her way.

He had only heard once more from the detectives investigating Dougherty's murder since they'd come to see him. Wittlin had called to let Warren know that they had located the cabbie that had driven Barbara and him home and had visited the Korean grocery the next day, and Warren's story had checked out. They'd also found a record of his call to Pete Giambi when he'd gotten home that evening.

Before it even dawned on Warren that they were establishing an alibi for him, Wittlin had cut Warren's indignation off at the pass. "Listen, Mr. Hament, there's a lot of money involved in your business, and we get paid to investigate every possible angle. You're probably in the clear. We're looking for the homeless guys now. It's our job."

"Guys? You think there was more than one?"

"Well, more than one was seen in the area. These vagrants are tough to track down. We have some possible forensic evidence from the crime scene, so we'll know if we've got the right guy. Don't worry, it may take a while, but we'll catch him." Warren could tell that Wittlin was frustrated. His conversation had the cadence of a cop's, but there was more behind it than just institutional efficiency. He had a cynical undertone that was almost self-mocking.

"Detective, I believe you will. Not McDermott, maybe. But *you* will." Warren had formulated one of his usual instantaneous judgments—he liked Wittlin and wanted him to succeed, even if he'd thought Warren was a suspect. Well, if they wanted him downtown, they'd have to wait, because he was leaving town for a while.

"Thanks, Mr. Hament. I wish I were really as confident. This town is getting to be a little too much even for me. This guy had two kids. Maybe fifty bucks on him. Ten, no, five years ago, he'd've been rolled, maybe messed up a bit. Now they kill 'em without a thought. How the hell can we keep up with them? If Dougherty wasn't such a solid citizen, we'd be off the case by now. Six months is a long time to be working on a homicide like this one. Listen, thanks for your time. I'll keep you informed if we get anywhere." That had been some time ago. Warren had wondered for a while if Wittlin was trying to make Warren comfortable, while still investigating him as a suspect, but the long period with no contact made his *Columbo*-inspired worries dissipate.

It was funny, but when Warren had told Larisa about the whole incident, she'd predicted that he'd be a suspect. She'd said he had the most to gain. Obviously, the police felt the same way. It didn't matter now because, fortunately, he hadn't chosen to walk home alone or go right to sleep. He couldn't help the nagging thought that, had Dougherty been killed before the state's big trade, all that commission would be credited to Warren. Who knew if Weldon would even pay out the commission now that Dougherty was dead. What a bad break. Just one week earlier…

Warren caught himself and shuddered. What was he thinking about, taking commissions from a dead man? Maybe this job was beginning to get to him a little. Sometimes he wondered if he had what it would take to last. Guys such as Dougherty just let everything run like water off their backs. Others—Anson Combes or even Holik—played the politics and were constantly destabilizing everyone underneath them, to avert any threats. Warren had actually believed the company line about customer service. He knew other firms, such as Goldman Sachs, supposedly indoctrinated their people with the need for at least the perception of ethical behavior, and Bear Stearns had their own internal police. He knew this was all a smoke screen for the same cutthroat activity as anywhere else, but at least they paid lip service to it. But, since he'd been at Weldon, no one had ever mentioned anything about ethics. Weldon's main concerns seemed to be making money, beating the competition, and being a "team" player. Alex Stevenson had said that *team* meant being willing to see 95 percent of every dollar you made go to pay senior management for getting dressed in the morning.

From Warren's bedroom window, the buildings along Central Park South loomed like sheer cliffs over the diminutive trees of the park. Lit up at night, the buildings had something almost alien about them, like giant machines grinding up the island. The view was addictive and was what had drawn Warren to the place.

"Warren, you just have to stop taking all this so much to heart," Larisa said, lying in bed next to him as he stared at the invading horde. "It's all just a very high-stakes game, with no rules."

"But there are rules. Remember? We learned them for the Series Seven Securities Registration exam."

Larisa laughed out loud. "Hah! That's rich! Sure, there are rules. But do you see anyone enforcing them? There's only one rule, and that's 'Don't get caught.'"

"I guess. But it gets a little wearing. I mean, sometimes it seems like everyone's out to screw the clients, but that's not even enough. They all seem to be looking to shaft each other too."

"Jesus, Warren, grow up! This is business! The only thing that counts is money! You didn't know *any* of these people a year ago, and if you died to-morrow, they would forget about you in a week. Or a day, like Dougherty."

Warren rolled over and kissed Larisa on the forehead. "My little angel. The sad part is you're right."

"Listen, it's no better upstairs. All the associates try to make the others look bad so they will make VP first, and all the VPs try to take all the credit so they will become MDs first. Hey, last week I made sure a few mistakes didn't get corrected in a big report this jerk Steve Morley was preparing.

Embarrassed the shit out of him at the presentation. Trust me, I'll be a VP two years before he ever will. He just left the file open on his computer where anybody could get to it."

"Jesus! How could you do that?" Warren was taken aback. Complaining was one thing when you could at least pretend to be above it all.

"How? That asshole *buried* me with Temenosa last month. Never told me their lawyers called urgently from court when I was in the bathroom. They had an embolism, and I had a hell of a time explaining. Every man for herself. All's fair in love," she said, rolling over on top of Warren, and pushing against him hard with her hips, " and especially war."

∼❧∽

Warren had told his father on the telephone later that week that things were moving so fast, he felt as if he were just riding this big wave. Larisa had overheard and told him when he hung up he'd better learn how to control his own destiny, or others would control it for him. She mentioned how he'd let Dougherty walk all over him and said that Anson Combes would do the same thing, only he was worse. He had real power in the company and could hurt Warren's career. Even his Dad had said sometimes he wished Warren would take command. "Killer instinct, kiddo. It's part of the game. Someone's got to win, and it may as well be you."

He knew that they were both right. He needed to somehow get more involved in the politics, cover his flanks, and gain some measure of control. He couldn't get past this naïve belief that if you produced big numbers, stayed within the limits of the law and ethics, and kept customers and traders happy, you would succeed. That was only marginally important compared to playing the angles. For someone everyone seemed to think was so smart, it just never got through. He'd have to start thinking more about geometry.

∼❧∽

It had been a while since Dougherty's death, but Anson had continued nosing around, albeit a little less obtrusively. Barbara Hayes had suddenly become distant and a little awkward with Warren. The business was still lucrative, with constant rebalancing, but she rarely called, and seemed generally cool to him.

The past few months, despite his efforts and a few trips up to see her, she had started to give more of her business to Drexel Burnham and sold some of the stronger, solid corporate bonds in her portfolio for higher-yielding junk bonds. Warren had tried to dissuade her, but even he had to admit the extra yield was enticing, whether or not Milken, the star head of Drexel's junk-bond department, made five or ten points on every trade. The last time Warren had been up to Madison, he was shocked to see that she had lost a lot of weight and started to dress less conservatively, and she had even driven him to the airport in a new Saab sedan, with leather seats and a manual transmission. She ran through the gears like A. J. Foyt.

Warren surmised that all the contact with the Street had given her more expensive tastes. The fancy dinners and wines, the private cars and extravagant bond conferences, had a way of infecting people. He imagined she'd saved every penny she earned at the state and could afford a few luxuries, and he'd gotten one of the secretaries to let out that Barbara had a top-secret new boyfriend. Good for her, he thought, remembering Dougherty's snarky comments about her and Giambi. Well, now she was hot and Dougherty was dead. Go figure.

twenty-five

When Warren got to Larisa's apartment, he spent a few minutes looking for the book he'd left there, *Winter's Tale* by Mark Helprin. There'd be plenty of time to catch up on his reading while she was away, he'd told her, and he wanted the book for his trip out West. He was starting to feel like it was the best novel he had ever read, and would pack it despite its considerable heft. It turned up in the bathroom, then he loafed around on the couch while she was in the bedroom packing for her trip to Dallas. A Knicks game was on TV, and she'd handed him a beer. They talked through the open door while she packed.

He tried to work around the issue, at first bemoaning how little they saw of each other. He talked to her about Plainscor, the company she was working on. Once she started talking, it might be easier to get something more than a glib response out of her.

Plainscor had lost a fortune in gas drilling and gone busted, but were trying to bail themselves out with an $800 million lawsuit against Jeremy Crow, the shrewd oilman who'd sold them the lion's share of his land rights and leases. It was a long shot, but they'd hired a sharp, famous Texas lawyer to represent them. His taking the case had made Plainscor's stock bounce up almost 20 percent.

"But, realistically, what's the chance they settle?" Warren asked. She had explained that half the reason for the suit had been the likelihood that they would convince Crow to settle in the high eight figures rather than risk a Texas jury. He was a high-profile loudmouth, and several magazine interviews could be interpreted to imply that he had gloated for years about playing Paul Donahue for a sucker. Plainscor's founder had trusted his instincts for years and ridden a string of huge finds to build a company with $3 billion in revenues. He wanted to take it to ten, and that was when Crow had picked him off.

"I think the chances are pretty good. It won't be enough to bail them out entirely, but it'll buy us some time." She was half shouting through the open door.

"Time to do what?"

"Isolate some of the valuable assets. Move some cash. The usual."

"Isn't that illegal? I mean, if the company's in trouble, isn't it some kind of crime to drain off assets from what's left?" He couldn't help but notice that the Knicks were getting their butts kicked. Moses Malone was lighting up Bill Cartwright.

"Nah. It's not strictly illegal. Not the way we're doing it, anyway. If they win, nobody's going to care much about this stuff. If they lose, believe me, it's only a drop in the bucket. Plus, the SEC doesn't give a shit about this stuff."

"Sounds like you better protect your ass on any advice you give 'em."

"Hey, we get legal opinions on every move. We throw Gordon and Crowell at 'em, to give 'em that Washington-slash-Texas big-law-firm flavor. They'd write a fairness opinion on the purchase of Manhattan from the Indians for the right price. Worry not." She leaned out of the doorway and blew him a kiss.

"Hey, how about Crabtree and Evelyn? Mantle and Maris?" Traders and salesmen generally hated attorneys. Commonly, unless they were being paid an exorbitant sum to provide an opinion that a transaction was fair, they just gummed up the works. "In a way, lawyers are just like women."

"Well, believe me, if their opinions are for sale, they ain't for sale cheap." Larisa tossed her suitcase on the bed. "Whatdya mean, 'just like women'?"

"Can't live with 'em, can't live without 'em. I guess you get what you pay for. There's the old joke too: 'The difference between hookers and lawyers is hookers will stop screwing you once you're dead.'" The Knicks game was clearly out of hand, and the conversation wasn't going anywhere.

"Fuuuuuny. Hahaha."

He got up and went in to keep her company. She was pretty much finished, and as soon as he plopped down on the bed, she walked into the kitchen to get herself a drink. Her suitcase was open, lying on the bed. It was hard to miss her birth-control pill case on one side, by a pair of slippers. She'd stopped taking them with him, opting for other methods, because she said they made her feel bloated and gross.

He sat still for a moment, staring at the bright blue evidence of her intentions. He couldn't help but wonder if she'd left it so obviously in view to send him a message as clearly as possible. Whatever her intention, he felt the anger rise in him, then subside, as he thought about whether he was really upset. He'd been completely faithful to her, except the moment with Eliza the summer before, for about two years. It was the longest he'd ever gone sleeping with only one person. Admittedly, the time pressures and strain of his work made it easy not to play around, but the opportunity had been there many times. They'd never talked about being in a monogamous relationship, but Warren felt it had been pretty much agreed. It was a little bit of a double standard, but he hadn't planned the liaison with Eliza. Christ, going to Austin's house for the weekend had been Larisa's idea.

Even so, knowing that she was sleeping with someone in Texas didn't hurt him half as much as he would have expected it to. He was sure it was one of her powerful clients, or maybe one of the attorneys. He was trying to convince himself he didn't care. The relationship had gotten pretty rocky anyway. He might have wounded pride or an insulted ego, but he had to face that it was probably time to move on. He stood up and finished the lukewarm Budweiser, then stepped into the living room and sat at the round table she used as a dining area. She came out of the kitchen and came over to him, pressing her flat stomach against his head, and hugging him to her. He eased away.

"Look, there's something we'd better talk about." He held her at arm's length, his hands on her hips.

She looked slightly quizzical and sat down, taking a sip of her beer. "You sound so serious. What is it?" She put down the bottle and leaned her hands on her chin.

"Listen, I've been doing some thinking, and I thought we should probably talk about this anyway. I mean, I've been trying but... well, you know, you've been so wrapped up in work lately—I mean, so have I—but, between work and everything else that's been going on, it's pretty clear that we both could use a change." He paused and waited to see her reaction.

She just stared at him impassively.

He pressed on. "I think that it'd be a good idea if we just kind of cooled it for a while. Thought things over. It would do us both some good—"

"Cooled it?" Her voice was full of bile, biting. "Thought it over? Isn't that kind of cliché? Why don't you just come right out and say it? If there's someone else you're seeing, just say it. Don't give me this shit. I don't need to listen to this shit." Tears were coming up in her eyes, and Warren faltered, but steeled himself.

"Listen, Larisa, don't get so self-righteous. I'm not seeing anybody else, and I haven't been. But that's pretty good. I mean, I may be a bit slow, but I've always packed a little lighter for my trips than you." He glared at her and pointed to her suitcase through the open door.

She didn't waver at all. "Oh, so that's what's on your pathetic little mind. Well, while you were poking around in my suitcase, did you happen to think about it for a minute? I wanted to start back on the pill because I know how much better it is for you, and it makes things so much more spontaneous. I thought you might want to say good-bye to me nicely and not have to worry. Obviously, you just wanted to say good-bye. Fine. Do all the thinking you want. I don't give a fuck. You're an asshole." The tears were flowing now, over her high cheekbones, and off the precipice of her sharp jawline. She turned half away from him and wiped her nose with the back of her hand, like a wounded cat with a downy paw.

Warren sat quietly for a minute, listening to the sobbing. She was beautiful. He couldn't help but notice how her breasts heaved slightly against her T-shirt when her chest shook. He marveled at his own body, responding sexually to the woman he'd just broken up with, mostly because he hadn't felt that response for so long. Men *were* pathetic. Nevertheless, he still had his doubts.

He rose from the table and smoothed her hair for a moment. Then he got his coat, and the book from the coffee table. He shut off the TV. He walked to the door and turned back to where she sat at the table, the sobs reduced to sniffles.

"I'm sorry. I am. I always loved you. Maybe I was wrong." He spread his hands in a gesture of supplication, and she rose to her feet, quickly crossing the room and stepping into his open arms. "I love you too. Maybe we can…" She stopped and kissed him hard, pressing her body against his, opening his coat to make room. Her hands slid down to his pants, unzipping and stroking him. She pushed her skirt up as she pulled him to the floor on top of her, guiding him into her, their tongues intertwined, his breathing heavy. She was crying as he made love to her in the entry foyer, and only as he exploded in the excitement and emotion of the moment did the thought cross his mind: What if she's bluffing?

twenty-six

It had been a long time since Warren had been in Los Angeles. His father had taken him there once when he was twelve years old. They had stayed in an oversize Mediterranean-style villa in Bel Air, the home of Marissa George. Her daughter was a promising junior, and Ken Hament had developed a reputation for working with younger girls. The tennis court was carved into the side of a hill, and a swimming pool was cantilevered over a sheer drop. Warren had spent the day like a movie mogul, sunning by the pool while his father pounded balls with Kelsey.

After three days, the fifteen-year-old had asked Warren if he played. His father had given him strict instructions to stay off the court with her, but she had started teasing him. Finally, after two hours of her insulting Eastern tennis and explaining how she could beat both of her brothers, Warren asked her if she'd ever played against boys her age. She had not.

"Well, if you had, you'd know by now that no girl can beat even a lousy guy." Warren had put all the condescension a twelve-year-old could muster into the comment. It led to an unrefusable challenge, a match, and Kelsey in tears, her confidence shot and the Haments' California vacation cut short. Ken had taken Warren to Disneyland anyway, which Warren had hated.

"Time passes, and every generation gets stronger and better," Ken said. "If I ever catch you being mean to a girl again, I will smack you silly." He was right. Warren doubted if he would stand a chance against the tiny but powerful teenagers on the women's tour now. The memory caused him a pang of regret for what he'd said to Larisa. She was working so hard, and he took her for granted, he concluded. Relationships between two fully engaged people were not exactly easy. It had to be harder for an attractive woman, with men undoubtedly hitting on her all the time. When she'd come home from Texas, she had tried to patch things up, but he was convinced she had been lying to him. He just couldn't get past it. They had drifted apart, and he could feel her anger whenever he saw her in the office. He was anxious for a chance to get away, and it came quickly.

Weldon Brothers sponsored an annual outing at Pebble Beach for some of its best clients. Warren had invited John Conklin from Wisconsin, and the two senior investment managers from Warner Savings, the large savings and loan Warren had been assigned when he started selling.

Warner had grown from a $300 million institution in LA that no one on Wall Street cared about, to one of the four largest savings and loans in California, at $11 billion in assets, in just a few years. Most of this growth had come about by selling certificates of deposit to their customers, and that money had been invested largely in junk bonds and mortgage-backed securities. Two men, Karlheinz Beker and Pete Largeman, were in charge of picking how the money was put to work. Warner's profits were determined by the spread in interest rates between those on the money they borrowed—the CDs and their deposits—and those on their investments. When the US Government insured all bank CDs up to $100,000 per bank, they suddenly gave investors motivation to buy whatever bank's CDs had the highest rates, regardless of the risks they took. If the bank failed, as long as you held no more than $100,000 of any one bank's debt, you were safe.

As the bank increased its liabilities by raising money selling CDs, it had to increase its assets by investing. Eleven billion dollars is a lot of money to invest, and suddenly Wall Street was in love with Warner. Every firm courted its investment business, trying to sell it anything they could dream up. In addition, the bank originated a lot of mortgage loans through its branches and often sold off packages of them to reinvest in higher-yielding assets or to diversify its holdings. The higher the rates on what it bought, the more the bank earned, and the more Karlheinz and Pete made in bonus and stock options. Warren had won more than a fair share of both types of business, and he was surprised when Anson Combes called a meeting with Warren,

Malcolm Conover, and Paul Jacobs, the head of the junk area at Weldon. Anson said he wanted to devise a strategy to get more of Warner's investment business and wanted to strategize before a big group of Weldon sales and finance people headed out to California.

"Look, they're a huge thrift, and we're missing a ton of opportunities," Anson had started. "Warren, you're doing a good job, but, let's face it, you're still pretty new at this. We need to hit these guys hard, bring in the big guns. I want to get out there and find out what's going on. I think I can persuade them to open up some of their mortgage deals to us, and the junk will follow." Anson pushed his glasses, which continually slipped down, back up onto the bridge of his nose.

"Well, Anson, I'd say that Drexel's got pretty much of a lock on their high-yield corporate business. You know, Mike Milken..." Paul Jacobs was an older man for Wall Street, in his late forties, and he spoke in measured tones. He had been a bit slow in developing Weldon's non-investment-grade corporate department, or junk-bond trading area, because he didn't really believe in it. Weldon had always been a top investment bank for the major corporations and governments of the world. The explosion of the mergers and acquisitions business had made Weldon a force in bringing new deals to the markets. By selling bonds, and creating clever new ways to finance takeovers, the acquiring companies could borrow money to finance their spending sprees. These bonds were risky—if a company went too deep into debt, it could fail and default on its obligations.

All this had forced the trading area to become a major factor in the firm's business flow, as several billion dollars of new bond issues were fed into the markets by their M&A department from their deal flow. Jacobs had constantly argued that many of the deals were shaky and had insisted that Weldon only handle well-structured ones.

Combes cut him off. "Milken? What is it with this guy? All you junk guys talk about him like he's God or something. Hasn't Warren been getting you good feedback on what they're doing? Malcolm? I mean, this is a major account. We've got product, research, deals. I want their mortgage business. They let Drexel sell a three-hundred-million-dollar package of loans last week that had to have a point in it. That's three million, minimum.

We could have done that deal. My department could have structured that in their sleep. We need to be all over them." Anson had smacked the table a few times.

"Um, Anson, I appreciate your feelings. We all want to do more of Warner's business. But you've got to understand the nature of their relationship with Drexel." Malcolm's diplomatic tone had visibly irritated Combes, who hunched his shoulders and looked up at Conover in a pose that had reminded Warren of Richard Nixon. "It's not that simple."

"Oh, Christ, I'm sick of this garbage. How am I going to tell Gustave Haupt and Mack Carter that we can't get in the door with Warner?" Anson brought in the names of the chairman and the CEO of Weldon. Warren knew that they both disliked Combes, even feared him a little, but respected the revenues he brought in.

"Hey, Anson, hang on a second." Warren's temper had begun to get the best of him. "We're not exactly getting shut out. First off, our Investment Banking Committee decided that we wouldn't sell Warner's CDs. That's strike one. Drexel sells ninety percent of them in the money markets, and one hundred percent of their commercial paper and debt. Strikes two and three. That means that Drexel basically raises all their money for them, and then sells them junk bonds as part of the deal. Still, I did two million gross with them last year, which isn't zero, despite all that. I opened them up to mortgage derivatives, and they do more of that business with us than with anyone—"

"Two million is nothing. We should do that on one trade. I'm telling you, we need to really put the press on these guys. I'm ready to do it." Anson was rolling. "You haven't been listening to a word I'm saying." That was actually Anson's code for his not caring what anyone else had to say.

Anson had then suggested setting up a meeting on their way to Pebble Beach. Warren explained that Pete and Karlheinz were coming on the trip—they were never ones to miss a free meal or golf game. The appropriately named Pete Largeman was one of the dumbest, heaviest, laziest investment managers Warren had ever met, so much so that his nickname around the Street was the Load. His partner, Karlheinz Beker, was one of the smartest and oiliest portfolio managers around and had masterminded Warner's growth on an inverted pyramid of debt and equity.

In asking Warren to set up an appointment at their offices in LA, Anson explained that he wanted to see their facilities and meet them in a business setting, not at some "boondoggle" such as the golf outing. Warren knew that Anson often used "business" trips to get to his house on a golf course or to visit his family in New Orleans. Only other people's trips were "boondoggles." Anson's were always important client calls.

The meeting adjourned, with an agreement that Warren and Anson would visit Warner, and then go on to Pebble Beach for the outing. Even though it meant dealing with Anson, Warren was glad to get away from his apartment and everything that reminded him constantly of Larisa. It had been almost two months, but the wound felt fresh. The closest he'd come to a date was when a stunning woman from Salomon Brothers had come in for an interview to join Weldon's sales desk, and she had openly hit on him. He'd resisted the temptation, and when Weldon didn't bite, she'd quit and moved in with a rock star.

As he left the office, Warren idly contemplated what the first meeting between Beker and Combes would be like. Sharks were generally loners, and a confrontation would be a rare and dangerous event. These two were flesh eaters of the first order.

The travel department had tried to book Warren on the same flight out of JFK as Anson, their normal practice, but Warren changed his flight to Continental out of Newark. Five hours alone with Anson, even in American's awesome first-class cabin, was a terrifying concept.

twenty-seven

❧

On his arrival at LAX, Warren was met by a pleasant man from the car-rental company, who had been standing at the baggage-claim exit with a small name sign. The Weldon salesman in Los Angeles who covered the largest money managers and pension funds, Howard Steinman, had booked a car for Warren and told him only that he'd be surprised. That was an understatement.

The Bentley Turbo R cost over $150,000 new, and was unbelievably ostentatious, but Warren had always been curious to drive one. A dark blue sedan sat gleaming at the curb, with a rich tan leather interior. Inside, the solidity and sumptuousness of the car was remarkable. The surfaces were all deeply polished burled walnut, the gauges beautifully arranged and labeled. Off the line, the car seemed like a rocket, albeit a velvet-lined one. In LA, he had been told by Howard, you are what you drive. If so, to other drivers Warren Hament was now a playful and self-indulgent English lord, motoring about in his new Bentley.

Evidently, the doormen at the hotel believed in the same auto-existentialism Steinman espoused. Warren got an incredibly warm reception, especially from the parking valet. Warren had driven directly to the Hotel Bel-Air, his memory of the route from the airport intact after all these years. He and his father had eaten lunch here once, and Warren remembered it as the most beautiful place he had ever been as a child. Steinman, who had once spent four months at the hotel after a gas explosion at his house, had put in a word for him. Warren had been given the hotel's most coveted room, a large one-bedroom suite, with a walled-off private garden that included a Jacuzzi, disguised as a round, tiled fountain, filled by a marble lion's head spigot, and strewn with petals from the bougainvillea that climbed the trellises around it. It was incredibly romantic, and it seemed like a waste to be here alone.

After tipping the bellman, he stripped down for a quick soak in the Jacuzzi, then took a shower and changed into casual clothes. It was only two o'clock, and Combes wouldn't be looking for him until the next morning. They had a seven-thirty breakfast scheduled. Although it was only the savings and loan, Warren mused that "breakfast at Warner" sounded perfectly Hollywood. He threw a blazer over his polo shirt and went to retrieve the car. He thought an exploration of Beverly Hills might be interesting, and he put on his sunglasses, hoping they helped him look the part.

twenty-eight

◆◆◆

Warren admitted to himself, cruising down Canon Drive, just off Rodeo, the car was kind of embarrassing. It was sort of discreet, but in an obvious way. He thought the car made him look as if he were trying too hard to be something he wasn't. By Wilshire Boulevard, he had made up his mind. He made a quick turn and zipped into the luxury-car rental lot just a few blocks down. In the tiny office, an extremely pretty girl was behind the counter, wearing the company uniform shirt draped over her own, with a name tag pinned to the pocket, labeled SAM. She was tall and thin, with straight, dark brown hair.

When Warren walked in, she put down a book and looked up." Hi. What can I do for you?" She had the twangy Southern California accent, but delivered the greeting almost deadpan, without the usual fake perkiness. Her green eyes were mesmerizing.

"I . . . uh . . . I wanted to trade in the car?" Warren tossed the keys on the counter. His eyes were riveted to the clerk, and his voice was a little tremulous. The woman was a complete knockout.

"The Turbo R?" She sounded surprised and looked over his shoulder at the car, which seemed to absorb the sunshine.

"Yeah. Maybe for a Chevy or a Lincoln." He couldn't help but sound a little wistful.

"Is something wrong with it? It was running fine when we sent it out to the airport." She sounded concerned, and Warren figured repairs must be unbelievably expensive.

"No, not at all. It's great. I just want something simpler. It's kind of embarrassing." Warren shrugged.

"Well, I've gotta charge you for it. It's the most in-demand car we've got. I've got to hit you for the one day." She actually sounded apologetic.

"Yeah, I figured. That's okay. I just don't feel right in it. It's not the money. And I could never drive it to my meeting tomorrow anyway. That car needs a movie star, or a chauffeur or something. Not me."

"You just a Chevy kind of guy? You don't look it." She smiled at him.

"I hope that's a compliment. Anything low-key will do." Warren smiled back.

"Well, whatever you say, but the simplest thing we've got here is like a Jaguar or a Mustang convertible. I think Hertz has Caddys or maybe a Marquis." She put her elbows on the counter and rested her chin on her hands. "You sure about the Turbo?"

"Nah. I can't keep it. Just bill me for it, and I'll figure something out." Warren felt bad about wasting six hundred bucks, but was resigned to it. Besides, Steinman had promised him that he had a way to get Weldon to pay for it. "Maybe you can get one of the guys to give me a lift over to the Hertz lot. Or Avis. I don't care."

'Tell you what. I'll drive you over. In the Turbo. But I'm going to go *real* fast." She picked the keys up off the counter.

Warren was surprised and reacted quickly. "Hey, if you're going to be my chauffeur, why don't I buy you a drink or something? Like dinner, after you get off work. It'd be the least I could do. I could come pick you up in my Citation." Warren had a nervous grin on his face. He'd never been good at delivering pickup lines, and he realized to his horror that he'd actually used the words *pick* and *up* in his pitch.

She gave him a long look and pulled out the rental form he had filled out at the airport. She nodded a few times. "New York ... Weldon Brothers? Is that like Warner Brothers?"

"No. It's Wall Street, not show biz."

"Oh, it's different? I didn't know."

Warren laughed. "Well, you may have a point."

"I like the way you laugh. Plus, you're not in movies or TV. ... Okay! We'll have a drink, then I'll drop you at Hertz." She yelled into the office behind her, "Carlos! I'll be out a while! Watch the desk!"—then came out from behind the counter.

"Sounds good to me! Let's go. Should I ride in back? Where's your hat?" Sam slipped off the striped uniform shirt, which she tossed on the counter. In her jeans, boots, and T-shirt, she looked like a magazine ad. Warren couldn't believe she was actually coming with him. They headed out the door. "You'll hold the door open for me, right?" Warren said. "And call me sir?"

"Don't push it, *Warren*." She punched him lightly on the shoulder, then waited elaborately for him to open the driver's door for her.

When she heard he was staying at the Bel-Air, she wanted to have a drink there. She said she loved the patio, then kept up a solid stream of small talk during the short trip down Sunset Drive to Stone Canyon, mostly about how she'd negotiated the deal for the Bentley originally, buying it from the girlfriend of a producer for less than 40 percent of its cost just three months before. The car valet was even more impressed the second time when he got a look at Sam, who Warren had decided looked better driving it than he ever could.

The outdoor terrace was beautiful, shaded by tall trees, and fragrant with bougainvillea and eucalyptus. While they waited for the drinks, which were martinis, they filled each other in a bit on who they were. Warren described himself as a failed athlete and Wall Street geek, and Sam described herself as a former actress who actually owned the car rental lot. Her business manager had put some of her earnings from a season on a sitcom and two national commercials into it. He'd stolen the rest of her money, along with most of the investment of a few studio guys who had also financed the lot. They had been arrested for drug dealing, and she wound up managing the place while they did time and she looked for a partner or a buyer. She didn't mind working there, and the lot was making good money, most of which she got to keep. She lived in Santa Monica, but came from San Diego. Her father was a surgeon, and her mother a nurse. They'd spent her junior high school years in Landstuhl, where he was a trauma surgeon at the big army hospital. To prove it, she ordered the next round in perfect German: *"Zwei weitere martinis, mein lieber!"*

She had one brother who was a golf pro, and another who flew F-14s for the navy. She had gone to UCLA film school, but discovered she hated everything about show business and wasn't too sad to leave it behind.

"Well, that's interesting. Do you not get enough to eat on the lot?" He pointed to the empty tray of olives and nuts, which she had completely demolished.

She smiled. "Fast metabolism. Gotta feed the fire!"

When Warren told her that he was in town to meet with Warner, her eyebrows arched; then he told her it was the bank, not the studio.

"Hey, aren't they the sleazeballs who buy all those crap bonds, or jerk bonds, or something?"

"Junk bonds. Yeah. How'd you know that?" Warren was genuinely surprised.

"I read about them. Plus, my crook business manager was in bed with the guy that runs that place and the old man who owns it. They did some big deal with this guy with a ridiculous hairpiece and dentures who was evidently a billionaire." She was looking at the bottom of her glass, which was empty.

"Sounds like Mike Milken. Ugh! Man, those were strong drinks. Where to next?" Warren stretched and yawned.

"You know what I'd really like to do?" She was tilting a little bit to her left, and the glass in her right hand was sideways.

"Please don't say go for a drive. There's no way I can get behind the wheel." Warren was spinning a bit himself. He rarely drank, and never martinis. The thought of a moving vehicle made him slightly nauseous.

"Nah. I wanna go for a swim in their pool. That's what I wanna do."

"Great idea. But I don't think they're big on skinny-dipping here. Maybe we can buy you a suit at the gift shop?" Just at that moment, the idea of seeing her naked made Warren's blood boil.

"Well, I've got on black underwear. Looks kind of like a bikini. I'm up for it if you are." She was serious, and no way was he going to offer any resistance to seeing her in her underwear.

"Okay. Let's go to the room, get robes. I've got a suit. Towels too. Then swim." His mouth was working slowly, and his mind had creaked to a stop, as another part of him took over the thinking.

"Hey, Tarzan. Get check. Pay check. Then go. Oomgawa," she mimicked him, and made an ape face. The waiter appeared, magically, with the check. Warren signed it and rose shakily to his feet. She followed him, and they made their way unsteadily down the narrow pathways and hidden court-yards to his room. He fished the key out of his jacket and opened the door for her.

"Hey, this is nice." She stepped into the foyer and past the dressing room, into the peach-stuccoed bedroom, and opened up the sheer curtains that shaded the French doors to the terrace. "Very nice. You must know some-body. Or they must know you. Is that what I think it is?" She nodded her head to the fountainlike Jacuzzi and opened the doors.

"Yeah. It's actually kind of nice. Wait, I'll get my suit." He started to rummage through his suitcase.

"To hell with the pool. This'll do just fine." She pulled her shirt over her head and unfastened her jeans as she stepped out onto the patio.

"You *are* wearing black underwear, aren't you." Warren couldn't help but notice she was in great shape, her stomach defined, small veins visible on her biceps and even at her pelvic bone.

"Yup. What color're yours?"

"Sky-blue boxers." He pulled off his shirt and stepped out onto the patio.

"You ever drive one of these things before?" She crossed back to the doors and unbuckled his belt for him.

"I've got a license and everything." He ran his hands down her shoulders. She got his pants open and pushed them down. She brushed his lips with hers.

"Then let's take it for a spin." She leaned into his arms, and as they kissed, he slipped the clasp and slid the straps of her bra down. She let it fall, and he kicked away his pants with his shoes. Her skin was a dark bronze against his paleness, and he broke the kiss to run his lips over her throat and down her chest, covering her breasts with small kisses. She held his head with her hands, pulling him back up for another kiss. His hands were running up and down her back, and over her bottom.

"Hey. How about that hot tub?" She turned in his arms and, with her back to him, slid her panties off. He reached around and cupped her breasts in his hands, and she stroked his thighs with her palms. She could feel him rising against her, and she reached back to the waistband of his shorts and tugged them down. They caught for a moment, then dropped. He moaned as the sensitive skin pressed against the smooth, cool skin of her rump, the downy hairs at the small of her back tickling him. He bent his head around as she leaned back, and they kissed again. He leaned into her, his hands moving down her flat stomach to probe her.

Warren turned her toward him, then lifted her in his arms and sat her on the edge of the tub. He knelt in front of her, with his head between her thighs, and gently caressed her with his lips and tongue. She held on to his shoulders, guiding him. He could feel her excitement peaking and intensified his effort slightly, as she rocked with a series of crests, making a small, squeaky grunting sound deep in her throat as she came. Her pace slowed, and he rose to his feet, placing himself in position as she slid forward slightly to accommodate him. Their eyes met for a moment, and as an answer to the question in his eyes, she reached down and guided him into her. His breath short and strained, his body taut, he moved until he felt himself ready to explode.

She sensed him building, swelling inside her, and slid her feet down off his back to the ground, giving her more leverage. She ground her hips with him, slamming against him, the force of his climax buckling his knees. He half collapsed over her, his body quavering with short spasms as he recovered. They rested in that position for a few moments.

"Jesus. Wow." Warren was still shaking and half rolled off her.

"I'll be right back. Meet me in the tub." Sam got to her feet and slipped into the room.

Warren climbed wearily into the tub after turning on the timer, discreetly camouflaged with painted Mexican tiles. In a minute, she reappeared, holding two small bottles of juice.

"I love minibars. But I'm drunk enough! I propose a toast." She handed him a bottle as she climbed in beside him. "To Bentleys and Bel Air!" She clinked his glass and drank hers off.

"I'll drink to that." Warren sipped his apple juice contemplatively. They were quiet for a minute. "This is pretty great."

"Mmmmmmmm." The two of them leaned back, and the bubbling, warm water lulled them both, until the hum of the motor and the gurgling of the fountain filled the air.

It seemed as if an hour passed as they sipped their juice and half dozed in the water. Warren noticed how he didn't have the tense, uneasy feeling he usually had after the few times he had ever had sex with a girl he hardly knew. She seemed familiar to him, and he was completely relaxed around her.

"You know"—her voice half startled him—"I don't feel like getting dressed and getting the hell out of here. Not one little bit." She looked him in the eyes and smiled.

"1 was just thinking the exact same thing. I was also going to say that I don't usually do things..."

"Me either. Except I don't *ever* do things like this." She smiled again. "I guess you're just lucky."

"Or irresistible. Like you. Actually, it's been a long time since I've done *anything*." He splashed water lightly in her direction.

"Charmer. Well, I'm still on the pill, but I can hardly even remember why. C'mon, let's get out of here. I'm just about poached." She stepped out of the tub and scurried for a towel, throwing him one as he climbed out. "I'll bet, if we tried real hard, we could get something pretty good to eat from room service."

"You know, you just may be right." He swung the patio door shut as they went inside, the pink afternoon light fading on the cypress trees.

twenty-nine

⌇

The next morning, Warren was surprised how well rested he felt when the phone woke him. Sam had stayed the night, and the room-service dinner had been just about perfect. They'd made love again, more slowly, and drifted off to sleep early. He had an hour to get ready, and when he realized they still had the car, he called Anson's hotel and left a message that he'd meet him at Warner's offices. Sam happily agreed to drop him off and take the car back to the office after she stopped at home. They shared a light breakfast on the patio in the morning sun, talking about his plans for the day, and she looked beautiful in the big terry robe, her hair a wild tangle.

"I know what's going to happen now." She had the sports pages of the *Los Angeles Times* open on her lap.

"What's that?" Warren had showered, shaved, and dressed, ready to go.

"I'll drop you off this morning, you'll call me from the airport, and I'll probably never see you again." She got a pouty look on her face, pushing out her lips.

"I sincerely doubt that. Want to meet me in Pebble Beach when my outing's over on Saturday? You play golf?" He wasn't sure he meant it at first, but as the words left his lips, he discovered he really did want to see her again, preferably immediately.

"The answer is yes and no. Hate the game. But I like those little carts. And you know what kind of a driver I am." She gave him a sunny smile.

"Well, since you're my new chauffeur, you'd better get hopping. I've got to go meet with the jerk-bond kings of LA, not to mention one of the most miserable human beings of all time, and it's getting late." He hooked his thumb in the air and bent over to kiss her.

"Oh, yessir! I'll git de ve-hi-cle right away, boss!" Her tone was mocking.

"Hey, lose the attitude. I don't pay you enough for that kind of sass." He spanked her on the behind with the *Times,* and she giggled happily on her way to get dressed.

Warren hopped out of the Bentley a block down Wilshire Boulevard from Warner Savings and Loan's Executive Office Building. The five-story, steel-and-glass monstrosity featured a billboard on its roof emblazoned with the bank's ludicrous coat of arms. The warm day was clear and bright, but, Warren noticed, he was the only person on the sidewalk though he was surrounded by office buildings and apartment houses. It was LA exactly the way comedians described it.

He turned into Warner's reception lobby, and cool air rushed past him as he opened the door. The receptionist sat behind a beautiful semicircular podium desk, made from tiger maple edged with brass. The floor was a carefully laid pattern of large ivory-marble blocks, and the walls were padded and upholstered in a rich art deco cream velvet. Warren couldn't imagine how much the tasteful and serene space might have cost.

"Hi. I'm Warren Hament from Weldon Brothers. I'm here to see Karlheinz and Pete. Also, there's another person from my office..." Warren was speaking to the receptionist, a pleasant-looking woman in her midforties.

"Yes. That's Mr. Combes. I've sent him up to the conference room already. Just take this elevator to the fifth floor. It's on your left, second door. Julie's Karlheinz's secretary, and she'll look to anything you need. Here's your pass." She gave Warren a nice grin, and he took the adhesive pass, thanked her, and stuck it on his lapel. He peeled it off as soon as the elevator door closed.

On five, he stepped off the elevator, which was an express, and turned to his left. He almost ran down Julie Gordon, Beker's assistant.

"Hey, Warren, take it easy. Nobody's in there yet except your guy." She was a trim, petite woman in her late twenties, smart and dedicated. He found it amusing that the receptionist had referred to her as a secretary. She had so much more on the ball than Pete Largeman that his time would have been spent more productively getting her coffee. Warren had met her when they came to New York. Warren discovered that he needed Julie's help to get ideas presented intelligently to Beker when he was too busy or distracted to take Warren's calls. Explaining things to Largeman was a waste of energy. He generally only wanted to talk about Dodgers tickets, or to plot out how he could arrange a business trip to his hometown, Chicago, which could tie in nicely with a Bulls, Blackhawks, Cubs, White Sox, or Bears game and dinner at Morton's. Recently, he'd taken up golf, and salesmen from all the Wall Street firms were lining up for the pleasure of escorting Pete, in his billowing neon double knits, onto some of the finest courses in California. The joke around the Street was that Largeman had played at Los Angeles Country Club more times that year than its head pro. Largeman still sported a 36 handicap despite the practice, and he was a consistent cheater. Caddies avoided him like the plague since he never tipped them more than the minimum.

"Jesus, Julie, sorry. I'm a little distracted this morning. You met Anson?" Warren touched her shoulder affectionately. She worked for a couple of low-lifes, but she always maintained her sense of humor, and he genuinely liked her.

"Yeah. Real charmer. Asked me for coffee, with Coffee-mate. Then gives me some stuff to copy. I was going to ask him if he wanted a blow job too, but I was afraid of the answer." Her sarcastic tone indicated she didn't really mind taking care of this stuff. It was normal business-meeting crap, and she knew she was stuck doing it because she was junior, not because she was female.

"Glad to see he's making an impression right off the bat. Where's Pete? Maybe he could jog over to Dunkin' Donuts for us all."

"Oooh. That's a good one." She laughed out loud. "The Michelin Man is in the head. Karl's on his way. Let me get this stuff copied. Oh, yeah, I got this message for you." She handed him a slip of notepaper. "Could you grab the coffee? It's over in that kitchenette. No Coffee-mate, though." She pointed to an open door down the hall.

"Yup. I remember. See ya in a sec." Warren stepped into the kitchenette, which had a full range of appliances, a pantry stocked with food, and a refrigerator filled with fruit, cheese, vegetables, and all sorts of interesting-looking snacks. A smaller, separate fridge held lunches people brown-bagged. It was all well planned and expensively done. The countertop was light gray granite. He started to reach for the tray and realized he still had the phone message in his hand. Kerry had called from New York and left him a message to call Mr. Wittlin. It took him a second to realize she meant Detective Wittlin, but probably chose to make the message a bit less conspicuous to a client. He stuck the paper in his jacket pocket, then grabbed the tray, which had been sent up from the company dining room, and balanced it with his briefcase as he crossed back to the conference room. He pushed open the door. Anson Combes was on the phone at the far end of the room, across an ocean of more tiger maple—a custom-made conference table with small teleconferencing devices in front of each seat.

Combes looked up and covered the mouthpiece. "Hey, Hament, you the coffee boy now too? Big step up, eh?" Combes laughed his hissing, nervous cackle and quickly scratched his left ear.

"Hi, Anson. Yeah, actually Malcolm had asked me to meet you at the hotel and carry your bags out for you, but I overslept. Sorry, no Coffee-mate. Will that be one lump or two?" Warren put the tray down and poured himself a cup from the thermos of coffee. Anson had turned his attention back to the telephone. Warren shrugged and poured Anson a cup too, then handed it to him. He was busy berating Brad Brooks, an associate, about some data-processing snafu. His tone was condescending, sour, and demeaning all at once.

"Yes, but, Brad, that's no excuse. We've got to have those numbers today, and they've got to be right. If they sent the tape in the wrong format, that's our fault for not telling them which one we run. This is inexcusable. You fucked it up, you fix it. I don't give a damn who else has to wait, I want those numbers now.... Yeah? Well, Holik's a fucking moron, okay? He bids what I tell him to bid anyway. He's a fucking loser. I know you agree. You wanna listen to that clown? I'm telling you, get those numbers to Diane now. Don't talk to Holik. I'll deal with him later."

Warren stood there impassively, knowing that, at a key moment in the future, Combes would use this conversation to put Brooks in a compromising position. Combes would say that Brooks had told him he thought Jamie Holik was a moron and a bozo, simply because Combes had said it and Brooks was too intimidated to demur. Whenever Combes started it with him, Warren would immediately change the subject, never agreeing with Combes implicitly or explicitly.

Combes had hung up on Brooks and swiveled his chair back to the conference table. Suddenly, as if some sort of drug had hit his system, Anson became friendly, charming, flattering, and funny. He complimented Warren on arranging the meeting, how well he had developed the client relationship and the business, and how much he appreciated the way Warren had included him. He said he was looking forward to the golf trip and hoped they could sit down and discuss some of Anson's ideas for the improvement of the mortgage department and explore some of Warren's own ideas. As Warren was figuring out how to respond, Karlheinz and Pete came in the room, followed by Julie with a stack of papers, which she distributed. Introductions were made, and Anson launched his pitch.

The papers were charts of Weldon's prowess and standing in all the various capital markets functions. These included its rankings as a seller of all the various categories of stock and bond offerings, and its "firsts" in financing structures. Anson whipped through them all quickly, summing them up by pointing out that Weldon was a top-five firm in virtually every area that could conceivably be of use to Warner. He heaped compliments on the bank's strategy and execution in the markets and expressed appreciation for the opportunity to meet with them. Finally he turned to Karlheinz Beker.

"Basically, Mr. Beker, Weldon—we—want to get deeper into bed with you. What do we have to do to get more of your mortgage business? If it means stepping up our junk business too, we can deliver. I've gotten the Investment Banking Committee to agree to sell your CDs, under certain conditions. We're pulling out all the stops."

Warren's jaw dropped. Not only had he not been informed that the IBC had changed their mind about selling Warner's paper, he was dead against it. He saw Warner for what it was—a bloated, overleveraged house of cards that relied on the federal government's guarantee of its deposits to borrow the money it lent to Mike Milken. If its returns on those loans—the junk bonds, partnerships, and other investments such as commercial real estate mortgages—should fall below the cost of its borrowings, the bank had enough capital to last maybe a couple months. Considering nobody could tell from their statements what half their investments were, Warren had agreed that selling Warner's certificates of deposit to Weldon's valued customer base was hardly a confidence builder for the firm or its reputation.

Karlheinz Beker slowly put his pen down on the conference table. "I appreciate the lengths you seem willing to go to for some of our business, Mr. Combes"—Beker's accent was not heavy, just a trace of Austrian intonation—"but, as I told you in our telephone conversation, right now we are very pleased with the service we are getting from Drexel on nonmortgage products. Perhaps at some point in the future, if our needs change, we can review the situation. It is not as if our firms aren't doing a fair amount of business together as it is. Warren has been doing a very good job of keeping us up with developments in the markets, and I must say that your mortgage trading desk seems first-rate, and very willing to work with us. Warren executed a rather large IO strip trade for us just recently." Beker reached into the case he had carried into the meeting and pulled out a stack of Weldon Brothers spiral binders. "I took the time to review these, and I wanted to return them to you. They were very helpful."

It was all Warren could do to sit still. From Beker's response he learned that Combes had called Beker at least once without even telling Warren, a serious breach of etiquette. He also recognized the binders. They were highly confidential preliminary reports on a bank balance-sheet management system that the sales group was developing in concert with Weldon's Asset Finance team. Basically, they were developing a computer-modeling program that could manipulate and reallocate an institution's balance sheet to take the greatest advantage of existing and future regulations. The plan was to put the finishing touches on the program, then parcel it out, on a fee basis, to the firm's best clients. They called it BIGS, but Warren couldn't remember what the acronym stood for. Combes had sent the guts of the project to one of the least trustworthy, sleaziest, and greediest people Warren had ever met. He could guarantee that Beker had sent copies directly to Drexel's Finance department, and they were busy replicating the system as they spoke. Warren took it personally, as he had spent many late evenings with Weldon's Asset Finance people building the model.

"Well, I understand that Drexel is really a top-notch firm in many of the markets you need access to, and that they can offer you certain products and opportunities that we cannot. But I think, if you consider it, that a broader relationship with Weldon will benefit Warner over the longer term, in terms of perception and bottom line, when markets and needs change. That's why I think that, if you give us your next residential whole-loan deal, you'll find that you have not only gotten great service from a superior firm, but you have also put one of the key blocks in the foundation of a long and mutually beneficial cooperative effort." Anson sounded like some kind of canned-tape player. Warren could practically envision slides of Weldon's board of directors, as dried out a bunch of Swiss as you could ever find, flashing up behind Anson. If there were a firm anthem, Warren would have expected it to be playing. It was about as subtle a pitch as "Do you come here often?" The thought brought an image of Sam to his mind, and he had to will it away to focus on Anson, who had gathered his papers into a pile and was looking down at them as he spoke.

Warren decided to jump in. "Karlheinz, I think what Anson's trying to say is that we are really pleased with the time you've given to our ideas, and with the willingness to work with us you have shown. Weldon just wants to be certain that you understand how anxious we are to take this to a new level, so that you can have the next generation of analytics and execution on line, with us. Drexel's great, but they are actually pretty far behind in many sectors. Working with a firm with the reputation and status of Weldon means something in the marketpace. Drexel is Drexel."

"Thanks, Warren. I appreciate your translation." Karlheinz gave him a cold, purely Aryan smile and turned to Anson. "I'll tell you what. I will give Warren the computer tape for our next loan transaction. We can discuss it after our little outing. I hope, Mr. Combes, that you feel the trip has been worthwhile." Beker nodded slightly to Anson.

"Absolutely. I think you'll be pleased with the results we give you, don't you, Warren?" Anson had that killer look in his eyes. The one he usually got just before he humiliated someone or fired one of his people.

"Yeah. That's great, Karlheinz." Warren was absolutely stunned. Anson had given one of the most simplistic sales pitches he'd ever heard, offered nothing new to Warner, handed them about $10 million worth of research, and Karlheinz, who never returned a favor if it would cost him twenty cents, had just opened the door to a new relationship. Something didn't add up, and

Warren's suspicions were not eased by the fact that Anson and Karlheinz had spoken on the telephone privately, or that Anson had sent the reports to Karlheinz, obviously with a fair amount of lead time.

The rest of the meeting went uneventfully, with Warren recapping the performance of some of the trades he had put Warner into. Largeman pitched in from time to time to take credit for the big winners, and after another half hour, Warren and Anson were back in the elevator.

"Still think it was a waste of time, Hament?" Anson had his teeth out. He called it a smile.

"Anson, you're amazing. I mean totally. You just absolutely bowled them over. Wow. I can't believe I didn't have you out here six months ago. You're like a cruise missile—a secret weapon. You should be in sales. You ..." Warren was laying it on as thick as he could, but started to choke on his own sarcasm. To hell with it, he didn't report to Anson Combes, and this whole meeting had been bullshit. "You know, come to think of it, you are in sales. You must be, because you called my fucking account without letting me in on it. Hey, Anson, maybe I could hear a tape of that call? I'd love to hear how a pro greases the skids." Warren's voice was shaking a bit.

"Hey, calm down, buddy boy. It was just a courtesy call. Malcolm knew all about it." Anson was serious now, and he pushed his glasses up. "Anyway, I bet we get that deal."

If he's so cocky, then he knows it's in the bag. I wonder how he arranged that? Warren thought to himself. They walked in silence to the door, past the depositors' big investment in rare woods. Warren caught himself. Maybe this business was getting to him a little bit. The one thing that consistently amazed him was how driven people such as Combes were over nothing more than ego gratification. When you thought of it, it was rare for a trader or a salesman to take home more than a relatively small fraction of his or her total production on Wall Street. Five to 10 percent was the norm, with an occasional 15 here and there. The other 85 covered the costs of office space, telephones, computers, and clerks ... and, of course, senior management. They got a cut for just one particular talent—being especially good pricks.

"Well, Anson, I'm just not used to having anyone call my accounts without letting me in on it. There's usually something I can help with to make things easier. You know, like telling you that giving Warner a copy of the

BIGS proposal'd be like sending out working drafts to Drexel and Salomon for comments." They had reached the lot where Anson's car was parked.

"Well, I think it's going to get us our first client for the program. You ought to relax. Go get laid or something. You'll never hit 'em straight at Pebble with all that tension in your shoulders." Anson slipped on a pair of sunglasses and opened the door to a Fleetwood with an Avis sticker on the bumper.

"Hey, Anson, what do I need to get laid for? I just got fucked, and I didn't even have to take off my clothes."

thirty

ﾖﾐﾖ

The drive from Los Angeles up to the Monterey Peninsula is one of the most dramatic in the world. Warren had decided to drive rather than fly so he could take some time to sort out his thoughts, and to see the coast. Sam lent him a Ferrari convertible, a two-year-old, black Mondial she'd bought from the federal Drug Enforcement Administration for about half price. They had seized it from a Hollywood lawyer who had been stopped for speeding with a kilo of coke in the wheel well.

The car hummed along, and soon Warren fell into a rhythm of shifting gears, accelerating, and braking, watching the sights slide by in the warm air. The hills that swept to the ocean from the desert fell away in sheer drops to the surf, and every few miles Warren would pass a few lonely horses or cattle grazing the dry grass of immense and deserted coastline tracts basking in the salt haze.

The past few months had been a whirlwind. After Dougherty's death, he had not only filled his shoes as a salesman, but improved the production dramatically. He had been working hard, and most of the portfolio managers he covered found dealing with Warren easier than with Bill. Warren was more state-of-the-art, conversant with the new derivative products and sophisticated investment strategies that Dougherty had not learned in depth. The business of managing institutional money was growing more complex by the day, as the amounts of capital to be invested ballooned almost beyond belief. Pension funds were growing by leaps and bounds, not just from an influx of new contributions from the weekly paychecks of a bigger workforce, but also from the staggering amount of income being generated by the existing investments. The California Public Employees' Retirement System, for example, had almost $45 billion in funds. This threw off almost $2 billion per year in interest and dividends to be invested, in addition to another $2 billion in new contributions. That was almost $100 million a week to invest, just for one pension fund in one state. Soon big pension funds would be pushing above $100 billion or $200 billion. And they needed to earn high investment returns to meet the unsupportable retirement benefits that public unions with their clout had forced politicians to give them. That meant the funds would have to take lots more risk every year.

Many pension funds had so much cash under management they would hire investment management companies to invest portions of it. One such manager, Warren's client Modern Investment Management, or MIMCO, ran almost $40 billion in assets for pension funds, universities, municipalities, and so on. At their fee of just over one-quarter of 1 percent per year, MIMCO earned almost $100 million per year. Almost 80 percent of that was pure profit. Pete Young, the senior partner, earned about $12 million per year and had some $125 million in equity in MIMCO by 1982.

Warren had to admit, driving an $80,000 car on a beautiful day, that the rewards of this business came fast and furious. But the rewards didn't just materialize out of nowhere. All that money being made by the investment managers and the Wall Street firms had to originate somewhere. Generally, it came from the pockets of the beneficiaries of the pension plans, the holders of the insurance policies, the buyer of mutual fund shares. The little guy who was too busy earning a living to pay attention to what stocks to buy or what bonds to own. Warren understood why stock managers got paid if they performed—it was like having an ace poker player on your side in the casino, and stocks were understandable to most people. Of course, most of the managers had a good year or two and then "reverted to the mean," in Giambi's parlance. But the bond managers were largely a different story. If one outperformed "the markets" by a percentage point per year, he was a guru. Two and he was a god. Most were measured in fractions of a percent. This brutal business required an increasingly sophisticated mind to master it as bond structures got more complicated.

Nevertheless, Warren was nonplussed by everything he saw in the business.

It was filled with young men who had virtually no focus or desire in the world except to make money. He had watched an almost endless stream of PhDs in engineering or physics fritter away their educations on building things like binary bivariate option contracts, which used unbelievably complex computer architectures to demonstrate the efficiency of Newton's First Law of the Capital Markets: "If almost nobody understands it, it will probably make you rich." Wizened deans of finance and academe were trotted out to herald the dawn of a new age of global capitalism, in which binomial trees somehow accounted for every possible outcome and could allow you to hedge your pension fund's exposure to fluctuations in the Polish zloty with a basket of options on other lesser developed countries' nondollar debt. Of course, the only reason any of this was relevant was that investment managers pushed into new areas desperately seeking performance. America was undoubtedly at the cutting edge of financial science. An image of the comedian "Professor" Irwin Corey, with his big wig and nonsensical babble, flashed into Warren's mind and made him smile. Perfect candidate for treasury secretary in the next administration.

Warren shifted down a couple gears for a hairpin turn that opened out to a massive vista of surf pounding a rock formation stranded offshore. The ozone tang in the air and majestic views couldn't rid him of the vague sense of guilt and hypocrisy that nagged at him whenever he had thoughts of superiority. Wasn't he just as guilty as the rest of them? Hadn't he sold his soul to mammon just as surely as Anson Combes or Bill Pike, who had given him such a hard time in his interview and turned out to be just as sour and nasty all the time? Maybe Warren was worse than them—he was always being told he was articulate, creative, sensitive, and talented—at least by his teachers right before they asked him why he didn't work harder. His parents had loved him, and he wasn't abused as a child. He could easily have found a way to bring happiness or joy into people's lives instead of kickout options on Fannie Mae 8s. He knew his father didn't understand the drive that had pushed Warren to business school or to the Street. Ken had always told Warren that medicine or entertainment were the most honorable professions. His uncle Buckley had dedicated his life to drug research, ignoring the lure of private practice and spending thirty years in laboratories and clinics that paid next to nothing. The man spent his free time delivering presents to children in his hospital's wards and had arranged a wholesale deal with a German stuffed-animal maker so he could afford to buy in quantity. Warren had to remember to send him another check.

As it had during all the other times that Warren's thoughts ran down this path, his mind slowly shuttered to the dilemma. The money was good, he tried to avoid screwing his clients, and he was always courteous to waiters and cabdrivers unless they attacked first. In the words of Bill Pike, Warren ate what he killed and packed out what he carried in. Simple rules, but ones that helped survival in the jungles, or on the fairways, as the case might be.

thirty-one

After about three hours, Warren pulled into a small deli/gas station perched alongside the narrow Coast Highway. He bought a Pepsi and a bag of pretzels, then went outside to sit on the hood of the car and feel the sunshine. It was always a relief to get away from the office, and the setting was superb. As he started to climb back into the driver's seat, his jacket caught his eye.

He remembered the message from Wittlin. It was a bit late, six thirty back in New York, but he grabbed the paper and went to the phone booth that stood across from the gas pumps.

Wittlin answered on the second ring. Warren introduced himself and asked what the detective needed. Wittlin didn't respond immediately, but wanted to know where Warren was calling from, the connection was a bit weak.

"Right now, I am standing in a phone booth with a great view of the Pacific Ocean. I'm in the middle of nowhere, about an hour north of San Simeon, on my way to Monterey, California." Warren reflexively looked around as he spoke, a New Yorker's motion, squinting as if to read the numbers on street signs.

"Well, then I guess I'll have to wait to see you until you get back. When you coming back to the city?"

"A couple of days. Why? What's up?"

"Not much, unfortunately. But there are some questions I wanted to ask you, some things you might be able to help with."

"You can't ask me on the phone?"

"No. Not really."

"Could you give me a hint?"

"Not really. Just a couple questions about your family, and other things."

"Gee, you're being communicative. I'll call you when I get back." Warren couldn't help being a little testy, even though he figured it wasn't a great idea to be rude to a policeman.

"I'll be here."

Warren grunted and hung up. The conversation struck him as odd. He pondered it as he drove away, shifting gears automatically. Why wouldn't Wittlin tell him what the questions were about? His *family?* Maybe he thought Warren would get nervous. But why? After all, Wittlin had absolutely no reason to think Warren had anything to do with Dougherty's death. He had a perfect alibi, and Wittlin knew it. No, Warren had nothing to be nervous about, but he was annoyed. Great. The call would probably stay in his mind and give him anxiety for the rest of the trip, he thought. Anxiety is not a good thing when you're hitting little white balls along the cliffsides. Combes had that right. Golf and tension don't mix.

He decided not to think about it if he could and sped up a bit to keep his concentration on the blacktop ahead. He was out on his own, on a narrow ribbon of highway twisting above the surf, with the sun low on the horizon, setting into an ocean on the wrong side of the road. The engine whined and the wind drove the worry from his head as the miles spun out behind him through the late afternoon, until the cypress forest sprang up from the blasted coastline, and he turned onto the lush peninsula at Carmel.

thirty-two

✦

The eighth hole at Pebble Beach is a golfing shrine, a mecca that inspires dreams and nightmares, joy and despair. The tee shot is blind and uphill, the target the corner of a house that is visible above the crest of the rise. A good drive will bring you to the edge of the abyss, a hundred-foot-deep crescent chasm that falls off to a charming aquamarine cove with sweeping surf and a pale sand beach. One hundred and seventy-five yards across this valley is a steeply pitched green, surrounded by powdery white-sand bunkers. The view is the grandest on any golf course in the world, and the hole is described by Nicklaus as the greatest par four in the game. The verdant green of the grass, deep blue sky, and boiling ocean water combine with the misty sea spray, salt-infused air, sunshine, and puffy clouds to make a tableau so rich and inspiring that a well-struck shot reverberates with the harmony of something divine. A par or birdie is a moment of pure ecstatic bliss.

When the designer sculpted this masterpiece, Pete Largeman from Warner was nowhere in his mind. From his pull hook off the tee to his second, third, and fourth shots into the water, he spewed a vile stream of obscenities while thumping his iron into the turf. His immense body was swathed in stretchy polyester of distinctly excremental hues, and he jiggled as he swore, with a cigarette clamped in his bovine jaws. Warren was waiting for Pete to enter cardiac arrest so he could compose himself for the four-iron attempt at the green, after a decent three-wood from the tee box. Finally, Pete's seizure abated, and Warren stroked the ball crisply, but to the left, and he saw a distant puff of white as the ball landed in a bunker.

"Hey, tough shot, Warren. It's a hard par from there." Pete was alluding to the sand shot that had to carry the sticky rough and stop on a slick green, or that risked a flier that cleared the green and went for a swim seventy feet below. Pete's comment made certain that, by the time Warren reached his ball, he would be terrified of the shot he faced.

"Thanks for the tip, Pete. Yours is a tough twelve from down there." Warren gestured to the beach far below. "Just hang out here. There'll be a chopper along any minute to take you down. I'd say it's a stiff 105-millimeter howitzer from there. Or a lob mortar. You're a prince."

"Hey, fuck you, asshole. I can't take more than a seven anyway, so it looks like I'm maxed out." Largeman was pretty jovial. He loved trading insults, which was a lucky thing. "Jeez, though, I'd hate to be looking at that shot of yours, man. Just hate it."

"Well, my good man, that's just exactly what you're going to do. Watch it. This one's in the bag." Warren actually had no clue how he was going to keep the ball on the green. He pulled his sand wedge out of his bag and tested its weight as his caddie advised him to aim two inches behind the ball, play it off his front foot, and finish the swing. After he got to the bunker and waited for the other players to chip on, he somehow managed to drop the ball lightly on the fringe of the green, and it rolled down the slope and stopped four inches from the cup.

Largeman clapped politely and knocked the ball away. "Nice sandie, Bubba. Great shot!" Even Pete Largeman had his moments. Pebble Beach was like that.

That evening, the group had drinks in the bar, and a big meal. Anson Combes had turned out to be a pretty good golfer, and his team was tied with Warren's for the lead in the little tournament that was set up every year by Larry Downe, a Weldon salesman from Cleveland. Downe was obsessive with numbers and ran a great tournament. There were prizes for just about everyone, from money, which everyone anted into the pot, to golf equipment and sweaters. Warren had started attending the outing the previous year, and even Combes's presence couldn't spoil it for him. After each day's rounds on one of the four courses, they'd meet in one of the hospitality suites, have drinks, smoke cigars, and laugh a lot until it was time go to dinner, which would be followed by more drinks, and an early lights out. The clients all had a ball, and nobody who was a part of the outing had missed one voluntarily for seven years. Virtually no business was discussed, and many real friendships had developed.

Combes was sitting off in a corner with Karlheinz Beker and Dick Leahy from Golden State, deep in conversation. Warren was debating whether to butt in on them and finally opted not to. Whatever Combes was up to, Warren would figure it out eventually. In the meantime, he just wanted to play golf and drink beer until Sam arrived the next day.

"Hey, Warren! Warren! C'mon over here a second." Anson was waving at him, smiling. "C'mere!" Anson was being jocular, a description Warren had somehow never matched up with Anson's tightly wound, highly controlled demeanor.

"What's up? You planning on covering these two guys from now on?" Warren did his best not to sound nervous or uneasy. After, all, the two men with Combes represented about 25 percent of Warren's business. He just hoped Anson wasn't annoying them.

"No. In fact, Karl was just telling me how happy they are that you started covering them. Bill, may he rest in peace, really wasn't on top of things the last few years. Dick pretty much agrees." It never failed to amaze Warren how immensely he disliked this man. In one sentence, after calling Beker "Karl," a mistake that generally enraged the man, Combes had gone on to sarcastically insult and demean a dead man, one whose death had evidently opened wide a door for Anson.

"Hey, we aim to please." Warren bowed his head and accepted the chair that Leahy had pushed back for him. Combes's mentioning Dougherty set off a cascade of questions in Warren's mind. Anson had started asking a lot of questions about Bill at the same time that someone was poking around their trades. Warren didn't even know that Dougherty had ever been assigned to Warner. As far as he had known, the bank was always covered out of the Los Angeles office. Was it just a coincidence, or was something going on? Combes was a scary guy, but Warren didn't take him for a murderer.

What possible reason would Combes have for killing Dougherty, other than maybe adding a little bit to his already huge paychecks?

"Anyway," Anson said, breaking Warren's intense reverie, "the three of us were talking, and we were brainstorming about how we can ramp up our business together, to benefit all of us. These two gentlemen have some great ideas. It's too bad that we didn't get a chance to sit down a few years ago." Warren could see that the two men were a bit into their cups, and Anson had clearly been putting on the press, or maybe plotting, with them.

"Yep. I think that you guys at Weldon have really got your act together. This is a great outing, and I think it's been worthwhile for us to talk." Dick Leahy gestured toward Anson and droned on for a while, the way senior executives do. He was used to having people listen when he spoke and felt no inhibition about going on. Beker started fidgeting a bit when Leahy spent a couple minutes talking about how Golden State was a leader, like Weldon, but, Beker got his turn and effused about Warner for a while.

The whole scene gave Warren the creeps. Anson Combes had somehow cozied up to Warren's two main accounts, and they had spent ten minutes stroking him. It was definitely weird. Dougherty's ghost must have been cringing. Nonetheless, Warren grinned and bore it. They sat and chatted about business for a while, then the talk shifted to golf. Warren complimented Anson on a great third shot into the eighteenth hole, and Leahy congratulated Beker on breaking 100 for the first time.

"Well, golf is a real test of character," said Karlheinz. "It's a window into the soul." In that case, Warren thought, you must be a first-rate cheater.

"I don't know," Warren said. "I've always thought that the only thing that how someone plays golf really divulges about about him is how good a golfer he is." One of the most honest men he'd ever met, a real estate developer who had an impeccable business reputation and had honored a handshake deal with Weldon's mortgage department that cost him over $8 million, was the biggest golf cheater Warren had ever played with, and when they had played a set of tennis at a resort he owned, he had called every close ball Warren hit out.

The conversation kept up for about fifteen minutes longer, and Warren wandered off to find some snacks. He excused himself to reach for some nuts at the bar, and the older man sharing a drink with a friend turned to him.

"Y'all seem to be havin' a damn good time." His drawl reminded Warren of Lyndon Johnson.

"Well, golf and alcohol are a pretty good combo. And besides"—Warren, using one of LBJ's pet phrases, nodded at Combes—"I've got that guy's pecker in my pocket."

The man laughed loudly. "Hey, that's a good one, son!' He smacked Warren on the back. "How I do miss ol' Lyndon. Jim Carruthers. Nice to meet ya."

"Warren Hament. Hey, aren't you with Temenosa?" Warren recognized the name from Larisa's constant updates about her work.

"Another good one, Mista Hament. How'd you know that?"

"My, umm—my ex-girlfriend is Larisa Mueller from Weldon. I work there too."

"Damn! That girl was *your* gal pal? You are one lucky man! You two split?" Carruthers had drooled a little of his bourbon in surprise.

"Afraid so."

"Well, I'm sorry to hear that, son. She's a fine-looking woman, and pretty much never stopped talkin' about you. You're the bond guru, right?"

"Guru? Well, not exactly." Warren chuckled slightly. "She talked about me? Hah! Well, actually, she always talked a lot about you!"

"Yeah, well, she always was tryin' to keep the wolves at bay. We were howlin' up the wrong tree there, that's for sure. Not a man in my office din't try. Rumah was maybe one succeeded, but I nevah knew who! Nope, she always tol' me you were the man if we ever needed someone to cover our pension plan. But, that'll be in the hands of the bankruptcy courts, I s'pose." Carruthers shrugged. Warren remembered Carruthers had pocketed nine figures a few years before in a management buyout paid for with junk bonds. Too bad for everyone else who'd gotten hammered while he drove the company into the ground.

"Well, thanks for the consideration. I better stop eating these nuts, looks like my guys are heading to dinner. It was nice to meet you and put a face to the name."

"Pleasure was all mine, son. Hey, put a good word in for me with your ex, wouldya? Ha! Jes' kiddin!... Well, maybe not. Lissen, if you wanna play the Point before you head home, gimme a call. You take care!"

They shook hands and Warren promised to take him up on the rare in-

vitation to play at Cypress Point, taking his card, then turning back to re-
join the group.

The bill was settled, and they wandered downstairs to two vans they had
rented and drove off to dinner in Carmel. Warren got wrapped up in the
good spirit of the twenty-eight men, drinking and joking, and generally acting foolish.

After dinner, a raucous affair with a full case of wine polished off along
with many cocktails, a drawing was held to see who would drive back to the
hotel. Obviously, no one in the group was sober enough to get behind the
wheel. They agreed to pay two of the caddies who were eating with them to
ferry them home, then send them back in a taxi. It took about twenty minutes to get the unruly group into the vans, and the temporary chauffeurs
filed out of the lot and back toward the entrance to the 17-Mile Drive.

"Hey, Hament, what'd we agree to pay these guys for the lift?" Larry
Downe, the Cleveland saleman, asked in his capacity as official accountant
for the trip. His words were slurred from the drink.

"Don't worry about it, Larry, I won't expense it." Warren had already
slipped each man a $100 bill.

"Aw, Christ, Larry, who cares?" Tom Shugrue, a rangy Southerner and
the best golfer in the group, drawled. "Don't sweat the small stuff." Most of
the repeat attendees liked to tease Downe about his thrifty and compulsive
attention to every penny. That he cheated a little on the golf course and
mistreated the caddies hadn't done much to endear him, but he did do a
great job organizing everything from the rooms to the dinner reservations.

"Hey, guys, I always gotta tell you twenty times, don't overpay the help!"
Downe was peeved, and he smacked his fist into his palm on each syllable.

"Umm, Larry, I believe you've got your caddies confused with your hookers," Shugrue drawled, and the whole van burst into laughter. Downe's bald
pate flushed bright red. Two years before, Downe had tried to hire a hooker at
a local bar, only to be turned down entirely when he tried to haggle on price.
The caddie who had been sitting next to him had reported the story to Shugrue the next day on the first tee, sotto voce, and Downe had never been allowed to live it down. He accepted the abuse as his dues for being one of the
guys. He was a bit of a stiff, and only covered small accounts, but Larry was
a good guy—his thrifty ways an unbreakable habit.

The vans pulled up in front of the Lodge, and everyone piled out. A few straggled in toward the bar, and others headed to the practice green for a late-night putting contest that might see a few thousand dollars change hands. Warren waved them off and headed toward his room, down the driveway toward the golf course and the ocean. He had booked a higher-priced ocean-front room, scrupulously advising Downe that he would pay the price difference himself.

It was eleven twenty when he got in, and the room had been prepared for the night by the housekeeping staff. The Lodge at Pebble Beach consisted of a row of low, white stucco buildings. The best rooms lined the famous eighteenth fairway, with large sliding-glass doors that afforded sweeping views over the grass to the Pacific breakers crashing on the rocks just offshore. The rooms were elegant and cozy, the décor warm California rustic, with neutral tones set off by rich patterned-fabric accents on the pillows and chairs. The huge bed was turned down, a fire was ready to go in the grate, the lights had been left dimmed, and the sound of the surf was drifting in on a light breeze. Warren shucked off his sweater and shirt and found a robe hanging on the door of the bathroom. He changed into a pair of shorts and a T-shirt, put on the robe, then brushed his teeth and washed up. He walked to the windows and cranked one open, letting the brisk salt air and the rhythm of the waves float through the room. He paused for a moment, then lit the fire, closing the screen. It sprang to life, aided by the gas jet, and he sat down on the bed, setting the alarm clock, then slipping under the covers, taking a moment to savor the light smoky scent of the wood now burning evenly. He took his pocket calendar off the nightstand, then picked up the phone. It took him a moment to find Sam's number, then he dialed. It rang about twelve times, with no answer, or answering machine. He figured either she was out or had turned off the phone, and neither possibility did much to raise his spirits.

"Oh, well," he said, half out loud, and reached for the light. A sudden movement at the closet door startled him. He sat bolt upright.

"I hope that call was to me." It was Sam, coming out of the closet, wearing a tiny nightgown. "I've been hiding in that damn closet for an hour. I hope you don't mind, but I ate the macadamia nuts from the minibar."

"Jesus. You scared me half to death." Warren's heart was pounding a bit, but he had a huge smile on his face. "How'd you get in?"

"Do you think there's a bellman in California who could say no to me?"

"Maybe not. Think there are any bond salesmen who could?"

She was climbing in the bed. "I can be very persuasive when I want to be. Nice shorts." She snapped the waistband of his yellow boxers.

"I wasn't expecting company. I would have—"

"Baked a cake?" She reached up and turned off the light. "Hmmm, what have we here?"

thirty-three

෧෨

The light on Warren's answering machine was flashing like crazy when he got home. It had been a long flight back on the red-eye, and traffic on the Van Wyck Expressway had made the cab ride from Kennedy into an ordeal. He dumped his bags and headed for the shower before bothering to listen. He plopped down on the bed, still wet, and stretched his back. He couldn't ignore the light and reached over to punch the button.

There was a call from his father, two from the office, one from the cleaner's looking for a mis-delivered suit, and one from Detective Wittlin.

"Mr. Hament, this is Detective Wittlin. Please give me a call as soon as you get back from California. It's important."

Warren was tired and wanted to get a few extra hours of sleep before he went in to the office, so he shelved the message. He had just dozed off when the phone woke him.

It was Wittlin. "Did you get my message?"

Warren said that he had, but the overnight flight had left him punchy.

"I told you the other day that I'd call you when I got back to town."

"Listen, Mr. Hament, I've got to be honest with you. We're not getting anywhere with the homeless-killer angle on this. My captain likes someone who knew him, disliked him, and maybe had something to gain. Maybe someone at work. Maybe his wife or a relative. Personally, I think he's read too many mysteries, but, he's a captain, and I'm not."

"So? What's it got to do with me? And I thought people saw a homeless guy there."

"It may not have anything. But I do want to ask you some more questions. I understand your father was in town that day. Did you see him?"

"What? My dad? No, I didn't see him. I didn't even know he'd been in town until the next day. He was home by the time we left the AC dinner, I'm sure. How about we meet in my office tomorrow or the day after?"

"Are you avoiding me?"

"That's a ridiculous question." Warren felt the anger rise. "Actually, it's outrageous."

"You're right. Maybe you should bring a lawyer." Wittlin's voice suddenly went hard.

"Hey, Detective, I don't need a lawyer, and you don't have to insinuate anything. You wanna piss someone off, catch the guy who killed Bill Dougherty."

"Well, Mr. Hament, that's just about exactly what I'm trying to do."

Warren was surprised at himself, how angry he'd gotten, and how quickly. "Listen, Detective, I'll be happy to meet with you anytime. We have our office Christmas party tomorrow night, and I'll be free anytime before then or the day after. You just let me know what fits you best. I would prefer, if you can, to have you come to my office or home because I haven't got a lot of free time to get away from the office. I expect you can get away easier than I can, since this is your job. Am I right?" Warren adopted a formal, conciliatory tone.

"Okay, Mr. Hament. I'll call you tomorrow and set it up."

"Super. No, make that super-duper." Warren clicked off, not at all pleased.

The Seventh Regiment Armory has the best address of any National Guard unit in the country. It sits, like a squat, medieval fortress, on Park Avenue between Sixty-Sixth and Sixty-Seventh Streets, completely surrounded by elegant prewar apartment buildings, home to New York's wealthy and its socialites. While most of the other armories in the city often double as homeless centers or soup kitchens, the Seventh Regiment, befitting its setting, moonlights as a tennis club and a party space. Four times a year, it houses antique shows, where $250,000 commodes and $500,000 paintings are picked over by women in $15,000 designer outfits at opening parties generally hosted by fabulous interior designers. Once a year, however, the armory is the venue for the Weldon Brothers Christmas party.

At about five thirty in the afternoon, the first waves of black sedans started dropping their passengers at the steps to the armory. The radio-car drivers would collect a voucher, then make a U-turn down Park Avenue, returning to Weldon's offices for the next crew. Some people arrived on foot, and several buses disgorged their loads. By six, the party was in full swing on the expansive floor, with a loud rock-and-roll band echoing in the cavernous space, four bars, and about a dozen tables loaded with food. Before heading up, Warren had spent a half hour with Wittlin and discovered that the detective had made little progress, except for an account that a scruffy, destitute-looking man had been seen either stealing or driving a BMW in the neighborhood of the NYAC shortly after the murder. Warren owned no car, or at least none registered in New York State. Wittlin had checked. Warren assured Wittlin he wasn't hiding a BMW in another state and had certainly not engaged in any used-car transactions while in California. The detective admitted Ken Hament seemed to have left the city well before the murder, and that Wittlin was just looking at every possibility. He had little to go on, and Warren was slightly annoyed that Wittlin had made it seem so important that they talk. Warren made the party hardly late at all.

Anson Combes stood apart from the throng of people at the bar, watching. The horn-rimmed glasses he wore constantly slipped down the thin bridge of his fine nose, and every minute or two, he'd push them back into place with his index finger. One of the new Finance associates, a heavyset Stanford business school student who had been working eighteen-hour days since June, had delivered a gin and tonic to Combes, who had thanked the young man and briefly talked to him about a new deal, complimenting him on his performance. The younger man drifted away, and Anson seemed lost in thought, the bright light of the ironic disco ball reflecting off his glasses. Something evidently amused him, and he let out a guttural snort.

"Whatever you're thinking about, or whomever, I kind of feel sorry for them. I know that snort of yours." Warren had come up behind him and was chewing on a stick of beef teriyaki. "It kind of sounds like tearing flesh."

"Funny, or maybe ironic, you should say that." Combes nodded at the stick of charred meat.

"Good party?"

Combes scratched his ear and let out a nervous titter. "Well, it was, right up until now. You?" Anson's tone of voice was brutal—it conveyed pure hatred, hidden behind a thin veneer of good-natured ribbing.

"So far. Say, how's Philippa doing? I saw her on Madison Avenue the other day. She must be due any day. I thought she looked terrific." Warren had been surprised when Combes had gotten married. He'd been divorced twice and, as Kerry Bowen had recounted, broken off an engagement with a gorgeous twenty-two-year-old associate just three days before the wedding a couple years ago. His new wife was pleasant, in her midthirties, but seemed antithetical in every way to the thin, model type Combes usually went for. She'd been four months pregnant at the wedding, which took place in the late summer.

"What?" Anson looked confused.

"I said that I saw Philippa—your wife, remember?—the other day, shopping on Madison Avenue, and I thought she was carrying the baby very well. She looked terrific." Warren had to shout a little as the band had picked up the volume.

"Yeah, she looks great—for a fat fucking pig." Anson snorted. "I call her the Waddler. It's just gross." Anson snorted again, and his glasses slipped down as he scratched his ear. He pushed them up.

"Jesus, Anson. Jesus H. Christ." Warren looked at Combes with disbelief. Stan Heifitz, a corporate trader, with his back turned to them, choked on whatever he was eating, having heard what Anson had just said about his wife. His savagery went beyond just business. Warren wanted to just get away from him. "Umm…I think I'll go ask Bev for a dance." Bev Gershon was the heavyset, maternal woman who ran the closing department. She was eternally single, ate constantly, always had a ready smile and a big laugh, and loved to get drunk and dance. She was across the floor, talking to a group of trading assistants, throwing back her curly hair and roaring in laughter, her glasses, attached to her neck with a beaded chain as always, bouncing on her chest.

"Yeah. That's a good idea. I could use a dance too." Combes looked around. "Maybe I can find that girlfriend of yours, Bonnie." Warren had been uncomfortable when a girl he'd dated for a few months back in college, an attractive woman from Hong Kong, wound up getting a job in the syndicate area.

Nobody knew they had once dated, and her familiarity with him had caused some comment. People speculated that Warren had a crush on her. He'd taken some teasing, most of it jealous and playful. He knew Combes had been hitting on her for a while and also knew Combes figured Warren was a frustrated suitor. This undoubtedly made Anson even more interested in bedding her, his peculiar one-upsmanship driving him and his marriage inconsequential. Bonnie was a grown-up and could make her own decisions. Warren let Anson think he was winning this game.

"Yup. Well, catch you later, Anson." Warren spun on his heels and wandered toward a group of salesmen who surrounded a waiter with a tray of shrimp puffs. He saw Larisa across the room talking to Anson's secretary, Annlois, and felt a slight pang. Larisa looked fantastic, in a fitted suit, her hair let down from its usual work ponytail or bun.

Dutch Goering had one hors d'oeuvre in his mouth, and two reloads in his left hand. He grabbed Warren as he walked by, spilling a little of the vodka from the cup in his right hand. Warren hadn't had a drink since he and Sam had drained a bottle of champagne sitting on a rock watching the seals play in Monterey two weeks before. They'd had a great two days together. Thinking about her made him thirsty.

"Hey. *Hey, Anson!*" Goering shouted over the music, but Combes didn't hear. "Aw, fuck. I wanted to know how it went with Golden State yesterday. That fucking psycho sees my buddy Dick Leahy and doesn't even call me in. Fuck him." Warren noted that Combes had met with First Cal again, this time in New York, and, as usual, completely ignored the professional etiquette of letting the salesman who covered the account know.

"Hey, Dutchie boy, easy on the sauce. We don't want the National Guard to be called out to their own armory. " Goering was notorious for his inability to hold liquor and his love for pouring it down.

"Hey, Hament, blow me, okay? I can outdrink you any day, you little Semitic pussy." Dutch was slurring his words only mildly, a sign that this was his first drink.

Warren seized the opportunity. "Yeah? Five hundred bucks says we both drink a glass of vodka and I can stand on one foot longer than you. What do you say, O brownshirt *Jugendmeister?*" Warren poked him in the ribs with the skewer from the chicken kebab.

"No fucking way. Let's do it." Goering knocked Warren's hand away.

"Right away, *Führer*." Warren made a beeline for the bar, where he got one straight vodka, and one light vodka and water, no ice. He walked back and offered the vodka and water to Goering.

"Give me that one, scumbag, I know your tricks." Goering grabbed the straight vodka. He saluted Warren with the cup, and they both chugged them empty.

"Oh, shit, why'd you go and do that?" Mike Barnes, a thin, well-dressed black man said as he watched in horror. "We'd better call the cops now and get it over with."

"Don't give up on him yet, Mikey. Pretty boy's got money on the line here. Maybe he'll be able to hold on this time." Warren smiled.

Barnes rolled his eyes. "Yeah, right."

"Hey, I'm shick of you fuckersh making fun of me. Ohhh, fuuuck! Look at the body on that fucking bitch over there. Fuuucck! How'd you like to have her sucking on your fucking giant bone, huh? Nah, you wouldn't like that at all!" Goering threw back his head and guffawed, his perfect, white teeth catching the light. He slapped Barnes on the shoulder.

"Hey, Dutch, I don't think that's a woman at all. I think that's one of the waiters." Barnes laughed. Warren was amazed at how much Goering got away with. Barnes acted like a buttoned-down Ivy Leaguer most of the time, like a badass gangbanger when he wanted to be cool, and a good old boy when he wanted to fit in. He accepted Goering's racist rants in good humor, which they were, but Warren knew even he must have wanted to knock Goering's teeth out just then.

"Yah, well, you just wish you could get the slack a good-lookin' white guy like me gets, don'tcha?" Goering roared again and made sucking motions with his hands and lips.

"Christ, Dutchie, you sure know how to sweet-talk. Your wife like it when you talk to her like that?" Barnes handed Goering a napkin to wipe off the vodka he'd sloshed onto his sleeve.

"Fuck that bitch. What's she going to do? She's got her cute little hubby-wubby and his nice fat paycheck. So what if I like to get a sweet fucking piece of ass? What's she going to do? Leave me? Take da baby-waby and go 'way? Aw, *boo-boo*!" Goering mimed wiping his eyes with both hands. "*Boo-boo!*

All my fuckin' dough's in the Channel Islands. She couldn' find it with a fuckin' telescope! Fuck her." He waved his hands in disgust.

"Poster boy for the American family." Barnes smiled.

"Hey, stud, you wanna just pay me the five hundred, or you want to give it a go?" Warren was perched on his left foot, the right one hovering six inches off the ground. His balance was perfect.

Goering scowled and tried vainly to keep his equilibrium, but he couldn't hold it for more than a few seconds. Hament laughed and waved him off. "Save your money. You'll probably need it to make bail later tonight." He knew Goering would never pay on the bet anyway.

"I tell you what I wanna do." Goering was having a little difficulty standing even on two feet.

"What's that?" Barnes asked.

"I want to fuck that little Chinee piece of ass Combes is trying to jam." Goering nodded to the dance floor, where Combes was dancing with Bonnie.

Warren looked over and smiled. The two were grinding slowly against each other. The cute associate and the married managing director with his first child on the way. There was nothing like the sight of true romance to gladden even the jaded heart.

thirty-four

❧

Some blocks in Greenwich Village lend the city a vaguely small-town feel. In summer, the trees are almost as tall as the brownstones, and their droopy leaves make a dappled shade that cools the asphalt. In the winter evenings, with a coating of snow, the streetlamps form pools of light, and the smell of wood fires wafts down from the old chimneys and kindles memories of other places, with a muffled serenity that echoes with the reverberation of faded hoofbeats and an era before time began to move so quickly.

Anson Combes had ridden in a cab to such a spot, the nobly named King Street in the West Village. It was a quiet night, and the couple were slightly drunk, intoxicated more by the sexual tension than the liquor. Bonnie Chian had decided this was not going to be a mistake. Anson was a good-looking man and kept himself in excellent shape. She knew he'd recently remarried and also knew that the word was he hadn't wanted to. His wife's Catholicism and his position had conspired to leave him no choice when Philippa turned up pregnant.

Having a managing director in her thrall, especially an attractive and dynamic one such as Combes, couldn't hurt. She hadn't slept with anyone for a long time, and the fumbling come-ons from the younger men at Weldon had gotten boring. Half of them were terrified of even approaching her because of the new, fierce morality enforced by Human Resources, at least on junior employees, and the other half were intimidated by her Eurasian good looks. Combes had an arrogant self-assurance that made accepting his

offer of a ride home easy. He expected her to say yes, and his kisses and ca-
resses in the car were clearly foreplay, not entreaties.

The cab pulled to a stop in front of No. 20, a four-story, brick Federal
that had been subdivided into four floor-through units. Bonnie's was the
third floor, and as she stepped into the elevator, Anson followed her and
held her from behind, kissing her neck and kneading her breasts. His glasses
had been pushed up to the top of his forehead, and Bonnie giggled as she
removed them. He was slipping his hand under her skirt on the landing
when she unlocked her front door, and she had to struggle a bit to get it closed
before he pulled her toward the couch in the living room. She saw that the
lock hadn't caught, but Anson was all over her, pushing her skirt up over her
hips, grasping her firm bottom in his palms, and pressing her down onto the
couch with his weight.

She moved with him now, pressing up against him, opening her mouth
to his kisses, helping him slide off his suit jacket. He had her skirt up and
was grinding his hips into her, his erection pressing through the cloth of his
suit against the slight swell at the front of her panties. She reached between
them for his belt, and he lifted his weight slightly to open a path. She worked
it open, then undid the clasp and zipper of his pants, ducking her hand inside
the opening to stroke him. He moaned slightly and worked the buttons of her
blouse open to reveal a floral bra, which he pushed aside, and covered her
breasts with his lips. He used his free hand to push his pants and shorts down
to his knees, then tore at her lacy underwear. She stopped him and simply
pushed the covering to one side, using the same hand to curl her fingers
around him, guiding him into her in a tangle of loose clothing.

Anson began pumping his hips frantically, his face a mask except for the
tight grimace of lust. She was responding to him now, almost forgetting who
he was and what she was doing. His pace slowed, then quickened again, and
she could feel that he was close to coming. She wasn't ready yet, but encouraged him with her moans. His breath was shorter, his eyes clenched tight.
She leaned her head back and closed her eyes, giving herself up to him,
casting away whatever doubts she had.

From the front door, her knees were visible over the back of the couch, as
was the back of Anson's head. The intruder had not expected the door to be
unlatched, and the entrance had been perfectly quiet. The figure paused for

a moment, head tilted down for a look at the scene being played out below, then reached out with a long, black baton, which fired blue sparks as it touched the back of Combes's neck. Combes went rigid, then started to shake slightly as the voltage passed through his body for two, then three, seconds. Bonnie did not notice the slight snapping sound. She felt an odd tingling, but before she could react to it, the intruder touched the baton to her knee, and the surge of electricity left her senseless before she could even open her eyes.

thirty-five

❦

I'm not sure I understand, Miss Chian. Let's try to get this one more time." Roger Wittlin was tired, pissed off, and frustrated, and McDermott gaping at her long, elegant legs wasn't helping things any. What the hell is wrong with men, anyway? he thought, disgusted that his partner couldn't keep his thoughts clean.

"Okay. Okay. I told you. We were on the couch, making love, and I kind of felt weird, then something hurt, and I couldn't breathe. I think I blacked out. When I got back up, Anson was in the bedroom like...like that, and then I called you. That's it. That's all I remember."

Anson Combes lay facedown in the bedroom, the back of his head crushed, evidently by a marble obelisk that lay shattered across the carpet. His blood had soaked into the rug, his naked body pale and limp in the light. A photographer was working, and two technicians were searching for fingerprints, fibers, hair, blood, anything that new forensic technology could help in turning a cipher into a suspect, or even a profile of a suspect. They seemed to be satisfied with their progress.

"You saw nothing at all, heard nothing at all? You don't know where those marks on your neck came from?" Wittlin jabbed his finger at two small, red bruises on her throat.

"I meant what I said, Officer. The last thing I remember is making love on the couch, then some pain, then this. If I remembered anything else at all, I would tell you. God, he was my boss, for God's sake. I can't fucking believe this." She was shaken, trembling, crying now, pathetic.

Wittlin patted her on the shoulder. "Hey, Wall Street's murder, right? Let's just be glad it was him they were after and not you. I think you got very lucky." Wittlin remembered something his mother had told him. She said she had married a Jewish man because they almost never drank and almost as rarely cheated on their wives. So he was a half-Jewish, half-Irish cop, which had probably explained why he'd taken to it and also done well on the police exams. Which reminded him. "And I'm not an officer, I'm a detective."

"Hey, Rog, we got some good shit in here," Stuart Jermon called from the bedroom. Wittlin got up and left the slim woman alone with her thoughts and a cup of Greek-diner coffee, picking his way into the bedroom.

"Where the fuck is the meat wagon? And tell those idiots downstairs to lay off the fucking lights, already. Let some people around here get some sleep." Seven patrol cars were on the street, all pulled up at odd angles, half on the sidewalk, although plenty of spots to park normally had been open. Four detectives were canvassing the building for witnesses, and forensics men were examining the stairs, halls, and elevators. The uniformed guys were hanging out on the street, their potbellies spilling over their belts, several slurping coffee and chewing on the doughnuts a rookie had picked up at the all-night grocery around the corner.

"What is it?" Wittlin looked up at the tall black man in a pair of cotton coveralls.

"Well"—Jermon held up a small, clear plastic envelope—"we've got some hair here. And a partial footprint there. He was wearing gloves for sure, and probably some kind of cap. He just walked in. The girl said the door didn't close. Bad luck. No struggle to speak of. I'm not the doc, but that looks like at least two whacks on his head over there, so I'd guess one smack with some kind of club while he's on the lady. It doesn't put him out, but gets his attention. Stumbles in here while our boy tries to choke her lights out, hence the marks on her lovely neck. He sees lover boy trying for the phone and finishes the job right there with that stone thing. Literally bashed his brains out. He nails the wallet and the purse, runs a few drawers"—Jermon pointed to some lightly ransacked drawers—"then bags it. This was not too big a boy. Took him a couple of good shots to put lover boy down for good, and he didn't go back to finish her. Probably thought he'd done 'em both, though, since she was out cold."

"Makes sense. What do you think we'll get from the samples?" Wittlin was pacing the room, glancing back and forth.

"Africanus Americanus. Shoe size maybe ten and a half. Probably Pumas from the sole grid. Done a little B and E before, pretty careful. The hair I got from the sofa. Maybe bending over to straddle our girl. Natural curl. Definitely belongs to neither of these two here straight-hairs. The lab tests will tell us more, but my money's down."

"So, we got a black male, probably five feet eight inches plus, light to medium build from the shoe size, record of B and E, not afraid to mix it up and add assault or homicide to the tab. That about right?" Wittlin was relieved to see the ME's personnel show up, despite the delay.

"Yup, that's my best first guess. But, no B, 'cause they didn't lock the door, remember? But *every*body was getting some E."

"Clever! Jesus, that narrows it down to thirty-two percent of the city. I can count out maybe a third of them, 'cause they're already in the system. I figure that leaves me two, maybe three hundred thousand prime suspects. That about get it?"

"Nope. Way high."

"Why's that?"

"First off, this gentleman missed some valuable electronics"—Jermon pointed to a small computer and an expensive miniature stereo system on the desk—"and second, there was a Knicks game on cable tonight, so one hundred and fifty thousand of those suspects minimum were at home, with a bucket of chicken, screamin' at the tube. That's got to narrow it some."

"Yeah, fine. By the way, in case you don't already know, you're a racist, self-hating misanthrope. But I'm wondering about something."

"What's that, Sherlock?"

"When the brilliant Miss Chian says she felt kind of weird and something hurt, do you figure that's how she describes sex in general, or just the way she felt about fucking her boss?"

"Hey, Detective Officer Wittlin, you can answer that better than me, because I know you've been dreaming about fucking your boss for years." The technician smiled and plucked one of the hairs from his own neat Afro and stared at it. "I am going to find you."

thirty-six

❧

"W arren, Carl Dressler and Pete Fowler would like to see you in Frank Tonelli's office, right now." Patricia Mulvey's tap on the shoulder had caught Warren staring idly into space, thinking about the interest-rate swap option he was trying to layer on top of a currency hedge, and wondering how it was that Anson was dead so soon after Warren had decided he'd been the one who could be nailed for killing Dougherty. "They say it's important."

Warren was up and moving instantly, reacting to the call, swiveling his hips to slide past chairs protruding into the aisle. His stomach tightened with anxiety because he knew that this was the call he'd anticipated. Pete Fowler was the head of the Investment Banking Division, and on the executive committee of the firm. Between him and Dressler, the only person more powerful at Weldon was the chairman. Fowler was a big, genial guy, a lousy tennis player who loved the game anyway. He'd always seemed a little out of place to Warren, a bit too decent a guy for his job.

"Hey, Warren, come on in and sit down. Hope we didn't interrupt anything." Dressler was standing at the glass wall to the office overlooking the trading floor. Fowler was seated on the small Queen Anne sofa. Frank Tonelli stood quietly in a corner.

"No, just a little daydreaming. Only about a deal, nothing important like women or golf." Warren plopped into an armchair. "What's up?"

"Well, you know Anson had a very tight relationship with Golden State. And you're the only one who really knows about the deals he's been working on. Do you have any read on how we should pick up on it, now that Anson's out? And what's going on with Warner?"

That was what Warren loved about this business—Anson hadn't been dead a day, and he was simply "out." Gone. That almost nobody liked the man made his disappearance even more seamless. Warren took a breath and dove in.

"Sure, Carl. The deal with Warner is a little unusual, but simple. Straightforward. Anson worked out a deal with them to buy their mortgages, both performing and delinquent. It's very promising. He's also got a couple more deals pending with Golden State. As you know, we made about twenty million on our last deal with them, and this potential deal with Warner could be much bigger. As far as Golden State, it seems Anson wasn't in that tight with Leahy, only with this broker, Tom Scholdice. All his business went through Scholdice as far as I could tell. Kelly Hughes at Golden State told me that they very much want the relationship to continue. I spoke to her this morning, before Goering came in." Warren wanted Goering out of the picture completely until he could add something of value. "I think we can make this work to our advantage."

"How's that?" Fowler had uncrossed his legs and was leaning forward, his eyes focused intently on Warren's.

"Well, Anson wasn't exactly loved around Golden State. If you went out there, Pete, to introduce them to a new finance team, I bet you could wrap the whole thing up."

"Hey, take it easy on old Anson. He may have been a psycho, but he was our psycho." Dressler had a grin on his face.

"Yeah. Great. It seems obvious that we've got to keep working with Scholdice, but we should also work on building a direct relationship with the rest of the people at Golden State. Anyway, that's how I see it. There's a ton of biz out there, and someday there's going to be a complete restructuring too."

"You mean we should get in there and buy out everything we can before the shit hits the fan?" Fowler was catching on.

"Look, all the California savings and loans are going to blow up someday. Probably soon. Once they're under a regulatory agreement, everything has to be competitive. Scholdice seems to have been able to direct a huge amount of business our way through Anson. If the bank goes under, that connection will be useless. After the regulators take over, if they want to sell assets, they have to hold an auction, and we'll have everyone from Goldman to Lehman in there bidding 'em up. It's got to work to our advantage that Anson had this angle to Leahy. Plus, if we do everything through Scholdice, Weldon can't be accused of getting special treatment later on. It's pretty amazing. Up till now, Anson had the exclusive on everything they sell because Scholdice doesn't let anyone else even bid. Don't ask me how, 'cause I have no idea. Dutch really hasn't been working this side, and we should not let it slide for a minute." Warren had thought this through, seeing an opportunity to take over Anson's relationship with Scholdice, move Goering out of the way, and start getting the credit for all the big trades to come. He let his enthusiasm show.

"Interesting." Fowler paused, rubbing his chin. "What do you know about this broker?"

"He's a guy that Leahy did a lot of deals with. He supposedly gets capital from some wealthy clients and generally gets in for a quick flip on residential whole-loan trades. He was the President of a big California insurance company a while back. He started profit sharing with Anson years ago—he basically took a cut of the profits in exchange for the contact and some capital. That way he wasn't just working for a quarter of a point, but he'd get exclusives and sometimes half of the upside." Goering was far from an expert on the financial structure of banks and thrifts, and Warren had volunteered, as a team-oriented guy, to help out with some presentations. He'd used the opportunity to check out what Anson had been up to. Cozying up to Annlois Baker, his secretary, had helped Warren get a lot of information. He'd taken her out to dinner at La Grenouille one night after she'd worked until eight o'clock typing up the final draft. All Anson ever did was allow her to order in Chinese food. She'd been flattered by the invitation and, after a half a bottle of Burgundy, opened up, explaining the setup, and the key role of Tom Scholdice.

"How he get the exclusives? Why would anybody even give him an exclusive to broker a big trade? What's he bring to the table?" Fowler, to Warren's amusement, seemed genuinely perplexed.

"Look, Pete, with all the business we did the last couple years, Scholdice had to pocket twenty million easy. That pays for a lot of schmoozing. I guess

Anson figured there was no upside to finding out how he got the deals. I think Scholdice might be German for goose, or golden egg, or something like that." The conversation had played out perfectly so far. Warren was getting to demonstrate how much he knew, while at the same time casting doubt on Anson's ethics and Goering's ability to cover the account. Warren knew this would appeal to all the managers in the room. They loved naked ambition.

After a second or two, Fowler stood up, and started pacing as he spoke. "Okay. You're now the senior coverage on Warner and Golden State. If you think there's more there, go after it. Keep Scholdice on our side. You know the salesman's motto: 'Dress British, think Yiddish.'"

"Sounds good to me. I'll get the ball rolling." Warren had to admit, as Goering would say, sometimes this shit was fucking great.

thirty-seven

❧

"Listen to me, will you listen to me? You're not listening to me." Frank Tonelli had his hands out in front of him, palms to the sky. He'd put his Diet Coke down on the desk, next to the chocolate napoleon he'd been eating before Dutch Goering had interrupted him.

"I'm listening to you, Frank." Goering stared at him impassively.

"You're not listening. I'm not saying—"

"This is a hell of a conversation you guys are having. He's not listening, and you're not saying. Wow! This is just like meetings at the UN or the Paris peace talks!" Warren interrupted the two. He always enjoyed watching and listening to Dutch Goering's conversations. Dutch's first name was actually Anselm, but he'd gotten the nickname from Sandy Stein years before in honor of a particularly blunt haircut. Goering was, beyond doubt, the best-looking, best-dressed salesman at Weldon, if not on the Street. Warren had a tremendous respect for his accomplishments because while he seemed at first not to be the smartest guy, underneath he really missed very little. The trainees had nicknameded him "General Fucketyfuck," in honor of his penchant for cursing, although at least two of the women in the class had slept with him, and any of them would have loved to be placed as his backup. Goering knew how to get business done and led something of a charmed life, with a beautiful wife and two perfect kids.

At that moment, Goering's chiseled features were puckered in anger, and he repeatedly shot his cuffs, pulled at his tie knot, and adjusted his cuff links as he argued with Tonelli and Hament. "Listen, Warren, if you want to say something, why don't you just say it." Goering's ice-blue eyes glared at Warren through slitted lids.

"Look, Dutch, Pete Fowler reassigned Golden State to me this morning. He did so in front of Carl Dressler, and then specifically instructed Malcolm to make the change. Or at least he sent a memo to Malcolm, because Deputy Dog hasn't blessed us with his presence today. I know you've been covering part of Golden State for a long time, but that's not the point." Warren was sitting back in an armchair, considering how to handle this. When money was involved, Goering always seemed to have a knack for getting his share. Warren didn't want him gumming up the works. "I've done okay with them on the money markets side, and I've gotten to know Leahy pretty well. I think it'll work out."

"Listen, Leahy is a good friend of mine. I guarantee you he's not going to want the coverage change. You guys are going to fuck up a good relationship here." Goering ran his hand through his thick blond hair and checked his watch.

"Listen, Dutch," Tonelli interrupted, "if the relationship's so good, how come we only did two-fifty gross on the long-term side with them last year? It's easily a two-million-dollar account. Easy." Tonelli could be fun when he was on your side, but Warren was afraid that this confrontation could get out of hand.

"Everyone knows the thrift business is dying. They're on the ropes. This is horseshit." Goering was beginning to get up a head of steam.

"Look, Dutch, I shouldn't have been in here to begin with. You're a good guy, and I don't want to get in a pissing contest with you. Combes was eating your lunch with this account, and butt-fucking you with management right from the start. I was there once when he called you a brain-dead pretty boy, and I mentioned the fact that you'd grossed fifteen million last year, which is pretty good for someone without a cranium. So, I'm not looking to screw you. Fact is, I'd be happy to split the commission with you because I'm sure we'll capitalize on your groundwork. In fact, I'd want you in with me when we're getting near closing. You're the best closer in the firm, and we should take advantage of that." It was a struggle to be so pleasant to Goering, but better to placate him than rile him up. He knew that Goering would lose interest pretty soon anyway, and wasn't worried about it. Besides, no one had promised Warren full commission on the account yet anyway.

"That's a great approach, don't you think, Dutch? Great idea, Warren. Super." Tonelli's relief was palpable—Warren had offered him an easy exit. "Yeah. Hey, why don't you two guys strategize in here for a while. I'm going to get some of that Chinese food, okay? I'll check back later." Tonelli moved his bulk to the door of the office and headed over to the ledge by the windows, where an assortment of fifteen or twenty foil trays of Chinese food had been spread out, a Thursday tradition of the sales force.

"Man, when he hits that line, bodies are going to start flying." Warren knew that Goering hated Tonelli. In fact, as far as Warren could tell, Goering hated just about everyone. "That fat fucking dago bastard. I'm sick of his fucking shit. I'm telling you, one day I'm going to get him back for this. Look at that fucking fat ass. Doesn't give a fuck about himself. Man, I'll bet he dies of a fucking heart attack by forty-fucking-five. Fuck him. I fucking hope he gets cancer and suffers a lot before he fucking expires."

The soliloquy reminded Warren of an incident when a junior trader had counted 143 *fuck*s in a single Goering joke about a pig farmer. Two hundred bucks had been bet on the over/under at 50 uses of some form of the word, with a 3:1 payout at 150. It was neck and neck.

"Hey, listen, it's just politics. It makes Tonelli and Dressler look better if they can tell Malcolm what to do. You know I'm not out to screw you. It works out better for both of us this way." Warren sat there while Goering digested that, and for a moment Warren felt a pang of guilt. When had he become such a Machiavellian manipulator? It felt as if it had happened overnight.

"And where the fuck is that fucking douche bag Holik? Why does he always keep his skinny fucking ass out of this shit? It's like a fucking freak show in here. The fucking Polack beanpole and the fucking guido whale. That Polack cocksucker. His time will come." Goering was looking at himself in the reflection off the dark wall of glass. He adjusted his tie and shot his shirt cuffs one more time. "Fucking fucker."

Warren stifled a giggle.

thirty-eight

❧

"Maybe it's hunting season on Weldon Brothers bankers this year." Detective McDermott was sitting down this time, and Wittlin was doing the talking. "What's going on around here?"

"Detective, if it's open season on us, I suggest you sell licenses over at Salomon and Morgan Stanley. They'll be strong buyers." Warren hadn't been surprised when the two men had shown up, commandeered a conference room, and started interviewing almost everyone on the floor.

"Nah. The Mayor would be pretty mad if we started letting our best taxpayers blow each other away. Unless, of course, you're Republicans. Hmm." Wittlin smiled at the thought.

"Well, anyway, what can I do for you?" Warren was anxious to get this over with. The more time you spent with cops, the less comfortable it seemed you got.

"Okay. First the routine stuff. You knew Anson Combes, right?'

"Absolutely. We worked together."

"You like him?"

"Nope. Can't think of anyone who does, offhand. Did, I mean."

"You know he got killed while popping a girl you used to date, right?"

"That's very tactful, Lieutenant. We hardly dated. Two or three weeks, years ago."

"Everyone thinks you were an item once."

"No, everyone *likes* to think that. Ask Bonnie. It went nowhere. She's way too smart and beautiful for me."

"Why not?'

"Why does this matter?" Warren found this unbelievably nosy.

"It might. Look, there were four hundred people who were with you when the guy got his skull crushed. No one thinks you had anything to do with it. Relax. If we can find any little thing, anything at all, to figure out who might have had a reason to kill this guy, that takes us out of a burglary/homicide and into murder by someone with a motive. It narrows the field, and maybe ties back to Dougherty somehow."

"I see. Sure. Okay. Bonnie and I didn't work out because she didn't think I'd be successful enough. At that time, I was talking about doing something a little less lucrative. Once she figured that out, she was gone. Good riddance." Warren waved his hand. Bonnie had always been one of those pretty women who figured they were destined for something special, one way or the other. When he'd said he had decided he wanted to be a teacher or a tennis pro, she'd bolted. "She liked to play with the big boys."

McDermott chimed in, "Well, she played with a lot of them."

"What's that supposed to mean?" Warren didn't like McDermott's tone.

"From what we can tell, she got cozy with about half the managing directors in her department. But what about Combes? What turned him on?" McDermott seemed to enjoy this line of discussion.

"I don't know, and I know I don't care."

"Well, you may not know, but if you did, there's a chance you'd care." Wittlin had a thin smile on his face.

"How's that?"

"I think the man had a taste for your ex-girlfriends."

Warren sat there speechless. He felt his face flush. "What exactly are you saying?"

"Well, it seems that your other ex at Weldon, Miss Larisa Mueller, had been spending some time with old Anson the past month or so. I don't think you two overlapped, but I can't be sure, and the girl's not saying." Wittlin actually felt bad for Hament. The Mueller girl was a knockout.

"Look, I stopped seeing Larisa before I went to LA. You spoke to me when I was there. It had to be a couple of months ago. I've got a new girlfriend, sort of. I don't really care who she's sleeping with. And, don't call her a *girl* to her face, or you'll be in trouble. *Woman.* She's a woman. A free woman."

He couldn't believe she'd had the nerve to start up with Combes. The thought made him sick. It hurt too. It didn't matter that they'd broken up, or even that she might have been cheating on him. It was that Combes had gotten to her. He was glad the asshole was dead.

"Okay, okay. I just thought I'd tell you." Wittlin judged that Hament hadn't known about it. His reaction had been too natural to be faked. Wittlin could read the pained thoughts going through the younger man's mind on his face right then. Scratch that motive. "Sorry, I guess you didn't know. Who's the new girl—or woman—or whatever?"

"None of your business, Detective. If I tell you, you'll probably wind up informing me that she's sleeping with Dutch Goering. Look, I saw Anson leave with Bonnie, which seemed to me like a perfect match. I was in the middle of winning a five-hundred-dollar drinking bet, and trying to keep Dutch from raping someone or starting a race riot. I didn't like Combes even a little a bit, but I'm sorry he's dead because it might cost me some business. Almost anyone who knew the guy probably wanted to kill him at least once or twice." Warren leaned back in the chair.

"Okay, okay. Calm down. First Dougherty, now Combes. Do you think it's a coincidence? A homeless killer and a murderous burglar? It doesn't sit with me." Wittlin was over by the window, admiring the view.

"Hey, Detective, this is New York City. Christ, Goering had his throat slashed by a mugger right in front of his door last year, when he was blotto, and almost died. Did you know about that?"

"Yeah. We looked into it." Goering had been attacked after telling a beggar to "fuck off." The guy who did it had been arrested after attacking a woman the next day, and had been in prison since." Okay, we're done. If you think of anything…you know the drill. Do me a favor, send in Goering next."

"Oh, Jesus, isn't he the pretty boy?" McDermott piped in.

"Yeah." Wittlin grinned again.

"Uh-oh. Better stop taking notes. Our captain is black. If we transcribe this guy, I think he'll tell us to shoot him on sight. He's too much." McDermott was smiling too.

thirty-nine

❧

Jed Leeds's head looked like some kind of melon ringed with hair. Jed was only twenty-eight, but had gone three-quarters bald already. With his heavy Queens accent, three-piece suits and watch chains, he gave the general impression of being a porn actor dressed like a banker. He always seemed to be smiling. He traded the CMO position for Weldon, which included some of the most volatile and exotic securities in existence. These were mortgage securities that had been restructured to reallocate risk or hide it, in part to meet investors' needs, and also to get around the rules and make some pieces eligible for sale to people and investment funds that should probably not buy them.

Most of the risk in mortgages was in prepayments. If interest rates went down, people would prepay their mortgages to refinance their loans. The owners of the securities created from those loans would get their money back at the worst possible time—since interest rates were lower, they would have to invest the money at a lower yield. CMOs took big pools of mortgage loans, made a series of bonds out of them, and focused most of the prepayment risk of those big pools into a small number of bonds, or "front" pieces. This insulated the other bonds from all but gargantuan changes in prepayments. By leveraging the risk this way, they created front bonds that were incredibly sensitive to small changes in mortgage prepayment rates. It was Jed's job to run Weldon's inventory, and to try to hedge and lay off that risk.

Some investors were willing to take the risk of leveraged prepayment in exchange for higher yields. Others were willing to accept lower yields for less prepayment risk and bought the back pieces of the CMO pie. But by far the favorite customer of the Street was the one who didn't know what the hell he was doing, but had lots of money to invest, and for some reason thought he was smarter than everybody else. As Leeds put it, generally, when the music stopped, the investment bankers and traders made lots of dough regardless.

On Warren's way back to his chair from the interview with Wittlin and McDermott, Jed called Warren over to his desk. He'd been badgering Warren for weeks.

"Hey, hitter, they going to fry you for doing Anson?" Jed's voice was nasal. His shoulders were dusted with dandruff.

"Nah. But they told me they'll be putting a tail on you for a few weeks. They think you were in love with him." Warren looked down at Jed's feet, which were tapping wildly to a tune only audible inside the trader's head.

"Well, they'll wind up with some nice pictures of me and Holik at Chowfun, getting our puds pulled." Jed was referring to an Oriental "massage parlor" frequented by Weldon's elite traders.

"An ugly, ugly thought. What can I do for you?"

"I need you to sell the Met some of these Zs. I got fifty of these and seventy of those. It's like a bakery. You want cookies? Cake? Whatever you want, I got. C'mon, can you get some of this shit out of here for me? I need you." It was becoming increasingly obvious to the sales force that Leeds had a problem with his position. He owned a lot of so-called Z-bonds. These back pieces were CMO tranches supposedly completely safe from prepayment, since they were the last $50 million or $75 million of bonds to receive prepayments out of $1 billion or so in each deal. They only prepaid after the other $800 or $900 million of the issue was gone.

Leeds and Carl Dressler had kept creating CMO deals, taking pools of FNMA-backed mortgages and structuring them, even though no customers would buy the Z-bonds in the current environment of dropping interest rates. Every deal made a huge profit, on paper. But they had built up a big inventory of Z-bonds and kept them "marked" at their theoretical value based on average prepayment rates. But as interest rates dropped, those prepayment rates started to increase dramatically. On top of that, they hedged the positions, and their hedges kept losing money. Normally, the value of long maturity bonds would increase as rates fell, but Z-bond prices were rapidly decreasing because investors were worried they would prepay much faster. Just one position in Leeds' book, $50 million of bonds from a deal backed by FNMA 10 percent mortgages, had been priced at $118 when the CMO was issued. Thanks to hedge losses, Leeds had marked the bond up to $142 on his books. In reality, the bonds were worth maybe $102 and would be almost totally prepaid at $100 within six months rather than eighteen or twenty years. That one position represented a $20 million loss. Leeds had dozens of similar positions.

No one except Jed, his clerk, and Carl Dressler knew the full extent of the problems, which were moving into the hundreds of millions in losses. It was already December, which meant there was no way to make back the losses before year's end. The rumor around the firm was that Leeds and Dressler had figured out some way to defer or even offset the losses, so they wouldn't affect the year's bonuses for people not on commission.

Warren had repeatedly tried to get his clients to buy the least overpriced bonds in Leeds's inventory. None of them were interested, and some responded by asking for bids on similar bonds they owned. It was a massacre. Warren tried not to think too much about it and concentrated on other areas. After all, Carl Dressler was the genius who had created the mortgage department, and the mortgage department had spun the profits that allowed Weldon Brothers to become a powerhouse in all the markets, competing with First Boston and Salomon. He would figure it out. In the meantime, Warren was focusing on Golden State.

"Hey, Jed, I've been trying." Warren said to deflect Leeds' pressure." Maybe I can sell some of that Freddie deal you brought last week. Really, Emerson's looking at it." David Schiff at Emerson Insurance had laughed when Warren showed him the bond. He'd asked how much of it Leeds owned. When Warren had told him 27 million, Schiff had asked if there was any way to short the stock of a privately owned firm such as Weldon. He advised Warren to start interviewing at other companies.

Warren walked down to the sales area and tapped Goering on the shoulder. He looked up from his telephone handset, mildly peeved.

"Hey, Dutch, the cops want to talk to you. Over in the Syndicate conference room." Warren jerked his thumb in that direction.

"What the fuck do they want?" Goering had covered the mouthpiece with his hand.

"Just to talk to you. Maybe about Sharon Tate. Or Jack Ruby. How the hell do I know?" Warren shrugged.

"I think they want my professional opinion on whether it was Bonnie's blow job that blew Anson's brains out, or some lawn jockey. That girl can drink soda through a garden hose." Warren was not surprised that Goering managed to turn even someone's death into an opportunity to boast of his broad experience and conquests while making a gratuitous racial slur. But it was funny.

"That must be it, buddy. You're up." Warren headed back to his seat.

He tried to focus on his afternoon calls, but had little success. He wound up staring at the blinking lights, with images of Anson and Larisa floating in front of him. He couldn't figure it out. She was so strong willed, and independent. Anson was basically a low-life WASP prick. He treated most women like shit, both those that worked for him and those in his private life. In fact, he treated everyone like shit. He was a decent golfer, but took it way too seriously. Otherwise, he was a lousy athlete, though he spent hours on the exercise bike, and Warren couldn't imagine that Anson had the patience to sit through Larisa's endless play-by-play about the nuances of her day. Maybe it was the old, nasty line from high school—to get a great girl, you have to treat her like a dog, since most men were intimidated by them. Maybe she needed to feel debased and subservient, to be put in her place, to be happy. He had never believed that about any woman and never would. Plus, she clearly liked being in charge in bed. It just didn't make any sense to him.

The longer he sat, the more he realized that his feelings toward her were unresolved. He was sure she had been sleeping with other men over the last month or two of their relationship—her disavowal was unconvincing, no matter how heartfelt it seemed. Somehow, her screwing Combes made Warren the loser in a contest that he didn't even fully understand. He figured out the best thing he could do for himself right then and did it.

Sam picked up the phone on the second ring. For a few moments, he put on a Jamaican accent and asked if he could rent three Jaguars for a reggae band coming to Los Angeles the next week. Then he asked if she could arrange for women for the band, and if not, how about just her for him? She bought it and handled herself pretty well, cutting him off before he could get too explicit about what he was going to do with her, and redirecting him back to the cars. She was only mildly pissed when he stopped the act and asked if he could speak to the manager.

"You asshole. Damn. I wouldn't have minded renting three cars for a week just now. Business is slow." Warren could hear the radio in the background.

"Hey, if business is slow, I've got a proposition for you."

"What's that?" She sounded a little wary.

"I miss you. Let someone else handle the office and fly here for a few days. We'll shop, talk, eat, and have fun. It's snowing a little today. You could stay until New Year's weekend. What do you say?" He really did want to see her.

"I don't know. It's been a while. Maybe you won't like me anymore, and then you'll be stuck with me." Her throaty voice made Warren uncomfortable in his chair.

"Listen, I'll get you the ticket. First class on American. Open return, whenever you want. I still like you. Lots." He felt almost silly, but the pleading was real. He desperately wanted to see her.

"Oooh. Big sugar daddy. Will I get to keep the headphones from the flight?" She sounded coy.

"Absolutely."

"Okay. I'll take the one thirty tomorrow. Don't sweat the ticket. I still like you too. Just be at that goddamn gate, or I'm going right home. You know, I haven't been to New York in maybe five years." Now she sounded happy.

"Pick you up at the airport? Are we that serious?"

"Well, *you* better be!"

"I'll be there. This is great!" He signed off with her, not wanting anything to spoil the moment or change her mind. He felt totally exhilarated. He'd have to cancel a dinner with Malcolm, but figured Conover would be pleased to reschedule. There was hope for a happy New Year indeed.

Just as he was beginning to feel a little upbeat, Annlois, looking drawn and upset, came over to his desk. She was a tall, thin woman, surprisingly mature for a secretary. Warren had seen her on occasion wandering on Water Street during her lunch break, seemingly distraught, talking to herself, and looking ill. He had mentioned it once to Combes, who'd shrugged it off and looked at him as if he were nuts. At this moment, she seemed worse than ever.

"Oh, Warren, hi. Sorry to bother you..."

"It's okay. Really. What can I do for you? Are you okay?" Warren realized she must be thinking about her job—no more Combes, no more Combes's secretary. "Listen, I'm sure they'll find a place for you. There's got to be a new head of finance, right? You're great."

"Oh, thank you. No, I...I, um, wondered if you could help me. With some things. Anson's things. You know, there are some things that should be sorted through."

Warren was surprised she would ask him to help look through Anson's papers. That was something he would have expected one of the other finance people to do. "Sure, Annlois, I'd be happy to."

"Yes, you see...um, I thought that you...because you were...well, Mr. Conover asked me to take care of it, and there are so many things I'm not sure about. It would be a favor, and if you wouldn't tell anyone...I don't, I mean I wouldn't want them to think that I couldn't..." She seemed a bit nervous.

"I understand. It's not a problem. Is everything in Anson's office? I could take care of it this evening if you'd like. Will you stay to help?" Warren was curious to see what kind of stuff Anson kept around. He couldn't turn down a chance to poke through them with Annlois.

"Oh, of course.... I didn't mean to do it alone...I mean for you to do it all yourself." She smiled, and Anson noticed how her lipstick was applied beyond the edges of her lips to make them appear fuller. The only woman he'd ever seen do that before was a friend's grandmother.

"Okay, then. Maybe around six. I'll come by when I'm all done." Warren smiled back at her.

She thanked him again, then moved back across the floor. She moved deliberately, and Warren thought that her shoulders looked slightly more square, her step a bit less leaden.

forty

꧁꧂

Managing directors' offices at Weldon Brothers tended to feel like suites at English hotels. They were filled with mahogany tables, upholstered armchairs and a sofa, and usually had a few current magazines on their coffee tables and prints of sailboats hanging on the walls. The one mark that separated a finance office from a trading office was the proliferation of Lucite tombstones—small copies of the newspaper ads run to announce big new bond deals sealed in plastic as a status symbol. The more tombstones, the more seasoned and the bigger a hitter the finance person must be. Anson's office had them everywheres, in all shapes and sizes, so many that he'd actually stacked maybe twenty on the floor in a corner. The view out the window was nothing particularly special, just the usual panorama of other office towers with a partial opening to the sky. Higher up in Weldon's building, the views became breathtaking and vertiginous. The chairman's office, on a corner, commanded a view from Connecticut to New Jersey, and on clear evenings, the late sun set it ablaze, seemingly turning it into a room of gold.

Warren came in through the open door to Combes' office. Annlois followed him. They were carrying folded corrugated-cardboard cartons from a large pile by her desk. She closed the door behind them.

"Why don't you start with the desk, Warren? I'll go get us some coffee." She opened up two of the cartons and set them by the left side of Anson's desk. Out of her dress pocket she fished a small key and handed it to him. "Just use your own judgment."

As she left, he noticed that she slipped the lock on and closed the door behind her. He stood there a moment, puzzled. Clearly, she wanted him to find something. Was it something that she was afraid of? Something she thought would embarrass Anson or hurt Weldon? Warren couldn't figure it out. But, whatever it was, it was probably in one of the drawers on the left side of Anson's desk, the only side that locked.

It took him just a few minutes to go through the large file drawer and two smaller ones. The files looked pretty routine. In the top drawer had been Anson's portable computer. Warren knew that Anson carried it everywhere with him. He'd spent close to $10,000 for it, all personal money. It was the first one Warren had ever seen that could fit in a reasonable-size shoulder bag. Anson used it constantly, but Warren figured the night of the party he must have decided it was too heavy to lug up to the armory. He took it out of the drawer and set it on the table. Its power cord wasn't connected, but Warren figured the battery might work. He opened the machine up and pressed the power key.

The machine was slow, but after about fifteen or twenty seconds, a log-on screen came up on the liquid crystal display, asking for a password. Warren turned the machine off. So much for that. He started on the rest of the desk. He hadn't found anything yet. Maybe Annlois was just a little spotty right now. The right side of the desk held nothing of interest. Most of Anson's files were in the long credenza. Warren figured that was his next stop.

Annlois opened the door, balancing two cups of coffee while she turned her key in the lock. Warren went to help, taking the cups and setting them on the desk. He pointed to the two boxes he'd filled with the contents of the desk.

"That's mostly personal stuff. You should send it to his wife, I guess." Warren shrugged. He peeled the lid off a cup and noticed it was light, the way he liked it, with no sugar. Annlois had been an excellent, old-time secretary.

"Yes. I'm sure...I...yes..." Warren saw her eyes go to the computer, which was open, but dark on the desk. "Well, you know, actually, I can probably handle the rest. I just thought you might be able to...I mean, well, is that your computer? Anson had one just like it."

"Oh, no—"

She cut Warren off. "Yes. He did. He was always telling me how he wanted to get one for his house, so he wouldn't have to carry it so much. Did you know his house had a name...Ledges, I think. Yes, that was it. The Ledges. I think it had a lot of stone or something. He loved that name. Anyway, I can handle this...." She swept her hand around in an arc. "You were nice to help. Oh, don't forget your computer."

Warren put his coffee cup down and paused. Hadn't the police searched this office? Wouldn't they have taken the computer? What was going on?

"Ann, wait a second. What's going on? Why is this still here? Come on." Warren felt he was missing something.

"Oh, Warren, you're right. I almost forgot. When the detectives were searching, they asked about Anson's computer. They decided he must have had it with him because it wasn't here or at his house. The nice-looking one—Wittlin?—said it must have gotten stolen. You better be careful with yours. Anson usually had me hold on to his when he was out of the office. They're so expensive."

Warren made up his mind to go with the flow. She wanted him to have that computer for some reason and had just told him the password. He picked up the computer with one hand, and his coffee with the other. "Okay, I will. Thanks, Annlois." He saw that she had a dust rag and was wiping Anson's desk off as he left the room. He noticed an empty brown paper shopping bag from a food delivery—maybe Anson Combes's last meal—sitting by the trash and put the computer and power cord in it.

It took only two tries. *Ledges* had opened the security lock, and Warren had access to the entire hard disk. Dozens of files were in the Lotus program, each named for deals Anson was working on or had completed. Warren spent four hours going through the spreadsheets, finding a maze of numbers and calculations. He was careful not to disturb anything. In the word processor, he found endless letters and notes, and even a chapter of what appeared to be a novel Combes had started. It was about an incredibly handsome CIA agent in Europe, seducing a lot of women, mostly with big breasts. It would've sold well, Warren mused. He also found most of Anson's e-mails, and there were several with Larisa, making plans to see each other. They were all couched as meetings to discuss deals, but the undertone was clear.

After seven hours, and a severe backache, Warren noticed it was two thirty in the morning. He was going to be exhausted when he picked up Sam. He was restless though, and Annlois's nervous and tense behavior had whetted his curiosity beyond sleep. He kept plugging away and left the word-processing files about midway to check out the personal calendar.

Dozens of names and phone numbers were in the address book, some familiar, some not. He found his own name and address when he searched for it. He found one odd item—a group of telephone numbers with no identifying names, just initials next to them, and someone's name, Klaustag. At the end of the address section were two columns of three numbers each, all with different area codes. He scribbled them down on a notepad and kept probing through the date finder. There was nothing unusual there, except a lot of nights out of town, and an awful lot of United Airlines flights. Warren wondered what would happen to all those frequent-flier miles.

As a lark, he picked up the phone and dialed United's toll-free number. After a short wait, he asked the operator if she could check his mile total and gave her the number from Anson's computer. She said she couldn't access that information, and he hung up. An idea cropped up, and he scrolled forward in the appointments section and found several plane and hotel reservations for upcoming trips. Chicago, Los Angeles, Dallas, all Ritz-Carltons. There was a convoluted reservation for a trip to Saint Kitts with his family in February, and a trip to Munich to visit the parent company after that. Anson went to Switzerland at least three or four times a year, often renting a car to drive from Munich and returning it in Zurich, an expensive proposition. Weldon was 50 percent owned by a large German bank, and they often had conferences or "off-sites" that were really just boondoggles, European-style. He noted some closing parties scheduled for deals, and various birthdays. It was pretty much a dead end. The reason for Annlois's giving him the machine and her hints was eluding him, at least for now, and gave up. It was after three. He shut the computer down and washed up. Whatever it was, it would have to wait.

forty-one

～

He woke up dog tired, and the day dragged on like death. At lunchtime, Warren slipped out of the office and went shopping for a gift for Sam. He wanted to impress her. At Tiffany, a salesman made him wait while he dealt with a trio of Japanese tourists. Warren complained that he'd been there first, but was ignored. Annoyed, he walked across the street to Van Cleef & Arpels.

As soon as the guard let him through the door, he realized he was in over his head. There were no real display cases, just a few ornate, gilded desks with carefully dressed salespeople seated at each. The manager, an elegantly dressed blonde in her forties, was on him immediately, asking if she could be of assistance.

Warren let a long pause stretch out before he answered, "I'm not sure. I hope so." He was aware that he was on the other side of the sales table when he shopped, and he emulated his best customers—he tried to be pleasant, but to keep the salespeople off-balance at all times.

"What is it that you are looking for?" The woman gave him a small, tight smile.

"A welcoming present for a friend. Nothing outrageous." He smiled his most charming smile and was led to the first desk on the left and seated in a French baroque side chair upholstered in a white moiré satin. The manager introduced him to Mrs. Denoyer, the saleswoman, and stepped away.

He was shown South Sea pearl earrings for $30,000, and a black-pearl ring for $25,000. He tried not to blanch at the prices—they were crazy. The pieces were beautiful, but he guessed he could buy the identical items for half the price on Forty-Seventh Street, where the discount jewelers were, and still be getting ripped off. He was enjoying the show, however, and Mrs. Denoyer, a petite and attractive woman, tried on every piece so he could see it in situ. After ten minutes, he explained that he wanted to think over what he had seen and would come back again later. She said she understood, and the guard passed him back to the street. Warren tightened the belt of his camel-hair coat against the wind and found a taxi. He was going to consult an expert.

Back at his desk, he dialed the interoffice number for Howard Steinman, the top salesman in Los Angeles. Howard was actually responsible for his meeting Sam in the first place—he had booked the Bentley for Warren that led him to her rental lot. It was also well-known that Howard had gotten jewelry deals for almost every trader in New York and had helped his biggest client negotiate the purchase of a seven-carat diamond ring for his fiancée. When Howard picked up, Warren explained the stuation, keeping the details to a minimum, lest gossip start too soon.

"I don't wanna spend too much. I just met her."

"Big hitter like you? C'mon. I say seven to ten grand."

"Hey, that's fine. I was at Van Cleef and Arpels, and everything was twenty or thirty." Seven thousand suddenly sounded cheap.

"VCA? Anything there you liked?" Howard was totally immersed. He called the store by its initials like some kind of old friend.

"Yeah. There were some earrings. Kind of leaf-shaped. They were diamonds and emeralds, though. And they were twenty-one five." They had been beautiful.

"Okay, here's the plan. They've got everything at VCA. It's the best for quality, and you're paying for the brand and the designs. They keep their value. Go in again, ask for Mrs. Durand. She's a stone buyer. It's not her real name. She's a Polish Jew. Tell her diamonds and aquamarines, ten grand tops, and that I sent you in. I buy a ton of shit from them out here, and she used to work here. Monica's like a fucking billboard for them. You'll be fine. She'll show you something with a fifteen price tag, offer it to you for ten or eleven as a favor. Pay her ten or ten five, and it'll be yours."

"Howard, c'mon, you don't back-bid at a store like that."

"Oh, come on, cut me a break! Jewelry? It's worse than this business. I'm telling you, just use my name, and tell her your limit. Seven five won't buy you anything in there. Oh, yeah, be sure and give her your Weldon card first. She'll figure you're young, you're just getting started, and you'll be back. They don't discount for the big fish, but a young guy? First the girlfriend, then the wife, the mistress, and the second wife. Building brand loyalty— it's good business."

"You sure?"

"Warren, it's not a problem. Trust me. Where'd you meet her?"

"Who?"

"The girl."

"I told you. You weren't listening. Los Angeles, actually. Wilshire Boulevard."

"I knew it. All the great trim is out here. How'd you pick her up?"

"I don't know. It was at the Budget lot, I was turning in that car." Warren was distracted by the blinking of another of his lines, but Kerry picked up the call. She shouted over that it was an account's back office calling for a price, and he spun his finger in the air to indicate that he would call back.

"Wait a minute. The Budget lot on Wilshire? With the high-end cars?" Howard sounded incredulous.

"Yeah. You got me the Turbo R, remember?"

"*Not* the girl who owns the lot? You mean Sam Kensett?"

"You know her?"

"Know her? I'm in fucking *love* with her. *Everybody*'s in love with her. Oh my God. Oh my fucking God. You slept with Sam Kensett? I don't fucking believe it." Howard was actually moaning now.

"Hey, Howie, you're starting to sound like Goering. Please, don't be so crude. Miss Kensett and I are seeing a bit of each other. I prefer to leave it at that."

"Oh, no. Nonononono! She's perfect. She's a goddess. Every producer and director in Hollywood has tried to date her. You can't buy this woman some cheap bauble. For her, a fucking tiara! A rock as big as your nuts! I cannot believe this! When are you coming out to give this to her?" Howard was excited. "Can you bring her to lunch with me or something? I just want to touch her once. I'd beat off for a week, I swear!"

"Look, Howard, I don't want you telling everybody about this. C'mon, I didn't know you knew her." Warren figured if word got around, the whole LA office would find a way to scuttle him.

"I'll keep quiet. But only if you take naked pictures of her for me." Howard laughed.

"I don't think so. I'm not coming out there. She's coming here. I've gotta pick her up at the airport tonight."

"*Tonight?* You're going to spend the night with her *tonight?* She's flying to New York to see you? I'm going to die. I can't stand it. You must have a two-foot dick. She's so hot—no, she's beyond hot. I'd give my right testicle for a night with her. And my left one. Afterwards. I wouldn't ever need them again, anyway, and Monica wouldn't notice. Maybe I could say I was you. It might work. I'll charter the Concorde. You're so lucky. It must be because my dick is so small. I mean, I'm Jewish. But, so are you. It's not fair. I'm going to throw up."

Warren was laughing. Howard was the best ego builder in the world. That's why he was also one of the best salesmen in it. "No, Howie, mine's nothing so special. Stop whining. You've got a beautiful wife, two great kids, a big house in Bel Air, and Dumb Ed Johnson for your regional manager. Life could hardly be better."

"Just wait. You'll marry this girl, have kids, buy the big home and the cars, then you'll wake up one day and realize you haven't had a blow job since the Carter administration, like me. Then it's prostate cancer and you're out. She takes the insurance and marries some big *shvartzer* who calls her 'baby' this and 'baby' that, and she does everything for him in bed because he's not too embarrassed to ask. You'll see. You're better off just beating off. It's cheaper, and you don't have to redecorate—ever. Trust me. I know."

"Oh, Howard, come on. I love curtains. Besides, she's a shiksa, so maybe we won't spend too much time on window treatments. Look, I gotta go. If I'm going to go hondle at Van Cleef, I better get moving." Steinman wished him luck and clicked off. Warren grabbed his jacket, asked Kerry to watch his lines again, and headed for the elevator. On his way down he marveled at how quickly he'd decided that $7,000 or $8,000 or even $10,000 wasn't too much to spend on a little welcoming gift for a girl he hardly knew. Then he started having his doubts. Not about the money—he was becoming accustomed to being able to afford almost anything at all. He was wondering if Sam would find it vulgar or something. His mother had said jewelry was always appropriate, but he doubted his dad had spent more than $200 on anything for her. He decided to get the earrings and figure it out later.

Mrs. Durand was happy to see him. The rule is, once a customer comes back a second time, there's going to be a sale. Howard's name also worked like magic. She brought out a pair of aquamarine and diamond earrings that were subtle despite their sparkle. They would set off Sam's hair and eyes perfectly. She'd started at $14,000, and he'd gotten them for $12,000. As she was writing the sale up on his credit card, he mentioned that there was a small possibility the recipient might not accept them. Mrs. Durand smiled and said she doubted there was a woman alive who would turn down these earrings from such a handsome young man with such good taste. But, if it happened, she'd be happy to give him a refund. Warren thanked her and slipped the small box into his inside jacket pocket. He checked that pocket every five minutes all afternoon.

At that moment, Warren had $206,000 in his bank account. That represented his life savings, mostly from his bonus last year and commissions after he had laid out a $100,000 down payment to buy his apartment. By a rough calculation, he expected close to a million dollars in his January check, less about $450,000 for taxes, even if Malcolm shafted him on the business he'd been doing without a formalized payout scale. As a team player, he knew that it would be bad form to bring formalizing this up until after bonuses were paid. The firm usually notified all employees of their bonuses between Christmas and New Year's and paid out in the first week of January. Tensions were building around the floor for the traders and finance people, who, unlike salesmen, were not on commission and were paid according to management's whim. Bonuses were generally 70 to 90 percent of a person's pay for the year. Warren felt the tension of uncertainty, and marveled that traders could survive the stress of a subjective bonus every year.

Warren knew that, just on his account base before Dougherty's death, his second-half commissions were over $500,000 even if he got nothing else. He'd done much more than that with the new accounts since. The $12,000 didn't seem so daunting. He slipped a $5 bill in the cup of a panhandler on the way to meet the car to the airport and wished him a Merry Christmas.

forty-two

❧

American flight 63 landed right on time. Warren had the driver pull the
sedan up to the baggage-claim exit and went to wait at the gate. He took
the driver's sign with him and wrote out KENSETT in big block letters. Sam
was the second one off the plane, after a nervous-looking Harrison Ford, and
smiled at the sign. She was wearing tight black jeans and a big white shirt,
with a small duffel bag in one hand and a navy officer's blue dress coat on her
shoulders. Her boots made her even height with Warren. He grabbed her
around the waist and gave her a long hug, which she returned, with a short
kiss, as other passengers bumped past them.

She told him that she had checked one bag, and they strolled arm in
arm downstairs to the carousel. The flight had been okay, and she watched
the movie. The guy next to her had tried to pick her up, and she'd tried
to pick up Harrison Ford. Both failed, she said, sad to report. Warren
smiled.

Her bag came out quickly, and they were in the car within twenty minutes of her landing. Warren went from being apprehensive about seeing her
to complete comfort. She was relaxed, and it put him at his ease.

"I think it was the Bloody Marys that did it," she said when Warren re-
marked she didn't seem the worse for wear. "I just love that Mr and Mrs T.
mix. I think I had four of them. I wanted to get my money's worth. I had the
steak, which was okay, and a hot-fudge sundae, and one of those little bottles of Kahlúa. Did you eat?"

"Yeah, I did. At twelve o'clock." Warren hadn't even thought about dinner—he'd been preoccupied. He had noticed Sam had a penchant for reciting menus.

"You hungry?" She slipped her hand around his waist and curled up against him.

"Hey, I can always eat." He turned toward her, and she met him in a long kiss. "Mmm. It's good to see you," he whispered in her ear.

"And it's good to be seen."

"That's warm. That's loving." She nudged him in the ribs. Warren thought to himself things were going their way. The ironically named Van Wyck Expressway had actually been moving, a major miracle, and the Grand Central Parkway was wide-open, the traffic light, three smooth lanes leading to the shimmering city.

❧

"Doesn't it strike you as strange?" The light was streaming in through the tall French windows, the view of Central Park South crystal clear in the crisp, cold air. Sam was sitting on top of the covers, with a plate of toaster waffles and syrup on her lap, eating them with sticky fingers. They had spent the night getting reacquainted physically, and they were both happily fatigued, having slept in until mid-morning.

"A little, I guess. But this is New York. People get killed here all the time. Whole families get caught in the cross fire. It was just a coincidence." Warren was leaning back against the headboard, his arms behind his neck, taking in the view. Sam's dark hair was tousled, her long legs showing from underneath the Rangers T-shirt he'd lent her. Her angular features caught the sun, and Warren felt for a moment a desperate loneliness, almost a panic at the thought that she hadn't been here yesterday, and that there might be a time when she was not here again.

"Yeah, but have you even known one person who's been killed before? Now *two* in a few months? Hey, maybe you're next." She pointed a maple-coated finger at him and shot him in mime.

"No, not really." Warren reached out and smoothed her hair, and his eyes met hers. She smiled at him, and didn't look away. "Funny, there were two girls in school at Columbia who died in accidents, but Anson was a son of a bitch. Dougherty was a good guy. That was sad. At least he had a lot of insurance, though. Evidently that's big with the Irish." Warren sat forward and plucked a corner of waffle from the plate. " Besides, why would anybody bother killing investment bankers? Usually, if there's going to be genocide based on financials, it's the Jews who go first. I mean, you didn't see Hitler herding the Hapsburgs out of the Deutschebank."

"What is it with you Jews? If someone else gets killed, you figure it was a mistake, and they were aiming for you. It's like there's a Holocaust in every closet." She was waving a waffle in the air for emphasis.

"Uh-oh. Do I detect a little of the fascist in you? This could be it! I always had a thing for Mussolini. Great outfits! He did the same thing with his food. Waved it around and ate with his hands. And you've got a similar figure. Better hair. I think I'll call you Il Duce." Warren ducked as the waffle came whistling at his cheek. He grabbed Sam's hand and brought the waffle back to his mouth. He ate it slowly, then licked the syrup off each of her fingers, working his way up her arm to her neck. "You have beautiful hands, did you know that?"

"Yuk. Your lips are all gooey." She made a halfhearted attempt to push him away. He resisted and got her plate onto the night table before he pushed her back onto the bed and started searching under her T-shirt for where she had hidden the other waffles.

They didn't make it out of Warren's apartment until almost noon. The sun made them squint as they went through the front door. Warren still managed to catch Angelo's glance as the doorman sized Sam up with an appraiser's eye. Invariably, Warren would get a critique the next time he passed through the lobby alone. His building only had doormen on duty from 8:00 a.m. to midnight, so he had to remember to get Sam a key for the lobby door.

Warren's two front rooms each had small balconies with planting boxes, which he had filled for the winter with ivy and miniature evergreens. He'd taken his first vacation from Weldon and spent a long weekend days furnishing the rooms in an eclectic collection of French country antiques mixed with Biedermeier and art deco pieces from antique stores in Brooklyn and Greenwich Village. His mother had always told him the way to make a room interesting was to blend periods and styles. Larisa had designed the curtains, which had been sewn and hung by a frail Argentinian gentleman who ran a tiny workshop on upper Amsterdam Avenue. His prices had been unbelievably reasonable, but he was so nervous that Warren had given him a glass of brandy to calm him down halfway through the day he spent putting them up.

Sam had complimented him on the décor, as it was unusual for a young, single guy to invest in anything more complicated than a sectional sofa and a couple of posters. She singled out the curtains, and the care taken in picking fabrics. Larisa had spent three days in the Decorators and Designers building obsessing over moiré silks, velvets, and the like, bringing him dozens of swatches, settling on an art deco printed velvet. He had thanked Sam for the compliment and shamelessly took full credit.

They hailed a taxi on the corner and headed east, through the roadway that cut across Central Park and emerged just south of the Metropolitan Museum. From there, they turned down Fifth Avenue. They both had some last-minute Christmas shopping to do. Warren had suggested Bergdorf Goodman as a likely source of gifts for her family, and he had to get something for his dad.

The store was bustling, but Warren found the layout confusing. In the small men's department, Sam picked out six pairs of boxer shorts with silly, colorful designs, two each for her father and uncles, and Warren was split between a heavy pigskin suede duffel coat and a brown leather polo bag. The overly helpful salesman was pushing him toward the bag, but Warren finally opted for the coat. The price was almost breathtaking, $1,200, but it was an awfully nice coat. He'd already sent his mother a handbag from Bottega Veneta.

Before they left, Warren wanted to look at some suits. They went up in the elevator, to a part of the floor divided into a dozen small niches, each representing a single designer. Warren recognized some of the names from Goering's clothes. After five minutes, he told Sam it was time to go. He hadn't seen a single item under $1,300. "It may be the 1980s," he'd said to Sam, "but those prices are just crazy."

Outside, in the cold air, Sam realized she was hungry again.

"Isn't it a bit late for lunch?" He felt as if he'd hardly digested the waffles.

"Lunch, dinner, who cares? C'mon, what's good around here?" Sam waved with an expansive gesture. Warren noticed that she started moving her hands a lot when it was feeding time.

"I dunno. Whaddaya want?" He shrugged his shoulders. Picking a restaurant in New York was impossible. There were simply too many to choose from.

"Oh, anything. Maybe seafood. Clams. Shellfish. Whatever." Her eyes half glazed over, and Warren imagined for a moment that little lobsters were floating in her eyes, like in the cartoons.

"Anything, as long as it comes in a shell?" Warren asked, picking up the scent.

"Yeah. Salty, maybe even briny. You know. That's what I want." She hugged his arm.

"How about the Oyster Bar right over there at the Plaza?" Warren pointed a gloved finger across the street at the famous hotel. "They have oyster pan roasts, you know."

"That sounds yummie. Okay!" The pair made their way across Fifty-Eighth Street to the side entrance to the restaurant. The dark walnut paneling, bright lighting, and red leather banquettes hadn't changed in almost a hundred years, since the days when men would think nothing of quaffing two dozen oysters and two or three pints of beer before a serious eight- or nine-course dinner. Sam ordered only one dozen Cotuits and a bottle of Sam Adams, to be followed by a half dozen littlenecks, an oyster pan roast, and finally by a plate of snow-crab legs. Warren had a dozen littlenecks and asked if she'd share her pan roast. She looked a little crestfallen, but agreed.

"Let me ask you something," Warren started as she inhaled the fifth oyster and took a pull of beer. "Do you always eat like this? How do you stay so thin?" He'd also ordered a crabmeat cocktail and a cup of clam chowder.

"I like to eat. No, I don't really put on weight, unless I go to town. Hey, once, in Austria, on a trip for work, I put on twelve pounds. I got hooked on buttercream. I think I had it on toast and maybe even on fish. It was this incredible stuff they had in their cakes. I had to dry out for a week or two when I got back. I did the same thing once with my ex-boyfriend." She jabbed a tiny fork into another oyster, then changed her mind and just sucked it down.

"Ex-boyfriend, eh? And here I thought I was your first man." Warren smiled and took a sip of his beer.

"Oh, maybe my first *real* man. Yeah, he turned out to be a cretin. Stole almost all my money." She put down the shell. "That really was not a great moment."

"I thought you said your business manager took your money?" Warren was confused. "Was this a habit with the men in your life?"

"No. They were the same. He was my boyfriend. Or so I thought. Told me he had a Harvard MBA. Put me into offshore hedge funds, leveraged buyouts, blah, blah, blah. They were all phony. Except the car dealership. Took about a million bucks. Six hard years of modeling, a house I bought and sold, two commercials, and a sitcom. Hey, but he nailed some Hollywood big shots for some pretty good dough too, so it wasn't just me."

"Oh, yeah, like who?" Warren was interested in gossip, though he denied it.

"Well, for one, this big, hotshot lawyer who represents all the singers and supposedly does these big deals, but actually just bails them out of trouble and helps supply them with drugs and chicks. She's married to this sleaze-ball art dealer. He used my boyfriend to sell me some bogus painting for eighty-five thousand bucks that was worth maybe ten, but who knew? He was selling stuff to these idiot studio heads for millions. They used to drive everywhere in this Rolls convertible, each of them talking on their own fancy car phone. So when Artie screwed them out of five hundred thousand, I didn't feel so bad about it. Uggh." Sam had finished the oysters and was working on the littlenecks. "These are good. Really cold and sweet. Want one?" She held the pinkish bivalve under Warren's nose.

He detested the slimy creatures unless they were cooked to a cardboard consistency. "No, no thanks. Well, I'm glad to see your experience hasn't hardened you at all." He looked the other way as she chewed the clam.

"C'mon. What about you? You think these are fun people I'm talking about? In *your* business? The world's full of them. It doesn't mean you have to be one of them, but it pays to know what you're dealing with. I wish I had a lot earlier." She put her beer mug down on the table with a bang. "Some people want to screw you in every possible way."

"I don't think I'm naïve. Hardly. I just think you've gotta look for the best in people rather than the worst. My dad always said he tried to find one thing to like in everyone."

"A noble idea. Most people do find one thing to like in everyone. Their hand in your pocket." She had made short work of the creamy pan roast—Warren had managed to spear only two bites before it ws gone—and was already halfway through the crab claws, picking the meat out expertly with the fork. "Could you wave him down and get me another beer?"

"Yeah, you're probably right, but I try to maintain a more positive attitude and just watch my butt, so there's nothing else going in someplace it doesn't belong. But you can only control so much." He put down his spoon and asked the waiter for another Sam Adams. "It's like Anson—the guy who got killed. He manipulated everyone at work, screwed lots of people, probably had all kinds of strange stuff going on. Then one day, despite all the plotting and planning, strategizing and tactical analyzing, he wakes up dead with his head pounded in, and none of it matters any more. He kind of deserved what he got, but that doesn't happen very often. Usually bad things happen to good people and vice versa."

"Well, if someone could catch up to Artie and bust *his* skull, I wouldn't be crying at the funeral." She punctuated the comment by cracking a claw with a resounding crunch.

"What happened to him? Didn't he get caught?"

"No. Guys like him never get caught." She was relishing the last few bites of the sweet, white meat. The second beer arrived and she downed half of it quickly. "He stole like ten million bucks and then moved it around all these countries. He took me to Liechtenstein, on my credit card, supposedly to visit these friends of his in a big castle for a vacation. We stayed three days. That's how long it took him to move my money from the Channel Islands through Liechtenstein to an Arab bank and then into never-never land. Two weeks later, he was *gonzo alonzo*. He spoke pretty good Greek and real good Italian, so everyone figures that's where he is—Greece or Italy."

"But they have treaties with the US. Can't you trace the money?"

"Nope. Between Panama and Liechtenstein, the banking laws are unbelievable. We got absolutely nowhere. The US Justice Department couldn't even trace the money. Besides, my investigator thinks he turned it into hard currency and smuggled it out. It's gone. I gave up, and so did everyone else.

He won. But he left me in the car-rental business with the Demecelli brothers. Thank God they're silent partners. Ten to twenty in the federal pen
will do that." She had finished the crab claws, drained the beer, and threw
her napkin on the table. "Great snack. Perfect choice."

"You're welcome. *Snack?* I can't believe he just got away with it." Warren
picked up one of the discarded oyster shells. "*Hey!* What's that in there?
What's going on?" He had palmed the earrings and seemed to pluck them
out of the shell. "We better ask the waiter what kind of oysters these are."

"What?" Sam looked confused. Then she saw the earrings. "Oh my God...
They're beautiful."

"They're for you. Kind of a welcoming present."

"Come on. Wait a second here. I can't be taking something like that from
someone I hardly—"

"You don't want to finish that sentence. We know each other pretty well
by now. At least, I'd like to think so." He still had the jewels in his outstretched hand.

"Yeah, well, maybe so. But, you know, jewelry puts things on a different
level."

"What, a more serious level? Maybe that's the level I want to be on here."

"I don't know. Isn't there some saying about this kind of thing? Like
strangers bearing Trojan horses or something?"

"Forget about it. Take them on a test drive, and we'll worry about the
levels later."

She tried them on, carefully clipping the posts behind her lobes. She
bent over to check herself out in one of the mirrored walls. "Jesus, they look
great. I can't believe it."

"Modesty becomes you, my dear. But those actually become you more."

"God, I think these are the nicest gift anyone has ever given me. Are you
sure..."

"Hey, I'm sure. I don't want you thinking this whole thing is about a
plane ticket and a couple of weekends. When you decide that I'm just a dull
bond salesman and dump me for some Hollywood big shot, at least you'll
have something to remember me by, or to hock when he steals the rest of
your money," Warren said with a smile creasing his eyes.

"Oh, yeah, that's right. I meant to tell you—Bob Redford just invited me down to his place for the weekend with George Lucas and Dustin Hoffman. Gotta go!...Come on, you're not dull at all! All your friends are getting killed all the time, you know all about jerk-off bonds, and you play golf, a very exciting game. This is kind of fun."

"Yeah, until they decide to kill me."

"Well, until then we'll have a good time and be well fed. Now, let's pay the bill, take a walk, and start discussing dinner. I like Italian food a lot."

"Are you serious?"

"It takes a lot of fuel to keep me going."

"Well then, what'll it be—regular or premium?"

"Umm...I think you know the answer to that question."

"I think you're right."

forty-three

After loafing around town with Sam, going back to work was something of a shock to the system, and a relief to the digestive tract. The week before Christmas is traditionally supposed to be slow on Wall Street, but according to most of the veterans on the trading floor, it never turned out that way. Warren had a backlog of calls to return, and the day passed quickly and stressfully, arguing with the treasury-bond traders about some prices they gave his clients for trades, and missing a lot of business to other dealers. By four o'clock, Warren realized he hadn't eaten anything since breakfast, and he'd only had time for a brief chat with Sam, who was at his gym getting a massage.

Finally, there was a lull, and Warren caught up with Kerry Bowen, who also looked totally spent, her hair mussed, and her eyes red. Warren was uncertain how to broach the subject of his pay with Malcolm Conover, as he knew he'd be earning a straight commission on his own accounts for the year, but wasn't sure how he would be paid for the work he'd done the past months with Dougherty's old accounts. Kerry had advised him to go right in to Malcolm the first week after Dougherty's death and straighten it out, but when he'd tried, Malcolm had been evasive and told him not to worry about it. She was writing out the day's last trade ticket when she felt Warren staring at her.

"Okay, Warren, what's up? I feel like the Gorgon is watching me. This has been the day from hell." She looked up from her work, sensing that he wanted to talk.

"The usual. It's driving me nuts. I'm going nonstop here, but I have no clue what it all means." He shrugged his shoulders.

"Listen, they're doing all the traders' final bonus numbers today. In fact, I think they'll start telling people after the close. I'm sure you'll be told, too. Relax, it's almost over, and there's nothing you can do about it, so why worry?" Kerry already knew to the penny what she would be paid for the year, since she was on a straight commission. Warren honestly didn't have a clue. On full commission, he'd be getting just under $2 million. The commissions on his base accounts were $750,000. He had increased his production 50 percent with them. It was a lot of money either way, but a huge range. In his heart, he figured they'd give him $1 or $1.1 million. What galled him was that the rest of the money, almost a million dollars, would probably be split up by the three department heads.

"Yeah, you're right. I should just sit back and enjoy the ride." His sarcastic tone elicited a wan smile from Kerry.

"C'mon. It's Christmas. It could be worse. You could be actually working for a living, instead of just pushing bonds. Cheer up."

At that moment, Malcolm Conover appeared behind Kerry. "Hey, Warren, got a second?' Malcolm gestured toward his office.

"Absolutely." Warren felt his stomach tighten. They must have finished preparing everyone's pay numbers early for a change. It was showtime.

Malcolm's office was smaller than Frank Tonelli's or Jamie Holik's, but had a better view out over the harbor. He had decorated the walls with posters from the Philadelphia Museum of Art. Warren knew that Malcolm had been a mediocre salesman in the Philadelphia office before being asked to come to New York as national sales manager. "Those who can, do; those who can't, manage" had been Bill Dougherty's favorite description of Malcolm. Warren took a chair and crossed his legs. He held his hands in his lap to cover his nervousness.

"Well, Warren," Malcolm started as he sat behind his desk, "you've had an interesting year."

"I'll say."

"Yeah. But it's been a pretty good year. You've done a good job with your own list, and a nice job covering for Bill. I'm sure you'll do just as well helping pick up the slack for Anson until he is replaced."

"Thanks, I've tried." Warren didn't like the choice of words. *Covering for Bill. Picking up the slack.* He hunched forward a little. It felt like a lottery drawing.

"Anyway, the point is, you're in a unique situation. Your own sales credits add up to seven hundred and forty-two thousand in compensation for the year. You'll be receiving a check for that, less your seventy thousand draw, in ten days, after New Year's. We've also decided to add something for the extra work you've done. That will be an additional twenty percent or so, another hundred and twenty-five thousand. We think you're doing a good job, and coming along fast. This is the most any second, full-year Fixed Income associate has ever made at Weldon, over eight hundred thousand dollars in total comp, and we think you should be proud." Malcolm looked up from the sheet of paper he was holding with a smile. "How do you feel about it?"

Warren actually felt kind of numb. He'd just been told he was going to earn over three-quarters of a million dollars at age twenty-eight, more than ten times what he'd expected to make just two years ago. But he was pissed. So pissed, he was sure the tingling in his face was evident as a flush. He started to talk, but stopped himself. Malcolm was looking at him, eyes wide-open, in an earnest look of almost paternal pride. Warren composed himself.

"Well, Malcolm, I want to thank you. It's a fortune, and I'm glad you gave me the opportunity to be sitting here. I am truly grateful. I know that the final numbers are in, and there is nothing that will change them. I am curious, though, about one thing." Warren heard his voice quavering just slightly.

"What's that?" Malcolm's look had changed to one of carefully furrowed eyebrows.

"Last year, you told me there was a cap that I didn't know about. This year I increased production 50 percent with my accounts, helped Bill book huge trades, and then in just two months, I produced almost nine million in gross with Bill's list. That's as much as he did in the first ten months. On his nine million, he got paid about a million three. How come I only get one twenty-five? How did you all come to that number?" Warren's tone was reasonable, not at all angry.

"Well, Warren, you are a second full-year associate. Which reminds me, you'll be promoted to VP in March. Generally, there is a formula by which second-year associates get paid, but you were on commission. We weren't going to add anything, actually, because, if you keep Bill's list, next year the sky is the limit. It's a great opportunity, one we want you to have. But I fought with Anson and Jamie to get this for you, and Carl agreed. We felt twenty percent of your earned commissions was generous. We hope you're happy." Malcolm handed Warren the sheet of paper, which spelled out the numbers. Warren knew the real number was not even close to 15 percent.

Again, Warren composed himself. Those four—now Anson had somehow been included posthumously—had basically stolen about a million dollars from him, and he could do nothing about it. In fact, he was supposed to thank them for it. He spent a few moments examining the sheet. He was now so angry he could hardly contain the shaking.

"I understand, Malcolm. And I don't have any more questions. You all have been generous with me. Maybe I'll stop by his grave and thank Anson personally." Malcolm recoiled a bit at the comment. "I'm sure I'll justify your confidence in me next year. Really." Warren stood up and shook Malcolm's hand.

"Warren, you should be thrilled. That's a lot of money for someone at your level. Have a drink. Celebrate. I thought I saw that girlfriend of yours down here earlier. Take her out to dinner. You're a big hitter." It was typical that Malcolm wouldn't even know that Warren and Larisa had broken up. Warren guessed Conover would make at least $3 million, working three or four days a week, and doing almost nothing except having endless meetings and looking for problems where none existed.

Warren felt his blood pulsing. "That's a great idea. That's just what I'll do. Thanks, Malcolm." Warren turned, opened the door, and walked slowly back to his desk.

Kerry looked up and blanched slightly. "Want to talk about it?"

"Fuck no. I want to kill someone. I'll get over it. Besides, that fucking piece of shit Combes is already dead." Warren plopped down in his chair.

"Easy, boy, easy. Keep it in perspective." Kerry reached across the desk space and patted his hand. "Just try to keep it in perspective."

"I will. Hey, maybe the guy who's knocking off people around here will take me out next, and then I'll get some real perspective. It's just that right now my foot would like to have the perspective from about three feet up Malcolm's ass."

"Nice, nice. Come on—no one's going to kill you except yourself if you don't calm down. And you're just part of a great tradition. You're still new at this. Next year, they can't screw around. Although I have heard they're considering dropping the commission system."

Warren's head snapped up.

"Just kidding. Why don't you go get a soda and think about it. Whatever they paid you, I'll bet you there isn't a single person that graduated with you that even made half. Chill out."

Warren decided that she was right on all counts, and to take a walk. "You know, you're absolutely right. I am gonna take a walk, and we are all grossly overpaid. I'm a jerk. Thanks."

"It's always my pleasure to help a dope realize he's a dork. See ya." She smiled and waved as he got up.

"I'm sorry. This is all beginning to get to me. I'll be fine. Thanks. You're about the only friend I've got around here. I'm just not used to proctology yet." He smiled at Kerry and picked up his jacket. "I'm outta here. See you Tuesday."

"Okay. Hey, have a good weekend, *big hitter.*" She put heavy sarcasm into the moniker.

"Thanks, babe. Oh, and merry fucking Christmas."

Nobody even looked up as he headed for the door.

The cold air was invigorating, and he headed toward Battery Park. It dawned on him that Kerry, whom he liked an awful lot, had probably earned more than twice what he had been paid. And, to be honest, he was already a much better salesman than she. He caught himself up short. These were miserable thoughts. The things he was saying and doing were completely absurd. He'd been paid a fortune for making phone calls and going out to dinner. Where did he get off venting steam at Kerry, or resenting what she made? She had been helpful to him at every chance and had never done anything to undermine him. He felt guilty for the nasty thought—he blamed it on the nature of their business.

What was the nature of this business? Wall Street was a label for the most avaricious and just plain vicious aspects of American, or even human, commerce. Yet, it thrived on a self-imposed image of respectability and honesty. Then, every couple of years, someone would get caught stealing millions or maybe billions in some trading scandal, and everyone would act outraged. Every seven years there'd be some huge financial crisis born out of some Wall Street scam. But wasn't it the same in every business? Car manufacturers would be found to scrimp on some safety detail to save a few bucks, and a thousand people would die. Cigarette makers would purposefully lie about their own health research or even target their advertising at kids. How old was the saw about the butcher with his thumb on the scale? Everyone cheated. Everyone tried to take advantage. If you weren't caught, you were called an aggressive genius. If you were, you went to jail. Unless you were in senior management, in which case the firm paid some puny fine and nobody got punished at all.

"Yeah," Warren said out loud to no one as he strolled the sidewalks that hugged the windowed walls of the valley of the money spinners, smoking a cigar, with a piece of paper in his pocket that said he was going to earn almost $900,000 this year, "this sucks."

forty-four

⚜

It was hard to get much sympathy from Sam. She listened to his story, then shook her head in disbelief. "Hey, only a complete asshole could be unhappy making nine hundred thousand dollars in one year. That's a fortune. God, my best year, I made four fifty, and I had to work like a dog and travel nonstop. And I was never allowed to eat! You're being ridiculous." They were facing each other across the living room. She was nestled in a big, velvet armchair.

"I know. But it's not just the amount. It's relative. I mean, that extra money went somewhere. It went into the pockets of senior management. They know I should have gotten it. They just took it because they could. It's not fair. Those guys are a bunch of jokers and bozos too. It's not like they do much of anything. That's the problem with a company like this—too much useless management." Warren was whining a little, and Sam cut him off.

"I don't want to hear any more about it. Fine, they stole your money. In the meantime, they left you with plenty. I can't even believe you're sitting here complaining about some guy who's dead. He may have been an asshole, but he's a dead asshole. If he was running around on his wife, so what? He's dead and she's loaded now. Screw him, he got what he deserved, right? Forget about him."

"I can't. This guy was up to something, and I can't figure out what it was." Warren had taken the small computer from Anson's office off a shelf in the armoire and was plugging it in behind the end table by the couch.

"What do you mean?" Sam was confused.

but the money was already gone. We got nowhere. Yeah, I know what these numbers are. They're how that slime took my life savings."

"Wait a minute. He stole your money, then sent it to Liechtenstein, and nobody, not even the US government could find it?" Warren found this hard to believe.

"Yup. He had all this cash bouncing all over the world. And now, nobody knows where he is, but we know what he's spending. Our money. Man, I'd like to kill him." She slammed her fist into her palm.

"Jeezus. Liechtenstein banks. What the fuck was Anson doing with accounts in Liechtenstein banks?" Now Warren was beginning to understand what Annlois had wanted him to find.

"Hey, I don't even know who Anson was, but it's a pretty safe bet he wasn't doing anything good. Didn't you say someone killed him?" Sam poked Warren in the arm.

"Yeah. But it was a robbery. If they were going to kill him to get the dough, why would they kill him while he was screwing Bonnie in her apartment? It doesn't make sense. Unless they had the numbers too." He was confused. Who were "they" anyway? What money?

"Bonnie? You say that like you knew her well. Maybe you and Anson had something in common after all." She smiled at him and grabbed at his shorts.

He pulled away. "Yeah, maybe we did. Maybe we did have something more than just Bonnie and Larisa in common." His mind was far away. Maybe.

forty-five

By February, Sam had settled in, and Carlos had shipped her most of her clothes and cosmetics. Warren was stunned that her makeup and various potions took up two large duffel bags, while her clothes fit in one. His bathroom couldn't come close to holding it all, and she'd commandeered the entire linen closet just for cosmetics.

"Hey, it's always summer in LA. All my stuff is light." It was true. She had bought several sweaters and two coats, but was always cold. The first time Warren had offered to pay for a coat, she pretended she didn't even hear him. The second time, she told him to stop, that she had her own money, and it was bad enough he was paying all the rent. She'd acquiesced when he'd pointed out she still had to pay the rent on her place in LA. "And a woman needs to take care of her skin."

Warren was convinced all the fancy creams were exactly the same, whether they cost $5 or $75. Sam started a long explanation about the various ingredients and how they were processed, which he interrupted by asking her what she thought the chances were the Giants would sign a new corner-back. To his utter amazement, she replied, "Their secondary is totally solid. Why would they do that? Their defense is like a rock. The real question is if Morris can stay healthy next year and bring home another Super Bowl."

"Who are you," he asked, "and what have you done with my girlfriend?"

"I've always loved football. But, I have to be honest with you. I'm a Forty-Niner fan. I know that hurts. We can talk about it, but—"

"You never fail to amaze me," he said, smiling broadly. "You can root for whatever team you want. And I'll learn about face creams, if we can go to a few games next season."

"If? Are you kidding?" She stepped across the small kitchen and gave him a big hug.

"Well, that's assuming we're still at liberty after our little master plan spins out," he whispered in her ear.

"You call the signals, Coach. I'll run the plays."

∽∾

Malcolm Conover wasn't too pissed when Warren told him he was going to take another week off. He'd only had a few vacation days the previous year, to visit his dad. Warren had also done a great job following through all the trades before Anson's death, and the firm had made so much money that it could afford the temporary drop in business that might result from his backup's taking over. Kerry was more than competent, even only paying half attention to his accounts, and Malcolm also made sure he'd know where to reach Warren. It wasn't as if there weren't any phones in the Black Forest.

Warren had accumulated enough frequent-flier miles to upgrade to two first-class seats on Lufthansa, which Sam insisted had the best little cosmetic kits of any airline. He also splurged and bought a bottle of Grands Échézeaux along in his carry-on bag, which added a touch of extra civility to the perfectly acceptable in-flight dinner, not to mention deepening the sleep afterward.

In Munich they picked up a sleek, black Porsche from a rental agency, and Warren rechecked the route. It would only take about three hours to make it to Vaduz, in Liechtenstein, and they would be there not long after its bankers unlocked their forbidding office doors.

The drive was beautiful, the snow cover fresh and clean, the roads clear and dry. They made such good time that they lingered over strong *Kaffee* in a charming Bavarian inn, and Sam sampled a few of the rich breakfast pastries for the extra energy. They went over the details they had rehearsed again and again before leaving and on the plane. Sam knew a lot about the banks from her expensive forensic accounting lesson at Artie's hands, but Warren took her through the intricacies of how they calculated and talked about interest rates on big, important accounts. It was hardly eleven o'clock when they pulled into

Vaduz's tidy central square and parked, just about twenty yards from the august entrance to the Wilhelmsbanken. Sam levered herself out of the low-slung car, looking elegant in a fur-lined, leather duffel coat, and tight stirrup pants tucked neatly into a pair of Hermès snow boots. Warren simply wore gray flannels and a white dress shirt under the shearling coat he'd bought at Barneys for the occasion. They looked healthy, wealthy, and very much in their element, their black sunglasses glinting in the clear mountain air.

A portly doorman in a black cutaway allowed them to pass, and Sam led the way to the inner sanctum. At the reception desk she did not remove her glasses, but in an imperious voice and perfect German, fine-tuned with a half dozen classes at Berlitz, addressed the older woman who looked up from her seat inquisitively.

"*Herr Schlusmann, bitte.* It is important."

"*Ja. Ja.* A moment, I will ring him. Please sit, if you wish." The woman gestured to two wing chairs and lifted her handset. She started speaking only moments after punching in an extension.

"Herr Schlusmann, there is a young woman and a gentleman to see you at reception. . . . *Ja.* I will tell them. *Ja.*" She put the receiver down and turned her face to Sam. "Herr Schlusmann has asked that I take you to his office." Sam nodded and gestured to Warren to follow.

"Ah, good. Then we will get this problem straightened out." Warren couldn't believe Sam's accent, and though he hadn't a clue what she was saying, she sounded convincingly pissed about something.

They followed their guide into a surprisingly bland office, where a round, well-dressed gentleman sat behind a large partner's desk, making notes on a report of some sort. He looked up pleasantly. "Yes. Hello. How can I help you?" His accent was clipped.

"Help me? I will tell you. I am quite upset." Sam still had the pissed-off tone, in what Warren assumed was excellent German. "There is a serious irregularity in my account, and I want to correct it right away."

"Irregularity? Of what sort? I'm certain we can correct it." The man sounded genuinely solicitous, and Warren couldn't help but think Sam's legs had something to do with it.

"When my brother passed away, his estate was held only in US dollars. Every account. Every bond. It is simply not possible. Not possible." She was now speaking to the man as if he were an idiot and actually banged a fist on the desk for emphasis.

"But I don't understand? What is not possible?" His voice was unctuous, soothing, practiced in assuaging the petulant demands of the rich.

"Some moron has responded to my inquiry by insisting that my account is held here in Swiss francs. That is absurd. It is dollars. Dollars only. Who is responsible for this stupidity?" Warren was sitting there, nodding gravely. He understood the part about dollars, and something about Swiss francs. He tried to look annoyed. "This is my solicitor, Herr Markus. We wish to address this problem right away." She gestured to Warren, who rose and shook Herr Schlusmann's hand.

"Well, that is a concern. There is quite a difference. Let me investigate. What is the account number, if you please." He was speaking to Warren now, but Sam butted in.

"Three oh eight seven six six three four two dash three is the first. The one with the problem." There was only one account at this bank, but she thought it was a nice touch. Herr Schlusmann jotted it on a slip of paper.

"*Ja*. I will see." He swiveled in his chair to a small computer terminal. Then paused, almost as an afterthought "Of course, if you will, I must have the pass code."

"The pass code?" Sam asked.

"Yes, of course, the pass code." Schlusmann swiveled imperceptibly back toward the desk.

"I will not give you my pass code. I will enter it on the computer in private as I always have. What is this lunacy?" She had a condescending bite that transcended language. She had committed to memory all the numbers in Anson's spreadsheet, and the moment of truth had arrived. If they didn't match up, they could have real trouble.

"Yes, of course, as you wish." The servile tone had returned. He spent a moment at the keyboard, then swiveled back. "At your convenience…"

Sam stood abruptly and stepped to the console behind the man, who did not turn to observe. She tapped the keypad a few times and stepped away. "*Ja*," she muttered.

Schlusmann turned again and spun through a few menus. His back stiffened slightly as a screen full of tiny numbers appeared, which even Warren could see contained an awful lot of zeros. Sam had to struggle not to show any reaction.

"But, as you can see, this is all in United States dollars! I cannot understand how you were ever told otherwise. Do you—"

"*Ach.* Idiot. I told her. Well then, good. Tell me, Herr Schlusmann, was the interest paid in last month, as scheduled? Twenty-five basis points under LIBOR, I presume?" The information Warren had gotten from one of the traders at Credit Suisse had been spot-on. This would apply only to a highly preferred account—most deposits here paid no interest.

"Yes, of course. But we have modified your rate to only twenty last September." The man was being so polite as to border on obsequiousness.

"So generous, Herr Schlusmann. I am sure it must cause you a great deal of discomfort." Sam was smiling now, deciding the time had come to ease up. She motioned to Warren, as if he were a servant, to follow her. He tried to look the part as he nervously snatched her coat and helped her into it.

"*Bitte,*" he muttered. He thought he sounded like Lili Von Shtupp in *Blazing Saddles.*

"*Danke. Danke schön, Herr Schlusmann.* I will notify you of where I wish my account transferred tomorrow. This bank should be most ashamed of itself. I do not blame you, but this is intolerable." The man looked crestfallen, shocked. He started to renew his apologies, to explain that the bank never made such errors.

She cut him off. "Herr Schlusmann, I do not blame you. Not at all. I will write a letter to your director complimenting you. I will even recommend you to the Faaringsbank. But I do not suffer such treatment easily. Now, I must be going. I will be in touch with you tomorrow." She tossed her Hermès scarf around her shoulder, and she and Warren exited briskly past the receptionist, whom Warren nodded to, and the doorman.

"Of course, madame, as you wish." Schlusmann walked behind her, looking dejected. He was clearly accustomed to brutal treatment at the hands of the extremely wealthy.

Outside, Sam looked a little dazed. They walked to the car quietly, and Warren held the door for her, then clambered to the driver's side and in.

"Jesus fucking Christ. I don't believe it." She had a smile as wide as the Alps on her face.

"What? What was it?" Warren was dying.

"Oh, only ninety-two million dollars. And the account is registered under a Klaust AG with a post office box in Grand Cayman for the address. No people's names at all. That means the pass code is the only ticket in and out."

"You're kidding me. Ninety-two million dollars? *Dollars?*" Warren had started to pull away from the curb, and he had to concentrate to make the shift. His hand wasn't steady.

"And change. A lot of it. Warren, that was just one account." She had an awed tone in her voice. "And he never even asked for my *name*! Can you believe it?"

"I know. It's scary. Jesus. What do we do?" His mind was racing. Where the fuck did 92 million bucks come from?

"Let's open the account, then think about it for a while, okay?" She smiled at him.

"You got it." He made a right-hand turn and drove a few blocks, pulling up outside another formidable-looking building, the modern, white, glass-and-steel offices of the Faaringsbank. This time, he went in alone. The tone of the bank officer was hardly as solicitous as Herr Schlusmann's had been, and when Warren asked to open a private account, he was treated to a long wait. A secretary dropped a sheaf of papers on the desk, and Warren started filling them out. Sean Sennet with a mailbox address at the General Post Office in New York. The falsified passport Artie had left behind had been in Sam's drawer for two years, and changing the picture had not been hard. God only knew what name Artie had used when he'd left. Finally, the woman escorted him into a small office and introduced him to a Vice President, Jurgen Dohlmerr.

"*Ja*, Herr Sennet, and what will the opening deposit be?" The conversation was in English, which the banker spoke with a magnificent British accent.

"If it is not too much trouble, Herr Dohlmer, I would like only to open the account today. Once you have provided me with the number and codes, I will have my bankers transfer in a substantial sum within the week." Warren was purposefully speaking quite slowly and formally. "I would like to register the account in the name of a confidential Liechtenstein trust, please, if you can complete that for me? I am only here in Liechtenstein to attend to

several private matters, and this is not a sum I wish to carry in any nego-
tiable form." Warren pursed his lips and put the bank's pen into his breast
pocket.

"I see. You understand of course that the bank has a minimum account
balance of two hundred thousand Swiss francs." The older man was letting
a hint of superiority creep into his voice.

"I would prefer an interest-bearing account, Herr Dohlmer. LIBOR even,
if you could." Warren smiled at the man.

"That would require a rather substantial balance, I am afraid." Dohlmer
obviously thought this American was an idiot. "This is not, after all, Citibank."

"Herr Dohlmer, I have not seen fit to insult you. No, this is not Citibank,
but neither is it Credit Suisse or even Wilhelms. I attended to this matter
myself because it is a private one, or I would have had it handled by my
family's fund managers. I am certain you will be pleased with the balance,
which will be *extremely* substantial. I plan to keep it here for quite some time
and add to it as other funds come available. Faaringsbank will do well with
me. If you would, please, the numbers. I must be on my way." Warren adopted Sam's regal tone and folded his gloves. "I would appreciate it if you
would move quickly."

Dohlmer paused, sizing Warren up, then nodded and walked to another
desk. The man there perused the papers, stamped them, tore off a slip, and
then consulted a register. In a moment, Dohlmer was back. He handed the
sheaf of papers back to Warren, less only the small slip. They'd never even
taken the passport. Dohlmer then pulled out another folder and swiftly executed the paperwork to create a private trust, which Warren named Sporty
AG after his neighbor's annoying Lhasa apso. The trust would own the bank
account, and the records of the trust, like the account, would be completely
protected by the country's secrecy laws—laws all sorts of despots, criminals,
and the occasional legitimate businessman relied on. If somehow the records
were released, they would lead to a post office box taken out in the name of
someone who didn't exist. No paper statements were sent out, so Warren
doubted he would even need to maintain the box for more than a few months.

One of the sheets of paper held wire-transfer instructions, and an autho-
rization for transfers out. The only record the bank now had was an account

number and a pass code. That slip and the trust paperwork would be kept in a locked vault, and only the commission of a crime in the nation of Liechtenstein itself was grounds for its release to any law enforcement authority in the world. The transfer of funds out of the bank would require a telephone call, telex, or fax, and so long as the pass code was correct, the money could be sent anywhere in the world by instantaneous wire transfer. Warren nodded, shook the man's hand, and stood.

"Herr Dohlmer, I will contact you tomorrow evening, to be certain you have received the transfer. I will allow you to set the rate you feel appropriate for the account balance, but if it is not fair, I will take my business down the street. My family looks forward to a long relationship with this bank." The older man thanked him, and Warren left, meeting Sam, who was on foot at the corner. They walked around the block to the car, without seeing another soul. Liechtenstein was, after all, a small country. Money, it seems, really takes up little room at all.

They made the scenic drive to Zurich, where they checked in using Sennet's name again. The Dolder was a grand old hotel in the forest, and the couple indulged in a lengthy session with their spa staff. Over the next two days, they checked the balances of all six accounts and transfered the three largest to Faaringsbank. It had been a bit of a letdown after the first, but Account 83713847 now had a balance of $224,622,400.39. It was earning interest at 4.5 percent, a highly preferred rate. When he had spoken to Herr Dohlmerr on the phone, his manner had changed remarkably, and he offered to take Warren to lunch anywhere in Europe, at any time. Warren had upgraded to a huge suite at the Dolder, the tall windows commanding a beautiful view out over the hills and the lake from one of the dramatic towers. Sean Sennet was a wealthy man.

That they controlled such a vast sum of money seemed momentous, and they had a feeling that the combined forces of Interpol and the FBI were certain to break in on them at any moment. Of course, except for the false identity and passport, shown only to the bankers and not to any government officials, they hadn't done anything wrong. As with all private accounts in Swiss and Liechtenstein banks, the papers executed by Anson or his cohorts when they'd opened the original accounts stated clearly, in any language you required, that the holder of the pass codes had full legal right to the funds. The signatures waived the bank's liability if the codes were inadvertently stolen or passed on by the depositor. Now that money was gone, transferred into another bank, with an electronic trail they would never divulge and would be expunged from any record within two years. Besides, no one seemed to be looking for any missing money, and the putative Sean Sennet was completely and absolutely guaranteed secrecy by the laws that supported Liechtenstein's entire economy. The small nation's only economic engine protected Sam and Warren from any prying eyes. It was strictly personal business, and the very soul of discretion.

They finished out the week and returned to New York and the hurly-burly world of commerce. Both Bill's and Anson's deaths were still unsolved, and Detective Wittlin didn't even call Warren anymore. He had brought up the coincidence that Ken Hament had been in town the day that Anson got killed as well, but, again, nothing linked him to the scene, and he had been at his hotel in Midtown having a drink with another tennis pro at about the time of Anson's murder.

Warren tried not to think too much about the money, but he spent weeks researching every deal that Anson Combes had done over the past seven years. Surprisingly, many of the deal files had been moved to an archive warehouse. Warren had filled out the retrieval requests and noted on the forms, in case anyone was curious, that he was working on devising a new structure for similar deals. He also ordered up unrelated deals by other people to cover his tracks.

There was only one noticeable trend in Anson's files. Almost every sizable deal Anson did was with Warner or Golden State, and almost every one of them involved a massive profit participation by the broker Scholdice. Welson would work for a point or two—great by normal standards. But Warren had added up over $375 million in the first two years alone paid out to Scholdice—about ten times what Weldon had netted. The total could eventually have been close to a billion dollars. The pattern had become pretty clear: Scholdice was working with the men at the banks and Anson to turn the banks' losses into huge payoffs for all the men involved. The money must have gone from Scholdice maybe first to the Caymans and then to Liechtenstein.

Warren went to Weldon's library of financial statements and, a check of the two banks' reports revealed extremely large loan-loss reserves stretching back over at least five years. The losses were covered by profits from other investments—junk bonds, real estate, and so on. The banks' losses were taken on the loans Anson bought, repackaged, and sold, at massive profits. Weldon earned a nice fee, but the bulk of the money went to Scholdice, who was clearly sending a share to Anson's account, keeping his cut, and, no doubt, sending a big chunk to the men at the banks as well. Warren was willing to bet that some of those European banks had accounts set up by Scholdice, with Karlheinz Beker and Pete Largeman participating in the spoils. They'd devised a brilliant scheme to sell off blocks of the banks' perfectly good assets, replace them with shaky, but not high-yielding ones, and skim the profits off the top. The plan also allowed the banks to avoid paying taxes on their profits on these questionable assets. Anson was a hell of an investment banker, after all. The financial press hailed these men as geniuses—they'd saved their institutions from the ruin of poor lending practices with brilliant investments. Their shareholders should be thrilled.

Ultimately, if the junk bonds and the leverage failed, the shareholders would be wiped out, and Uncle Sam would foot the bill. There would be no obvious theft because all they would see were the collapsed junk bonds and real estate; the "bad" mortgages had been sold off long ago. The losses on the loans had been well reserved for, and $200 million or even $1 billion was a drop in the bucket over time. It looked to Warren as if this had been going on for at least four or five years. By the time anyone caught on, it'd be impossible to accurately reconstruct the whole scheme. The press was right. These guys *were* brilliant.

Then why was Anson dead? Had he stiffed them? His share did seem pretty large. Did Dougherty figure out the scam, and is that why he was dead? Maybe that's why Anson was so interested in Bill. Or maybe Anson was worried about Warren's finding out. It all made his head spin. One thing for sure, Warren didn't want anybody connecting him with any of this. He returned the files and stopped snooping. The thought of all that money, sitting in that quaint, little bank, felt like having Aladdin's lamp in your bag, but not knowing if the genie was good or evil. He wondered what would happen when, or if, Scholdice or Beker or whoever went looking for the cash and discovered it was gone. But then, why would they if they'd already gotten their share? All that money must have been Anson's. There's no way they'd all trust each other with that kind of untraceable money.

Sam decided to stick around New York for a while longer. She never mentioned the money, although Warren kept her informed about his research, and under the guise of returning to her own investigation, she reaffirmed with her attorney that no one could, without proof of a serious financial crime under local laws, compel the banks in Liechtenstein to divulge where the money had been transferred to or by whom. She had tried for years to track the real Anschutz through Liechtenstein, and even with clear evidence of his crimes in the United States, the banks and their government ignored the FBI and Sam's lawyer, not even replying to their inquiries.

The happy couple were falling into a pleasant rhythm—Warren would take off for work in the mornings, and Sam would run any errands they needed. She'd spend an hour or so on the phone to Carlos at the lot, where business was good. She had turned it into a real moneymaker—Carlos was putting over $8,000 a month into her account and still holding a surplus. The biggest volume of business came from the film studios. They would use her cars both as props and as executive transportation. Carlos had solved one thorny problem when a studio production head was arrested with an ounce of cocaine and two prostitutes in one of Sam's Maserati sedans. The police wanted to impound or even seize the car, and Carlos had gotten his cousin, a detective, to intervene. Two days' use of an antique Corvette had convinced the officer to lay off. Carlos was a hard worker, and trustworthy, and she called the bookkeeper and told her to give him a 40 percent raise and a $50,000 bonus. He was speechless—this was double the amount he'd ever made in a year.

"Listen, I may not make it back to L.A. for a while," Sam had changed the subject while Carlos stammered his thanks into the phone. "Could you send me out the rest of my shoes?"

"I think maybe this is serious, no?" He had been on the lot for six years and had helped her learn about the business when she'd taken it over. He never minded doing things for her. "I am a lucky Mexican, Samantha. I have a good job and a good boss, a green card, and my family with me. I drive nice cars, and you know how Mexicans are about cars. For you, I will do anything."

"I don't know, Carlos. Maybe it's for real. I hope so." She was telling the truth.

"I hope he is a good man. Not like the last one, eh? He better treat you right." Carlos had hated Artie and was offended at the abusive way he drove the cars he was constantly borrowing. He had ruined the clutch on a Lotus Turbo Esprit and worn the rubber off the tires of at least a half dozen others. Carlos had said to Sam that a man who treated automobiles that way would not treat women or clients any better. She hadn't listened.

"I think he is, Carlos. He has a good heart. His job makes him angry sometimes, but he is sweet to me." As she was talking, she realized, for the first time, how much she was in love with Warren. It wasn't just that he was funny and they had a good time, and that he was successful and generous. She loved the way he was basically naïve and hated the way his work was making him jaded. He never made her feel as if he were a threat to her in any way, and he genuinely paid attention to her happiness. "God, I hope he is," she had added, and Carlos, three thousand miles away, had smiled into the receiver at the fullness of her voice.

forty-six

~≈~

Almost three months passed, and there had been no noise about any problems at Warner or Golden State. Warren noticed that some of their business started slipping away to other dealers, particularly Sacramento, the brokerage arm of the huge insurance company. They were raising a lot of money for Warner, and without Anson pushing, Warren hadn't wanted to get Weldon involved. He knew that the two banks were not what they seemed, and while he wasn't about to tell anyone, it was easy to let the business go elsewhere. When Malcolm questioned the drop in production, Warren attributed it to other firms' being overly aggressive to get the banks' business, and to Sacramento's willingness to sell lousy credits to its dumb-money retail system. Philo Clarke, a business school classmate, told Warren an amazing story. Sacramento's mortgage sales desk had knowingly misrepresented a big new deal they had sold to thousands of small investors through their retail brokerage system. The head trader, for whom Philo worked, had balked, insisting on a letter from the sales head acknowledging the head trader had nothing to do with the obvious lie. "He says, 'You idiots are gonna get sued!' So the head of sales says, 'Fuck the moms and pops—we're making seven goddamn points!' and signs the letter," Philo had told Warren. Within three months, all the small investors who'd bought it had lost over $50 million of the $75 million they'd invested and filed a huge lawsuit. Sacramento had been forced to make them whole, losing $53 million. It was par for the course at what Philo called "this fucking wire-house, black-Irish, boiler-room bucket shop."

Warren had picked up the slack in production with Emerson Insurance, helping Schiff put together a whole restructuring of their asset base, and into a bullish stance on interest rates. Schiff felt strongly that the country was on the brink of a huge recession, if not in one already, and wanted to position to reap the maximum benefit if long-term interest rates declined to facilitate a recovery. Tax reform had began to hit, and Schiff was convinced things would get rough by mid 1989. Despite his usually conservative bent, they went on a shopping spree together, buying mortgage derivatives and treasury strips, and extending the maturity in every one of the firm's accounts. Schiff reasoned that his company had a huge surplus, and if his bet was wrong, they would still be in a solid position. Warren concurred. Still, his own paranoia made him document Schiff's full understanding of the risks he was taking with a comprehensive acknowledgment letter Warren had Weldon's legal department prepare. Schiff had obtained his board's consent—essentially he was risking only the gains he'd made by being right on the markets so far. It was a good gambler's strategy.

One day, Schiff had taken Jed Leeds out of $157 million of principal-only strips. These were securities that paid no interest, but received all the principal from a pool of FNMA-guaranteed mortgages. They sold for fifty-two cents on the dollar. If interest rates went down, it would become easier for the homeowners whose mortgages were in the pool to refinance, and the prepayment rate on the pool would climb. This meant that Schiff would receive the principal back, at 100, much faster than projected, making him a big profit. If he was wrong, and repayments slowed down, he would be hurt, getting his money back more slowly. What made the mortgages attractive was that they were already prepaying so slowly that little room was left for them to get any slower.

Jed had been long in the position for two months as the markets had fallen during a lull in the building rally. The bonds had lost almost ten points in value, and he was desperate to sell them. When Schiff had agreed to buy them, Jed ran across the floor and kissed Warren on the top of his head. He paid Warren a $2 million gross commission. Malcolm called Warren into his office to congratulate him. It was the biggest single commission anyone could remember on one trade. Warren had to admit he was happy. Everyone on the floor was high-fiving him, and even Annlois came by to congratulate him.

"Say, Annlois," he had said before she left, "have you got a second?" She looked to both sides and, seeing that no one was paying attention, bent over his desk. "What was it you wanted me to find in that computer?' Warren couldn't help it—she was the only link between him and Anson's accounts.

She looked nervous and whispered to him, "I knew that Anson was seeing your girlfriend, and that he kept his dates on his calendar and some e-mails. I wanted you to find out for yourself, rather than from someone else. You're a nice young man. I'm glad the two of you aren't together anymore. I don't like her very much. She's pretty, but uses people."

Warren nodded thoughtfully. "Thank you, Ann. I did find the calendar. But the police told me about Larisa first."

"Oh. I'm sorry."

"No, it was for the best. We had already broken up."

"You know, Warren, it's funny the way Anson would always ask Larisa about you. It was like he wanted to know what you were thinking about him all the time. He used her too, I think. He was a hateful man." Annlois looked sad.

"I don't think anyone could use Larisa Mueller without her knowledge and consent. Not her." Warren smiled at Annlois, and she patted his hand warmly before she walked away.

Gossip. Interoffice romance. Not $200 million in a European vault. The woman had given him the secret to protect his feelings. He couldn't help but chuckle. It had been completely personal. Not just business.

In the odd way things always seem to happen, Warren ran into Larisa the next day. He hadn't spoken to her often since their parting tryst. He hadn't told her that he knew about Anson, hadn't let on that he knew her whole indignant scene about the pills had been a charade. Why start an argument? She knew the truth, and he didn't mind her seeing him as a sap.

He had gone to the thirtieth floor for a short meeting with members of the Insurance Group. These analysts appraised the values of the stocks of all the major publicly held insurance companies, and they had decided to add Emerson to the list of companies they followed. If they gave it a harsh review, it could hurt Emerson's stock price and their business, but a good one might help. Warren had been relieved that they were positive on the company.

Larisa worked on the thirty-second floor, but the copy center was one flight below. She ran into Warren as she headed for the staircase with a pile of reports. He stopped to talk, and the others continued on. She looked tired, and he could tell that she'd been working hard. She'd put on a few pounds too. It actually made her even prettier, softening some of the hard edges.

"So. How're things?" she asked brightly. "I hear you're setting all kinds of records down there." She smiled at him.

"Yeah. Things are going pretty well. I can't complain." He shrugged.

"I always knew you'd be a star. And so fast." She started her familiar gesture, a playful push on his shoulder, but caught herself and dropped her hand.

"Well, I think that karma—or fate, or whatever—has made things happen a little quicker than they might otherwise. But you gotta take what you can get, right?" That two men who had either stood in Warren's way or disliked him had died was not lost on him. He had no illusions that his rise hadn't been aided by their bad luck.

"I'll say." She stopped for a minute and looked into his eyes for a long moment. "You know, I miss you, Warren. Things are so different now."

He looked at her and couldn't hide his discomfort. "Well, I think it worked out for the best. You know what they say, 'The truth will set you free.'" He regretted the shot. "I may have been wrong about what I said, but I do think things will be better for both of us."

"You weren't wrong, and I'm sorry for what I did. But I'm not sure you're right about this. We were good together. I always felt like you supported me, and you know I was always on your side. We just lost sight of each other." She reached out and brushed her fingers over his hair. He flinched. She saw it and turned away. "It's a shame."

"Larisa, the past is the past. Whatever you did or I did doesn't matter now. We've both got our careers, and you're going to wind up with everything you want. I know it." He felt a patronizing tone creep into his voice, but in reality he felt little for her other than sympathy. She'd picked out Combes as the coming star and hitched up to it, and now he was gone. That he was married hadn't mattered. She'd probably believed him when he'd undoubtedly told her he was going to leave his wife. It was a miscalculation, and she'd paid the price for it, but she was on her way to becoming a huge success on her own. He couldn't deny a big part of him had held strong feelings for her, but Sam was incredible, and he was as happy as could be. Larisa would have to sort it out for herself. He thought about Chas Harper for a moment—Larisa had picked him over Chas and a sure life of wealth and comfort, then dumped him for a shark like Anson. Who could figure it? Warren always led with his heart.

"Look, I've gotta get back downstairs. We'll talk later. I'll call you." He turned toward the elevator bank.

"I know. You should know that I miss you, that's all. Take care." She said it with a finality that he couldn't miss. It gave him a pang in his stomach, but the relief was stronger. She walked to the staircase, and he watched her long, slim, muscular legs climb slowly out of sight.

forty-seven

❧

The light shocked him awake, and startled, Warren twisted his neck. He instantly knew it would be stiff later in the day. "What? What is it?" He turned to Sam, who had turned on the lamp next to the bed and was sitting bolt upright

"I thought I heard something. I was up, but I thought I heard something in the other room." Warren shushed her, and they both sat tensely, listening. There was no sound.

"I'll go look," he said wearily, and eased himself out of bed. He walked over to his closet and reached up to the shelf. His hand came down with a steel-framed tennis racquet.

"Who are you expecting? John McEnroe?" She laughed at the sight of him, in his boxer shorts, hair tousled, holding the bulky, silver weapon in front of him.

"If there's a burglar in the house, he's going to get a circumcision."

She laughed again, but looked worried. "Be careful. Want me to come? Why don't you call the doorman?" She started to get up.

"No doorman after midnight in this building. You stay here. Just be ready to call the cops if you hear me yell, 'Let! First service!'" He opened the door slowly and stepped into the dark hall. He carefully searched each room, but found nothing. The doors were locked tight. It was unlikely anyone other than Spider-Man would have climbed up the façade to the tenth floor, but he checked the windows anyway. They were secure. While he was up, he walked to the fridge and pulled out a carton of orange juice. He thought about getting a glass, then just pinched it open and drank from the container.

"It's so gross the way guys do that." He had to gulp fast and lean forward not to spill the juice.

"Jesus!" He said, wiping his mouth. "You scared me."

"Oooh. You coulda spit orange juice all over me if I was a burglar." Sam nodded toward the racquet, which was on the table between them. "Nobody to smash?"

"Nah. Everything's shipshape. You must've been dreaming. Personally, I keep seeing visions of Herr Schlusmann inviting me into the showers." He put the carton back into the fridge and picked up the racquet. "Whoever it was woulda been in big trouble." He made some chopping and slicing motions. "I would've used that Connors punch volley first, then kicked him in the nuts."

"If you're such a hotshot tennis player, how come you're not a pro?" Sam opened the fridge and took the juice out, then hunted for a glass.

"I dunno. Concentration. Desire. Killer instinct. I clearly lack them all. Just not that kind of material." He shrugged.

"Well, now that we're up"—she put down the glass and moved toward him—"and there's no cat burglar in the house"—she was now pressed against him—"and you're only in those little shorts"—she pulled the waistband—"maybe we can work on that 'desire' part you clearly lack." She teased him through the thin material, then looked down. "Hmmm. You look like a promising student."

forty-eight

❦

"…Just give us twenty-two minutes, and we'll give you the world.…"

The clock radio showed six thirty, and Warren reached out feebly to silence it. First, he had to move the blue boxer shorts that covered it. His head felt heavy, and his neck was sore, every fiber of his being screaming at him to lie back down and go back to sleep. Sam stirred, her hair fanned out over her face and the pillow, the arch of her haunch draped by the sheet. He couldn't help but admire her in the soft morning light, her even features and arched brows, long legs and slim hips sweeping to full breasts carried by a strong rib cage and wide shoulders. She was a thoroughbred and slept the sleep of the dead.

"Traffic and weather together on the…" He located the right switch and hoisted himself to head for the shower. He was on autopilot as he bathed, shaved, brushed, combed, spritzed, and dried himself, picking out a charcoal, subtle Glen-plaid, single-breasted suit, white shirt, and rust-colored Hermès tie. Sam had introduced him to patterned socks, and he slipped on a black-and-maroon-check pair, then laced up the Bally wing tips. A final check in the mirror told him he looked every bit the young investment banker, and he went to the kitchen for coffee.

With the morning sun slanting in from across the park, the white room took on a buttery glow. He had agonized over the cabinets when he'd renovated and wound up having them made from sycamore wood and a greenish bottle glass. The countertops were a heavily veined white marble, and the floors antique limestone. It was his favorite room, and he'd taken out the second bedroom to make it larger. The owner of the building had decided to take it co-op, and Warren had immediately agreed to buy the unit at the "insider" price, which was so cheap it seemed like robbery. New York City's rent laws were incredible.

The Wilson steel racquet still lay on the breakfast table, catching the sun with a blinding flash. He realized he'd forgotten to fill and set the timer on the coffeemaker the night before, so he stepped to the sink and filled the Krups machine with water and grounds, flipping it on, then closing the canister of coffee. The back door to the apartment opened into the kitchen, and Warren had asked the doorman to be certain always to leave the newspaper there for him. It was lying on the mat when he opened the door, a picture of George Bush staring out from the first page. The vice president's picture held his eye for a moment, but as he stood, something else occurred to him. The door had been single-locked, and he always double-locked it.

"Angelo?" Warren spoke normally into the phone, but held the receiver about a foot from his ear.

"Yes? Right here!" Warren had anticipated Angelo's habit of screaming into the phone like Bell calling for Watson.

"Hey, Angelo, it's Warren Hament. Could you ask Gabriel to come upstairs for a second?" The doorman had shouted his assent, and after a few sips of coffee, Warren heard the service-elevator door open and greeted the superintendent by the back door.

"Gee, I don't know, Mr. Hament." The unctuous, condescending tones of the Polish émigré never failed to annoy Warren. "I'll check the log, but I would be surprised if any of the staff would have come into the apartment without telling me." The building had a copy of Warren's keys for emergency access.

Warren smiled unconsciously. The super never actually did anything himself. He'd have one of the doormen or a handyman do it. He just wanted the tip himself. Warren knew that every other staff member in the building hated Gabriel. Nonetheless, Warren didn't have time to worry about it, so he fished a twenty out of his pocket. Another $20 tip, he thought, just the cost of living in New York, like the parking tickets, the taxes, and every other maddening expense made necessary by the endless inability of the city government to clean up its own corruption and convince the poor that any work was better than welfare or crime. "God," he said out loud to himself, coming up short, "I'm starting to *think* like a fucking Republican."

Warren poured and drank the rest of his coffee while reading a heartening summary of the Rangers' hockey game the night before. The team was improving, but Warren knew better than to hope for a Stanley Cup anytime soon. Still, it could happen. He put down the paper, his neck stiff and painful. He got up and poked around in a drawer, finding some aspirin, and downing them with juice. He stopped for a moment. Coffee. Aspirin. Orange juice. Jesus, he might as well pour some battery acid down there, too. So, he searched around some more and came up with a pack of Rolaids. He popped a few in his mouth, and the rest in his pocket. He crept into the bedroom and gently kissed Sam on the forehead. She opened her eyes, the indirect light making the green irises almost translucent.

"Gee, you look nice," she said, sitting up. "You know, you're better looking than you think."

"God, a compliment at this hour? What did I do to deserve *that*?"

"Hey, I know I might have told you that looks don't matter to a woman, but I'm starting to realize that you're the cutest guy I've ever gone out with."

"*Gone out with?*" Warren spread his hands wide. "I think we're a little past that."

"Hmmmm. Yeah, maybe. Well, we'll have to talk about that later." Sam stretched back out and pulled the covers up to her chin. "I need at least three more hours here."

After the taxi ride to the office, and a few minutes getting organized, Warren began the ritual of another day. He was amazed how quickly everything had become a mundane repetition, even though it involved moving billions of dollars around in increasingly arcane ways, and at how having at best a modest talent made young professionals into arrogant, free-spending millionaires. The work was deadening and largely filled with limited and shallow people. Increasingly, the engineers and quant jocks were the stars of the Street, and their peculiar patois could kill the conversation at any cocktail party.

Warren couldn't keep himself from pondering Liechtenstein, and the events that had led to the treasure so carefully buried there. Frankly, he wasn't even certain how illegal Anson's activities had been. The money technically was only brokerage fees and trading profits earned by a middleman on some fantastically lucrative transactions. Unless the bankers had been completely fraudulent in writing down the loans, there was no crime there. Combes's taking a big cut of the profits was obviously against the firm's rules but... Warren stopped himself. This was all a stupid rationalization. He knew that Combes and his cohorts had stolen the money from the banks, just as surely as if they had done it with a gun. If money had been passed back to Beker, that was probably a felony. If the shareholders and regulators were too sloppy or stupid to notice it, that didn't change anything. The right thing for Warren to do would be to march right off and tell the FBI or the CIA, or somebody. Hell, he thought, if I told the guys at Weldon, they'd probably just try to figure out a way to take the money themselves. Besides, Warren hadn't engaged in any of the criminal activity. He'd just stumbled upon the pirates' buried treasure. He wasn't sure what that made him.

He'd seen lots of instances where management had approved trades with insurance companies or banks to help them avoid accounting problems. They were illegal, but they were profitable for Weldon and hard to define. Malcolm had always had some plausible-sounding explanation. Once, Kerry had asked about paying one of her banks two points more for a package of adjustable-rate mortgages than they were worth, in order to sell them a different bond at a four-point markup. To sell them and buy the CMOs made a lot of sense, but if they sold the mortgages for their true market value, they would take a loss, which would result in lower earnings for the year, and that would result in lower pay for the men who ran the bank. So, if Weldon paid a price that would allow them to break even or show a profit, then made up the difference by also selling the bank the CMOs at an inflated price, Weldon would make lots of money, the bank would look falsely profitable, and if a regulator figured out what was done and actually did something about it, they would all wind up out of the business or in jail. Malcolm okayed the trade.

"Well," he had said to Kerry, "you know those are some pretty weird ARMs they're selling. They could be worth a couple points more. Who knows? I've seen it happen before." While many unusual securities, particularly in mortgages, *were* hard to price accurately, that trade had been an obvious and egregious violation. Nothing ever came of it, except for Weldon's $2 million profit, because the regulators were generally people with little or no knowledge of what they were regulating and rarely checked transactions anyway. Profits from that trade helped fatten Malcolm's year-end bonus, in addition to allowing Kerry to earn a big commission. The firm's compliance department rarely raised a stink if a supervisor signed off on a trade—after all, those same supervisors set the compliance department's bonuses. This system ensured that problems or bad deeds would generally be ignored or covered up. There was no reward for a compliance officer to uncover misdeeds. In fact, Warren had heard more than once that the officers got pushed aside or even fired.

Warren's mind returned to the larger question. If the money wasn't really "missing"—since no one seemed to notice or care about the markdowns at the banks—that meant no one would be looking for it. There had been absolutely no sign of any investigations or inquiries, and most of Anson's records and files had been distributed to the groups working on each transaction or archived. Warren and Sam had broken down the computer into tiny pieces, roasted them in his fireplace, then scattered them in trash cans all over the city. There was no sign that anyone thought Anson's death was anything more than a tragic example of the growing crime rate. It just didn't make any sense. There was no such thing as the perfect crime. If Anson Combes had died, Warren reasoned, it was because someone wanted that money. Otherwise, some dumb burglar had killed one of the wealthiest men in New York and left with only a few bucks and some jewelry.

Thinking about the whole situation made Warren anxious, and he buried himself in his work. The corporate trading desk had been at the morning sales meeting, hawking a big new deal for an airplane leasing company, so he hunkered down and started studying the financial summaries to see if he wanted to sell it to his clients. He'd gone about halfway through the pack of Rolaids in his pocket already, the chalky, mint flavor somehow soothing to the spirit as well as the belly.

Unlike many Weldon salesmen, he tried to screen out the garbage before attempting to sell anything to his accounts. All Street firms needed the revenue from new deals to keep the machine greased, so some stinkers would inevitably sneak in, even at a relatively conservative place such as Weldon.

Larisa's Temenosa deal had been a prime example. One day, the firm is raising money selling bonds for Temenosa, supposedly a hot, growing diversi-
fied oil services company with fabulous cash flow. Seven months later, all
the money raised in the bond offering is gone, spent on a lousy acquisition,
investment-banking fees, and a lot of executive compensation, and the firm
files for bankruptcy. It seems the bankers on the deal had been a little too
optimistic about that cash flow. Oh, well, there went a billion dollars or so.
The amazing part was that Weldon got assigned the plum reorganization
advisory job by the bankruptcy court. Since they already knew so much
about the company, the receiver would save the expense of a new firm's
starting from scratch. The fees were generous, even though the company
itself was virtually busted. It was all a funny joke, as long as you were on the
magic gravy train.

It took Warren about an hour to decide that the leasing company was a
house of cards that would collapse almost immediately if the airline business softened even slightly. With all the new debt, it would actually fail if
business just stayed the same and didn't improve. Meanwhile the CEO and
majority owner lived like a king and would no doubt use a chunk of the
bond proceeds to fund his lifestyle. He stuck a prospectus in an envelope
with a printed "For Your Information" card and scratched out *Information,*
substituting *Amusement,* sending it off to David Schiff. He loved this kind of
deal. They could laugh together as it crashed in flames.

Thinking of Larisa again made Warren a little uneasy. She had seemed
genuinely sad when he'd run into her. She was a tough cookie who had gotten where she wanted to be, but paid a price personally. She had been made
one of the youngest vice presidents in Finance at the firm and was on the
path to be an MD within a few years. It may not have worked out with him,
or even with Anson, but she'd find someone new. Besides, having kids or a
family was something that would wait. At the pace she was going, she'd be
able to retire and have a brood at thirty-five. He could see her point and
couldn't fault her logic, although her sleeping with the guy he was most
scared of hadn't exactly warmed his heart. For a minute he wondered if she
might have known about Anson's accounts. He dismissed it—she had always
warned him never, *never* to do anything even in the gray area between legal

and questionable. He felt that she was not yet resolved as a part of his life somehow, and that thought did not make him comfortable. He had a great girlfriend, a good career in a tough business, and a great big bag of salty pistachio nuts that the shoe-shine man had sold him that morning. All was right, or at least allright, with the world. For now.

forty-nine

A cold hand ran down his spine, grabbing at his stomach and squeezing hard enough to make him gasp. A yawning pit opened inside him, and hot flames shot up from his groin to his cheeks, setting his skin afire, and his heart ablaze. He felt himself shrinking suddenly and violently, until he felt like a pin dot, white-hot, searing down through his seat, the floor, and into the earth and bedrock below.

"Warren, there's someone from the police here to see you" was all the receptionist had said to him, and he struggled for his breath as he answered, "I'll be right out." In the three months since they'd returned from Europe, there hadn't been so much as a peep. It had lulled him into a sense of calm. It only took an instant to shatter into a billion shards, and his composure returned only slowly as he walked to the elevator foyer as if to the gallows.

The familiar and intelligent face of Detective Wittlin peered up from a copy of *Forbes* magazine, which he was flipping through. The round, smiling face of Donald Trump stared out from the open page.

Wittlin closed and dropped the magazine back on the small coffee table and greeted Warren with a handshake. "Hey, sorry to drop in on you unannounced. I needed to talk to you right away." Wittlin swiveled around. "Is there someplace we can go?"

Warren held up a finger. "Mary, are any of the conference rooms open? The detective and I need some privacy."

The receptionist consulted a logbook briefly. "Only the War Room, and only until two."

Warren looked at Wittlin, who nodded approval. "Fine, pencil us in." He showed Wittlin the way, through a set of double glass doors, and down a short hall. The War Room was actually a big conference room, with the most advanced teleconferencing technology available. Every branch office of Weldon had a room just like it. From this room priority sales calls were made, and senior executives could address every employee in the firm simultaneously. It was ridiculously large for just two men, but they sat at the corner of the immense conference table.

"Okay. What is it?" Warren crossed his legs and tried, quite successfully, to look relaxed. His heart was pounding.

"I have something I want you to take a look at." Wittlin reached into his coat pocket and pulled out a manila envelope. He slid out of it a small stack of photographs and handed them to Warren.

They were obviously from a security camera in a building foyer or lobby. A distorted overhead view showed two people, quite clearly Anson Combes and Bonnie, entering the foyer. A second showed a lone figure, head covered by a hat and some kind of face covering, leaving. Warren started to flip through the others, but Wittlin stopped him.

"That's the one I wanted you to see." Wittlin reached for the rest.

"Can I see the others?"

"You don't really want to. They're shots of the body. Pretty rough stuff."

Warren pursed his lips. He was beginning to feel relief—Wittlin was asking about the murder, not about European bank accounts or sham mortgage sales.

"I guess not." Warren studied the shot. The shadowy figure was completely covered by a big parka and the hat. On closer inspection the mask appeared to be a scarf, and Warren could make out some kind of pattern on it. "What can I tell you?"

"We think that's the killer. The timing seems right. No one else in that building remembered going out or having a visitor. It has to be. I wondered if you could tell anything from it?" Wittlin looked Warren square in the eye inquisitively.

"Why'd it take so long to get this? It's been, what, about five months?"

"Yeah. Well, we were checking it out, computer enhancing it, and following up leads. We got nowhere. I figured I'd take a shot and see if anyone else could get something from it." Wittlin shrugged. "We're just about out of gas on this case."

Warren nodded and studied the picture again. Something about it unsettled him. The posture of the man? The scarf? He spent a long minute scanning it before he handed it back. "I'm sorry, Detective. I'd like to help. But I can't see anything there that you can't. It's somebody walking out of a building. Could be anybody, any building."

"I know. Listen, I appreciate you taking the time. I'm afraid I'm going to let you down on this one. Some of the jewelry from the girl's place turned up—the watch anyway, on a kid we arrested uptown. Not a killer, just a pusher. He bought it from a fence we know, who couldn't even remember his own name. Twenty bucks, for a three-thousand-dollar Rolex. A woman's watch, too, on some punk crackhead. Anyway, that makes the B and E look real, and we'll probably scale it down." Wittlin looked sheepish.

"Look, Detective, if it makes you feel any better, Anson Combes was a world-class shit. Nobody liked him, probably not even his wife, who he was cheating on with more women than just Bonnie. Hopefully, she'll get remarried, and her kid will have a decent father. He is not missed around here, I can tell you that." Warren risked the candor because he felt bad for Wittlin.

"I know. It's amazing, everybody says the same thing about that guy. If you had to look at everyone that hated him as a suspect, you'd bring in anyone who ever met the guy. Still, some perp is laughing his ass off at me and may do it again. This fucking job can get on your nerves. Do you know the lab guys identified the hair and skin samples to a black male, probably twenty-five, type O positive blood. There's about a million suspects in that category, just like about sixty percent of the murders in this city. Same basic profile for the guy who killed Dougherty. Similar samples, different blood type, different DNA. We can test for that now.

"So it wasn't the same guy. Just the same act, ending a man's life." Wittlin had gotten up and was slouched over as he talked, disheartened.

"Well, if anything else comes up, I hope I can be of more use next time." Warren held the door for the detective and escorted him back to the elevator landing.

"Thanks again, Mr. Hament. You gotta understand. The DA's office won't arrest anyone without almost a signed confession these days. We have to build an air-tight case. And listen, you be careful, okay? This is a rough city for you bankers these days." Wittlin smiled, and they shook hands again.

"Detective, believe me, everyone here has been a lot more careful since this all happened. Christ, the secretaries have a subway pool—no one rides home alone anymore. Take care." The elevator door closed behind the man, and Warren turned back to the trading floor.

He stopped in the bathroom and washed his face. The fear that had seized him was irrational. He hadn't done anything. Wittlin's inquiry was a wild-goose chase. Still, something in that security photo drew Warren in, something he felt he should have noticed, should have seen. He checked his wallet. Wittlin's card was still there. If it came to him, Warren could call. But, he wondered, if it did, would putting Wittlin on the trail inevitably lead to Faaringsbank, and the snotty little Herr Dohlmer? Or would keeping quiet lead a young, maybe black man with a special mission and a peculiar talent to decide that Warren Hament's house was the next one to burglarize?

fifty

❧

Angelo was surprised to see Warren in the middle of a weekday after-noon. The building had a fair number of retirees and wealthy dilet-tantes, most of whom would often linger for idle chats with the garrulous Italian doorman. He was something of a font of gossip about the building, and if you caught him slightly off guard, or after a lunch that included a little wine, there was no telling what you might find out.

"Hey, Mr. Hament, nice to see you." Angelo touched his cap as he opened the taxi door. He was a little wobbly, a sign that his lunch break had been well catered by Mrs. Ingrisano. Warren generally tried to remember to bring home the tiny service bottles of wine from his plane trips to leave for An-gelo. That way, at least the portion would be small. He knew Angelo's favor-ite was a Sutter Home cabernet.

"Same here, Angelo." Warren climbed out, then paused to check the seat behind him, an old habit that had saved him countless umbrellas and several wallets. "How's tricks? There are some bags in the trunk."

"Not bad, not bad, Mr. Hament." The older man smiled under his salt-and-pepper mustache and motioned to the driver to pop the trunk lid. "Of course, not anything like you. Not at my age." The lascivious grin was meant as a compliment to Warren's taste in women. Sam was definitely a hit with the doormen and car valets on both coasts. Angelo struggled a bit with the two large shopping bags, which were not heavy, and Warren helped him with one.

"Yeah, well, Angelo, you never know. This one looks like it might last a while." He paused in the lobby, a beautiful marble hall with elegant neoclassical moldings and a circular plan. It always irritated Warren that the board of the building was too cheap to give the walls a good cleaning, but the patina of age was not badly served by the layer of dirt. It almost suggested an unearthed ruin, a Pompeian tomb, but with an automatic elevator.

"Oh? I'm happy to hear that. Umm, your most recent...I mean, the young lady...before..." Angelo was lost for a tactful way to refer to Larisa, as he had obviously forgotten her name.

"You mean Larisa, my last girlfriend?" Warren came to his rescue.

"Oh, yes. Exactly. Larisa. Well, I hadn't seen her around for a while, and what with the new one, I sort of figured..." Angelo's grin was huge.

"Well, we'll see, won't we, Angelo?" Warren handed him the $5 bill he'd gotten in change from the cabbie. "See ya."

"Oh, yes. Thank you, Mr. Hament. And good luck!" Angelo called to the closing elevator door.

Sam was out for the day. She'd gone to New Jersey to visit her cousin, a physics professor at Princeton. She'd hit Warren with a ball of socks when he'd asked if they were going to discuss the behavior of high-energy plasma in a supercooled nongravitational state, or just girl talk. He missed her, but there were some things he needed to do, and he'd taken the day off from work. She had been with him for months now, and he'd stocked up at the discount drugstore for himself and picked up some items on her list. He also bought three new pairs of shoes at Bally, which he dropped in the bedroom. He dumped the bags full of shampoo and moisturizers in the bathroom and had just sat down at his desk when the phone rang. He let it ring a second time before he answered it, a habit he'd picked up somewhere along the line.

"Hi. Is this Warren Hament?" The voice on the other end of the line was unfamiliar, a circumstance that had never meant anything to him before. These days, it provoked a distinct bit of anxiety. He acknowledged his own name.

"Hi, Warren. My name is George Charpentier. I'm with Julian Jameson, the executive recruiter. Do you have a second, or is this a bad moment?"

"George, I hope I never have a bad moment. What can I do for you?" Warren couldn't help it; his pulse quickened just a bit. He'd heard about these calls. These were the guys who did all the sniffing around for Street firms looking to raid talent from the competition. The right sniff could mean a multimillion-dollar contract. Warren wasn't sure what his situation might be, but he wanted to listen.

"Well, Warren, we've been retained by an investment bank here in town to help find candidates to build up their sales effort with the top Fixed Income accounts, mostly on the East Coast. Your name came up as a prime prospect. I wonder if you might like to pursue this. I know they'd love to talk to you."

Warren smiled at the *here in town*. He could never see New York as a town. "Well, what kind of firm is it? A major?"

"Well, no. It's a second-tier firm that is starting to invest in a push to move into the top tier. They are extremely strong in retail and have a presence on the institutional side."

"Well, it's hard for me to respond one way or another. I'm pretty happy at Weldon. Before I can say yes or no to talk, I obviously need to know which company it is."

"Sacramento. They've gotten the okay from their parent company to make a three-year campaign to hit the top five. They just hired two top investment bankers from your shop. Senior guys. Generous terms too. They're negotiating right now with a major name to head up Fixed Income. As far as capital is concerned, they've got far more than Weldon, and they're also hiring new traders. It's actually pretty exciting. You could wind up a key guy at a major player in a year or two."

"I know they're a lower-tier firm now, but it's hard to dismiss Sacramento. If the parent company is really behind them, they can't miss. After Pru, they're the biggest financial company in the world." Between the life insurance company and the investment management and mutual funds business, Sacramento Mutual Life controlled $293 billion in assets. They were also one of the biggest clients of Wall Street.

"That's true about Sacremento, but both they and Pru are basically retail shops, they sell to moms and pops, not the big institutional money managers and institutions like we do." Warren couldn't help but have a bit of the bulge-bracket snobbery.

"Yup. That's true. But they want the prestige, and they've gotten sick of letting all the other firms take their fees and business because the investment bank they own can't handle the assignments." The implication of an inside track to Sacramento Life's business was immense.

"Would I get to cover them—the parent company? On commission?"

"It's possible."

The salesman at Weldon who covered Sacramento had earned $1.3 million in net commissions from that one account alone last year, without any favored-nation status. "Who would I be meeting?"

"The first guy would be Bill Cunningham. He's the head of Fixed Income Sales and Trading. Then Jack McDougal, National Sales manager. After that, it's up to them."

"What's their background?"

"Well, they both came from B. H. Koger, I believe, when it broke up."

Koger had been a reasonably successful company about ten or fifteen years before, Warren knew, that specialized in trading US treasury bonds and agency debt, such as the paper of the Federal Home Loan Banks or Fannie Mae. It had been dissolved when it suffered some big losses and its partners pulled their capital before it was completely wiped out. He didn't know much about the firm other than that its ex-traders had populated many of the Street's trading desks after the blowup, and that most of them had retired by now or been fired. They were dinosaurs from an earlier age when margins were bigger, and the amount of money that had to be made to be considered a successful trader was measured in the single millions, not in the tens or hundreds. They were also known as an Irish firm.

"Do these people know anything about mortgages or corporates? Or are they just agency traders and retail geeks?"

"Ask them." George clearly wanted to get Warren in the door for the interview, as any good headhunter would. You can't make a sale if the customer isn't in the store.

"You know, George, I don't think so. I think I'm going to pass."

"Really? Warren, this is a huge financial powerhouse, and they'd be ready to guarantee you much more than you made this year against commissions that could easily double or triple your pay." Charpentier was not about to give up.

"George, I get it. This was my first year making any real money. I'm cheap right now. I should be able to double my take-home next year at Weldon. So, they'd be getting me low. I made a million bucks this year. If they'd guarantee me two point five per for two years with a bigger payout *and* covering

Sacramento along with two of the top-five pensions and another insurer in the top five and one in the top ten, we could talk. Otherwise, I'm only interested in a bulge bracket firm." Warren had no interest working at a third-rate firm. They were filled with third-raters and legal departments that treated their own employees like the enemy, waiting for the chance to screw them.

"Jeez, Warren, you sure you're not a trader? Those are some pretty steep terms." George was a bit deflated.

"Hey, I didn't call you. But I do have a question for you."

"Sure, what's that?"

"I heard you are consulting with Merrill on their associates program?" The giant investment shop had recently started overhauling how it hired college graduates, looking to broaden its reach from just the top colleges.

"Yes, I am. They're looking for college grads outside the usual finance or econ majors."

"Well, there's a kid I interviewed here the other day who was really exceptional, but it turns out he can't work here because his mother does." This wasn't true, but Warren figured a good turn for someone made up for a fib.

"Really? So?" George actually sounded vaguely interested.

"Well, I think he'd be a great fit for Merrill. He understood mortgage derivatives amazingly well for a college kid, and I know those guys are trying to beef up. You really should get him in there ASAP. I liked him, and I like his mom a lot. Whether or not things work out for me. His name is Harold Baker. His mom is a great lady." Warren had given Annlois a thick publication on derivatives to send to her son and hoped he'd actually read it.

"Hey, seriously, that's great! I was just talking to the head of the program, and he was saying he wished they could use recruiters to screen all the applicants! Harold Baker. Tell him to send me his résumé, and I'll get him into the rotation." Warren liked the way headhunters called themselves executive recruiters. "I'm sorry you're not interested in Sacramento. Let me know if you think any of your colleagues might be."

"Have you talked to Alex?" Warren figured something like this might appeal to the perennially depressed mortgage trader.

"Hah! Many times. He's afraid of his own shadow. I had him two mil at

Bear Stearns last year and he said no. He's a hopeless waste of time who would rather complain than do anything."

The two signed off, and still at his desk, Warren paid a few bills, then went to unpack the new shoes and toss the boxes. They were identical black wing tips, and he took the old, worn ones and stuffed them in the bag, making a mental note to see if one of the doormen wore his size. They weren't in bad shape, but Warren had decided that buying new shoes every year or two wasn't too big an indulgence. Not for a big hitter like him.

fifty-one

❧

Warren felt like a nominee on Oscar night. Everything seemed to take forever. He was impatient, waiting for the moment, and everyone else was just lollygagging along. The past couple of months at work had drive him crazy, even the frantic trading floor seemed to move in slow motion. Sam noticed his agitation and tried to soothe him, but he was inconsolable. She said he was getting her all worked up too and wondered if he wasn't just trying to transfer his anxiety to her. He denied it, but had to admit she was perceptive. He wanted her tensed up. This situation had to resolve itself eventually. Two men were dead, over $200 million was sitting in a foreign bank, and there had been no closure. He couldn't stand it. It had been over six months, and everything seemed quiet.

At the office, he told everyone how happy he was. He had a gorgeous girl-friend living with him, and they were getting along great. Sam had started taking graduate-level classes at NYU in Art History and Finance. Kerry made gagging sounds when he brought in three framed photos of Sam, including one of them together, laughing at the top of a ski run in the German Alps.

He called Frank Malloran, who had heard all about him and Larisa, and was anxious to meet Sam. Warren asked if Malloran thought that the four of them should go out sometime. Frank said he'd ask Karen, but thought it might be a little awkward for her. He was willing to try, but sisters tended to stick together, and she might still be on Larisa's side. He told Warren that Karen had commented that it didn't take Warren long to find someone new, and someone so pretty.

"God. It was Larisa's doing. She was screwing some hotshot in Dallas. I'm not proud. She broke my heart." Warren paused, his eyes hot. It was the first time he'd ever admitted this to anyone, and maybe even to himself. He preferred not to spread around that he knew about her and Anson. "Things weren't great, but I loved that girl...uh...woman. See? I probably still do just a little. I feel sick every time I see her, even though Sam is a twelve in every way—definitely a huge trade up. Larisa may say she still loves me, or something, but, look—she's a lot more calculating than I am. My conscience is clear, but my soul is still busted."

"I know, that's what I said too. You might be the only truly nice guy in this business. But, let's just...I tell you what. I'll take you two out alone. What do you say? No Karen, no stress. okay?" Frank sounded buoyant.

"Okay. Next week. I'll check in with you." They agreed and hung up. Warren sat and contemplated for a moment. He had wanted Karen to meet Sam, get a good look at her and report to Larisa. Why? What good would it do? It was hard for him to sort out his feelings about Larisa, but throwing Sam in her face for no reason would be pointless and mean to both of them. Maybe Frank knew that and was trying to avoid being involved in such a stupid plan. He was a great guy—maybe Frank was wrong about Warren and he wasn't so nice after all.

As luck would have it, it all made little difference. A week later, Warren called Sam up and said he'd be a little late at the office. He asked her if she would meet him for a drink, and maybe a bite. She agreed and came by on schedule at six thirty. He showed her around the empty floor, then escorted her downstairs and into the bar of the charming Italian place just across the street. He ordered two dry martinis, then two more, and was nuzzling Sam's neck and talking about skipping dinner, which Sam rejected, when a big group of Weldon Brothers finance people came through the front door. Warren saw Larisa before she saw him and quickly became fully absorbed in what Sam was saying. He could actually feel it when Larisa's glance fell on them.

She surprised him. She strode right up to the bar, and smiled at him. "Well, Warren Hament. I'll be damned." She laughed warmly and patted his arm. "How are you?"

"Oh. Umm, great. Great! Larisa, this is Sam. Larisa's an old friend." Sam threw him a fiery look, then turned and greeted Larisa with a firm handshake and a smile. He watched the two take each other in. His own comparison confirmed his feelings. Sam was a little older than Larisa, and life had given her more reason to be jaded and bitter, but it didn't show. There was, at once, strength and vulnerability. He knew Larisa could see it too. Sam was formidable. She was smart, beautiful, and confident.

"Hi. Warren has told me quite a bit about you. It's nice to meet you." Sam disengaged her hand and tossed her hair slightly. "He says you're the smartest woman he knows."

Larisa smiled at the comment and looked at Warren. "Well, maybe he doesn't know that many women."

"I've always been of the opinion that one can never really know a woman anyway," Warren said, and dipped his head a little as if dodging a punch.

"Well, it was nice to meet you, Sam. And good to see you, Warren. I've got to join the group. Keep in touch." Larisa's jocularity was so practiced that it took a sharp ear to hear that it was forced in any way.

Sam watched Larisa as she walked away. "Well, now I know why you brought me here. Want to tell me what this was all about?" Sam looked at him, more curious than angry.

"I swear to God, I had no idea she would come in here!" Warren had had a tight smile pasted to his face, which now faded to an exhausted grimace.

"Come on. Cut the crap. What was this all about? You have something going on. I want to know." Sam prodded him with a finger.

"No, I really don't. I'm not that strategic a thinker."

"Maybe you should be. She seems to be, from what you've told me. Man, I wouldn't want to piss her off. Anyway, she certainly is attractive. Great calves."

Warren was always amazed at the details women noticed about other women. He figured whatever they were self-conscious about on their own body was what they noticed in others.

"Are you kidding me? You've got the best legs in Christendom. Much better than hers. A national treasure!" Warren wasn't passing an idle comment. Sam's legs were a great natural resource, her upper thighs thin and muscled, almost concave.

"Flatterer. I'm starved. No way I'm skipping dinner. Can we eat somewhere else?" Sam nodded her head toward the back.

Warren didn't reply. He was lost in thought. Strategic thought, he mused. Something had just lit up the inside of his skull like a bonfire.

"Hellooo? Food? I'm asking for sustenance? Anyone home?" Sam waved her hand in front of his eyes.

"Wait. Gimme a sec. I'm thinking about something." Warren put up a finger.

"Hah! I thought I smelled something burning." Sam shrugged and contemplated her drink for a second, then fished the last olive out of his glass.

Warren came back to life with a start. "You know, I suddenly got this idea. If I'm right, maybe the pressure is off. If I'm wrong, all I did was piss off an old girlfriend. Trust me?" He drained what was left of his martini. Sam stared at him for a moment, sifting his tone, the look in his eyes. She broke the eye contact first. "Whatever it is, I'm in. I've come this far. To hell with it, you only live once, right?"

"That's what they say."

"I always thought the lottery was for suckers," she said, still chewing.

"Ever win anything?" he asked, more than a little edginess in his voice.

"Two bucks, once. One of those instant poker games."

"This is a bigger ticket. And it costs more than a buck to play." Warren tried to force a grin.

"And I think we've overextended that metaphor just about to death. Just let me know when it's over, okay?" Sam plopped her napkin on the bar in the universal signal that it was time to go.

"Hey, you know what? I think you're going to be there. I think you're going to know."

"Oh, boy. Something to look forward to," she said sarcastically. "What I'm thinking is lobster."

fifty-two

～

Like most social engagements for people in their business, five or six weeks passed, but Frank called Warren, and reminded him about that dinner. Karen wanted to come after all. The Post House is just off Park Avenue on East Sixty-Third Street, an elegant version of the traditional New York steak house, befitting its location in the middle of the most expensive residential real estate in Manhattan. The two couples arrived almost simultaneously and checked their coats. Karen lingered a moment to be certain that her fur got a wood hanger, then they headed into the dining room. Every male head swiveled when she and Sam led the foursome to their table. Karen's height and blond hair made her an obvious object of admiration, but Sam was dazzling. She had, at Warren's insistence, tied her hair back with a black velvet bow and worn a short and tight dark green velvet dress they'd picked out at Valentino, with her new earrings. She wouldn't let Warren pay for it, as usual. She wore almost no makeup and looked elegant, sophisticated, and sexy. The two men couldn't help but swagger a bit as they followed along.

The first half of the meal saw the two friends playing catch-up after that entrance. Sam snagged the wine list and after a brief perusal commanded a magnum of Château Palmer, 1966. The captain's eyebrows went up, not so much at the price tag, but at the sophistication of the choice. It was actually a bargain, an unreplaceable gem from a good vineyard.

Sam looked at Warren with a sly grin. "Hey, before my ex stole all my dough, he taught me how to spend it on what I drank. Oh," she added, turning back to the captain, "please open that right away and decant it. And be sure that the glasses are rinsed and dried before you pour it."

"Now, I forgot, which one were you again, Ernest or Julio?" Frank cracked with a smile.

"In this town, more like Joey and Kid Blast," Sam rejoined.

Warren never ceased to be amazed by Sam's library of arcane facts. "Jesus, how do you know about the Gallo brothers?"

"*Desire.* That and *Blood on the Tracks* are probably Dylan's greatest albums," Sam replied.

"'*Born in Red Hook, Brooklyn, in the year of who knows when . . . ,*'" Frank sang in a nasal imitation of Bob Dylan.

"'King of the streets,' Joey Gallo," Warren added. "Great song!"

"Well, maybe you'll be King of the Street, anyway." Frank laughed as he said it. "Until someone comes and blows you away."

"Well, Sam already does that," Warren responded, and took Sam's hand as he said it.

"Awwwwwwwww," Sam said, and leaned over to give him a peck on the cheek. The sommelier arrived with a large bottle of wine and made a ceremony out of preparing the neck of the bottle and operating a simple corkscrew.

"An excellent choice, madam," he intoned ceremonially as he handed her the cork.

"Yeah," Karen chimed in, "it's nice to have someone along who knows more than just the highest price."

"Hey, given what's been going on, blowing away you Wall Street guys is no joke anymore," Sam said, nodding to the server. He began decanting the wine into a crystal carafe while examining the thin red stream in front of a lit candle on his tray.

Frank looked at Warren and shrugged. Sam and Karen launched into an analysis of the menu, debating lobsters versus steaks versus lamb chops. Sam suggested that women who weren't sexually satisfied generally ordered steaks. Karen said she felt like the double-cut porterhouse. Sam called the busboy over and asked if she could have a whole-rib roast. He looked at her in utter confusion.

"Okay, okay, you two, c'mon. We give up." Warren waved his napkin like a white flag. Then he steered the conversation to the trip that Frank and Karen were planning to Anguilla. Frank could be counted to be on the cutting edge of resorts—if it was about to become a hot spot, he'd just gotten back.

"Yeah, well, last year we went to this neat place on the Pacific coast of Mexico. It was built by Goldsmith's daughter—you know, the Englishman who owns about a thousand square miles down there. It was great, but the water was too rough. This year, we're trying this spot called Malliouhana if it opens on time. Sounds more laid-back."

"The beach looks great, the rooms are supposed to be amazing, and we're just going to go and relax," Karen added.

"Sounds awesome. It is interesting, though, how one of the big topics of conversation in this town is getting out of here." Sam had noticed this about New Yorkers. "I mean, in LA everyone's always talking about real estate or movie parts or other people's sex lives. Here it's all about vacations and summer houses."

"Well, generally, that's because life is so miserable here that the only thing that makes it worthwhile is going away," Warren explained.

"And no one except us has a sex life," Frank chimed in.

"So why don't you just live somewhere else?" Sam replied.

"Because it's the only place we can do what we do and get paid so much to do it," Frank said with a grimace.

"Do you really like living in LA so much?" Karen asked Sam.

"No. I actually hate it. But I was doing pretty well there, then my boyfriend ran off with my life savings, and I'm stuck with a house I can't sell in this market, and that's where my car business is. So, I've gotta stick around there, for now." Sam took her first sip of the wine, which had been breathing for a few minutes. "Wow!" She nodded approval and the sommelier poured everyone a bloodred glass.

"Where would you rather live?" Frank asked pointedly.

"Well"—Sam looked at Warren—"I kind of like New York, except for the cold weather. San Diego is nice. I could live just about anywhere, to be honest. I love Europe too. Didn't you live in Geneva?" Sam lobbed the conversation back to Karen, and it bounced around through the crab cocktails and well into the steaks and the dregs of the wine, which grew into a massive, powerful, and mature claret the equal of any of the great first growths. Sam and Frank had a too-long debate over what had led to the downfall of the LA Rams as a franchise, and then everyone had agreed to split a single piece of cheesecake with coffee.

Out in the cold air, they paired off, with the two men smoking good-size Cuban Romeo y Julieta cigars that Frank had brought in from Montreal, and Karen and Sam strolling about twenty paces ahead. The car that Warren had hired for the night followed them as they walked up Madison Avenue.

"That's some hell of a girl you found yourself there, pal," Frank said, exhaling a cloud of fragrant smoke over his shoulder.

"Yeah. I think so too. You think that Karen will be able to tolerate her?" Warren had noticed her warming up to Sam as the evening progressed.

"Well, like you said, it was Larisa who was screwing around. I mean, loyalty to your sister is a great thing, but, in this case, I think she'll get past it."

"What do you think she'll tell Larisa?"

"I'm sure she'll tell her you two look like a match. She knows it won't serve any purpose to try to protect Larisa's feelings, if she still has any. That ain't exactly what I'd call a sensitive Susie." Frank smiled and tried, unsuccessfully, to blow a smoke ring.

Warren snapped off two perfect halos and flicked the ash off his cigar. "That's the understatement of the year. It's funny how I seem to have totally misjudged her. I guess people aren't who or what you want to believe they are."

They walked on in silence.

"It seems like you two guys may be in it for the long haul," Warren broke in.

"It could be. It very well could be. It's a frightening concept." Frank rolled the cigar in his fingers. "I never thought I'd even consider a second shot."

"Hey, that's what marriage is all about, right? You'll never know unless you take a chance." Warren thought about his parents. They had seemed so perfectly complementary, and yet it didn't last.

"Now, let me see. Do I detect a hint of rationalization in that statement? Am I imagining things, *ahem*, or are you saying what I think you're saying?"

Frank elbowed the smaller man in the side, and he stumbled to regain his balance.

"Well, we haven't talked about it or anything, but it's a distinct possibility. Hey, I'm circling thirty. That's old enough."

"I think that'd be great. Listen, I had some SC buddies check her out. This girl has a sterling rep. One of them almost had a heart attack when I told him my friend was seeing her. Word is she told Warren Beatty to get lost once when she was like eighteen! Hey, we could do one of those double ceremonies. Very sixties." Frank waved his hands in the air in a gesture evidently meant to be psychedelic.

"Nah, I'm too young for that. If I get married, I'm going to have it performed by some shaman from a primitive tribe somewhere where there's lots of ocean and blue sky. With maybe six people there."

Up ahead of them, Sam and Karen were having a similar conversation. Karen had confessed that she wanted to marry Frank, and that she would have Warren to thank for the introduction.

"Warren set you guys up?" Sam was a bit surprised.

"Yup. He was dating Larisa then, and Frank had been divorced from his first wife for a while. She left him for his boss. It was pretty ugly."

Sam hugged herself against a cold blast of wind and idly stared at a display of wild, unwearable clothes in the window of the Gianni Versace boutique. "What happened with Warren and Larisa? He doesn't talk about it much."

"Well, from what she tells me, he dumped her right before he met you. From what Frank tells me, Warren caught her having an affair with someone else. Knowing my sister, he probably did catch her, but she probably wanted to have her cake and eat it too. She always knew how to pick a winner, but also hedge her bets. I personally think she made a big mistake. Warren's a pretty great guy. Are you two serious? It seems like it to me."

"I think so. Do you really think she was cheating on him? I'd hate to think he dumped her for no reason. She seemed to be a little pissed at him when we ran into her the other day." Sam brushed the hair out of her face. "I mean, the last guy I trusted basically destroyed me emotionally and financially. I don't want to go through that again."

"It wouldn't surprise me. She always had a couple of guys on the line in high school. In college, she dated half the football team—actually led most of them on. Guys literally used to fight over her. I think she's actually pissed off that she got caught. Now, she doesn't have a fallback if the other guy, whoever he is, doesn't work out."

"Your sister sounds like a real sweetheart." Sam couldn't help but notice the undercurrent of disapproval in Karen's voice.

"Well, let's just say that she deserves whatever she gets. Years ago, I was dating a great guy. He was on the UN staff, from Rhodesia. Great looking, from a wealthy family, and with his heart in the right place. He spent three years working against apartheid in South Africa, even though he kept getting death threats. It was like living with Gandhi, but he looked like Dirk Bogarde and drove an Aston Martin. Larisa met him when she came to visit me in New York right before I went to Geneva. I was working one weekend, and he takes her out to dinner because I had to help prepare a speech for the Ambassador. She gets him drunk and takes him back to his apartment and sleeps with him. Of course, Mr. Saint has to tell me about it because he feels so guilty."

"Gee. Sleeping with your sister's boyfriend is definitely not too cool."

"Yeah. And once I knew about it, what am I supposed to do? He said they got back to the apartment and she started crawling all over him, and after all, he's a man, and she was this nubile little teenager. She always had those big boobs, too. She got them for both of us. I mean, it isn't like you can continue a relationship with a man who has slept with your sister. So, that ended it, and she apologized and everything, but I know she still kept seeing him. He was in an ambush in Soweto last year and lost a leg. So he suffered, but not old Larisa. We had a tragedy in our family when we were kids, and Larisa has always thought my parents blamed her. Somehow she managed to turn my brother's death into being about *her.*" Karen's words came out in a torrent, and Sam could hear the pain and bile just behind them.

"Jeez. I had no idea," Sam responded. "Warren said that he didn't think you'd come to dinner because you were angry at him over what happened with Larisa. I guess he was misinformed."

"I wasn't going to come because I was worried that I'd have to sit around and defend my sister. Warren's a great guy, and Frank thinks Larisa really screwed him over. I'm tired of doing that. She gets what she wants when she wants it and thinks five moves ahead. She thinks that what happened to our brother gives her a pass for any kind of behavior. So I decided that I wanted to meet you. All Frank ever talks about is how pretty you are, and I wanted to see for myself so I could tell Larisa how Warren's got a gorgeous new girlfriend, and they're so happy together. I know she'll call for the details. And I'm going to give 'em to her, in spades. She hates losing."

"I don't think it was a competition, but thanks anyway." Sam smiled at the compliment, and they walked on quietly for a block. Warren and Frank had stepped up their pace and caught them at the corner of Seventy-second Street, in front of the Ralph Lauren store that had opened in a huge French neo-Renaissance mansion.

"I've had enough. Let's take the car, okay?" Warren was feeling a little woozy from the wine, beef, and cigars, even in the bracing air.

"You guys go ahead. We'll make it on foot from here." Frank's apartment was four blocks away, on Seventy-fifth off Park.

"Okay. Hey, it was great to get out with you two. You set an example for us. Young love and all that. At your age, Frank, infatuation takes the years off." Warren gave him a playful shove.

"Well, you're hardly the one to talk. Sam, it was absolutely our pleasure. You make sure he gets tucked in early so he can sell lots of bonds bright and early tomorrow. The fate of the free world hangs in the balance."

"In that case," Sam said, "the free world better have a contingency plan." She accepted Frank's hug, and a kiss on the cheek from Karen. "That really is one hell of a coat," Sam said to Karen as they separated.

"Thanks. You two be good, now. Oh, and let us know where you're going to register, would you?" Karen gave Warren a big hug and whispered in his ear, "She's great. Larisa never should have let you get away."

Warren waved at them as they walked off, arm in arm, and when he turned, Sam was holding the door of the car open for him. "All this time, and I'm still holding doors for you," she said. He half tackled her into the backseat and mumbled the address to the driver, asking him to take the park drive, then burrowed into the nape of her neck.

"I say Tiffany and Christofle." Warren gave her a light kiss on the lips.

"What?" The taxi had entered Central Park on Seventy-second Street and Fifth Avenue, and the light covering of snow that had fallen a few days before made the lampposts into pools of soft light in a sea of white.

"I said I think that Tiffany for china and Christofle for silver would be timeless, yet sophisticated choices."

"What on earth are you talking about?"

"If you even want to go through all that. Personally, I'd rather just do the deed and buy our own stuff. I don't have that many friends, anyway."

"Excuse me, but did I miss something here?" The driver had merged to the left and was coming up the slight rise to the Bethesda Fountain.

"Say, driver, would you do me a favor?" Warren leaned into the front seat. "Just pull over on the right up here for one second. I just want to show my girlfriend the view up here. She's from out of town."

"Yeah, okay, but hurry up. The park's not safe at night, and I don't wanna hang around too long."

"What's going on? Why are we stopping in the middle of nowhere?" Sam looked a little apprehensive.

"There's this great view right up here, by the balustrade over there. It's amazing at night, with the ice and the snow." He opened the door as the car stopped. "Just for a second. Nobody'll be out in this cold. We're safe."

At the top of the hill, a wide, brick esplanade led to two immense stone staircases that descended to a large, circular piazza. The Bethesda Fountain was a Victorian landmark, with a soaring statue of a winged female figure. Although the water had been drained for the winter, it was illuminated by floodlights, and from the balustrade between the staircases, a sweeping view of the lagoon, iced over, but reflecting the towers of Central Park West, unfolded, a peaceful and private vista on a deserted winter night.

"This *is* pretty," Sam said as they leaned on the stone railing for a moment.

"Yes, it's beautiful. This was my favorite spot in the whole city as a kid." The tension in Warren's voice made her turn to him. He kissed her fully and held her against him for a long moment. "I love you, Sam."

She could see the emotion in his eyes, and she stroked the side of his face. "I love you too," she said simply. They stood like that for a moment.

"There's something I need to tell you. It's important." He took the hand that was on his neck and kissed it.

"What? Tell me."

"Okay." He took a deep breath and drew his other hand out of his coat pocket. In it was a ring, a platinum band with diamonds set in a pattern of steps, which he pressed into her palm. "I want you to marry me. I want to marry you. I love you more than anyone I have ever known, and I don't want to wait until someone or something comes between us." He stopped and saw the reaction on her face. There was some surprise, but he could see the tears come up in her eyes.

She looked at the ring in her hand, then took it in her fingers and put it on. "And I have something to tell you." She looked up at him, with tears now streaming down her cheeks.

"Tell me."

"There is nothing in the world that I want more. I want to marry you."

They came together again for a long kiss. They were both smiling.

"You know, the first time I ever saw a girl naked, I was standing right here," he said.

"When was that?" She wiped away the tears, grateful for the transition.

"I think it was around 1968 or '69. There was a moratorium—an antiwar protest—here, and a bunch of hippies climbed the statue and took off their clothes. I think I was about ten or eleven." The memory was vivid in his head, the warm summer day, the bongo drums, anti-Johnson chants, and the smell of pot smoke and horse manure from the mounted police. It seemed as if only a minute had passed, yet it was a million miles away.

She took his arm, and they turned back to the car. "I bet you were the cutest little boy at the moratorium," she said, and for twenty yards, they were both children again, their dreams still ahead of them, in a night that held no threats, only promises.

fifty-three

❧

It was hard not to feel silly, with the sunglasses and the driving gloves, but they were both practical, and she looked great. The engine made a growling sound as she ran through the gears, accelerating up the entrance ramp onto the Northern State Parkway, then punching the throttle and easing into the left lane. A serene, almost blissful look was on her face as she banked into a right-hand curve after a quick downshift, gaining speed through the turn and topping ninety on the empty road.

Warren had turned off the radio, wanting to enjoy the whine of the exhaust and eliminate any distraction for her. He was settled down into his seat, with a light mohair blanket on his lap, relaxed, enjoying the scenery as it sped by.

When Robert Moses had constructed this highway through the heart of Long Island, he had claimed enough land on either side to guarantee a permanent buffer of trees and woodland. Even now, in late winter, one could rarely see any sign of civilization other than the roadway and its signage, and in light traffic it was like a personal touring track.

Warren had agreed to deliver the car to East Hampton for Cornelia Harper, who offered them the use of her house for the weekend as recompense, although the drive alone would have sufficed. The Aston Martin DB5 belonged to Ray Karr, Austin's dad, and Cornelia was storing it for him in her garage. Chas had confided in Warren that his mother and Ray Karr had been seeing a bit of each other, and the car had been the only thing Ray's ex-wife had let him take from their house in Far Hills. He and Cornelia had taken off for the Alps and asked Chas to look after it. When Warren mentioned that he and Sam had been planning to spend the weekend in Montauk, Chas had hatched the alternative plan.

The powerful Aston was perfectly maintained, and they'd agreed to split the driving. At the speed she was going, though, her forty-five minutes would get them most of the way. Although he spent so much of his childhood there, it was difficult to recognize much of the Hamptons. In the daylight, unlike on the trip he'd taken before with Larisa, he'd was disgusted at the way the land had been developed, the houses springing up like deformed shoe boxes in flat potato fields, the Hollywood types and Wall Streeters competing for who could build the most square footage. As with so many other places, the conversations he heard about the Hamptons sounded like supermarket talk—everyone was simply comparing house prices, just as they did with their art collections and their takeover bids.

Warren decided to let Sam do all the driving. She was enjoying herself, and he would get to look out the windows. Plus, she was a much, much better driver than he would ever be. When they reached Southampton, he directed her to the back roads, rather than the main highway, so she could enjoy the driving, and he could investigate the changes. They went down Flying Point Road in Water Mill, then back to Cobb Road and across the highway again. Everywhere, Warren saw the ungainly developments and the new houses shoehorned in next to two-hundred-year-old shingled farm-houses and manors. The old Henry Ford estate had been converted into a dozen monstrous white elephants, with spindly trees already dying from the underestimated winds and salt spray. In Sagaponack, smaller, cheaper versions nestled on sparsely vegetated cul-de-sacs. They stopped briefly at the old general store that sat among the fields on Sagg Main Street, and Warren was amazed to see a display of designer food and a half dozen $30 pies where he'd once found only bottles of Coke and sandwiches made on Wonder bread. A snack cost twelve bucks, but he had to admit the seafood salad was fresh.

From the general store, it was only a few minutes back to the highway, then down Buckskill Lane to Baiting Hollow and Hedges and they were on Lee Avenue. A left, then a quick right, and they found the Harpers' at the end of Terbell Lane—a large, but not massive, shingle-style house sur-rounded by trees on a slight rise overlooking Hook Pond and, farther on, the

Atlantic. As promised, the garage was unlocked, and Warren hoisted the door for Sam to drive in. He grabbed the two green duffel bags from the tiny boot and located the front-door key in the Martinson's coffee can on the floor. The gravel crunched under their feet as they crossed back to the house, which felt warm and cozy once he had gotten the door open and the lights turned on.

Gal Harper had bought the Terbell house almost fifty years before, eschewing the grand manors on Lily Pond Lane and Lee Avenue. Like Ray Karr, he didn't want oceanfront property on a flat, unprotected sandbar, as he referred to Long Island, and he wouldn't have owned a house there at all except that his wife liked to spend summers on the East End. He had given the house to his daughter on her twenty-fifth birthday and, once his wife passed away, had never visited again.

His first child, Peter, a fullback at Yale and his heir, had broken his neck and drowned while bodysurfing at the Main Beach in a summer squall in 1947. His body had washed ashore and lain unnoticed for several hours until a local boy, out digging for crabs, had stumbled across it. After that day, Gal Harper almost always had an excuse to stay in the city or travel to Maine in the summer.

Cornelia Harper had mourned her older brother just as she mourned her younger brother when he died in Korea. She had worn black and been sad, even though Peter had been a bully and beaten her up until he'd been sixteen, and Charles had always resented her. She had taken photographs of her two brothers to a portrait painter on Park Avenue, and the two canvases hung in the dining room in East Hampton in curious homage to sudden and untimely death.

A note from the caretaker was on the foyer table, which Warren read out loud as they toured the house. Three main rooms were on the first floor, all with large picture windows, which opened out to the lawn, the marsh, and the dunes beyond. The kitchen was surprisingly modern and bright, and a small library was tucked into the eastern corner of the house, with French doors that opened to a summer garden, now evidenced only by the neat flagstone grid and canvas-covered evergreens that delineated its beds and borders.

As he read, Sam opened the refrigerator, well stocked, as promised. They climbed the stairs to the master bedroom, an L-shaped space with gabled ceilings, decorated in hunter green and white, with toile-de-Jouy wallpaper and delicately flowered curtains. Two piles of towels were laid out in the master bathroom, which had wide, chestnut plank floors and Portuguese tile around the sink and bath, which sat by another large window open to the wetland vista.

They also poked their heads into the five other bedrooms, each immaculate, carefully decorated, and cheerful. The house had an air of space and comfort, not ostentation or great wealth. The only people meant to be entertained in this house were its occupants and a few close friends. Warren and Sam felt at ease. The architect, a hundred-odd years earlier, had understood how to design rooms and proportions that did not intimidate or confine.

"I think this will do," Sam said happily, plopping down on the cream-colored sofa in the living room. "I am very happy here."

"Yeah. This is pretty easy to take." Warren was poking around in the liquor cabinet and found an open bottle of single-malt Scotch. "Care for a small drink?"

He poured them each an inch of the liquor and nestled down next to her on the couch. "I guess it pays to have incredibly wealthy friends with great houses."

"I guess. I can't believe you grew up out here."

"Why not? Besides, we left when I was pretty young. And our house would have fit in the garage here."

"I don't know. It seems so Puritan out here or something. Like the natives are all fishermen or oystermen or something like that. Were you some kind of quahog-digger or something?" She was taking the tiniest sips of the strong Scotch. "Jesus, this stuff tastes like Sterno that's been strained through peat moss."

"Aye, lassie, that's the bite of the true Highlands," Warren said in a decent Scottish brogue.

She laughed and put the drink down on the walnut coffee table. She thought twice and picked the glass back up, slipping one of the magazines underneath it to protect the finish. The smile faded, and her expression shifted slightly.

"What is it?" Warren picked up on the change immediately.

"Look, we, like, never talk about it, but I think we ought to. I mean, it's not just some fantasy or something. That trip was real. Those bank accounts were real. That money *is* real. What are you going to do with it? What is your plan?" She sat up and looked at him. "We can't just pretend none of it ever happened."

Warren nodded and sipped his drink. "I know. I know. You're right. It is real. Very real. And I do have a plan. Look, I don't know if anyone is looking for that money. There's been nothing unusual at the office, and it's been a pretty long time. No inquiries, no questions, nothing. Nothing at the banks either, as far as I can tell. They're still doing business. I think Warner's going to go under eventually, but it may take a while yet. The money isn't going anywhere. If everything works out, maybe we keep it or donate it to charity or something. If not, maybe they'll find it and figure out a way to take it back. Just so long as are not connected to it until it's all over. There's just one piece that's missing."

"What's that exactly?"

"Who killed Anson and Bill. Somebody killed them both, and I don't believe it was a coincidence. If it weren't for my alibis, the cops would have arrested me for it. I think they may figure I hired someone to do it. It doesn't matter, though, because they'll never be able to prove that I did."

"Because you didn't, right? I mean, I'm not engaged to a murderer, right? You're not going to knock me off for the insurance or anything, are you?"

"What insurance?"

"The life insurance you want to take out on me."

"I don't want to take out any life insurance on you. What are you talking about?" Warren turned to face her, completely flabbergasted.

"Come on. I got that letter and application from your company's insurance agent."

"You're kidding me, right?" Warren was smiling. "Good joke."

"Warren, I'm dead serious. I thought it was nice, you adding me to your medical coverage. And I thought it was generous that Weldon allows you to insure your fiancée."

"They don't. I didn't. I mean, I would, but I didn't. What application? Did you send it in?"

"No, not yet. What do you mean you didn't send me the application? If you didn't, who did?" She was sitting straight up.

"I don't know. But it sounds like a problem."

"A problem? Someone sends me an insurance application? That's a weird problem. I can see how you'd be concerned if I'd made an appointment to talk to a salesman or something. Actually, that's worse than dying. But who would bother?"

"Someone who is trying to set me up?"

"But set you up for what? Dental coverage?"

"Think about it for a minute." He tapped his head.

"Oh, thanks for pointing. I forgot where to think." Sam paused for a moment. It was obvious. "But, if they were trying to set you up to look like you killed me, isn't it a little simpleminded? What difference could a half a million dollars make? No one would believe you'd want to kill me to collect a half a million bucks of insurance. That's no money to you big investment bankers."

"An obvious setup might be something a clever guy like me would do to cover his tracks."

"You read too many cheap mystery books. Jesus. Take out insurance on me to make you a suspect, but then point out that you're way too smart and sophisticated to do something so stupid, therefore the insurance policy would actually have been a way to prove it wasn't you. And you'd get to keep the money."

"The application itself could start a fight. You could start to suspect me. Who the hell knows? All I know is that you could be in trouble. Or I could. I can. There's too much money at stake here. I don't get it. Why try to set me up? These are some very confusing bad guys. Why don't they just ask for the fucking money back? It's not like I can tell anyone about it. They could threaten me. Threaten you. My mother. My father. Kneecap me. Break my fingers one at a time. Disfigure my face. Offer to kill me quick and painlessly if I tell them without a struggle. I'd crack eventually."

"I've got news for you. You've already cracked. Boy. I thought you had a plan."

"I thought I did too. Hmmm. Insurance policy? It just doesn't make sense. Unless..."

"Hey, maybe someone in your benefits department heard you were engaged and sent you the insurance forms. Maybe you're paranoid," Sam said.

"Maybe. Probably. Or, it could just be a warning. Threatening you."

"I can take care of myself."

"Yeah. But two people who were pretty tough business are already dead. I think this is gonna have to work itself out soon, or I'm going to just kill myself so I won't have to deal with the anxiety."

"Oh. Okay. How much insurance is there on you? Can I be the beneficiary? Are you worth more dead or alive?"

"Nice. Let's go check out that bed up there, then you can answer that question. All this thinking is wearing me out." Warren stood up and stretched.

"Why is it every time you say you're tired, I wind up feeling like I'm in some nature show about rutting antelopes or wildebeests?'

"I dunno. Meet me in the *Wild Kingdom*. I'm going to take a shower and think all this over." He tugged her up off the couch, and he tickled her as they climbed the stairs.

"Hey! Cut it out!" She whacked him on the shoulder. "You're gonna get it!"

"That's what I'm afraid of...." They turned down the hall, giggling, for the time being.

fifty-four

❧

When he got back to work the next week, he had a busy schedule. First, Warren asked Annlois to book him on a flight to Los Angeles and reserve a room for three nights at the Beverly Wilshire. He told Malcolm that he needed to catch up on things with the banks, that Karlheinz had asked him to come out and review their strategies for the new year, and that he would stop in at Golden State as well. To build up some background, he put in a call to Bill Scherrer in the Reorganization Group and chatted with him for fifteen minutes about some of the bank recapitalizations that Weldon had been hired to complete. It seemed, Warren explained, that the West Coast thrifts were all going to need to be restructured eventually, and getting in the door early couldn't hurt. He'd met Bill through Larisa and thought he was bright and capable.

"Say, would it be helpful if I joined you in LA? I could clear the deck." It never failed to amaze Warren how willing people at Weldon were to fly off to sunny Southern California at the drop of a hat right up until June.

"I tell you what. Why don't you see if you can leave it open for Wednesday, and I'll give you a call tomorrow from out there and let you know."

"Okay. I can ask Larisa if she can cover for me if you need me." Bill knew that Warren and Larisa had been involved with each other, but it had momentarily slipped his mind. "I guess," he added hesitantly.

"That's a great idea. I'm sure she'll be happy to. I appreciate it. I'll give you a call no later than five tomorrow, and you can grab the Wednesday-morning flight for an afternoon meeting if it looks like a go." Bill had agreed, and they'd disconnected. Warren had anticipated that Larisa would have to be notified about the trip—the Reorg group was always stretched thin.

Once the plans were made, he called up Frank's house, to ask Karen if Frank was home. She sounded surprised that he wasn't in the office. Warren shuffled some papers, then apologized. "I forgot. I thought he was going out to LA this afternoon, and I wanted to fly out with him. He actually canceled the trip, and I plum forgot."

"You're going to LA?" She sounded interested. "You and Sam going to ask for her father's blessing?" Frank had told Karen about the engagement.

"No. Actually she's staying here." His voice sounded strained.

"Is everything all right?" Karen's interest perked up.

"Yeah. She just didn't feel like going. Why aren't you working? Playing hooky?"

"No. I'm only working three days a week now. Frank wants me to quit after the wedding. He says he wants to 'keep' me."

"Yeah, well, that's why you're not his first wife. You keep the job or you'll just wind up fighting to keep him. Idle minds are the devil's something or other. You know."

"Oh, you don't see me as the Suzy Homemaker type?" Karen said sarcastically.

"I don't think that's in the Mueller genes. You ladies need to apply those minds of yours. Making cookies in a lightbulb oven isn't a life's work, you know." Warren laughed. "Larisa always said you wanted to be the next Albert Schweitzer."

"Says you. How long you going to be gone? Want me and Frank to entertain your betrothed while you're away?"

"Till Friday. Sure, if you feel like it. . . . Oops, I've gotta jump, duty calls." He knew Karen understood how conversations on a trading floor were subject to instant cancellation if a customer called. He figured that Karen would tell Larisa that she'd spoken to Warren, and that he was going to California without Sam.

Before leaving, Warren briefed Kerry about everything he had going on and gave each of his accounts a call to let them know he'd be out for a few days. He wasn't ready to leave until four thirty, and most of the business for the day was finished anyway. He got his coat and two-suiter from the closet and waved good-bye to Kerry. A car was waiting for him downstairs, and he tossed his bag on the seat.

"Newark, right?" The driver shot a quick look over his shoulder and pulled away from the curb.

Warren grunted and settled back in his seat. "You mind if I change my clothes back here?" The driver shrugged, and Warren quickly pulled a pair of black jeans and a gray, long-sleeve T-shirt out of his bag. He wrestled himself around for a while, waiting to change his pants until they were in the Lincoln Tunnel. By the time they arrived at the airport, he was casually dressed, with a baseball cap and sunglasses, and his suit was carefully stowed in the garment bag. He signed the voucher and hopped out of the car, rushing through the doors like all the other travelers trying to make their flights.

fifty-five

❧

S am had settled in with a couple of videos and a book on Renaissance art. Warren marveled at the thick, impenetrable volumes she read and teased that they were her equivalents of sleeping pills. He grabbed one from her once and quizzed her, amazed when she remembered almost every date, name, and detail.

"I could fill my mind with useless *garbage*, like you, or I can fill it with useless *knowledge*, like this," she'd said, and gone back to reading.

From the window, in the evening light, the trees were just beginning to break their buds. It had been a warm day, and the chilly winter weekend in East Hampton seemed separated from the coming season by months, not days. She pushed the first cassette into the VCR and settled back in the bed. It was *Year of the Dragon*, with Mickey Rourke. Warren had recommended it, though he warned her it was pretty violent. She remembered that it had been panned by the critics, who all thought Michael Cimino, the director, was some kind of irredeemable war criminal for making *Heaven's Gate*. She had actually liked *Heaven's Gate*.

She enjoyed the film, and the gore didn't bother her much. It was just the movies, and she'd seen how they faked it when she was working. Rourke had been good, and the action taut. She wandered into the kitchen for a beer and turned out the lights.

It was almost eleven o'clock, and Sam changed into a pair of Warren's flannel pajamas before settling back in bed and reading for an hour. Before turning in, she picked up the phone and called her parents' house, but the housekeeper told her they were out to dinner, so she brushed her teeth and buried herself under the covers in the dark room, the lights of the skyline throwing a pale shade across the wall, the clock on the MONY Building read 12:05.

∾

The key turning in the lock of the service door barely made any sound at all. Certainly not enough to disturb anyone inside. It was almost three in the morning, and the city was sound asleep. The carpeting in the hall muffled the footsteps as a shadowy figure carefully made its way toward the half-closed bedroom door. In its right hand, a steel blade reflected the weak light that filtered in through the window as the intruder turned and quietly entered the bedroom. At the door, the figure stopped, scanning the room. Out of a pocket came a small plastic bag, which was silently opened and a finely shorn combination of hair and fiber cuttings shaken out on the carpet. This done, the figure slowly stepped toward the bed where Sam lay, her body under the comforter, and her head mostly covered by pillows, a habit to keep out any noise or disruption. The knife hand swung around, poised.

"Why don't you put that thing down?" Warren's voice came from behind, and the figure jerked in shock. He was standing in the open closet door, holding his steel tennis racquet in front of him like a shield.

Behind the ski mask, the killer's eyes flashed around the room.

"I mean it. I'm pretty good with this thing." He took a few short swings.

"Fuck you, Warren. Fuck you." It was a woman's voice and the tension went out of her body as she turned to face him.

"Come on, Larisa, don't do anything stupid." He took a half step back as she stood on the floor, the knife still in her hand.

"Don't do anything stupid? Don't do anything *stupid*? It's too late for that." She took a step toward him and spat out, "I am stupid. I did stupid things. For you. I did everything for you. You should be in fucking LA right now. You should let me take care of all this. I always have."

"You didn't do anything for me, Larisa. You did it all for yourself. Even Anna's ski accident." He held her off by brandishing the racquet again, and she pulled off the mask, her blond hair exploding over her shoulders in the half-light.

"Fuck Anna. She had everything handed to her. She shouldn't have been skiing out of bounds anyway. All I did was point her the wrong way. You're an asshole, Warren. You're just like the rest of them. No better. Don't kid yourself." She still held the knife. "What are you going to do? You and your fucking tennis."

"No. You're going to put down the knife, and we're going to get you a good doctor. Maybe in another country. We can both afford it. So you killed Billy and Anson. Who cares? They were useless sacks of shit anyway." He backed up a little, and Larisa moved away from the bed toward him. "Come on. I'm on your side. I still love you. We'll figure a way out of this."

"I killed them for you. You have to know that. They were in the way. That pompous idiot Dougherty, he was already dead, he just didn't know it. Inbred moron. You are so much smarter than him. And Anson? I only fucked him once to find out what he was going to do. He was trying to get you fired, you know. He would've too. But he liked me. He told me everything. In Dallas, that time. I stopped him. For you." Her eyes were wild. "I didn't even kill that bitch he was screwing when I smashed his fucking skull. But I should have. Fucking slut." Larisa reached down with the knife and, the blade turned backward, slit the turtleneck shirt from the bottom to her throat. It hung open, showing her chest.

"Larisa, stop now. It's enough. How was Anna for me? To open up a recruiting spot for you?" Warren couldn't back up any farther. He was against the closet doorframe.

"It just worked out. She was drunk and tired, and all I did was point her the wrong way. And Serena too. She went down those stairs like a sack of potatoes. But I cracked her head on the stair after, just to be sure. She would have gotten your spot, you idiot. Anna would never have beat me out for the spot at Weldon, but the chance came and I took it. I didn't even have to push her, she just skied right past me and over the edge." Larisa laughed. "You shoulda heard her wail. But, besides, I had *you* working for me, right? I was in no matter what, Mr. Superstar. That was a long time ago. Come on, Warren, finish it. Everything is always my fault anyway, right? Take this knife away from me. Put it right here." She ran her hand between her breasts, then cupped one, rolling its nipple between her fingers. "You love my tits, don't you? All you fucking assholes love these things. Dutch Goering used to tell me how he wanted to fuck me there. He had such a nice cock too. I loved to suck on it." The knife was coming up slowly.

"Jesus Christ, Larisa, come on."

"What? You can't take it?" She had the knife up now, slowly moving toward him. "Come on, Warren, you walked out on me. I knew you would come back to me once this useless cunt was dead. Now let's see if you've got any guts."

"Larisa, cut it out. Put the knife down. I don't want to hurt you."

"Hurt *me*?" She laughed and kept coming, backing him up to the wall, still held off by the steel racquet. She paused for a moment, looking for an opening, and he took the opportunity.

"It's time for you to meet someone." Warren pronounced the words loudly, a preset trigger to action.

"That's about enough, Miss Mueller." The light came on by the bed, behind her. Detective Wittlin, who looked a little silly with Warren's pajamas over his clothes and a bulletproof vest, held a 9 mm pistol in his right hand. "We don't need anybody else getting hurt." He had climbed out of the bed behind her while she was confronting Warren. He stepped around it while she was still stunned, and twisted the knife out of her hand with a smooth motion, then stepped away. "Mr. Hament, do me a favor and put that thing away before someone makes a stupid joke."

Dick McDermott and a uniformed officer came into the room, with Sam trailing them. The patrolman couldn't help but notice Larisa's chest, and he took off his jacket, handing it to her with a look of remorse. She put it on as if in a trance, then Wittlin handcuffed her.

A compact, wiry man came out from under the bed. "I think it came out perfectly." He had a bulky recording deck with him, which trailed a thin wire to a tiny camera on top of the armoire. "The new night-vision camera worked pretty well."

"You're pathetic, Warren," Larisa spat at him. "Pathetic." The impact of what was happening had finally hit her. "Without me, you're going *nowhere*. You fucking *idiot*." She spat the words at him, enraged.

"I'm sorry, Miss Mueller. You are under arrest for the murders of Anson

Combes and William Dougherty, and Anna Meladandri. And Serena, who-ever she is. I am Detective Lieutenant McDermott of the New York City Police Department Homicide Squad. I want to advise you of your rights. 'You have the right to remain silent. Anything...'"

As McDermott read Larisa her rights, she looked at Warren with disgust. "You pansy. You fucking wimp. You owe everything to me. You'd still be some little trainee in diapers." McDermott paused while she spat out the words, then kept going. The tech collected the machinery, and Wittlin sat on the bed.

Warren looked at her, his shoulders sagging. "Larisa, I had everything anyway. Not everyone is in the rush you were. It was enough for me." She was a striking sight, her arms pinned behind her, the long red-gold hair fall-ing over her shoulders, her eyes ablaze, her mouth curled in contempt. She struggled a bit when the policemen took her away, but didn't say anything.

"I don't believe it." Wittlin shook his head from side to side. "We only had to follow her for two nights, and she showed up like clockwork. How did you figure it out?"

"It was the photo from Bonnie's building. I thought I might recognize the scarf." Warren smiled and sat down next to Wittlin.

"So why didn't you say something?"

"Because I didn't even realize it until much later. Also, I figured she'd have gotten rid of it, and then if you'd asked about it, she'd have known you were on her case."

"That's complicated reasoning. Okay. How'd you know she was going to try for your girlfriend here?"

"Fiancée, Detective." Sam smiled at him. "Well, I guess I tried to pro-voke her. Make sure her sister told her how awesome Sam is, let her know I wasn't without options. Then she sent a spousal life insurance application to Sam. I asked HR. They didn't send it. It was a dumb mistake, but her temper got the best of her." Warren gestured in bewilderment. "I guess she wanted to punish me."

Sam walked over and shoved him down on the bed. "Options? I've al-ways wanted to be live bait. Big step up from car-rental jockey."

Warren let out a little laugh.

"Insurance application? Why didn't you tell me about it?" Wittlin seemed annoyed.

"No insult intended, but having the police department suddenly sniffing around HR could only have tipped her off. You told me yourself you had no evidence, that the DA would only indict with a confession. So I made their job easy." Warren got up. "I got them their confession."

"Yeah. The DA is kind of a joke with investigations, that's true. But, I've gotta be honest with you . . ." Wittlin looked a little sheepish.

"I know. You guys figured I had something to do with it all."

"Yup. Or your dad. He was in town for all the murders. I guess there is such a thing as coincidence. McDermott owes me a hundred bucks, though. That's why he was so testy."

"Well, I'm glad you had faith in me. I'm flattered." Warren touched his fingers to his brow in a mock salute.

"Don't be. I laid off fifty of it with our captain." Wittlin stood up. "Anyway, I'm glad to see this case closed. If we lost any more investment bankers, the whole city'd shut down." He walked to the door.

"Yup, that's why we get the big money. Solving these big cases. Are you going to need us for anything?" Warren had his arm around Sam.

"Tomorrow we'll need to take statements at police headquarters. You two get some sleep tonight. If you can."

"Detective, tonight I'm going to sleep like a baby." Sam smiled.

"I'll see myself out. Take care now." As Wittlin walked out of the bedroom, his voice trailed off down the hall, "I'd change those locks if I were you, especially if you've got any other ex-girlfriends I don't know about."

Sam gave Warren a hug, and they stood still for a moment.

"If you do—" she started.

"Yeah, I know."

"—I'll kill you."

fifty-six

◈

J esus, Dutch, that whole story is kind of hard to swallow."

"I'm tellin' you, it's true. Jojo's too fuckin' dumb to make something like that up."

"But Mats's dad is the chairman of Jones Fyfe, for crissakes. Jason Leeson's been on top there for ten years already. They may be a second-tier broker, but he must have put fifty or sixty million bucks in the bank by now. There's no way his kid's gonna do something so stupid. I mean, I've met some of the people over there. There are some dummies, for sure, but that whole thing's too far gone even for them."

"Listen, Jojo heard it from this babe he's poking on Jones's repo desk. That fuckin' dope Mats was hiding bad trade tickets and blaming the mismatches on the back office! I heard he dropped about seventy-five mil before they shut him down. That slimeball Grant Bradley's his boss. This broad tells Jojo that Bradley's been on the take from all the guys in Jones's finance side for years—pieces of their deals through Bahamian shell companies— that kind of stuff. Anyhow, even that sack of shit had to cut Mats loose. Of course all those dumb Irish guys over there couldn't figure their way out of a paper bag with a machete and a chain saw, so no one ever noticed the books didn't balance."

"Man, what is wrong with that company? They can't do anything right. God, the parent company must just be pissing blood about it!"

"I guess. But, hey, they hired the fuckin' guy. Remember when he was down at Bache, and they booted him for that bank deal?"

"Dutchie, that was a little before my time ... you're showing your age."

"Come on, you remember the fuckin' story. He and Anson were big buddies back then too. He was trying to get us to hire that fucking goofball Bradley Savings and Loan. They were doing all those S-and-L deals with Scholdice. Said Bradley' was one sharp fuckin' cookie."

"Oh, yeah? Anson and Bradley were pals?" Warren knew that Grant Bradley was well-known around the Street for being a second-rate talent who had a big job at a third-rate firm. Just like Jason, the chairman of Jones Fyfe Securities, they both were big players in the world of retail stock brokerage, but regarded as lightweight sleaze in the higher-powered milieu of institutional investment banking and trading. Something was falling into place. If everyone thought Bradley was on the take from the S&L and bank deals his firm did, and Anson and he were friends, it wouldn't be much of a stretch to think that Anson had cooked up his own scheme to salt away a real fortune. That the chairman's kid had tried to hide losses and then blown up was interesting, but not material to Warren's situation. It wouldn't be too hard to hide the missing money by creating losses on the trading desk and blaming the kid. A perfect crime with the boss's son as the fall guy. He'd lost his job, but mismarking positions wasn't technically a crime unless you worked for a commercial bank. And if he split $75 million or so with his dad, well worth it

"Fuggin' A. They were at Hahhhhvard together, don't you know? Coupla peas in a fuckin' pod." Warren doubted Goering could get through an entire sentence without using some form of the word *fuck*.

"Jeez, Anson went to Harvard? Really? I never knew." That got a good laugh from Goering. He had been the first to notice that Anson somehow made certain that everyone found out his alma mater within five minutes of making his acquaintance—a not-uncommon trait among Harvard alums. As Goering had put it, a conversation about sheep mating habits in the Australian outback could somehow include the interjection "It's funny ... when I was at Harvard, I had a professor who did his master's thesis on bovine ..." and so on.

"Well, at least you won't have old Anson sticking his nose into your business anymore." Warren sighed.

"Me or you, pal," Goering said. "Man, it's hard to believe that fuckin' broad of yours actually knocked two guys off. God, if I'd only known, there were a few fuckin' people she could've taken care of for me. I mean, what'd she have against them?"

"Well, technically, it was four people. She pushed a girl off a cliff in B-school and killed another shoving her down the stairs. And she may have pushed a girl in front of a car in high school. But she didn't have anything against them. It was nothing personal." Warren shrugged. What could be more personal than murder? "But, hey, I've gotta ask you something. And you've gotta tell me the truth."

Goering's eyebrows shot up. "Oh? Depends. What's the question?"

"Did you nail Larisa while I was with her?"

Goering laughed, his even, white teeth showing. Tears almost began to roll out of the corners of his eyes, and he slapped his thighs. "Whoooeee! I've finally got your butt just where I want it, don't I, poopsie pie?"

"God, if I'da known you were going to get such a big kick out of it, I never would have asked." Warren waved his hand dismissively at Goering.

"Hey, no problem, son. I tried. Lord knows, I tried, but I could never get anywhere with her. She only liked the big hitters, not the fuckin' peons like me."

"Well, it's nice to know even a vicious killer has some standards. Thanks for trying to seduce my girlfriend, though. I appreciate it."

"Touchy, touchy. What about that old school pal you nailed after she got engaged?" Warren had forgotten he'd told Goering about Eliza. Despite his show of being crude and his reputation with the ladies, he had to admit that Goering was actually a loyal friend and had a moral compass when it came to business and his family. And knew how to make a buck.

"You're right. There's no honor among thieves."

"Never was. That's a fuckin' myth."

"Hey, Dutchie boy, I've got some news—so are you."

fifty-seven

❧

The streets of Vaduz didn't seem as narrow as he remembered them. Sam looked relaxed and happy in the passenger seat, and the big Mercedes sedan slid around the corners quietly. The wedding had been small, simple, and pleasant. Cornelia Harper had invited them to hold it at the beautiful party space in her apartment house on Fifth Avenue and held the reception in her apartment. The honeymoon was a trip to Europe. They had spent a couple of days in London, followed by a quick trip to Stuttgart to buy the car for shipping home—after all, he was a successful young bond salesman with a seven-figure income, and she had an import license for used cars for her rental lot.

In the months since Larisa's arrest, it became clear that the money Warren and Sam had found in Anson's accounts was not the subject of any sort of search or investigation. The two West Coast banks had taken the markdowns exactly as Warren had surmised, and in a seemingly innocent conversation Warren had with Scholdice, the broker had announced his retirement and relocation to a ranch in Australia: "Warren, this business has been good to me, but times are changin'. My accounts are all headed for a big bust, and the days of easy money are over. Me and my pals made hay while the sun shone." Beker and Largeman had left Warner as well and set up a money management firm.

Warner had been audited twice by the Federal Home Loan Bank Board, and nothing had come of it, except that the bank was clearly in trouble, like all the S&Ls that had overleveraged in the mortgage markets once the effects of the new tax laws passed by Reagan hit home on real estate. Warren could see that all the "missing" money had properly been accounted for as write-offs that were balanced by other profits on their new investments and income each year, and the last thing the regulators wanted, it seemed, was to find any kind of scandal. Of course, if those profits proved ephemeral over time, the focus would be on those bad investments, not on what had happened years before. Warren could only wonder how many other schemes to milk money out of the savings-and-loan industry there were. It looked as if Mike Milken at Drexel was in some serious trouble for many such schemes on a much grander scale. The one at Warner had clearly been good for at least a half a billion or more and was essentially untraceable.

Meanwhile, Reagan's second term was producing big gains in the markets, and the Street was prospering. If anyone looked, the couple's side trip to Liechtenstein looked like just a shortcut to Geneva, where they were going to visit Warren's brother, who was doing a research fellowship, and spend a day with Frank and Karen, who were engaged and to be married in June. Warren and Sam spent a day reviewing the procedures that they had gone over with the lawyers Schiff had referred them to. Warren had told him the funds were part of an inheritance from Sam's family in Germany and England. She did have extremely wealthy distant cousins in Frankfurt, so it seemed plausible if anyone questioned it, and the paper trail would lead nowhere. They had spent hours agonizing over the money. It hadn't really been stolen, they rationalized. Warner had written down loans and sold them and bought high-income products to cover the losses. It had been possible it would all work out, until the tax law change clobbered real estate values, and interest rates dropped. If Warner failed, the main losers would be the Mexican family that owned 90 percent of the stock, but the run-up in its value had largely been based on false earnings anyway. Warren chose to believe the rumors that the Sanchez family was laundering money for Mexican drug cartels—it made what they had done seem almost victimless.

Sam had handled the transfer transactions perfectly. About half of the money was repatriated through the Caymans, necessary taxes were paid, and the other half had been transferred into the Faaringsbank account of a new firm, Flickflack AG, named after a horse she had owned as a kid, that was listed on the Luxembourg stock exchange with ownership through an anonymous Liechtenstein trust. Sam became the chairwoman and owned all the shares.

The company also endowed an academy in Jupiter, Florida, where Warren's father offered scholarships for full room, board, schooling, and tennis and athletic training to two hundred underprivileged children from all over the United States. The operating budget consumed only a fraction of the income that the company was earning through the decisions being made by its chief investment adviser, David Schiff. Through a combination of good luck and Schiff's excellent timing, he had moved the Trust into bonds as they rose, and then into stocks. Lately, Schiff had been enamored with discount retailing and computer-software companies for the long-term. They looked like good growth areas for the late eighties and early nineties, he'd explained, because they offered real products that everyone would need. By mid-1989 the Flickflack trust had assets of almost $300 million, even after paying some $50 million in federal taxes.

"Look," Sam had told Schiff, "take all the risk you want. We want to be aggressive. We won't cry if we lose money. Warren says you have a nose for underappreciated assets. We'll trust it. You get five percent of everything you make, and you can still run your company." Schiff agreed, but insisted he simply match all the investments he made for Emerson so there would be no conflict. He saw trouble coming, in 1990, and believed the early nineties would be a buying opportunity for depressed assets. The riskier purchases would be handled separately. He also donated most of his share to the environmental causes he favored and used some of the balance to fund activist shareholder lawsuits against abusive corporate practices, particularly in the insurance business.

The board of directors, of which Sam was the sole member, decided that the operating company needed to own residences in the areas where its likely clientele resided—Islesboro, Hobe Sound, Malibu, and Paris. With the exception of Whales End, they were comparably modest, charming, and likely excellent investments, all bought during the lows of the 1990/91 recession.

Just over 50 percent of all income in the trust and corporation was paid out to various charitable organizations, which Sam spent a lot of time interviewing and choosing. The balance of the trust income was available to Sam to spend or invest as she chose, as the trust did not seek nonprofit status and paid taxes in the United States.

With the pressure off, Warren didn't mind the work at Weldon so much anymore. His rich wife gave him the liberty not to take any guff from Conover or anyone else, and he had a growing reputation as an honest salesman who wouldn't recommend trades to clients just to earn a big commission or enjoy the adrenaline rush. As a result, his business grew quickly, and he became the top producer at Weldon. After long discussions with Schiff and some of his analysts, Warren diligently guided his accounts to areas of the bond markets where the returns more than balanced the risks. He advised them away from the exotic, structured products that the finance guys kept devising. As Goering put it, "If you're playing Hide the Salami and you don't know where the salami is, you shouldn't bend over!" Some of Warren's clients didn't care—they were after big returns—and he soon released them to other salesmen. He took a lot of vacations, but he was allowed the latitude. He planned to stay at Weldon until he and Sam had kids, then find something that would allow him to spend as much time with them as his dad had with him. He had been hitting again regularly with his pal Neal, and his game was sharp again.

In the meantime, Sam had spent her free time refreshing her college major in art history, after dropping the pre-med idea despite getting nothing but As, and Warren had brought his mom in to work with them, making the operating company, called Gordian Fine Arts, a viable enterprise. She and Sam became advisers to several corporations in managing their art collections, and consultants to a growing group of collectors who were knocked out by the two women's combination of looks, brains, scholarly knowledge, and nose for a deal. Chas Harper had married a beautiful private banker at the Bessemer Trust who had helped him manage his family's money, and Nicole had been thrilled to refer dozens of their clients to Gordian rather than the usual art dealers and brokers, who could hardly be trusted.

One such assignment had taken Sam to Chicago, where she helped a major client acquire a $15 million Winslow Homer oil painting, then convinced him to bequeath it in his will to the National Gallery in Washington from his estate. She waived her commission in favor of a deductible donation paid directly to the Florida Academy and caught a flight to La-Guardia, and from there, a commuter plane to Camden, Maine.

The air had been smooth, and the Whaler met her at the dock for the cruise across the harbor to the house, where Warren was waiting. She took the pair of sunglasses Jimmy offered her when she climbed on board. It had been a long trip, but a good one. The boat powered out into the channel, the sun low on the horizon and the lights coming on in the waterfront shops and the large houses, reflected in the almost-black water, across the bay. The breeze was soft in her hair, and she settled deep into a cushion, looking forward to a warm, comfortable ride home.

ACKNOWLEDGMENTS

⸎

A work of fiction is no different than a good joke—there is an element of the truth in it that makes you laugh, or if poorly told, uncomfortable. In that regard, the truth is that I could never have written this book without the love of my father, who encouraged me to write later in life, because he wanted his son to be prosperous and happy, and my mother and brother who allowed me to grow up, knowing I was cared for. And, of course, my wife, who has made my adult life the envy of any man—not only is she beautiful, loving, and brilliant, but also a professional juggernaut who has never once settled for less than being the best at anything she does, pulling me along with her.

Also important are the panoply of miscreants and clowns (at least one of them an *actual* clown) who taught me that neither intellect, morals, nor taste were required to succeed in finance, so that even so lucrative a failure as my own might not reflect on my character. But there were also those rare dedicated and decent people who worked with me, and made what success I had not just possible but occasionally fun. Without them I wouldn't have lasted a month. Sharing every day since with my wonderful children and incredible wife, and a small group of special, caring friends, was a treasure I hope someday to deserve.

Finally, my heartfelt thanks to the editors I have worked with in my brief career as a writer—Richard Story, Deborah Frank, Katie Gilligan, and Melanie Fried there to greet me when I returned from the yawning